John Wilson Croker, Louis J. Jennings

The Correspondence and Diaries of the Late Right Honourable John Wilson Croker

Vol. III

John Wilson Croker, Louis J. Jennings

The Correspondence and Diaries of the Late Right Honourable John Wilson Croker
Vol. III

ISBN/EAN: 9783744715959

Printed in Europe, USA, Canada, Australia, Japan

Cover: Foto ©Raphael Reischuk / pixelio.de

More available books at **www.hansebooks.com**

THE CROKER PAPERS.

THE

CORRESPONDENCE AND DIARIES

OF THE LATE

RIGHT HONOURABLE

JOHN WILSON CROKER, LL.D., F.R.S.,

SECRETARY TO THE ADMIRALTY

FROM 1809 TO 1830.

EDITED BY

LOUIS J. JENNINGS,

AUTHOR OF 'REPUBLICAN GOVERNMENT IN THE UNITED STATES.

IN THREE VOLUMES.—VOL. III.

SECOND EDITION, REVISED.

ʌWITH ‖PORTRAIT.

LONDON:

JOHN MURRAY, ALBEMARLE STREET.

1885.

CONTENTS OF VOL. III.

CHAPTER XXIII.

1843–1844.

CHAPTER XXIV.

1845–1846.

CHAPTER XXV.

1847.

CHAPTER XXVI.

1848-1849.

CHAPTER XXVII.

1850-1851.

CHAPTER XXVIII.

1852–1853.

CHAPTER XXIX.

1854.

CHAPTER XXX.

1855–1857.

LETTERS, DIARIES, AND MEMOIRS

OF THE

RT. HON. JOHN W. CROKER.

CHAPTER XXIII.

1843–1844.

Mr. Croker's Acquaintance with Samuel Wilberforce—Article on "Rubrics and Ritual"—Dr. Wilberforce on the Tractarians—His Review of certain Episcopal Charges—Bishop Phillpott's Remarks on Newman and Pusey—Mr. Henry Drummond on Jewish and Modern Ecclesiastical Architecture—The "Young England" Party—Mr. Croker's reference to it in the *Quarterly Review* — Lockhart's description of the Leaders—Sir James Graham's Opinion—"Disraeli alone is Mischievous"—Sir Robert Peel's Sketch of the Political Situation— "The times are out of Joint" — Mr. Lockhart on Alison's History —Lord Brougham and the Corn Law League—Criticism of Jesse's Life of Selwyn—Letter from the Duke of Rutland—Lord Ashburton's Advice to Peel to "Nail his Colours to the Mast"—Peel's Reply— Letter from Sir Peter Laurie—Carlyle on "Cromwellian Confusion" —Disturbed State of Ireland—Prosecution of O'Connell—Subsequent Proceedings in the House of Lords—The Reversal of O'Connell's Conviction—Mr. Croker's Letters to the King of Hanover—His Opinion of Railroads.

ONE of Mr. Croker's most frequent correspondents at this period was Archdeacon (afterwards Bishop) Wilberforce, who had been rector of Alverstoke, where Mr. Croker had a house. Their communications related to a variety of subjects, but generally they were upon questions concerning the Church, in which Mr. Croker always took a profound interest. In May, 1843, he wrote for the *Quarterly Review* a long article on " Rubrics and Ritual," in which the Tractarian movement was incidentally discussed. This article was carefully revised before its publication by the Archdeacon, and soon afterwards—in April, 1843—he wrote to Mr. Croker about a difficulty in which his younger brother had become involved respecting a curate. " It is," he said, " a long and to me a sad story. It is, however, greatly exaggerated, foolish and wrong as entailing evil, as I think the act was. In one word, the thing he did was this : a sick man, whom he had visited for months, and of whose state he was satisfied fully, sent for him in the delirium preceding death. Thinking the man past the voice of reading a prayer, he took a *Cross*, and bade him fix his dying thoughts on Him who hung upon it. Taken alone this might have inflamed a parish, but coming as it did, as one of many equivocal acts, it stirred up a perfect conflagration. However, my brother (my youngest brother) is more tolerant of such ineptiæ than I can be in so serious a subject matter : and 'he curate, being a very good and a very zealous man, he as ar as possible defends him." In another letter he referred to the wish of the Tractarians to " sweep the church clear of all pews and seats, save the stone seat round the walls for the cripples and infirm." He continued : " There is a lunatic at Haslar, perfectly harmless (I believe, the cook) but obliged to be shut up because he has that peculiar sensitiveness about the honours due to the Virgin Mary that he would kill any one who speaks disparagingly of her. I think this would well illustrate, in one of your well-turned sentences, the growing Mariolatry of the Tract Doctors." In the same month of April he briefly reviews several episcopal charges which had recently been delivered, and remarks that the

" Bishop of Worcester's was *essentially* un-Church, but it seemed to me from absolute ignorance of his subject, with a very high degree of general ignorance ; well flanked by a remarkable unacquaintance with the written vernacular."

The following is the conclusion of the letter :—

But the charge of my excellent cousin, the Bishop of Chester was of another stamp, and seemed to be, from the thorough ingraining of Puritanism, essentially at variance with every principle of our Church.   I do not remember to have heard from any competent and unbiassed judge, two opinions as to its essential error as well as its mischievous violence.   In his first edition he singles out Gladstone's statements for dogmatic censure : in his second these are in great measure withdrawn, and a quotation from the ' Tracts for the Times ' is substituted.   This quotation receives the full vials of his wrath, as embodying a dangerous heresy ; but upon examination it appears that the passage is a quotation from one of the most universally approved and best-considered dogmatic treatises of his Lordship's greatest predecessor, Bishop Pearson. It is this sort of violence which gives their real strength to the *Tract Leaders*, and which, carried out into detail in the administration of his diocese, is making it next to impossible " to gather in ' *these* the harvest of food ' which they have prepared for us."   I was very glad to hear you thus express yourself, as I am convinced that it is indeed our wisdom.   By the way, my admirable brother here strikes me as a remarkable exception to your rule as to those who go all lengths with N. [Newman] and P. [Pusey].   There is not a touch of insanity in its remotest development upon him, and yet—he is an *amiable* man.

I trust that Sir Robert will not yield an inch to this Dissenting clamour as to his Education Bill.   It seems to me the very crisis of the moral power of his government, and deeply anxious as I am for its stability and renown *hereafter*, I watch every step with the keenest anxiety.   I am afraid that Sir Jas. G. [Graham], at least, does not estimate the relative strength of Dissenters and the Church aright.   The weakness of the Church a few years since, and the marvellous change which has come over the mind of England, have so entirely altered the position of all questions with which they are connected, that a man formed to official life in the old groove, can hardly be prepared for the present state of things. Do you think that he has realized the fact that, out of the 16 or 17 millions of our population, the conduct of Government on this question will cordially attach to them some 12 or 13 millions, if it stands by the Church; whilst no concessions will do anything *really* to attach the 4 millions besides, who feel in their inner hearts that they are severed in truth from our politics by a gulf which no concession or assimilation can bridge over. This at least is my conviction; and I wish that *your* powerful influence would suggest it to Sir R. Peel.

The Bishop of Exeter (Dr. Phillpotts) to Mr. Croker.

Bishopstowe, May 2nd, 1843.

MY DEAR SIR,

1. I differ from you in what you say is the general result of your opinion, that *whatever is, is right* in respect to Ecclesiastical rituals, &c.

I go thus far with you, that, considering all things—especially that the Church has not been permitted to legislate, nor to deliberate for itself, for 120 years, nor in calmness and sobriety for 40 years more—it is marvellous that things are so well as they are.

2. You differ from me about Convocation *less*, probably, than you suspect. I wish it to sit again, only for the purpose of synodically devising a better Synod than itself; one, more like Synods of the early Church—in *one* house, with less of *power* to Presbyters—but more of means of counsel and aid from them to the bishops than their separate House gives. I need not tell *you* that Convocation is not the ancient Synod of our own Church.

We need—and *must have*—a legislative body, sitting for real business from time to time. It ought to consist of bishops either solely (in the presence of Presbyters who should have a right, not to debate with them, but, hearing what they discuss, to represent by writing their opinions, when they think it necessary) or of bishops and such divines and representatives of the clergy, as shall be found necessary, securing a real preponderance to the bishops.

I write—not without having previously thought on this matter—but without ever drawing out my thoughts on paper, and, therefore, securing a full right to change my opinion on conviction.

But I am confident, that it is hardly possible for us to go on long without restoring to the Church a real church legislation. If you were a bishop, you would feel the necessity as strongly as I do, for you would not be content to let things slip smoothly and gently down, without an attempt to keep up the fabric committed to your charge. You would strive to restore what we have lost—and very much have we lost—as well as to preserve what we still hold.

Of the *Rubrics*, I think very few are really obscure, still fewer impracticable. I am favourable to the restoration of obedience to them, though perhaps I agree with you in not thinking very judicious the manner in which this was dealt with in the charge you refer to. There is not perhaps enough needing amendment in the *Rubrics*, of itself, to require a Synod.

But of *the Canons*, this cannot be said. Many of them are indeed impracticable, and therefore not only these, but many that are practicable, have fallen into desuetude. There are few which are fitted to the present state of things. They must be altered if the Church is to last in England, under the pressure of all that is opposed to it in the privileges (supposed or real) of Dissenters—and with the little of real power of restraint over it's own members, even it's clergy, which it at present has.

That there are not incalculably wider departures from what is right in the state of our Church, is a most astonishing testimony to the faithfulness of the clergy.

3. I give up *Newman and No.* 90 fully.

For *Pusey* (the most guileless of men, the most disinterested, the most truly evangelical) I feel too warmly to give him up, much as I think in him to be not right.

Of the *effects* of the tracts—and of that movement—my opinion is what it was. I rejoice in heart, and am humbly thankful to God, for what I see of the young clergy—whose feeling and views are, almost without exception, in some degree influenced by that movement. It is true, that only little has fallen under my eye, as Bishop, of the foolish extravagances, which I have heard of elsewhere.

I write immediately on the receipt of your letter, and in the midst of much occupation.

If, after what I have written, you still think I can be of use to you, command me.

If I find you quite disengaged, I will, with your leave, run down some day to Molesey. If it should happen that you let me in when the Solicitor-General * is with you, I shall the more rejoice : for [of] him I think more highly—as of a man of a right mind, as well of as of rare ability—than of any one else of our public men. I heartily wish that he were taken from that profession in which he has no rival, and, with an independent fortune, placing him out of any occasion for the emoluments of office, fixed permanently among statesmen among whom he soon would have no equal.

> Yours, my dear Sir,
>
> Always with real regard, most faithfully,
>
> H. Exeter.

Mr. Henry Drummond to Mr. Croker.

[Without date.]

My dear Croker,

You seem to forget that a wise man can ask more questions in a minute than a fool can answer in a year, but *Je ferai mon impossible* to please you.

You will remember that the Tabernacle was built east and west, so that when the sun rose in the east, it, shining in at the eastern door, illuminated through it the whole Holy, and Holy of Holies. The Temple of Solomon was built on the same plans, and the other temples by him at Baalbec and Palmyra are north and south, though the entrance is at the west to the Atrium. The Christian churches were built with the altar to the east for the reasons stated in a tract which I enclose. The Pagans could only imitate the revealed worship whether Jewish or Christian, because the creature never could imagine *how* the Creator should be worshipped. The worship of Pagans consisted only of the sacrifices of beasts, because that only could they *see* in the Tabernacle ; they never could know nor understand the things of the Holy, such as the candlestick, the golden altar of incense, and the table of shewbread, and had nothing whatever analogous. The Portico was always called the front ; even where there was no entrance except at a side. No doubt the earliest Heathen

* [Sir William Follett.]

temples were mere copies of Solomon's, as Wilkins has shown
in the preface to 'Magna Græcia,'* and would therefore,
wherever attention was paid to the points of the compass,
stand the same way ; but then, as now with Pugin, who
writes an elaborate article in the *Dublin Review* to show that
churches should have the altar at the east, and then forthwith
builds the cathedral at Southwark and places it at the west,
so the ancients did not always stand to their own principles
even if they knew them. The heathen knew nothing of worship:
they only knew the preparation for it, which is sacrifice. I
wish you would come here some day and talk this matter
over : I can send for you to the station at Woking, and you
are sure to find us, for my poor boy is so ill that we cannot
leave him, and shall not so long as he is spared to us.

Always yours faithfully,

HENRY DRUMMOND.

The "Young England" party, under the leadership of
Disraeli and Smythe (afterwards Lord Strangford), was now
beginning to attract the attention of the country. Mr. Croker
made a slight, and not unkindly, reference to it in a footnote
to one of his political articles. It consisted, he said, of "four
or five young gentlemen who are known, it seems, by the
designation of *Young* England. Their number is so small,
their views so vague, and their influence so slight, that it may
seem superfluous to allude to them, but our respect for the
personal character of those amongst them of whom we have
any knowledge — our favourable opinion of their talents,
though rather, it must be confessed, of a *belles-lettres*, than a
statesmanlike character—and a strong sympathy with many
of their feelings—induce us to express our surprise and
regret that they should not see, even with their own peculiar
views, the extreme inconsistency and impolicy of endeavouring
to create distrust of the only statesman in whom the great

---

* ['The Antiquities of Magna Græcia,' by William Wilkins, Architect
to the H.E.I.C. Cambridge, 1807.]

Conservative body has any confidence, or can have any hope. We make all due allowance for 'young ambition,' even when it neglects Shakespeare's wise advice, of beginning with a little diffidence ; but we can still find no sufficient justification for the conduct which these gentlemen have recently adopted —particularly for their support of Mr. Smith O'Brien's motion —the most offensive to *Old England* which has been made for many years. We beg leave, in all kindness, to warn them against being deceived as to the quality of the notice which their singularity has obtained ; it has in it more of wonder than of respect, and will certainly confer on them no permanent consideration with any party or any constituency : a few stray and unexpected shots, fired in the rear of an army, attract more notice than a cannonade in front ; but it is an evanescent surprise, soon forgotten, or remembered only to the disadvantage of those whose indiscretion created it."

There is no letter of Mr. Croker's to be found in reference to the "Young Englanders," but he appears to have written to Mr. Lockhart to make some enquiries.

Mr. Lockhart to Mr. Croker.

DEAR CROKER,

P. Borthwick was a notorious man in the Scotch newspapers of 1822.

B. Disraeli published his 'Vivian Grey '—the only work that has been at all successful—eighteen years ago I am sure. He must be forty or close to that.*

You omit G. Smythe, Lord Strangford's son—very young— the cleverest of the set I believe.

Cochrane † is, I suppose, twenty-five or thirty. Son of Sir Thos.—grandson of the Honourable Sir Alexander the Admiral. Mr. C. has a good estate in Scotland through his mother.

---

* [Mr. Disraeli was at the time thirty-eight. The first volumes of ' Vivian Grey ' were published in 1826.]

† [The present Lord Lamington.]

I don't know that Borthwick ever published poetry.
Nor do I know that G. Smythe has published verse, though
it is likely he has in the annuals.
Milnes, Disraeli, Cochrane, are poets. Cochrane not the
worst of the three. He is a Cochrane . . . but not a bad
fellow. A little *notice* would have made him and Smythe all
right. Disraeli and Borthwick are very necessitous, and
wanted places of course.
I fancy Young England has in some degree at least associated itself with *Urquhart.*

Ever yours,

J. G. L.

Sir James Graham to Mr. Croker.

Whitehall, August 22nd, 1843.

With respect to Young England, the puppets are moved by
D'Israeli, who is the ablest man among them : I consider him
unprincipled and disappointed ; and in despair he has tried
the effect of bullying. I think with you, that they will
return to the *crib* after prancing, capering, and snorting ; but
a crack or two of the whip well applied may hasten and
ensure their return. D'Israeli alone is mischievous ; and
with him I have no desire to keep terms. It would be better
for the party, if he were driven into the ranks of our open
enemies.

Very truly yours,

JAMES GRAHAM.

The general demoralization of politics, and the great discontent which prevailed among the working classes, gave the
members of the new party many an opportunity of distinguish-
ing themselves. They went to Manchester (in 1844) and
attended meetings of the operatives, and Mr. Disraeli showed
how strongly he held the opinions which he afterwards
developed in 'Sybil, or the New Nation,' as the book was at
first called, the sub-title being afterwards changed to 'The
Two Nations.' He had not yet denounced the Conservative

party as an "organised hypocrisy," or begun his fierce attacks upon Sir Robert Peel. In Peel's letters to Mr. Croker, there is not a single allusion at any time to Mr. Disraeli, nor does Mr. Croker ever mention him till towards the close of his life, as will be seen in a later chapter. That Peel, in 1843, felt the pressure of the difficulties which surrounded him is obvious from his own rapid sketch of the situation.

Sir Robert Peel to Mr. Croker.   Extract.

Whitehall (Sunday Night), [April (?)] 1843.

My dear Croker,

The times are out of joint. и this makes party out of joint.

Four years of successive unfavourable harvests, affected trade injuriously; five years of deficient revenue affected finance injuriously.

There is a schism in the Scotch Church—a schism in the Church here. Puseyism has alienated the Wesleyans, and redoubled the hostile activity against the Church, of other Dissenters, and made many sober and attached friends of the Church lukewarm in its defence. To govern Ireland by means of an exclusive Protestant party is impossible. The attempt to govern it impartially—after it has been so long governed through one party and the other—forfeits the confidence of both.

The attempt to revive trade by lowering the cost of subsistence, and to provide a remedy for such a state of things as that which left us with 14 or 15,000 persons in one town, during the last winter, without the means of providing food by labour, and yet at the same time to do this cautiously and with due regard to the interests of agriculture, is what is called a half-measure. The agriculturists forget the danger to which hunger and want exposed property a few months since, and resent the fall of price which averted it.

Commerce, inflated by extravagant speculation and the issues of joint-stock banks, and really suffering by the competition of other countries, demands some remedy or other from the hands of the Government.

Then Ireland, and an opposition ready to take advantage of Irish discontent and agitation for party purposes.

A minority able and willing to obstruct public business, not by moving adjournments and the *gross* abuse of parliamentary privileges, but by captious objections, incessant talking; twenty-two divisions in two nights, and trumpery amendments to trumpery clauses; each division consuming nearly a quarter of an hour. All these things together, do certainly constitute great difficulty.

The mere attendance on the House of Commons, eight and nine hours every day, almost precludes the proper performance of his real duties by a minister. Just conceive what *I ought* to do, and what I must continue to do in some way or other during the remainder of this day. All this is beside your proposal, or at least ᵏ very much akin to it, and my wandering from it is, pₑ ₃, a sufficient indication that I know not what to advise.

Ever affectionately yours,

R. P.

Mr. Croker to Sir R. Peel.

[Marked "1843," but no proper date.]

West Moulsey (Tuesday Night).

MY DEAR PEEL,

You must have thought me an oaf this morning, when I was talking to you about Corn Laws and Tariff; but I had not *then* seen either the *Morning Post*, nor even read the article in the *Foreign Quarterly Review*, attributed to Gladstone— to be sure, if I had known of either I should have mentioned *them* to you rather than the very unimportant circumstances *in the same direction* which had reached me.

I trust, I do trust, that is, I at once hope and believe that Gladstone has not written nor encouraged anything that can be perverted into an intimation of further change. What has been done, has been wisely and, I believe, safely done, and the country will stand by it—or by anything that looks like stability; but if it sees reason to suspect *your Government of wavering*, mind, I tell you, we are all lost.

Affectionately yours,

J. W. CROKER.

Mr. Lockhart to Mr. Croker.

December 6th, 1843.

Dear Croker,

Alison deserves all anybody can say of his negligence, and also of his coxcombical pomposity and preachification, and worst of all, his affectation of liberalism here and there by way of extenuating to the wicked his really good principles, political and religious. But he *is* a good old Tory, and a good, honest, amiable man, and he has spent twenty years on this big book, and looks to it (he thinks not in vain) for pecuniary help to a large family. I think, therefore, it would meet your wishes to be gentle to him—and certainly the contrary line would give me personal pain, we being very old acquaintances, and he the sheriff of my county, whom I must meet often whenever I go to Scotland. It occurs to me that you might do him a real kindness by pointing out his blunders; but it might be done in terms of respect and civility, and without any expression of severity mingled with regret. This is, however, *if* you *could* speak with general respect of his work—and I fear you could not; and if you could not—why, the article is all alive with interest and can spare a note, however good and however amusing.

Is not he led wrongly by some prior writer or writers who might be shown up with a long whip, without calling the heavy sheriff by name into the ring ?*

Yours truly,

J. G. Lockhart.

* [Alison was much annoyed that his *History of Europe* was not reviewed in the *Quarterly*. He wrote, "Considering that my History was a great effort made in favour of the Conservative cause at the period of its lowest depression ; when the press almost universally had gone over to the Liberal or revolutionary side : and when the author by publishing it had of course precluded himself from all chance of professional promotion from Government, I felt that this silence on the part of the *Quarterly* was unjust, especially as the Editor was an old personal friend." He little suspected that it was *because* the Editor was his friend, that his work was not reviewed, or the severe treatment from which he was thus saved.]

Mr. Croker to Lord Brougham.

West Moulsey, February 19th, 1843.

MY DEAR BROUGHAM,

I am very sorry to find that you think the professed object of the League *a good one;* I think your own arguments in favour of agricultural protection unanswerable, and unless you yourself can answer them, I am sure no one else can. I look farther, much, than the mere questions of prices of corn and rates of wages, which are what, to a logician, I may venture to call mere *accidents;* the *substance* is the existence of a landed gentry, which has made England what she has been and is; without which no representative government can last; without which there can be no steady mean between democracy and despotism; without which *you* would have found no ποῦ στῶ for your splendid elevation, nor I any security for my humble happiness; and, good God! what a chaos of anarchy and misery do I foresee in every direction, from so comparatively small a beginning as changing an *average* duty of eight shillings, into a *fixed* duty of eight shillings, the fact being that the *fixed* duty means *no duty at all;* and *no duty at all* will be the overthrow of the existing social and political system of our country. There's a corn law lecture for you.

J. W. CROKER.

Mr. Croker to Mr. J. H. Jesse. *

West Moulsey, December 5th, 1843.

MY DEAR SIR,

I am much obliged by your kind attention in sending me your Selwyn volumes: but to be candid with you, I can by no means approve of the publication of letters of so peculiarly a private, and in many instances scandalous, character. I cannot, I honestly confess, understand what authority can exist for such a ripping up of private life. I am sorry also to observe some few considerable, and many small errors, in the notes. Some of them are probably typist errors, but some are not.

I am, my dear Sir, faithfully yours,

J. W. CROKER.

* [Author of 'Selwyn and his Contemporaries,' 'Memoirs of the Pretenders,' and many other works.]

The Duke of Rutland to Mr. Croker.

Stanton Woodhouse, December 10th, 1843.

My dear Croker,

Mr. Burton's authority respecting the Chatsworth conservatory is undoubtedly very good and undeniable. I have often thought of the dispute you and I had on the subject of the architect of that wonderful erection, as we sat together at the Longshawe dining-table.* There is such a strong impression on my mind as to Paxton having more to do with the design and execution, that I wished to obtain the evidence of the Duke of Devonshire, and unfortunately he left Chatsworth on Thursday and I arrived here on Friday.

Many thanks for your good wishes that the Royal visit at Belvoir Castle should pass off well, and for the flattering things you say of the castle. We *were* blessed with fine weather, or I know not what we should have done; for notwithstanding all you kindly say, the reception at Belvoir was marked principally by hearty and loyal welcome, and by a desire to make the Royal guests *comfortable.* To all this there was added at Chatsworth a splendour and magnificence to which I neither could nor did aspire.

The Queen and Prince Albert seemed in joyous spirits while at Belvoir. I am all anxiety to learn the result of your conversation with the Chancellor of the Exchequer on the subject of gun-metal for Wyatt.†

Believe me, my dear Croker,

Yours very truly,

Rutland.

Sir Robert Peel to Mr. Croker.

January 28th, 1844.

My dear Croker,

Many thanks for the extract from Ashburton's letter. I read over two or three times that part of it which advises *the nailing of colours to the mast.* This is good advice from

---

* [It will be remembered that Sir Joseph Paxton's design for this "wonderful erection" prepared the way for the great Exhibition of 1851.]
† [For the Duke of Wellington's statue.]

Ashburton. I never heard *him* make a speech in the course of which he did not nail, unnail, renail, and unnail again his colours.

There is a barge passing by this window with a flowing tide, and the colours are nailed to the mast. . In five minutes the barge will be at Westminster Bridge; the colours will remain, but the mast will be lowered—by the prudent Ashburton, who is steering the said barge.

I am at this moment engaged in a fierce controversy with Sir Francis Head—I defending Lord Ashburton; Head denouncing him for having regretted that an *apology* was not made by England to the United States for the destruction of the *Caroline*.

Ever affectionately yours,

ROBERT PEEL.

Sir Peter Laurie * *to Mr. Croker.*

Park Square, November 8th, 1843.

MY DEAR SIR,

Having been at Brighton, I did not get your letter in time to be able to send before, what I am not sure will quite answer your purpose. I believe that the first attempt at something like a drop in hanging criminals was at the execution of Lord Ferrers at Tyburn in 1760, but whether it did not work well, or was considered too aristocratic a mode for common vagabonds, or was a patent mode—if patents existed in those days—it was not adopted as the general mode of execution till 1783, when ten felons were executed on the 9th of December in that year for the first time in front of Newgate, on a new drop or scaffold hung with black very similar to that now used. No execution upon the old mode took place in front of Newgate. The last person executed at Tyburn was John Austin, who suffered on Friday the 7th of November, 1783, for a robbery committed on John Spicer

* [The worthy Alderman who was long known by his favourite phrase, "Put it down." This letter was no doubt written in reply to some inquiries which Mr. Croker was then making in preparation for his article on "The Guillotine," which was published in the *Quarterly Review* in December 1843, and which met with a large sale when reproduced in a separate form.]

with very aggravating circumstances. The gallows used at
Tyburn was purchased by a carpenter who, having no sentiment in his composition, converted it into stands for beer butts
in the cellars of a public house called the "Carpenter's Arms"
in Adam Street. I imagine that the drop introduced and
first used on the 9th of December, 1783, must have been an
experiment, as I find that on the 25th of November, 1784,
the Court of Aldermen "referred it to the Committee for
repairing the gaol of Newgate, to enquire into the expense of
a *platform* and bell used at the public execution of criminals."
The removal of the place of execution from Tyburn to Newgate was made at the instance of the Sheriffs, Sir Barnard
Turner and Thomas Skinner (1783), in consequence of the
mischiefs which arose from the long parade of criminals from
Newgate to Tyburn, and not from "the fury of innovation"
as Dr. Johnson has it. I must refer you to Croker's 'Boswell's
Johnson,' a work which you may have heard of. The inhabitants of the neighbourhood of Newgate petitioned against
this, but ineffectually, and I believe that if the place of
execution were now to be removed, the inhabitants would
petition for compensation.

I am, my dear Sir, yours very faithfully,

P. LAURIE.

Mr. Croker to Lord Brougham.

Alverbank, Gosport, July 7th, 1844.

MY DEAR BROUGHAM,

It is very natural that W. * should look with apprehension
to your accession, as he happens to hold the place that public
opinion, I believe—that private opinion certainly—would
assign to you; but I do not suppose that his feelings go
beyond that kind of very natural disinclination. The misfortune it seems to me was, that when Ellenborough's going
out offered room for an arrangement, W. was not made P. S.
[Privy Seal] instead of the Duke of B. [Buckingham]. I
have a constitutional prejudice against putting—not ministerial ladies—but the ladies of Ministers, about the Queen.
It is certain to make an embarrassment. For the present, I

* [Lord Wharncliffe, Lord President of the Council, died in November
1845.]

see nothing to be done; the line you are taking seems to me to be the very best you can adopt, and before another session, affairs must take a more decisive turn and you will be at full liberty to shape your own deliberate course. For my own part, I see nothing but mischief if you do not get into the boat to *row*, instead of hauling or shoving her from the shore. For your own sake I would rather have seen you in judicial office, where you would have been in a condition to render great, incontestable, and unenvied services; but in one way or the other, something must be settled, or the House of Lords will become more unmanageable than the Commons. I shall probably pay a flying visit to town, or more than one, before the session is over.

Ever yours,
J. W. CROKER.

Lady Ashburton to Mr. Croker.   Extract.

[No date.]

Talking of octogenarians, the Berry girls are established in London, and all the wit and fashion of the deserted metropolis rallies about them.

I had a long and amusing letter from Carlyle. He is correcting the proof sheets of Emerson's new work, but speaks of it with qualified praise.*

Poor Carlyle writes, "I am in such Cromwellian confusion, in ugly drudgery and sorrow, and shall not see the beautiful face of the Grange, or any beautiful thing, for I know not what long months or years."

Lord Ashburton to Mr. Croker.†   Extract.

April 7th, 1844.

I always thought our friend too severe in his notions of party obedience. Pitt and some other great men left a

---

* [In 1844 Emerson published the second series of his 'Essays,' which was carefully revised for the press by Mr. Carlyle. See his letters to Emerson of Sept. 29 and Nov. 3, 1844. A previous note will render it almost needless to explain here that the writer of this letter is not the Lady Ashburton referred to so frequently in the Letters of Carlyle and his wife, published in 1883.]

† [This letter refers to the Factory debates of 1844. Lord Ashley's

greater licence for caprice in non-essentials for persons not
in office, and as old Hunt said of Manners Sutton as Speaker,
he rode them in a snaffle.   Peel likes to drill his men as our
great Duke does his guards, but gentlemen with various
whims and fancies want a little more freedom, and are in the
end better governed by it.   The same disposition was shown
when, in opposition, many of his very good friends differed
from him about Drummond's privilege question.   In the
present case, however, I consider Graham's half threat is
merely a manœuvre to frighten back some of the stray sheep
into the fold, for in truth a real change of Government is
impossible where there is really nobody to take the reins and
succeed our Apollo in driving the chariot of the Sun.
Although, however, not a question of sufficient dignity to
cause the death of an administration, I do not consider it
otherwise than very important.   Interference with manufacturing, or indeed any other labour, is a serious matter, and
in this case it is the interference of very foolish people.   I
do not know enough of the case to be a critic of the relative
merits of a ten, eleven or twelve hours' restriction, but I
should be sorry to incur the responsibility of any restrictions
at all.   These are questions not safely to be judged *à priori*.
Experience can alone test them, but unfortunately a false
step is not easily retraced.   Your rivals having once passed
you in the race, they are not again easily overtaken.   I would
therefore fight to the last against this false principle of
meddling, but to talk of resigning the whole government is
too bad a joke for anybody to believe you.   But there must
be many means of defeating this bad measure.   What is
our Lordship's house good for ?   The most mischievous men
of our day are our conceited political economists and our
ultra humanitarians, good men some of them, but theirs
is a description of cant just suited to the capacities of the
majority of our electoral body, and they therefore bully us,
and will continue to do so.   There is, however, a large stock
of common sense left among us, and with prudent, steady
government, I am not afraid of them all—Philosophers,
Chartists, and Repealers.

Ten Hours' Bill, for women and children employed in factories, was
opposed by the Government, which proposed to fix the limit at twelve
hours, and at one time talked of staking its existence on the point.
A compromise was adopted.]

The disturbed state of Ireland in 1843–44 again forced Irish grievances upon the notice of the whole country. O'Connell's agitation was at its height; at one vast meeting he promised the people that before a year had elapsed an Irish Parliament should once more be sitting at College Green. The excitement of the people rapidly increased, and in the early part of October, 1843, a general "rally" was summoned at Clontarf. The day before the meeting was to take place, a proclamation was issued by the Government prohibiting it, and O'Connell and his son were indicted for a conspiracy. O'Connell defended himself; his son was defended by Sheil, in a speech which even Sheil had rarely surpassed. O'Connell was condemned to imprisonment for twelve months, and to pay a fine of 2000*l*. The defendants appealed to the House of Lords, and the hearing of the case gave rise to some remarkable circumstances. The law lords having given their decision, the lay lords claimed their right to vote upon the question, and Lord Campbell admitted their technical right, but contended that, as they had not been present at the hearing of the appeal, it would be improper for them to vote. Eventually they retired, and the law lords reversed the decision of the Dublin Court, and O'Connell was set at liberty. These are the general facts which are referred to in the next letters.

Sir James Graham to Mr. Croker.   Extract.

Cowes, September 15th, 1844.

My DEAR CROKER,

It was unlucky that you happened to be absent on the day when I called at Alverbank. I wished to see you, for in a letter I can hardly describe the impression produced on my mind by the judgment of the House of Lords. The view taken by Follett * is correct with respect to the *cause*. Jim. Parke

* [Sir William Follett, Solicitor-General.]

[Baron Parke] is responsible; if he had not raised doubts, of which he was evidently ashamed, even Denman would hardly have dared to pander, as he did, to popular passion; but the *effect* is much more doubtful.   It has inflicted a deep, perhaps an incurable, wound in a very tender part.   Trial by jury in Ireland is the weak place, which renders the civil government of that country all but impossible; and this fatal judgment will render the administration of justice according to law more difficult than ever.   The decision really rests on technicalities, which, triumphing over the merits in the last resort, bring law and reason and justice into contempt; but, at the same time, the merits and the technical niceties are so interwoven as to make the distinctions hard to be understood, and the confusion cloaks the dishonesty of the judgment, and raises a prejudice in the public mind in favour of the accused. I fear that no Irish juries will ever again convict in a political case; and it will be hard to find judges bold enough to do their duty when the House of Lords betrays its trust; and no public prosecutor will have the heart to proceed with boldness and confidence, when having triumphed over minor difficulties and dangers, he is exposed to certain failure in the supreme tribunal, from the malice of political adversaries, in defiance of justice and of law.

I am, yours very truly,

J. R. G. GRAHAM.

Sir James Graham to Mr. Croker.

Whitehall, October 14th, 1844.

MY DEAR CROKER,

You have on many occasions kindly tendered your assistance; I have never asked for it in vain; and it has more than once been given with triumphant effect.

In Ireland, that bog where Will o' the Wisps abound, Federalism, I am afraid, with growing discontent, is gaining ground; and the pamphlet of Mr. Porter and the speech of Dr. Maunsell are symptoms of the progress of the disease.

The absurdity of the project is no security against the danger of it; but the full extent both of the absurdity and of the danger should be demonstrated in a manner which may rouse the apprehensions, if it cannot operate on the reason, of the Irish Protestants, who are the owners of the soil, and also of those Roman Catholics who hold land under the title of confiscated estates.

When I remember your early picture of Ireland,* as it was and as it is, I know no hand like yours to do real justice to this subject, which is at once grand and difficult.†

If you would undertake the execution of this work, the opportunity would be the next number of the *Quarterly*, on the eve of the meeting of Parliament; and Mr. Porter's pamphlet is a subject for dissection not unworthy of the knife; for a publication in favour of modified repeal from the grandson of a Protestant Irish Bishop, from the son of a Protestant pluralist in the Irish Church, from the High Sheriff of the county of Fermanagh, from the heir to a large landed estate, and an *emeritus* Orangeman, is surely a *lusus naturæ*, which a skilful anatomist ought to place on his table, and to examine for the instruction and warning of the public.

I am, my dear Croker, yours very truly,

J. R. G. Graham.

Lord Redesdale to Mr. Croker. Extract.

Batsford Park, December 9th, 1844.

My dear Croker,

Even if you take Brougham's reasoning, which is that a peer unlearned in the law may vote on a difficult point of law if he has only had patience or curiosity enough to sit out all the speeches of the counsel who argued it before the House, surely in the case in question that attendance was unnecessary. It was universally admitted that nine-tenths of the argument was of no use whatever. The decision was come to on one single point—for Cottenham would give no opinion on Denman's "jury" matter, and Campbell a very doubtful one. The whole turned on "the one bad count." Now, if those who are unlearned in law can qualify themselves to pronounce an opinion (as Brougham held they may), would not any peer who had attentively studied the written opinions of the judges, seven one way and two the other, and attentively listened to the speeches of the law lords on *the morning of the day itself*, two one way and three the other, be far

* [Mr. Croker's "Sketch of Ireland, Past and Present."]

† [Mr. Croker wrote an article of seventy pages on the subject in the *Quarterly Review* of December 1844.]

better qualified to decide on the single point thus brought before him, than one who had attended the hearing *six weeks before* of the various speeches of the numerous counsel on both sides, containing lengthy arguments on many other points which all agreed to set aside as irrelevant ? I know how I, and I think every man possessing common-sense, would answer that question.

Yours sincerely,

REDESDALE.

Lord Redesdale to Mr. Croker.   Extract.

Batsford Park, December 13th, 1844.

MY DEAR CROKER,

We agree very much in our general view of the case, but differ in matters apparently perhaps of detail, but which, on a careful consideration of this very important subject, will, I think, be found essentials. You say that we might fairly have "ruled to support the judges," and that "on mere legal questions the House ought always to defer to the judges, and not to the law lords, except as supposing them to speak the sentiments of the judges."

My view is this: That we ought in the case in question to have held that the opinion of the judges was a safer one for the House to follow, than that of the majority of the law lords, but I by no means admit that the House (though it calls for it) is *always* to adopt the opinion of the judges in opposition to the law lords. The contrary has been frequently ruled—by Lord Eldon among others—and any decision of the general character you propose, would be only setting up in our House another "*imperium in imperio*" (to which you so justly object)—the judges, instead of the law lords. I claim for the House the right of deciding which opinion it thinks best or safest to follow; and I agree with you that *on a point of law* it would be *generally* the safer course to follow the judges. The law lords being political characters, are more likely to allow *expediency* to rule, and not *law*, than the judges are.

Much stuff has been talked about the House having abandoned its principles, &c. It is unquestionably the privilege of every peer to vote, *if he thinks fit*, on every legal question, whether he may have heard it argued or not, and whether with or against the opinion of those learned in the law. All privilège is open to abuse, and this would be an exercise of it which has only to be mentioned to be condemned.   We are a *deliberative* assembly.   All our rules, orders, and practices are for debate before decision, and the *principle* is that our conclusions are formed on the reasons adduced in debate.   In political matters peers are supposed to understand the subject under discussion, and often vote without hearing the debate, giving their confidence to those who they may consider best qualified to advise them on, and to direct public affairs, which principle is openly allowed to belong to the constitution of our House, which on all. such questions authorises the voting by proxy. In our judicial character we properly lay aside political feeling, attend no longer to our political leaders, but to the opinions of those qualified by their profession to decide on legal subjects, and defer to their judgment.

REDESDALE.

Mr. Croker to the King of Hanover.

West Moulsey, December 28th, 1844.

It seems that the Repeal Bubble in Ireland has burst, and, although Mr. O'Connell will no doubt continue his agitation, it is not, I think, likely to have any serious duration, and will give way to some other, I hope less dangerous, mode of getting the populace into the payment of the rent.   There was a considerable apprehension felt in the autumn that some of the Irish Protestants were about to join the Repeal agitation under the disguise of *Federalism,* and no doubt some of the northern *Whigs,* anxious to play into O'Connell's hands, were busy about such a design ; but I never suspected that the Irish Protestants could ever be so mad as to desert British connexion, and I think the result proves that I was right. Except a few adventurers, speculating on their interests, I am sure that *not one* Protestant has joined O'Connell.

Our country gentlemen have not been much pleased with the Ministry's policy on agricultural protection, and some dissension in the ensuing session has been calculated upon, but, I think, erroneously ; the country gentlemen, like the Irish Protestants, know that any move would be still worse for them, and that Sir Robert Peel is at least a safer minister than Lord John.

The literary world is at this moment interested in the memoirs of the first ten years of George III., by Horace Walpole. They are written in even more than his usual spirit of malignity against my old and revered master, your royal father, founded chiefly on the old calumny that Lord Bute continued to be a favourite long after he was Minister, and managed the King and kingdom by the Princess Dowager and the back stairs. I remember his late Majesty George IV. assured me that there was no pretence for this, and that George III. never saw Lord Bute after he left the Ministry but once, and that was in the garden of Gunnersbury, and that the King was angry with Princess Amelia for having permitted Lord Bute to be there. I have some reason to suspect that on the accession of George III., Horace Walpole made some advances in the way of flattery, not only to His Majesty, but to Lord and even *Lady* Bute, and that, when they had not the effect he hoped, he turned round and abused them because he could not dupe them. You will be amused, in spite of your indignation, to read that Queen Charlotte was for many years kept *prisoner* by the Princess Dowager, and indeed there is nothing so bad that Walpole does not say it of the princess, whom he seems to have especially hated.

J. W. C.

On one of the last days of 1844, a resident of the suburban parish of Hornsey wrote to Mr. Croker, to complain that two railroads were about to be made through the village, and that one of them proposed to run a tunnel through a "very beautiful place called the Grove," originally laid out by Topham Beauclerk, and which Dr. Johnson used "frequently to visit." The correspondent hoped that Mr. Croker would be able to "do something" about these intruding railroads. Mr. Croker's reply shows that he took far more liberal views on this and kindred questions than have generally been attributed to him.

Mr. Croker to an Inhabitant of Hornsey.

West Moulsey, December 28th, 1844.

SIR,

I have read of Mr. T. Beauclerk's having laid out the ground of a villa at Muswell Hill, but whether for himself or some friend I know not ; but we know so much of the details of Dr. Johnson's life, that I think that we may venture to say that he did not visit Hornsey so frequently as to justify the appropriation to him of one of the walks as " Dr. Johnson's Walk." As to the railroads, I confess I do not at all participate the reluctance which you and Mr. Wordsworth feel at what you consider their intrusion into picturesque scenery. I say nothing, because nothing need be said of the preponderance of considerations of *public utility*, but even in the mere landscape view of the matter, I do not see why the *millions* who travel by railways are not as much entitled to enjoy picturesque scenery as the half-dozen idlers and sketchers who now once or twice a week wind through your valley or wander through your wood. I myself have been near half a century a resident of London, and have never yet seen your rural beauties ; but when the railroad shall be completed, I daresay I shall be as familiar with them as with Wandsworth or Wimbledon. I know persons who were adverse to railroads, and who would now give 500*l.* a mile to have them nearer their residences. I add one further consideration, that the railroad is the most innoxious to the neighbour's land, through which it only passes, of all possible communications ; it not only brings no vagabonds, tramps, or beggars, but forcibly excludes them ; and, except for the moment that one of these wonderful productions of art, a train, enlivens *en passant* the uniform features of nature, it can in no serious degree alter the prospect of a house even overlooking it. A railroad runs through the beautiful valley of the Derwent, and I think that triumph of art sets off, as well as renders more accessible, the natural beauties of the scene.

I have the honour to be, Sir,

Your most obedient humble servant,

J. W. CROKER.

CHAPTER XXIV.

1845—1846.

THERE are few more interesting years in English political
history than 1845 and 1846. They witnessed the triumph of
the Manchester school, and the introduction of a new system
into the commercial policy of England ; they saw the desertion of the Conservative party by its leader, and the subse-

quent downfall of that leader in the midst of his apparent triumph ; the appearance of a remarkable man, who succeeded in rallying the broken columns, and in exciting the curiosity and expectation of all observers, and was then suddenly, and almost mysteriously, taken from the world ;—the slow rise of still another leader, long distrusted and despised by his party, but eventually followed with enthusiasm, even when he was guided by principles which seemed to have been borrowed from the statesman whose life he had condemned as " one great appropriation clause." The personal records of these two years are as full of startling surprises as any of the great dramas which absorb the attention of mankind. There is the picture of a knot of discouraged agitators becoming so great a power in the State, that each party has since lived chiefly by adapting itself to their principles. There are the contrasts presented in the career of Sir Robert Peel, who seemed destined to enjoy as long a lease of power as Lord Liverpool, and who fell by the hands of the party which he had sacrificed, and of the men whose system he had adopted ; the unprecedented incidents which surrounded the brief presence on the scene of Lord George Bentinck, down to the moment when he went out for the morning's walk from which he never returned ; the resolute struggle for supremacy which was made by the pamphleteer and novelist, who was so little known or comprehended by the Conservatives of the older school, that they could not even manage to spell his name correctly. This is not the place in which the whole of this " strange eventful history " can properly be set forth, but a brief summary of some of its incidents will form a necessary introduction to the letters and documents which tend to throw a new and powerful light upon it.

It was evident to many men, even in the early part of 1845, that the Administration of Sir Robert Peel was not so

strong as it seemed. The landed interest was alarmed, and
yet the people were not being won over. Sir Robert Peel had
estranged many of his supporters by his cold and haughty
manner, and a still larger number by the tendency which he
had more than once shown to make rapid changes of ground,
on the most important questions, without notice or warning
to his supporters. The discontent in Parliament soon found
a voice. It was in the month of February that Mr. Disraeli
may be said to have begun that series of attacks upon Peel
which eventually drove the Ministry from power. Some
of these attacks were excessive in their asperity, and were
disfigured by a certain florid tone which occasionally went
dangerously near to making them ridiculous ; but in the main
they served their purpose. It was then that Mr. Disraeli
described the Prime Minister as having come upon the Whigs
bathing, and run off with their clothes. A few days later he
declared that Protection was in about the same state that
Protestantism was in 1828. He contended that if the country
was to have Free-trade, it ought to have it from Mr. Cobden,
not from the statesman who was pledged to the defence of
Protection. In April the Bill for increasing and re-arranging
the endowment of Maynooth was introduced by Peel, and
Mr. Disraeli stigmatised him as the "great Parliamentary
middleman," who "bamboozles one party and plunders
the other." He told the nominal leader of his party, that
"cunning is not caution, and that habitual perfidy is not high
policy of State." The Maynooth bill was carried, but it did
not appear that Sir Robert Peel had strengthened his position
either with his party or with the country.

Towards the end of January, Sir James Graham, who, it
will be remembered, was the Home Secretary, wrote to Mr.
Croker, calling his attention to the hostile tone of the press.
"The cry of the pack is general," he remarked, "and they are

inclined to run us down." He was disposed to attribute this to some want of "management" 'on the parts of the Secretaries of the Treasury; in reality it was a sign that the beginning of the end was come. Sir James Graham went on to say * :—

" The Press in a united host against the Government is a powerful adversary, and in the long run must do us mischief. There are, however, advantages in our independence from the thraldom which the fear of the newspapers rivets on those whose *first* aim is popularity. The hostility of the *Times* has somewhat abated : it has burnt itself out; but the approaching Session, I fear, will add fresh fuel to the fire. Stanley and I have had our share of abuse; yet we survive it."

Lord Ashburton † to Mr. Croker.   Extract.

March 12th, 1845.

MY DEAR CROKER,

I know nothing of the Dutch saint mentioned in the Malmesbury papers,‡ but the first time I meet Dedel will ask what he knows about him. I ran away from Holland the night before Pichegru entered Amsterdam, and in 1797 I was occupied in courting my Lady in Philadelphia.

As I see you are busy with these curious memoirs, the historical fact will not escape you of the great eagerness of Pitt for peace in 1797, and the desponding view of affairs taken both by him and Canning, checked by the dogged obstinacy of Grenville. This was the year of the mutiny and of the most critical event of that great war, the *Bank suspension,* an event

---

* Letter to Mr. Croker, dated Whitehall, January 29th, 1845.

† [This was Alexander Baring, first Baron Ashburton, signer of the Ashburton Treaty, mentioned in vol. ii. pp. 393–403. He was born in 1774, and married in 1798 Anne Louisa, eldest daughter of Mr. Bingham, of Philadelphia—a senator of the United States. Lady Ashburton, as well as her husband, frequently corresponded with Mr. Croker, and they were next door neighbours at Alverstoke, where Mr. Croker had a marine villa. Both Lord and Lady Ashburton died in 1848, one in May, and the other in December.]

‡ [In the *Quarterly Review,* No. 150 (March, 1845) was an article by Mr. Croker on the ' Diaries and Correspondence of James, first Earl of Malmesbury,' which had just been published.]

which set us at our ease, and enabled us to borrow without stint down to the battle of Waterloo, when our great Duke's victories just came in time to save us from bankruptcy—from this fatal facility of what Falstaff calls " scoring up."

I doubt, however, whether this event is more than deferred, seeing that our generation are unwilling to do anything towards the reduction of our score in the thirty years of peace we have now enjoyed.

Ever affectionately yours,

ASHBURTON.

In March, the signs of dissatisfaction were so unmistakable that Mr. Croker no longer hesitated to speak plainly about them.

Mr. Croker to Sir James Graham.   Extract.

West Moulsey, March 21st, 1845.

MY DEAR GRAHAM,

I hear from all quarters that the country gentlemen are greatly out of *temper*, or perhaps I should rather say out of *spirits ;* and you may depend upon it, are in a state of mind very unsatisfactory, not to say precarious and alarming.   You know that I was, and am, favourable to the new Corn Scale. I think it decidedly protective, though I wish now as I wished then, that the scale had run on to 25s. or 30s. more; for I remember Peel's telling me that autumn, that he had a letter from New Orleans, saying that the Mississippi wheat would be able to meet our 20s. duty in London.   Nor was I, nor am I, afraid of the general operation of the tariff; but I am, I confess, of Canada corn ; and I am not surprised that all these and several other smaller circumstances, light indeed, but all going in the same direction, should alarm country gentlemen, whose turn of mind is towards immediate and tangible interests rather than prospective, circuitous, and consequential advantages.

I do think that some occasion ought to be found or made, if not of doing, at least of saying, and strongly too, something comforting and gratifying to that great interest, which is, after all, the only safe basis of a Government in this country.

Ever yours, &c.,

J. W. CROKER.

Sir James Graham to Mr. Croker. Extract.

Whitehall, March 22nd, 1845.

MY DEAR CROKER,

I am aware of the fact that our country gentlemen are out
of humour, and that the existence of the Government is endangered by their present temper and recent proceedings.
We have laboured hard, and not in vain, to restore the prosperity of the country, and to give increased security to the
aristocracy, by improving the condition and diminishing the
discontent of the great masses of the people. We have
effected this object without inflicting any real injury on the
landed proprietors; yet we are scouted as traitors, and are
denounced as if we were time-serving traders in politics,
seeking to retain place by the sacrifice of the interests of our
friends.

The country gentlemen cannot be more ready to give us
the death-blow than we are prepared to receive it. If they
will rush on their own destruction, they must have their
way: we have endeavoured to save them, and they regard us
as enemies for so doing.

If we have lost the confidence and good will of the country
party, our official days are numbered; and the time will
come when this party will bitterly deplore the fall of Sir
Robert Peel, and when in vain they will wish that they had
not overthrown a Government which its enemies could not
vanquish, but which its supporters abandoned and under-
mined.

I am, my dear Croker, yours sincerely,

J. R. G. GRAHAM.

The Maynooth Bill was opposed by large classes throughout
the country, and many a speaker declared that the measure
would bring down upon the nation the wrath of heaven.
Mr. Gladstone resigned office, because in his work on ' Church
and State,' he had expressed opinions on the Maynooth grant
contrary to those which he at present held—so great was
the importance which he at that time, in common with Sir
Robert Peel himself, attached to the virtue of consistency in
statesmen. Sir Robert Peel was identified as the veritable

Antichrist, and Dr. Croly proved that George the Fourth came
to a premature end, and the Houses of Parliament were
burnt down, because Catholic Emancipation was granted in
1829.   Mr. Disraeli attacked the Prime Minister with
great virulence within the walls of Parliament, and the
press was equally active outside.   But Peel was in no way
discouraged.

Sir Robert Peel to Mr. Croker.

Whitehall, April 22nd, 1845.

My dear Croker,

The opposition to the Maynooth Bill is mainly the opposition of *Dissent* in England—partly fanatical, partly religious—
mainly unwillingness to sanction the germ of a second establishment, and to strengthen and confirm that of the Protestant Church.

Oxford and Cambridge are quiet—well represented by
their respective members.

We have with us almost all the youth, talent, and real
influence from public station in the House of Commons.

Many of our opponents merely yield to the wishes of dissenting constituents.

Tariff—drought—46s. a quarter for wheat—quicken the
religious apprehensions of some; disappointed ambition and
the rejection of applications for office others.

All this raises a storm at which I look with much indifference, being resolved on carrying the Bill, and being very
careless as to the consequences which may follow its passing,
so far as they concern me and my position.

Affectionately yours,

R. P.

*Sir R. Peel to Mr. Croker.**

Whitehall, June 9th.

My dear Croker,

You will see in the Irish Debates of 1795 the petition
from the Catholics presented by Grattan.

The first Maynooth Bill was framed by Lord Fitzwilliam's

* [This is the last of Sir Robert Peel's letters which the Editor has been
able to find among Mr. Croker's papers—with one exception, to be referred
to hereafter.]

Government with Grattan's knowledge. See Grattan's speech on moving the Address in 1795.

Though Grattan presented the petition against the Bill at a later period of the Session, he took an active part against it. I believe the Bill was the same substantially with that of which he spoke on moving the address.

The Archbishop of Canterbury (Moore) was consulted by the Duke of Portland on the second Bill, and I believe approved of it. At least, there is no record of any objection. I am sure he did not object.

Lord Normanton wrote the other day to Lord Somerton, his son, expressed the utmost indignation at his son having voted for the second reading of our Bill, and ended much blustering eloquence by a pathetic lamentation that the grandson of Charles Agar, Archbishop of Cashel (at that moment disquieted in his grave by such backsliding on the part of his descendant) should have committed such an enormity.

But I have a very plain, sensible letter from Lord Camden, saying that one of the parties whom he confidentially consulted on the first Maynooth Bill, and who approved of it, was this same Charles Agar (was his name Charles?), the inflexible Archbishop.

Now as to your second point, the rejection of the Bill in 1799.

I believe at this moment no human being but myself knows the real truth on that point.

It was an act of sheer mischief and mutiny of Lord Clare, who perhaps then had a foresight of diminished influence on the passing of the Act of Union.

He rejected the Bill without communication with the Irish Government.

Lord Castlereagh gave an assurance in the Commons, as you will perceive, that no prejudice to the College should arise from the proceedings of the Lords.

Have you Plowden's ' History of Ireland '?

> Ever affectionately yours,
>
> R. PEEL.

I feared the worst when I last saw Follett. I refused to receive his resignation, which he tendered, and wrote him the kindest letter I could.

Alas, for great professional eminence, and the severe struggle to maintain it!

> " Nocitura togâ . . . . petuntur
> Et sua mortifera est facundia."

Ever affectionately yours,

R. P.

The postscript of the foregoing letter refers to the condition of the Attorney-General.   In 1844, on the elevation of Sir Frederick Pollock to the bench, Sir William Follett had succeeded him as Attorney-General; but his health, which had never been robust, completely broke down under the strain of work.   He went abroad in the hope of recovery, and on his return, once more endeavoured to undertake the duties of his office.   The circumstances attending his death, which occurred on June 28th, will be found at the commencement of Chapter XXVI.

The storm which the Maynooth Bill had raised soon passed over, but the real difficulties and dangers of the Ministry had not begun.   In the month of August, the first signs of the potato disease, which resulted in the great and memorable Irish famine, made their appearance.   As the autumn advanced, the disease spread rapidly, and simultaneously with it there occurred a most unfortunate season for English and Scotch farmers.   The rain fell night and day.   The fields were flooded, and most of the crops were ruined.   The Corn Law League had all but broken down, notwithstanding the immense sums of money which it had raised and spent.   It now took fresh courage.   There were apprehensions of a general and disastrous scarcity of food, and Mr. Cobden and his friends redoubled their exertions.   Their biographer has stated as a simple matter of fact that it was the weather which won the day, and not their arguments.   " It was the rain that rained away the Corn Laws."

Sir Robert Peel, who was always extremely sensitive to any manifestation of opinion in the country, had been much impressed by the operations of the League. In October he appears to have come to the conclusion that it was gaining ground rapidly, and that it would be necessary to shape his own course in accordance with its undeniable progress. He has since told the world that he had adopted at an early period of his public life, "without much serious reflection," the "opinions generally prevalent at the time among men of all parties, as to the justice and necessity of protection to domestic agriculture." * If he adopted these opinions carelessly, he at any rate held them tenaciously down to the apparent turning of the tide in public opinion in 1845. In October he wrote to Lord Heytesbury to express the opinion that legislative remedies would have to be found for the "great evil" with which the country was threatened. "The remedy," he added, "is the removal of all impediments to the import of all kinds of human food—that is, the total and absolute repeal for ever of all duties on all articles of subsistence."† Lord Heytesbury was not a member of the Cabinet, and the policy distinctly foreshadowed in this letter was not communicated to that body even when it met on the 31st of October. The "three courses" which proverbially accompanied the recommendations of Sir Robert Peel, were thus indicated :—"Shall we maintain unaltered—shall we modify —shall we suspend—the operation of the Corn Laws?" Not a word was said about their "total and absolute repeal for ever." Still less was any information given to the Conservative Party with regard to the important change which had taken place in the opinions of its leader. Sir Robert Peel, in his 'Memoirs,' admits ‡ that he was subjected to reproach

---

* 'Memoirs,' by Sir Robert Peel, Part III. vol. ii. pp. 98, 99.
† Ibid. p. 121.   ‡ Ibid. pp. 318–321.

on this ground. He urges in defence that the "peculiar character of the unforeseen emergency," and "the peculiar position of the Cabinet in respect to the measures to be adopted," prevented him making that "unreserved communication" which he had actually "contemplated." [It is no part of our duty here to discuss the validity of this defence; it is sufficient to say that no commentator on these events, whether of Liberal or Conservative opinions, has ever accepted it as a justification of the line pursued by Sir Robert Peel towards his party.

In 1847, Sir Robert Peel again defended his conduct in a letter to Lord Aberdeen. In that letter he remarked, " In December, 1845, I thought their repeal [the Corn Laws] indispensable to the public welfare." It appears from his letter to Lord Heytesbury that it was in October, not December, that he came to this conclusion. He left his party and his colleagues in ignorance of his intentions nearly three months longer than, in 1847, he thought he had done._

On the 22nd of November Lord John Russell addressed a letter to the citizens of London which gave fresh alarm to Sir Robert Peel. " It justified the conclusion," he remarks in his memoirs,* "that the Whig party was prepared to unite with the Anti-Corn Law League in demanding the total repeal of the Corn Laws." Lord John Russell had, in fact, plainly stated that the Government " seemed to be waiting for some excuse to give up the present Corn Law," and he called upon the people to " afford them the excuse they seek." " Let us then," he said, "unite to put an end to a system which has been proved to be the blight of commerce, the bane of agriculture, the source of bitter divisions among classes, the cause of penury, fever, mortality, and crime among the people."

* Vol. ii. p. 174.

On the 29th of November, Sir Robert Peel circulated another memorandum among his colleagues, calling their attention again to the danger of a short supply of food, but still breathing no word of his intention to *repeal* the Corn Laws.   The following is an extract from this memorandum :—

> "Time presses, and on some definite course we must decide. Shall we undertake, without suspension, to modify the existing Corn Law ?   Shall we resolve to maintain the existing Corn Law ?   Shall we advise the suspension of that law for a limited period ?
>
> "My opinion is for the last course, admitting as I do that it involves the necessity for the immediate consideration of the alterations to be made in the existing Corn Law, such alterations to take effect after the period of suspension.   I should rather say it involves the question of the principle and degree of protection to agriculture."

There are hints here of suspension " for a limited period," of "alterations," of the "degree" of protection to be afforded to agriculture ; but nothing to lead any one to suppose that the Premier had long before decided in his own mind that *total repeal* was the only suitable remedy.   But by this time several of Sir Robert Peel's colleagues saw that the path upon which he was desirous of entering must inevitably lead to repeal, and two of them—Lord Stanley and the Duke of Buccleuch—resigned.* The position taken by the Duke of Wellington, then and afterwards, is very clearly defined in his own letters.   His first duty was not to maintain the Corn Laws, but to "maintain a government in the country."   He therefore followed Peel, though not willingly, in his great surrender.   But it is evident that he had no suspicion how complete was to be the surrender down to the last moment. On the 6th January, 1846, he stated to Mr. Croker that he "really did not know" what Sir Robert Peel intended

---

* The Duke of Buccleuch afterwards returned to his office.

to propose.   He evidently believed that it was to be an
"alteration" of the Corn Laws, not their total abolition.

On the 5th of December Sir Robert Peel, feeling, as he
says, that the "assent given by many [of his colleagues] was
a reluctant one," thought proper to resign.   Lord John Russell
was invited to form an Administration, but he did not succeed, on account of the refusal of Earl Grey to sit in the
Cabinet with Lord Palmerston, of whose foreign policy he
disapproved.   On the 20th December, Sir Robert Peel returned to power, Mr. Gladstone taking the office of Colonial
Secretary, which had formerly been held by Lord Stanley.

Mr. Croker to Sir R. Peel.*

Kensington Palace, November, 28th, 1845.

MY DEAR PEEL,

I had a letter from Mr. Murray last night to say that Lord
John Russell's letter was looked upon as the manifesto of a
new revolution, and asking me whether time and *other circumstances* would allow of an article in the next *Quarterly
Review* (about three weeks distant) to meet this danger.
I hear also from Ashburton that he is much alarmed, and
I learn from other quarters that there is a great ferment
in the minds of the country gentlemen.   I need not tell you
how *I* feel on this—not to me unexpected—alliance of the
whigs, leaguers and radicals.   It was no great extent of foresight to anticipate it, as I did in my article on the Corn
Laws four years ago.   Nor need I say how much I wish in
my declining years I could assist in staying the plague, but I
recollect the *telum imbelle sine ictu* of the old.   But that is
not all—I know not what your Government feels on this
momentous question.   The papers announce a change of
sentiment, and I myself have seen indications (in one or two
circumstances) that some Members of the Cabinet are inclined to a *modification* of the existing law.   I hope I may
be mistaken—*any* change in the line of concession at this
moment—when in my opinion the Corn Laws are proving
practically the wisdom and policy of their principle—would,
I believe, be ruin to the monarchical party and to the country

* [No answer to this letter has been found.]

—and I should abandon in despair all attention to public affairs, and follow, or rather slide down, the facilis decensus Averni—that is, Democracy.⟩

But I neither wish to take any step forward or backward without receiving, if you think it proper, and worth while to give it, your opinion. The *Quarterly Review* can be silent —at least so far as I am concerned—but its line, if it does speak, is marked out by the former article which I have just mentioned, and also—though that is a minor consideration— by the apparently unanimous opinion of all the classes which support it. It may happen that you should have some difficulty in answering this, or you may be willing to let the press take its own unbiased line. In either case you will take no notice of this letter, and the *Quarterly Review* must follow its own judgment, either in saying nothing, or in strong opposition to the new revolution. My own active participation in the review is drawing rapidly to a close, but I am confident that the *principles* which it has advocated, especially that of maintaining the landed interest, afford the *only safe*, and would prove, if pursued with courage and determination, ultimately the *most popular* basis of Government in this country.

Ever yours,

J. W. CROKER.

The Duke of Wellington to Mr. Croker.

Strathfieldsaye, December 11th, 1845.

MY DEAR CROKER,

Although there is no more sincere well wisher to the existing Corn Law Sliding Scale than myself, and although I have done and will do everything in my power to maintain it, my position is not the Corn Law ; but it is to maintain a Government in the country.

For that I have always contended and always will contend.

I am very sensible that any influence which I may have, the good which I may aid in doing, and the evil which I may aid in preventing, must depend upon the kindness and good offices of friends.

Such influence may easily be written, or cried, or even talked down.

Be it so ; I cannot avoid that evil.

But I positively and distinctly decline to take a step, which must have the effect of dissolving a Government which Her Majesty has formed, of which the dissolution must be followed by the loss of Corn Laws and everything else.

I will not attempt to reason upon these hypothetical views of Sir Robert Peel's propositions. I hope even to see what they are. In the meantime I endeavour.to prevail upon those who desire to have, or are willing to read or to listen in conversation to my opinions, to wait to see what he will propose before they decide upon the course which they will take upon his propositions.

This would be reasonable in any cause, excepting possibly in one involving party politics.

Believe me ever yours most sincerely,

WELLINGTON.

Mr. Croker to Sir Robert Peel.

Kensington Palace, December 16th, 1845.

MY DEAR PEEL,

When I wrote to you three weeks ago about Lord John's letter I little thought that so tremendous a crisis as your own resignation was so near at hand. It has *atterré'd* me. I am in despair—I came to town with a cold which I increased at the Bishop of Oxford's consecration, and I have not been out of doors since, until yesterday—but my cold should not have hindered my calling on you had I had any consolation to give or receive, and in truth even in more cheering circumstances, I never like to trouble you when serious businesses are in hand with my now useless and idle visits. I kept away gladly while you were making your Government. I keep away in despair while you are dissolving it—for with *it* go all my hopes of the salvation of the country. As I am now able to go out, we return to Moulsey to-morrow or Friday, where I shall await the final stroke, like one in a condemned cell. I cannot explain to you my ignorant wonder at our position. There is no scarcity —I fear no chance of one—for if to-morrow corn would only rise to scarcity prices, to the price even of 1839, there would be nothing to differ on. We are dying with all the symptoms of health. In what I have been very reluctantly forced to write for the *Quarterly*--not having seen or heard from any one who knew anything of what was going on—I was obliged to touch all that regards the resignation with the vagueness of profound ignorance, following in the few words I have said the hints of the *Standard ;* but I have re-asserted, as against Lord John Russell, the sliding scale and our doctrines of 1841-2 which I conscientiously believe to be the only safe ones ; and the carrying of which I believe to be the greatest service of all the great services you have done your country. And has it all been in vain ? and is the great Conservative Party dissolved ? and are the Landed Interests, and ultimately the aristocracy, and the monarchy, to be handed over to the fierce democracy of the *League ?*

The soberest party might be intoxicated at such a triumph —but it will drive—indeed it seems, has driven the League mad—and the Landed Interest and their advocates are already designated to public vengeance as *" murderers."*

Being wholly ignorant of, and not desiring to know before the rest of the world, your own share, views, and motives in all this dreadful catastrophe, I know not what to hope (if there can be hope) or fear—but black as the whole horizon looks, I cannot persuade myself that *even yet, you* could not save us. If you can't, we are all lost—you and all of us.

> Ever my dearest Peel,
>   Your affectionate and afflicted,
>   J. W. CROKER.

Mr. Croker to the Duke of Wellington.

Kensington Palace, December 13th, 1845.

MY DEAR DUKE,

I was busy writing an article in defence of the Corn Laws for the *Quarterly Review,* when this bomb burst. Neither I nor the *Review* can change the opinions which two years ago we published under Peel's own sanction. *Something* the *Review* must say, because the Conservative party have looked to it on all such occasions, and it could not now with decency or safety desert its colours.

Is your Grace at liberty to give me any clue as to the line it would be best to take. I do not venture to ask for details, nor anything like State secrets, but merely such an indication as will enable the *Review* to keep in harmony with your sentiments. I think there can be no impropriety in my asking you for as much light as you may be at liberty to afford me. ⌈I daresay Peel intended some large system, which he thought would afford by its compensations and balances adequate protection.⌋ I doubt the possibility of any adequate compensation, but even if it were certain, I do not think that this was a safe time to propose any great change, nor, above all, such a one as should risk so great a calamity as placing the *League* at the head of affairs.

J. W. CROKER.

The Duke of Wellington to Mr. Croker.

Strathfieldsaye, December 14th, 1845.

MY DEAR CROKER,

I have received your note of the 13th, and I shall be happy to give you every information in my power; but I don't like to write about matters of which I have a knowledge only as a member of the Cabinet.

The foundation of the Corn Law difficulty is the apprehension of the consequences of the potato disease, the nature of which is misapprehended, and their account greatly exaggerated.

You and I for the last forty years have known of some four or five instances of the consequences of the common practice of the cottier and labouring population of Ireland choosing to be the producers of the root which they are themselves with their families to consume as food; and mortgaging their labours for weeks or months to the landlord or occupier of the soil which produces the root, in order to pay the rent for the same.

Then comes the partial, or in this case the expected nearly total, failure of the produce of the root by the soil: the labourer is obliged to work for the rent; or at all events, if dishonest, to get food, for eat he must: and then observe, that if money was thrust into his pocket he is not accustomed to go to market or to shop to purchase food, and he must therefore be paid for his labour in food.

This is the real difficulty in Ireland; but I do not believe that there is even there scarcity of food, between potatoes and oats, to feed the people for the year.

The oat harvest there, as well as in England and Scotland, has been most abundant. In England and Scotland the consequences of the potato disease have been different. Potatoes in England, and I believe in Scotland, are not so much a necessary as in Ireland; but a sort of luxury to the poor. They give them a cheap hot meal, and are excellent used with their bacon or any other meat.   The best of the rural population suffer the most.   I mean those which have allotment gardens attached to their cottages, which they generally cultivate by growing potatoes, very rarely cabbages.

The loss of the potatoes to this class is a severe privation; as is—consequent upon the disease—the dearness of potatoes throughout the country to the labouring population in towns.

But in other respects I happen to know that the country never was better provided with food than at the present moment: and that, in fact, the United Kingdom is in a situation to bear the shock of the potato disease better than that of any other in Europe at least!

The harvest of 1844 was excellent and abundant beyond example: the produce of 1844 has not yet been all consumed. We had lately in bond 850,000 quarters of wheat, besides other grain; and observe that the average demand for the consumption of the country beyond its produce does not exceed a million quarters, and foreign corn is still coming in weekly to the amount of from 17,000 to 20,000 quarters a week.   However, all these figures you can and ought to have officially.

Then the harvest of 1845 has been good in England, Ireland and Scotland, and the price is moderate, indeed provokingly so, as the rise of price and decrease of duty might have opened the ports, and have put an end to all question and difficulty.

I have here given you the elements and outlines of the question.

I am staying here and shall be happy to see you if you will come down.

Believe me, ever yours most sincerely,

WELLINGTON.

The Duke of Wellington to Mr. Croker.

Strathfieldsaye, December 26th, 1845.

MY DEAR CROKER,

I return the inclosed,* of which I cannot make out one word, however curious to make out its contents, and diligent as my efforts [have been] to attain that object.

* ["The enclosed" was most probably a letter from Lord Brougham. Mr. Croker speaks in the next letter of sending *copies* of two of Brougham's letters to the Duke.]

I will do my best to keep matters right. The truth is, that if the Government does not make an arrangement of the Corn Laws satisfactory to the landed interest, it cannot hope for its support; and cannot carry on the Queen's business!

Ever yours most sincerely,

WELLINGTON.

Mr. Croker to the Duke of Wellington.

West Moulsey, December 28th, 1845.

MY DEAR DUKE,

I send you copies of two of Brougham's hieroglyphic epistles. You will see that he guessed very rightly that Lord John could not form a Government, but you will observe some errors, very natural to one writing at such a distance.; and that great mistake about *Irish landlords;* for the truth is, that O'Connell has hardly what can be called a landlord in his whole tail—they are all his *creatures* and those of the priests, and would vote *anything* that he should desire. But you see what he says about the *land*—*that*, depend upon it, is the only foundation for Government; and I have that confidence in you, that as you are (I know not, and enquire not, how) in the new Cabinet, it is to me and to all England, a pledge that we have at least our best bower anchor still in the ground. But then we cannot account for the reconstruction of the whole Cabinet, minus one; and the exchange being of such a man as Lord Stanley for such a man as Mr. Gladstone. Brougham, you see, never imagined such a reconstruction of the Government. My own private notion is that the present Cabinet can never make the Queen's Speech. You have consented for the public good to appear to hold together for a time, but whatever broke you up on the 10th December, was equally in force when you re-united on the 20th. This is *my guess*, but I don't ask yours.

Ever, my dear Duke,

Your most attached,

J. W. CROKER.

Since I wrote my letter I have heard from town that Mr. Gladstone went to Mr. Murray's shop on purpose to tell him that "he disapproved of every word of the Corn Law article in the *Quarterly.*" This volunteer declaration seems to confirm my suspicions that we are on hollow ground.

The Duke of Wellington to Mr. Croker.

Strathfieldsaye, December 28th, 1845.

MY DEAR CROKER,

I am most obliged to you, and shall be happy to see Lord Brougham's opinion.

I think that the decision founded upon the potato disease was erroneous. But the course taken could not have been otherwise, as the decision was founded upon a *bonâ fide* opinion of the necessity of the case.

This was very unfortunate!

The consequence of the resignation, and of the negotiations for the formation of a new Administration, was that those charged necessarily became acquainted with the cause and circumstances of the resignation.

These persons failed in their efforts to form an Administration, and there is no doubt but that Sir Robert Peel went down to Windsor on Saturday the 20th with the firm determination, if so required, to become Her Majesty's Minister again; and to enable Her Majesty to meet her Parliament, even if he should stand alone, rather than oblige her to seek for a Minister among the Radicals! Nobody could do otherwise than approve of Sir Robert Peel's conduct.

It must be observed, however, that his position in relation to the Corn Laws was greatly altered in comparison with what it had been in the end of the Session, 1845.

His opponents heard of the opinions, however erroneous, and circumstances, which had induced him to recommend to Her Majesty to endeavour to form another Administration.

He could no longer resume his old ground on the Corn Laws.

He must consider of some alteration; and if he means to carry on a Government providing for the interest of the public with credit to himself, he will take care that the alteration shall be of a nature to provide for the interests of agriculture, and to satisfy the just claims of the owners, occupiers, and cultivators of the land.

This is what I hope he will do. It is what the interests of the Queen and those of the public and his own credit require.

In respect to myself and other members of the Cabinet, who differed in opinion with Sir Robert in respect to the Corn Laws in October and November, we are in this position. We

may and do wish that the Corn Laws could be maintained,
but we know that none of us could form a Government in
order to maintain them; nor, indeed, could any other individual that we know of.

This fact was ascertained during the progress of Lord
John's negotiation.

It is impossible for us to do more than make every effort
that the system which will be proposed to Parliament may be
of a nature to give security and satisfaction to those interested
in the prosperity of agriculture. I admit that this is very
unsatisfactory.

But it is the best prospect that I can hold out.

> Believe me ever yours most sincerely,
>
> WELLINGTON.

The Duke of Wellington to Mr. Croker.

Strathfieldsaye, December 29th, 1845.

MY DEAR CROKER,

Since I wrote to you yesterday I have received yours of
the 28th with the copy of Lord Brougham's, which is very
curious.

Our position is undoubtedly a critical one, and I do not see
my way clearly. But I have better hopes than I had some
days ago. I feel that some of the landed interest are disposed
to wait and see what Peel really intends!

I am most concerned for the loss of Lord Stanley. He
could not possibly take the course which I have taken. I
believe that he has been speaking lately at Protection Associ-
ations.

Excepting in his case we shall have all our offices well
filled.

You have not perceived the difference between Peel's situation on the 10th and on the 20th of December. On the
10th, erroneously thinking that a material alteration of the
Corn Laws was necessary on account of the potatoe disease and
its consequences, but opposed by his colleagues in the Cabinet,
he informed Her Majesty that he could no longer conduct
the affairs of Her Majesty, and advised her to send for others,
who consequently became acquainted with the exact cause for
the breaking up of the administration of Sir Robert Peel.
When Lord John Russell failed in forming an administration

on the 20th of December, a movement of enthusiasm induced Sir Robert Peel, when sent for, to determine, before he saw the Queen, that if required he would stand by her, even alone if necessary, to enable her to meet her Parliament, rather than reduce Her Majesty to the necessity of calling upon Mr. Cobden and others whose names I have no right to indicate as his associates, to serve Her Majesty as her Ministers.

I participated in this movement, and at once consented to give my assistance to the Queen in her difficulties.

Sir Robert Peel at that time, the 20th of December, stood in this situation in relation to the Corn Laws : His opponents, Whig as well as Radical, knew precisely the situation in which he and his colleagues had stood. Right or wrong in taking that position, Sir Robert Peel could not on the 20th resume the ground on which he had stood in the Session of 1845.

He must therefore deal with the Corn Laws as he would, or nearly as he would, under the impressions which induced him to relinquish office on the 10th of December.

As to the members of the Cabinet formed on the 20th of December, they must feel that although their opinions and wishes on the Corn Laws were the same as they were previous to the 10th of December, they cannot expect from Sir Robert Peel and those of his colleagues . who have agreed in opinion with him, that they should defend the existing law.

All that they can do, and that which I am endeavouring to do, is to prevail upon those who have undertaken to prepare the measures which it is intended to propose to Parliament, to keep in mind the necessity that they should be such as to give satisfaction and security to the landed interest, and to induce the cultivators of the soil to continue their efforts to improve and increase its produce.

I quite concur in your notion of the importance in a national view of the prosperity of the agriculture of the country; and in a party political view of the landed interest.

In truth, Sir Robert Peel, aided and excited by his enthusiasm in the service of the Queen, will do Her Majesty but little good, and acquire but little credit for himself, unless he can rally round his Government the support of that party.

I hope the attainment of these objects is not yet out of the question.

I am doing all that I can in every way to attain it.

Believe me ever yours most sincerely,

WELLINGTON.

Mr. Croker to Lord Ashburton.

West Moulsey, December 30th, 1845.

My dear Ashburton,

I hear no news, nor am likely to hear any, for I am now on the *wrong* side of every post, except the 'Morning Post,' but see from Macaulay's letter* what our friends have brought us to. I am as much in the dark as ever as to the real state of the case in the Cabinet before or since the break up, but I have been forming my own conjectures—most likely, very groundless, but here they are—that Peel never imparted his Corn Law intentions to the Cabinet as such, though I now believe that he was modelling his Cabinet for the ultimate purpose. Potato famine was a godsend which enabled him to open a long conceived design; that some of the Cabinet took it *au serieux*, and debated the potato question as if it was a real matter, and the majority rejected it, as neither necessary nor opportune, nor if anything were proper, the proper thing. Peel having with him Graham, Aberdeen, Lincoln, S. Herbert, of course his disappointment and vexation must have been extreme at that, I suppose, his first check in so dutiful a Cabinet, but it was much worse when Lord Johnny dashed forward to take the bread out of his mouth; then, no doubt, he developed some evanescent plan, such as we have heard of, and that being equally, or rather more unpalatable, he tendered *his* resignation. So far everything seems to tally, except only that I cannot reconcile to my own confidence in Peel's fair dealing, and the Duke's and Stanley's sagacity, that they should not have had occasion to see his real intentions long before he produced his famine argument; but what followed is much more difficult to guess at. Why are they all in *statu quo* except Stanley? he was but one of six or seven. If they could stay, why not he? If he could not, how can they? And above all, how can they, when the death of Wharncliffe and the introduction of Gladstone turns the balance the other way? Of the importance of Mr. Gladstone

---

* [A letter written by Macaulay to a Mr. Macfarlan, a constituent, in which he said, " You will have heard the termination of our attempt to form a Government. All our plans were frustrated by Lord Grey." The letter was published without Macaulay's consent, and caused him much vexation. *Vide* Trevelyan's 'Life and Letters of Lord Macaulay,' ii. 169-172.]

in this matter, I must give you a slight indication; he volunteered to go into Murray's shop a day or two ago, to tell him that he disapproved of *every word* of the Corn Law article in the last *Quarterly*—of *every word,* mark that.   How can the Dukes and Ripon, and G. Somerset and Haddington be consenting to the triumph of a principle opposite in *every word* to the enunciation of their own doctrines?   My belief is, that the reconstruction is not solid, nor sincere, but rather than have the country longer without a Government, they consented to go on in their respective offices, which *they* had never resigned. adjourning the great question to the moment when the making the Queen's Speech would bring it to a practical issue.

Yours ever,

J. W. CROKER.

Lord Ashburton to Mr. Croker.   Extract.

The Grange, Christmas, 1845.

MY DEAR CROKER,

I agree with you in thinking that we shall see some strange party scenes on both sides when Parliament meets, and a pretty condition the poor country will be in among all these blunderers.   The best part of the squires are holding back till they see what is proposed, and I shall endeavour to persuade my old Essex colleague, Tyrrell, who comes here to-morrow, to do the same; but I cannot conceive that they are likely to be satisfied, and unless the conjurors perform some unexpected feat, my own speculation is that the land will show more strength in the House and in the country than is expected.   Your article, which I have read quietly, is perfect, and will form an admirable text both for Parliament and the hustings.   You will have seen that the *Times,* after some very feeble remarks on the party view of the case, promised to dissect the argument, which it has never touched since.   You may boast of having done great service to a good cause.

Macaulay's indiscreet letter will force Grey to say why he disappointed his Whig friends, and why he disapproves of Palmerston, so that the latter will gain much by this disclosure.

This common gossip not only tells his Edinburgh friend, who published it to the world, the secrets of his party, but

what he should do in the Cabinet, when he got there, with
the Irish Church. A curious specimen of statesman-like
discretion, and a further proof that speech making is not
always a proof of fitness for great affairs.

Yours ever,

Ashburton.

On the 4th of December, the *Times* created a profound
impression by announcing that the Cabinet had resolved to
recommend to Parliament the total repeal of the Corn Laws.
The Conservative papers, which had been left, like the
Cabinet, without any definite information on the subject,
were struck with consternation. One of them settled the
question by protesting that the *Times* had perpetrated an
atrocious fabrication. Very few persons were disposed to
receive the report without question. But Mr. Croker, whose
relations with Sir Robert Peel were now interrupted, appears
to have had a suspicion of the facts. The statement of the
Times, he remarked in his article in the December number
of the *Quarterly Review*, " is unfortunately nearer the truth "
than the contradictions of the Conservative organs. But
evidently he had not yet lost all faith in Sir Robert Peel.
He could not believe that so great a change as total repeal
was meditated. " We affect to be in no secret," he wrote,
" but we are satisfied that the *Times* was entirely misinformed
in attributing to Sir Robert Peel such a wide and general
change of policy, or to the Duke of Wellington any such
wavering of opinion at all, as its statement would indicate.
It is not in their characters." But his confidence began to be
shaken before the time arrived for the meeting of Parliament,
and in the early part of 1846 he addressed a despairing appeal
to the Duke of Wellington. The Duke's reply is characteristic
of the man whose sole anxiety in the midst of a crisis was to
find out " how the Queen's Government was to be carried on."

In reply to Peel's Cabinet memorandum of November 30th, 1845, the Duke had written, "my only object in public life is to support Sir Robert Peel's administration of the Government for the Queen. A good government for the country is more important than Corn Laws or any other consideration ; and as long as Sir Robert Peel possesses the confidence of the Queen and of the public, and he has strength to perform the duties, his administration of the Government must be supported." *   In the same spirit he wrote to Mr. Croker in 1846, avowing that he regarded himself as a " retained servant of the Sovereign," and protesting that he would never be a party to placing the Government " in the hands of the League and the Radicals." He little foresaw at the time that this was the precise result which Sir Robert Peel's policy was destined to bring about before six months had passed.

Mr. Croker to the Duke of Wellington.

West Moulsey, January 4th, 1846.

MY DEAR DUKE,

I firmly believe that the only trust of the country is in your Grace's consistency and firmness ; and I confess I cannot see what right Sir R. Peel can have to drag your Grace through the mire of his own changes of opinion. He may say with truth and candour, that *his* opinions are changed, but can your Grace say so ? Why should not he have the whole responsiblity of his own conduct ? What has your Grace to do with the affair ? You were deceived in the first instance ; you were taught to believe that the proposed measure arose out of the Irish famine. It is now admitted that that was a mere pretext, and I and others know, what was concealed from your Grace, that there was a long conceived design of attacking the protection system. Your Grace's resignation of the cabinet key might embarrass Sir R. Peel, but the difficulty is of his own making, *not yours ;* and he, before he made it, ought to have known how he was to *unmake* it. I admit that

---

* 'Memoirs,' by Sir R. Peel, vol. ii. p. 200.

he, having declared his opinions, and confirmed them by his resignation, cannot well go back; but why should your Grace and the majority of the old Cabinet follow him ?   Why prefer *his* character and consistency to *your own ?*   *You* marked your dissent to Free Trade quite as strongly as *he* marked his assent.   Why are you, and the rest, to forfeit all your pledges in order to help him to keep his *last ?*   I entreat, I implore your Grace to reconsider your position as to stirring *one inch* in a course, the end and object of which is avowed and visible to every eye.   I was in hopes that your authority might have stopped the movement; if you too join it, even as I have said for one inch, all is lost.

Your Grace, I hope, will excuse this honest expostulation. I may be wrong, but you know I am sincere. Peel is my dear friend. I have left public life ; I have no personal object in the advice I venture to give; but I am impelled by what I consider the imminent ruin of the country, and by my deep anxiety for your Grace's glory, and my sincere affection for your person.

Your Grace, if you have read so far with patience, may perhaps say, that if you retire from the Cabinet (not from the Horse-Guards) the Government will be broken up, as others must go with you. I hope so—that is the natural and straightforward result—but then you ask, where is a Government to be found ? I reply, Let Peel answer *that*. Let him make a Government of those who agree in his opinions, and not of those who *don't*.

Ever, my dear Duke, affectionately yours,

J. W. CROKER.

The Duke of Wellington to Mr. Croker.

Strathfieldsaye, January 6th, 1846.

MY DEAR CROKER,

I return Lord Ashburton's letter.   Since it reached me I have received yours of the 4th, and I am most flattered by your favourable opinion.   But I think you have taken an erroneous view of my position, with which you are not so well acquainted as I am myself.

I am the *retained* servant of the Sovereign of this empire. Nobody can entertain a doubt of this truth, as applied to my professional character.

I have invariably, up to the latest moment, acted accordingly.

When required, and the Sovereign has been in difficulties, I have gone further, as in 1828, I became the Minister of George IV., and in 1832 and 1839, I undertook to form a Government for William IV.

After Lord John had been sent for, and had undertaken the commission of forming a government, I, as well as others who had formed a part of Sir Robert Peel's administration, was required to state whether any or all of us would undertake to form an administration for the Queen on the principle of maintaining the existing Corn Law. I answered, No! Because I knew that be the vote in the House of Commons what it might, there were no persons in that assembly capable of sustaining in debate the existing Corn Law against Cobden and the League, Lord John Russell and the Whigs, Sir Robert Peel and those of the Conservatives who should think that the existing law ought to be altered.

I besides felt that the existing Corn Law is not the *only* interest of this great nation; and whatever confidence I may feel in my own judgment, I do not think that an administration could be formed in the House of Commons capable of conducting the affairs of the State, consisting of persons only who are of opinion that the existing Corn Law is preferable to any other.

When Sir Robert Peel wrote to me on the 20th of December, after Lord John Russell had resigned his commission, that if desired to resume his position he would resume it, and stand by the Queen and enable Her Majesty to meet her Parliament rather than that Her Majesty should be under the necessity of taking Cobden and Co., members of the League, as her Ministers, I applauded his determination, and determined to stand by him. Here again I acted as the retained servant of the monarchy; I was perfectly aware when I did so, of the embarrassed position in which Sir Robert Peel would find himself, even if disposed to maintain the existing Corn Law, as Lord John Russell, the Whigs, and the League must, as the first step in undertaking to form an administration, have obtained an accurate knowledge of the cause of their having been sent for; namely, that Sir Robert Peel having wished to propose to Parliament a material alteration in the Corn Law, could not persuade his colleagues to support the proposition.

You say that it would be better that Cobden should be the Minister, and propose the alteration of the Corn Laws.

I have a good deal of experience of the evil which can be done by a Minister of whom it is thought that it would be preferable that he should be the person to carry a bad measure.

I recollect that in 1832 it was thought that a government might be formed which in completing the Reform Bill might prevent some of its mischiefs! Some thought, let the Whigs and Radicals, who proposed the measure, complete it.

They were successful; the formation of the new administration failed, and the Reform Bill was carried; all the improvements intended were rejected, and some of the very worst parts of the Bill, the Metropolitan Boroughs, the Scotch and the Irish Reforms were carried after this failure.

I answer therefore, that happen what may about the Corn Laws, I will not take a course which may have a tendency to reduce the Sovereign to a necessity of requiring such men as Mr. Cobden to be her Ministers.

But I don't despair of the Corn Laws. I really do not know what it is that Sir Robert Peel intends to propose. I believe that he intends to submit to Parliament a proposition which has for its object to relieve the land from some of the burthens which fall upon the land exclusively. I don't know in what manner he proposes to attain his object, or what alteration he will propose in the Corn Laws; but I will endeavour to render them as little as possible objectionable to the landed interest.

But having done everything in my power to prevent the dissolution of Sir Robert Peel's administration, previous to its dissolution early in the month of December, I should be ashamed of myself if I was to run away from it now that it is reunited and on the eve of meeting.

I do that which I have requested our friends the great landed proprietors to do. I will see and consider what is proposed; will endeavour to render those propositions as beneficial as possible to the public interests. I know that without their support Sir Robert Peel cannot carry on a Government with advantage to the public or with honour to himself.

But I will not be instrumental in placing the Government in the hands of the League and the Radicals.

I am aware that I shall be in a difficult position; that has always been my fate.   But I feel no hesitation, and I doubt not I shall get out of it.

Ever, my dear Croker, yours most sincerely,

WELLINGTON.

Mr. Croker to the Duke of Wellington.

West Moulsey, January 8th, 1846.

MY DEAR DUKE,

When your Grace has deliberately taken your position, it would be presumptuous in me to say any more.   But I think that either at Torres Vedras or Waterloo you would have changed your mind and your place if you had found that the enemy had slipped behind you into Lisbon or Brussels, and that the place you wanted to cover was already in their possession.   One word I must add in my own defence.   The Queen could have been in no want of a government; Sir Robert and Lord John, either or both together could, and if they had been left alone, *must* have made a free trade Administration.   To be sure, with your Grace commanding an army of observation, they could have done no great mischief, and above all, could not carry the repeal; that would have been just as it ought to have been.   On all other subjects your Grace would have made them easy.

And as it is, are you sure you will enable Sir Robert to destroy (for the principle once admitted the rest must follow) the gentry and aristocracy, and the monarchy, whose " retained servant" and mainstay you are.   Will even your Grace not lose your power to save us by losing the confidence of the country ?

And then suppose the Whigs and League should, on the ground that what you propose is inadequate, join the country gentlemen in resistance.   What is to become of your half-and-half administration ?   But I have done.   Pardon my freedom, which springs from affection and respect; but it shall not be repeated.

Ever most sincerely yours,

J. W. CROKER.

Mr. Croker to the Duke of Wellington.

West Moulsey, January 9th, 1846.

My dear Duke,

As your Grace is, I see, at Strathfieldsaye, where I know
you have the *Quarterly Review*, I would beg of you to get
the 72nd volume and read a couple of pages, 553, &c., of
that journal for September, 1843, particularly in page 560.*
You will there see what I was then permitted to say about
Sir Robert Peel's Corn Law policy. I don't mean to say that
Sir Robert Peel is responsible for my views, nor do I recollect
whether he read this paper before it was published; he
perhaps did, but at all events, it expressed the opinion which
he then gave me, and he never after, till this last autumn,
gave me any reason to suppose that he had changed that
opinion. My preceding articles on the Corn Laws and on
the League were written under his eye. I wish your Grace
to be aware that my opinions now are just what they always
have been, and such as Peel himself and Graham inspired
me with.

Ever, my dear Duke, most sincerely yours,

J. W. CROKER.

The Duke of Rutland to Mr. Croker.

Pall Mall, January 22nd, 1846.

My dear Croker,

I partake of all the feelings which you describe yourself as
entertaining as to the present state of the country and its
rulers. My belief is that a tide of Democracy is hurrying us
on upon a downward course with a force that no minister can
stem, and that consequently it is found necessary to make
attempts at palliation and temporising. Have you the
slightest idea that, if the League had not been in existence,
the measures we are expecting to be developed next week

* [An article on the "Policy of Ministers," in which Mr. Croker
contended that it was the "first duty of a nation to feed itself," and
expressed confidence that Sir Robert Peel was convinced of the "funda-
mental truth, that there can be no safety—much less prosperity—for any
country but in the encouragement of its own industry, and the development of its own resources."]

touching agricultural protection would have been dreamed of? Then the coming measure must be a matter of triumph to the League; and is it to be supposed that, with their organised material, they will quietly disband and become peaceable citizens, after having carried their object and discovered their power? We had a large dinner yesterday at Apsley House (more than fifty), but I saw several at table whose course on the coming measure is very undecided; and Lords Hardwicke, Talbot, and Redesdale were absent, who have been regular attendants in former years. The latter I know has taken his line against any change in the Protection laws. I conclude that "Ministerial Resignations" in the last *Quarterly* proceeded from your admirable pen. The Duke seems wonderfully well. I felt it necessary to address a long letter to him ten days ago, in which I promised to wait the development of the forthcoming measures before I form or express an opinion.

Ever, my dear Croker,

Yours most truly,

RUTLAND.

On the 22nd of January, 1846, Parliament was opened by the Queen. There was no direct reference to the Corn Laws in the Speech, but Sir Robert Peel told the tale in the remarks with which he followed the mover and seconder of the address. He declared that his opinions on the subject of protection had "undergone a change"; that he could not "undertake to direct the course of the vessel by observations taken in the year 1842." The main grounds, he said, "of public policy on which protection has been defended are not tenable." Mr. Disraeli then made his memorable retort conveyed in the story of the Turkish admiral who was entrusted with a fleet intended to save the empire, and who took his departure, amid the blessings of the Sultan and the prayers of the muftis. "Away went the fleet; but what was the consternation of the Sultan when the lord high admiral steered at once for the enemy's port." These incessant

and irresistible attacks upon Peel had already made Mr.
Disraeli the leader of a party, though it was then but a very
small party.

Five nights afterwards—on the 27th—Sir Robert Peel
produced his scheme. It was to repeal the Corn Laws altogether at the expiration of three years, and in the meantime
to allow duties only on a very low scale—10s. when the
price was under 48s., decreasing 1s. per quarter up to 53s.,
and remaining at 4s. when the price was 53s. or more. After
1849 a merely nominal duty of 1s. per quarter was to be imposed.* It is worthy of observation that the average price of
wheat in 1845 was but 52s. per quarter—a price which has
been greatly exceeded many times since the repeal of the
Corn Laws,—and that in recommending his measure to the
country Sir Robert Peel laid stress upon an argument which
had been much used by Mr. Cobden, namely, that if England
adopted the principle of Free Trade, other nations would be
compelled to follow her example. He said :—

" When your example could be quoted in favour of restriction, it was quoted largely ; when your example can be
quoted in favour of relaxation, as conducive to your interests,
it may perhaps excite at first in foreign governments or foreign
boards of trade but little interest or feeling ; but the sense of
the people, of the great body of consumers, will prevail ; and
in spite of the desire of governments and boards of trade
to raise revenue by restrictive duties, reason and common
sense will induce relaxation of high duties. Our last accounts from the United States give indications of the decline
of a hostile spirit in this respect."

This last sentence has made its appearance, in some form

---

* The existence of this was forgotten by the general public, although it
brought in an appreciable sum to the Revenue, until attention was drawn
to it by Mr. Lowe striking it off in 1869.

or other, on many occasions since; but the fact remains that
the tariff duties of the United States are much more hostile
to the manufactures of Great Britain to-day than they were
in 1846, and that in 1884 both the great political parties
carried out the Presidential contest on a purely Protectionist·
"platform."   Mr. Cobden fixed five years as the outside
period which Europe would require to become converted to
free tariffs. This prediction he made in 1846. Sir Robert
Peel, with greater shrewdness, assigned no specific time for
the fulfilment of his prophecy.

The debates on the Corn Laws occupied the public attention
so largely that little notice was taken by the public of a new
Coercion Bill for Ireland, which was introduced into the House
of Lords on the 23rd of February. It is probable that Sir
Robert Peel himself attached comparatively slight importance
to this Bill, and it is certain that he was without any pre-
sentiment that it was the rock on which his Administration
was fated to be utterly wrecked. The events of the few
succeeding weeks have nowhere been related with so much
fulness and force as by the leading actor in them—Mr.
Disraeli. * He has told us that when the Corn Law Repeal
Bill was passed, the desire for "vengeance" filled the hearts
of the defeated party. "The field was lost, but at any rate
there should be retribution." The great and only question for
the moment was, " How was Sir Robert Peel to be turned out ?"
Every step in the subsequent proceedings was devised by Mr.
Disraeli and Lord George Bentinck, and the final *coup* was
possibly timed with an eye to dramatic effect. On the 25th
of June the Repeal Bill was finally passed by the House of
Lords ; on the same evening the Government was defeated in
the Lower House, on the Coercion Bill, by a vote of 292 to
219. At what seemed the very climax of his power and

---

* In the ' Life of Lord George Bentinck,' chapters iii.–xvi.

success the Minister fell, to rise no more; other men were henceforth to lead the Conservative party. But for a long time it had no prospect of getting back to power. All hope for it seemed dead. Lord John Russell was called to office, and held it till long after Peel's death—from 1846 to 1852.

It is now necessary to resume the thread of the correspondence.

The Duke of Rutland to Mr. Croker.

Belvoir Castle, January 25th, 1846.

MY DEAR CROKER,

Your mention of Granby's * speech on the present Corn and other Duties Abrogation Debate, and the report which you have heard of his speech, give me the sincerest gratification. He came here last night, and I shall take the liberty of showing him what you say, for there is no greater encouragement to a young debutant than *laudari a laudato viro.* He is very shy and requires encouragement, but he has good sense and judgment. I have likewise a very satisfactory report of my son John's † speech, but then he is more accustomed to the trade, and has less fear of hearing the sound of his own voice. *Conçois tu !* that after sixteen days from the commencement of the debate, they should be able to come down here to hunt two days, with the certainty of being in time for the division.

Every day I think the *mess* in which we are worse and worse. And what is to be the final result—who can tell? Then in the midst of it comes this great disaster (though victory it be!) in India.‡ How are we to stand such losses? We are about to vote an additional 10,000 men to the ranks of our army, but *now* that number ought to be swollen to 15,000.

Perrier has sent in the French Corn Protecting Duties, which seem very stringent. If they close their arms to us,

* [Lord Granby, the present Duke of Rutland, who had resigned his post at Court in order to oppose the repeal of the Corn Laws.]

† [Lord John Manners.] ∽•

‡ [The beginning of the great Sikh war, distinguished later on by the victories of Ferozeshah and Sobraon, the occupation by the British of Lahore, and the total capitulation of the Sikhs.]

while we open ours to them, we shall play at a game which a
sharper once played with a dupe, intituled, "Heads I win,
and tails you lose." *   I cautiously avoid forming my final
opinion on the whole subject till the measure is in the House
of Lords in the shape of a Bill.

Ever, my dear Croker,

Most truly yours,

RUTLAND.

Mr. Croker to Lord Brougham.

West Moulsey, February 4th, 1846.

MY DEAR B.,

It is very good of you to enlighten my darkness, if
indeed, I can call it enlightening when you yourself are
in so great an obscurity ; but you at least enable me to grope
out somewhat of the present posture of affairs, and I
believe the wisest and the best informed of any party
must be in an extreme doubt as to what is to happen.   I
agree in all you say about the composition of the Cabinet.
I have seen the principle that you indicate ever since the
move of Stanley to the Lords, which I now begin to think
was a preparatory step to his late retirement.   As to Ellenborough, it was so necessary to his position, and so gratifying
to his ambition to be in the Cabinet, that to obtain that
object, he would have swallowed not merely the Corn Laws,
but the gates of Tenmouth.†   The person in the worst position
after the Duke is Goulburn, who seems reduced not merely to
eat his words, but to eat them in silence, and become a cypher
in his own proper department.   He is a most excellent and
honourable man, with high principles, both moral and
political, and can only have been, like the Duke, forced into
his present circumstances by the dread of worse.   They are
really, I believe, sacrificing themselves for the sake of the

---

* [It is scarcely necessary to point out that this is the principle on
which the whole world, including our own colonies, has since acted.]

† [In the letters of Mr. Croker which were copied or dictated to an
amanuensis, there are many errors, some of them of an utterly baffling
nature.   The above is a favourable specimen, for it admits of an easy
solution.   Obviously the gates of Somnauth are meant.]

country. I was never anxious for Peel's return to power; I always saw in him a disposition which was fitter, I thought, for the leader of a Conservative opposition than of a Government, and I thought, and *think*, that, since the Reform Bill, the best chance of governing the country on anything like the old principles, was by a Whig Ministry and a Tory Opposition. Peel has, however, now dissolved everything like a Tory party, and I should be rather inclined, if I was to indulge my own hypothesis, to wish that Peel would coalesce with Lord John and the Whigs as the best chance of resisting the storm which he has raised.

Nothing can be more foolish or unfortunate than the mode in which the Conservatives are conducting the Opposition. I wish I had any conciliatory influence with either side, but even if I had, I hardly know what, except more moderate language, I could advise, for the evil appears to me beyond all human remedy. What is to follow I know not and fear to guess. I feel that God rules the political, as certainly as He does the moral and natural world, and will not suffer any *long* anarchy, but He may, and probably will, inflict a *severe* one. I fancy and fear that all the passions of the masses will receive a new impulse from what they will regard as Peel's timidity, and that in the works of party and public character, there will not be found *stamina* to form a Government capable of resisting anything; and then I think the next most probable transition will be a federal republic after the American fashion. This, as I once thought it, frightful extremity, is now become my Euthanasia as what may be accomplished with the least agency of murder and confiscation ; of both there will probably be a lamentable extent, certainly of confiscation; but, on the whole, our electoral forms may slide into the substance of an elective government with less violence than any other possible transmutation. In truth, what are we now but an elective government?—a nominal monarchy with republican institutions.

Ever sincerely yours,

J. W. CROKER.

Mr. Croker to Lord Brougham.

West Moulsey, February 8th, 1846.

MY DEAR BROUGHAM,

I need hardly say I partake all your apprehensions of a
Whig Ministry, but I do not see the possibility of avoiding
it.   The Tory party is broken up, Sir Robert, strong in his
own talents, and for the moment strong by the support of his
and our natural enemies, will carry his question no doubt in
the Commons, perhaps even in the Lords, by the terror of
something worse.   But if I have any political sagacity *that*
will end his power, and the *party* having already been
destroyed, we shall be at the mercy of the Whigs, and then
new combinations will arise; the victorious Whigs will split
into the two classes that always did and always will divide
mankind—the advance and the resistance; and the Russells
and Palmerstons will find themselves in conflict with the
Brights and Cobdens, and then we shall have the same game
to play all over again.   If the dissentient part of the Cabinet
had held together, and Peel only *gone on* or *gone out*, the Tory
party might have been kept together, very little weakened,
and always strong enough for a rational control over the
Whigs; but I now consider that party irretrievably destroyed,
irretrievably I mean for any present or early use.   I lay aside
for the moment all my own notions that Peel's measures
will ruin the landed interests, and probably accelerate a
revolution; but looking at the affair as a mere practical
question of party, I do not see any possible escape for the
Tories.   Those who follow and those who oppose Peel are
equally, to use a vulgar, but never more just metaphor,
cutting their own throats.   Do you see any extrication, and
in what direction? and have you arrived at any opinion as
to what would be best for the Conservative party—Peel's
success or his defeat?

Yours ever,

J. W. CROKER.

Sir James Graham to Mr. Croker.   Extract.

Whitehall, February 18th, 1846.

MY DEAR CROKER,

I have no doubt whatever that before the next potato
crop some distress will be suffered in many districts of

Ireland; and relief from the public purse must be given to a considerable extent. That unhappy country has ruined many Administrations, and has been the stumbling-block which has caused the downfall of the greatest men. It has not lost its malignant influence, and it will do its accustomed work again.

I am, yours sincerely,

J. R. G. GRAHAM.

Mr. Croker to Sir James Graham.

West Moulsey, February 21st, 1846.

MY DEAR GRAHAM,

In circumstances so serious as those in which we are now placed, I cannot refrain from noticing a part of your last note, which is, I think, founded on a misconception. You seem to attribute our present difficulties to *Ireland.* Now, that there are difficulties enough, aye and stupendous ones, about Ireland, I fully concede; but that Ireland has had anything to do with the grand convulsion that has overturned the edifice that we were all so proud of having erected in 1841, I cannot concede. Ireland has had no more to do with it than Kamschatka, and I think facts will show, hereafter, that the only way that Ireland is concerned in the revolution is that the measures taken in England, and for English views and no other, have increased the dangers and misery of Ireland.

J. W. CROKER.

Sir James Graham to Mr. Croker.   Extract.

Whitehall, April 2nd, 1846.

One of the great benefits and blessings which I anticipate from the Repeal of the Corn Laws, is, that at last there is some hope of surviving the din of this odious and endless topic of democratic agitation.

Mr. Croker to Sir James Graham.

West Moulsey, April 3rd, 1846.

MY DEAR GRAHAM,

To the last paragraph of your letter in which you say that " one of the great benefits and blessings you expect from the repeal of the Corn Laws, is some hope of extinguishing democratic agitation."

I cannot refrain from honestly telling you that my aversion to it is on exactly the opposite ground. I am deeply convinced that it will encourage, increase, and render irresistible, democratic agitation.

My experience is eight eventful years longer than Peel's, and twelve than yours, and

> "Old experience doth attain
> To something of prophetic strain;"

and I tell you, in all the sincerity of sorrow, that your measure will have speedily, widely, and permanently, the very contrary effect from what you hope for, and that your repeal of the Corn Laws will *feed* nothing but agitation. Its effects on agriculture and the general condition of the country I believe will be very bad, bad in whatever proportion it may be successful; but it is exactly κατ' ἐξοχήν the *moral* and *political* effects that I think the most immediately fatal. You have rendered it quite impossible to constitute a strong Government. You have divided the only party on which *any* Government could rely for stemming agitation. I wish I could describe to you the mixture of feelings of friendship and of fear, with which I sympathise in your personal struggles, and pray for your *political defeat*.

Yours most sincerely,

J. W. CROKER.

Sir James Graham to Mr. Croker.

Whitehall, April 4th, 1846.

MY DEAR CROKER,

I am sincerely obliged by the kind and friendly tone of your letter. I may be wrong; I have no overweening confidence in my own judgment; but I do not anticipate from Corn Law repeal consequences half as fatal as must have resulted from a protracted but hopeless struggle. Much hereafter will depend on the conduct of the Conservative party. If their resentments be stronger than their reason, or their regard for their own safety and interests rightly understood, great national disasters will ensue. The re-

sponsibility will be rightly awarded hereafter. I do not
shrink from my full share of it.

I am, with sincere regard, my dear Croker,

Yours very truly,

J. R. G. GRAHAM.

Mr. Croker to Mr. Goulburn.

West Moulsey, March 28th, 1846.

MY DEAR GOULBURN,

I have been just finishing a most painful duty imposed
and pressed upon me in a way which I found irresistible—
the following up of my former articles in the *Quarterly
Review* against Free Trade.

You know under what auspices we were led to take so high
a line in that discussion, and I must honestly say that the
information which you and the other offices furnished me
with, corroborated by all that has been recently produced,
have created and confirmed my opinion that all that you are
doing is as unjustifiable by reason and policy as it is by
every consideration which ought to bind men in a party.
However, strongly as I feel this, I would have left the task
to others; but so strong an appeal was made to my *honour*, as
having brought the review into that line of Protectionist
politics, that I could not help doing my painful duty. I dare
say that many of my friends feel that the changing their
(not opinions but) votes, has been a duty equally painful.

Yours, &c.,

J. W. CROKER.

Mr. Croker to the Duke of Wellington.

West Moulsey, April 5th, 1846.

MY DEAR DUKE,

I beg leave to thank your Grace for your goodness to the
grandson* of your old friend Walter Scott, whom you have
just named to a cornetcy in the 16th Light Dragoons *without
purchase.* When I mentioned the matter to your Grace, I

---

* [Walter Scott Lockhart, second, and at this time only surviving son
of J. G. Lockhart. He died Jan. 10th, 1853.]

did not hope for this latter favour, which is very sensibly felt both by his father and me.

You have been all my public life doing me kindnesses, of which I am so far worthy as to be very grateful.

You remember that I told you something that you did not know about *our friend's* [Peel's] conversion to Free Trade doctrines. I can now perhaps also tell you what you cannot but suspect, but may not positively know, which is, that it was nothing but the result of *fright* at the League. I always thought this, but I have had within these few days the most decided and authentic evidence of the fact. I could prove it in a court of justice by an indisputable witness, and yet he still goes on persisting in the humbug of the potato famine. I am more and more alarmed at the consequences of this truckling to *agitation*, and for once in my life hope *you* may be defeated when the Bill goes to the Lords.

Ever, &c.,

J. W. CROKER.

The Duke of Wellington to Mr. Croker.

London, April 6th, 1846.

MY DEAR CROKER,

The influence of fear is certainly very strong; it acts in secret, and it is difficult to have evidence of it.

I cannot doubt that which passed under my own view and frequent observation day after day. I mean the alarms of the consequences in Ireland of the potato disease. I never witnessed in any case such agony.

However, other feelings may have prevailed at the same time.

Ever yours most sincerely,

WELLINGTON.

Mr. Croker to the Duke of Wellington.

West Moulsey, April 7th, 1846.

MY DEAR DUKE,

You were not deceived as to the *fact*, but only as to the *cause*. The agony was real and intense, but it was the agony of a man who was deluding and betraying his conscience and

F 3

his colleagues. He was in a case like one that I have heard
of, in which a man seemed to be dying of a sabre wound,
while the surgeon did not know till after death that he had
a bullet in his body. Recollect that I told you before the
Government was reconstructed that I had reason to know,
long before there was any suspicion of the potato failure
that he was veering about to Free Trade. I have suspected
it these two years, and attributed it to fear of the League. *I
now know it.* I think if you will recall all your own recollections, of what passed from day to day, you will see that a
disturbed conscience, and the fear of being anticipated by the
Whigs, was the real cause of the agony; that the potato
failure was the sabre-cut, but that the other was the fatal
bullet in the body.

Ever, my dear Duke,

Your most attached and affectionate,

J. W. CROKER.

*Mr. Croker to Sir Henry Hardinge.**   Extract.*

Alverbank, Gosport, April 24th, 1846.

MY DEAR HARDINGE,

At the distance at which we are, you may be anxious to
hear my version of the extraordinary revolution which has
taken place in our internal policy, of which the result is, that
I am in as decided *opposition* as a private gentleman can be
to the Queen's Government. You know, I think, as well as
any man, how I loved Peel, quite disinterestedly, for I was
the greater man of the two when I began to love him; and
as we have gone on in life, I think I am almost the only
early friend to whom he has not done a personal favour,
unless making Barrow a baronet was meant as a favour to me.
But for all my affection for him, I cannot excuse this late
tergiversation, and above all, the deception of endeavouring to
attribute it to the potato failure in Ireland. I can venture to
assure you from my own knowledge that this Irish panic has
had no more to do with it than the disturbances in the
Punjaub. The design was formed before the potato crop was

* [Then in India. He was created Viscount Hardinge on the 2nd of
May of this year, 1846.]

planted, and the failure, singular and serious in fact, was
seized upon, and (as the Methodists say) improved into an
ostensible excuse for the measure that was already resolved
on, and waiting only for some pretext.   What the real cause
of the change of opinion was I cannot *positively* assert, or
rather I cannot apportion, for it may have been twofold.
There was, perhaps, some *original* disposition to abstract free
trade, and the advancement of the manufacturing interests,
and some latent hatred of the " proud aristocracy."   But the
main and immediate cause was terror, cowardice.   This I
know ; and I would not tell you if I did not—terror of the
League, which he felt ought to be put down, but he had not
nerve for doing that *de front,* and so he hit on the expedient
of dissolving them by submitting to their dictation, as he will
pacify O'Connell by repealing the Union.

I suppose all your correspondents will talk to you in the
colour of the times.   I tell you what I know to be true.   The
fatal consequences are that Peel, by betraying the precise and
specific principle upon which he was brought into office, has
ruined the character of public men, and dissolved, by dividing,
the great landed interest—the only solid foundation on which
any Government can be formed in this country.   I care
comparatively little about his actual corn law experiment ;
it will fail, and England will right herself from this fraudu-
lent humbug ; but while that process is going on, we shall be
running all the risks, if not suffering the actual infliction, of
a revolution.   On the principle on which we have truckled
to the League, how are we to resist the attack on the Irish
Church—the Irish Union—both much worse cases (in that
view) than the Corn Laws.   How to maintain primogeniture,
the Bishops, the House of Lords, the Crown ?   Sir Robert
Peel has put these into more peril than Cobbett, or Cobden,
or O'Connell, or they altogether could have done, and his
personal influence has carried away individuals ; he has
broken up the old interests, divided the great families, and
commenced just such a revolution as the Noailles and Mont-
morencies did in 1789.   Look at father and son, and brother
and brother, and uncle and nephew—thrown into personal
hostility in half the counties of England, and all for what ?—
to propitiate Richard Cobden.   Our dearest friend the Duke,
feels, I believe, and I know felt, as I do in all this.   I lament
that he has permitted his old age to be dragged into the

honourable disgrace of maintaining a position which he disapproves of. He submits to take a part, only, as he told me, for *fear of worse;* and if there had been any man of nerve or talents in the House of Commons, the Duke, I am satisfied, would never have resumed the Cabinet key. He does not, I am told, conceal from those who consult him, his aversion to what he is doing, which is only exceeded by his perplexity as to what else is to be done.

J. W. C.

Mr. Croker to Lord Brougham. Extract.

West Moulsey, May 5th, 1846.

My dear Brougham,

I should be quite as little dissatisfied with Lord John as with Sir Robert, and though upon the whole I had rather that Sir Robert were driven to a dissolution (that we might get at something like an expression of public opinion) I see great inconveniences from it, and it would not, I think, in any case, tend to make way for a strong Government. A strong Government I never again expect to see, and I think it the worst feature and consequence of Sir Robert's strange panic, or whatever it was, that it has sown the seeds of distrust, division, and dissension amongst those on whom alone any stable Government can depend for support.

I have not been in London since I saw you, and have no correspondent in the House of Commons. But I am glad to hear what you say of Lord George Bentinck; with him in the House of Commons, and if they had you in the House of Lords, the Protectionists might have stayed the plague; but I am sorry to see that you have taken the other line. I ought hardly to say *sorry,* for if you have taken it with a clear view of your own future course, and if it can eventually tend to clear your personal position, I shall be glad of it for your sake, though I had much rather that you had taken the other side, as more in consonance with your own early opinions, and more conducive, I think, to your political influence. But no doubt you have thought of all that, and I am only lecturing Hannibal on the art of war.

Yours sincerely,

J. W. Croker.

Lord Ashburton to Mr. Croker.   Extract.

Piccadilly, May 26th, 1846.

Stanley's speech last night was magnificent.*   I do not
know that I have heard a sounder or better connected argument put together with so much eloquence.   Brougham very
flat, an awkward bidding for the Seals, and not a shadow of
an argument.   Ripon miserable.   I think Stanley made impression on a very full house and gallery, but I fear there
will be no impression on the vote, though one should rise from
the dead.   Parties are pledged together in various shapes
to do what not ten men in the House approve.   The Whigs
at Lansdowne House on Friday resolved to stand together
and support the Bill.   Melbourne bounced and complained,
but at last yielded, saying that seeing you are as a party
resolved to eat any dirt Peel may make, I will not refuse my
mouthful.

Ripon made out that he had been a free trader all his life,
and that he was insincere in all the Protection Bills he had
brought in for the last thirty years.   Yet he told us the other
day that "he was armed so strong in honesty," &c.

A.

Mr. Croker to Lord Hardinge.   Extract.

West Moulsey, July 10th, 1846.

MY DEAR HARDINGE,

My letter of April last will have prepared you for the
events of the last fortnight, so far as the dissolution of Peel's
Ministry, but even my dismal forebodings did not prognosti-
cate such a finale as his parting speech last Monday week.†

This has done him more harm than all the rest.   His late
colleagues complain, that having re-united them in December
last, expressly to keep out the Whigs, and Mr. Cobden *by
name*, he has now brought in the Whigs, and lauded Mr.

---

* [On the motion in the House of Lords for the second reading of the
Corn Importation Bill. The motion was carried, and the Bill read a
second time, on the 28th.]

† [This was the speech in which Sir R. Peel declared that the name
which " ought to be, and which will be, associated with the success of
these measures "—the repeal of the Corn Laws—" is the name of Richard
Cobden."]

Cobden to the skies. They complain also that he resigned without the slightest notice to them, and they, not one of them, had the least inkling of the kind of speech he was about to make. The Duke is very angry at this contemptuous treatment, and so are others of the Cabinet, and I suspect all. All this is part of a system which he has been all along pursuing, but which he never avowed till yesterday, of belonging to no party, and disclaiming all party connections.

Lyndhurst went to him yesterday morning to talk to him about conciliation and re-uniting the party. Peel told him at once that he would have nothing to do with party—*that he stood alone* with his *individual* opinion, and would neither influence nor be influenced by any other person's. He told him that he meant to go down and take his seat on the Opposition bench in front of Lord John. This was complained of as unfairly embarrassing his late party. The real Opposition having thrown them off, he ought not, they contend, to usurp the place that by universal practice belongs only to the leader ; and there was some talk of pre-occupying the seats, and not making room for him, but I am not at all in the confidence of the Ultras, and know not what they mean to do. In the Lords there is almost unanimity—that is, they are all rallied under Stanley—Peelites and Protectionists ; but in the Commons the reconciliation is more difficult, if it be at all possible. The Protectionists abhor the Peelites so thoroughly, that even the example of the Peers will not, they tell me, produce a reconciliation. What effect Peel's renunciation of party attachments may have I know not, but I think a little of the *frost* of opposition will connect and bind together all the Conservative fragments, though not, perhaps, till the general election. The appearance of the House of Lords on the first night of the new Ministry was striking—the whole of the Opposition side was crowded, so that some could not find places, and sat on *that* end of the woolsack and of the cross benches, while there were not fifteen peers—ministers, bishops and all—at the Ministerial side. If the reconciliation should be effected in the Commons, something of the same kind will occur, but not to such an extent, for some of the Peelites will certainly adhere to Lord John.

Ever, my dear Hardinge, affectionately yours,

J. W. CROKER.

Lady Ashburton to Mr. Croker.   Extract.

[No date.]

MY DEAR MR. CROKER,

Pray tell us what you hear, for you are always better informed than we are. My Baron is busy, and not without hope of doing some good. He will probably consult you ere he takes a step. The Peelites are very violent, and I grieve to say that the harmony of our family is disturbed by difference of opinion, not on our side, but *they* are so sore that they dread an allusion to the one absorbing subject, however slight. Sir Robert is lost in public opinion, and his friends flatter themselves that a coalition with the Whigs may be the result of his treachery. I saw several Whigs yesterday, and am convinced that they will *repudiate* him. They will have free trade in opinions and no dictator. Ch. Greville said to C. Wood, who told me, " Upon my word and honour, I can see nothing to justify Peel for having brought forward this measure." The new asseveration is " May Peel protect me if," &c.

Ever most truly yours,

A. C. A.

Mr. Croker to Lord Lonsdale.

From my Hermitage, West Moulsey, June 7th, 1846.

MY DEAR LONSDALE,

Nobody feels more deeply—few can feel so deeply as I do —the deplorable conduct of Sir R. Peel, or more sincerely desires to see him suffer the penalty of his unhappy tergiversation, but I hope the Tories will not be provoked by *his* change of principle into a forgetfulness of theirs. The only permanent Government possible in this country must be founded on the landed interests. I hope, therefore, that the landed interests will not join either Whigs, Radicals, or Irish Repealers, in opposition to any measures (even though unpopular) which have a tendency to strengthen the governing power—for instance, the Coercion Bill—a bad bill, a cowardly bill, and one that will fail in its effect ! Let our friends tell Sir R. Peel that *such* is his measure, but add that as an Act of Government, proposed as necessary to the peace and safety of Ireland, however inadequate they may think it, they cannot undertake the responsibility of rejecting it; and on all other questions that may arise I would entreat them to recollect that the day cannot, I hope, be far distant when they themselves will have to form and carry on a Government.

If there is any one inclined to a different course, with whom you think my opinion would be of any value, you are at liberty to show them this suggestion—the result of near half a century of political experience.

Ever affectionately yours,
J. W. CROKER.

Lord Lonsdale to Mr. Croker. Extract.

London, June 15th, 1846.

DEAR CROKER,

I hear *Israeli's* [*sic*] gun is loaded for a shot to-night; that the Premier's narrative of his Catholic question does not agree with that tell-tale 'Hansard,' or that some other information has been got to enable Israeli to give a heavy broadside to-night.

Faithfully yours,
LONSDALE.

The following letter refers to Mr. Croker's article on "The Close of Sir Robert Peel's Administration," which appeared in the *Quarterly Review* in September. The proofs of the article had been previously read and revised by Lord Ashburton, Lord Stanley, and Lord Brougham.

Mr. Croker to Lord and Lady Ashburton.

West Moulsey, June 19th, 1846.

Thank you, my dear Lady and Lord for your joint and several letters. They have been most agreeable, and *very useful* to me; and your American newspaper has, by a happy accident, furnished me with the *best hit* in the whole paper I am writing. That paper, I regret to say, must make a final

separation between Peel and me. I deeply regret it, for I
love him, yes *love* him, and would gladly have quitted literary,
as I have done practical politics, when I differed from him,
but I could not; he had involved me and I had involved
others, in a line of politics which, though he may be able to
escape from, *we* cannot, and I was summoned as a man of
honour to support my friends in the struggle into which I had,
by Peel's own instructions, led them. I shall come up on
Monday to send my paper to the press, and I shall stay a day
or two to see it in shape; when it is so, I must ask my Lord
to favour me with his advice about it. It would be of great
importance to my arguments to get an account of the importation and distribution of the Indian corn in Ireland—
surely some of the Irish Tories could tell us.

I suppose the great question—in or out—will be decided
in a few days. Those who seemed most sanguine that Peel
would weather the storm, seem now to abandon their hope.
What I see and hear of H. B. [Brougham] surprises me; he
seems to attack Stanley, and yet I hear, he thinks *Stanley's
party* on the whole the safest in the country. I have been
in my article like Macheath at the end of the ' Beggar's Opera.'
I have been *dancing my hornpipe in fetters.* I have been
afraid and ashamed to say all that I think truth requires
about Peel.

Yours ever affectionately,

J. W. CROKER.

Mr. Lockhart to Mr. Croker. Extract.

August 6th, 1846.

The ' Modern Timon ' is not, I think, by a *poet,** but it is
the work of a clever man, and who understands the con-
struction of lines and the rhythm, and in short, all that people
can learn without inspiration. I should suspect the *Timon*
to be by Bulwer or Disraeli, or possibly Dicky Milnes :† but
I am sure the 'Orlando' is from some mere reporter or
penny-a-liner. He also sends his work to me, and perhaps
I may, when I have read it through, be able to guess better.

J. G. LOCKHART.

---

* [The ' New Timon,' by Sir E. Bulwer-Lytton, passed through three
editions this year.]

† ⌐Lord Houghton.]

Mr. Croker to Mr. Lockhart.

Kensington Palace, August 19th, 1846.

MY DEAR LOCKHART,

As I leave town to-morrow, I went to take leave of my dear old friend at Apsley House ; and if you were astonished at the ex-Chancellor's letter, you would have been much more so at the language of the Duke.   Nothing can equal his disapprobation, I should almost say despair, at all that has been done, all that is doing, and his apprehensions as to what is coming ; and *all* the blame, where you and I would only put *part* (to be sure the largest part) of it.   He, however, is all for amnesty, " *Christian Charity,*" which he says is as great a duty in politics as in morals.   He is very much shocked, and indeed indignant, at the apathy with which the cause of the mischief looks at the ruin, not only of the party, but of his own *followers and friends.*   He went into all this in pathetic detail.   He told me, as what I would not believe, that he had never seen *Peel in private* since his resignation, except once that he met him *riding,* and they rode a short way together, just long enough for Peel to ask what the Lords would do with Lord Hardinge's Bill, *not a word more !* and that he had not even seen his face for weeks (I doubt whether he did not say months) before the resignation—I suppose *he meant,* " except in full Cabinet."

It was on the whole a remarkable conversation, of which I have not time to-night to recapitulate more than is necessary for our present purpose.   In conclusion, he advised us to take our political line from *Stanley,* of whom he spoke as *our* leader.   He added what I have before told you of Peel being *unwell.*

Yours ever,

J. W. CROKER.

Mr. Croker scarcely needed the advice which was given to him by the Duke of Wellington, to " follow Lord Stanley." He had no faith in Mr. Disraeli, who seemed likely to become the acknowledged leader of the Protectionists—for it was not until 1847 that this position was formally taken by Lord George Bentinck.   Lord Stanley had been called to the Upper

House in September, 1844, in his father's barony, and his speeches had immediately given him a commanding position in that House. His communications with Mr. Croker were frequent, for it is scarcely necessary to say that the old friendly and confidential intercourse between Peel and Croker had now entirely come to an end.

Lord Stanley to Mr. Croker.   Extract.

Knowsley, August 23rd, 1846.

I confess that it is very difficult to draw a line which shall at once open the door of reconciliation to the least prominent of Peel's followers, and at the same time refuse to acknowledge the repeal of Protection as a *fait accompli*, or to acquiesce in the tergiversation, not to say treachery, of those by whose instrumentality the present change has been effected. Yet I feel confident that we should run counter to the best feelings of the country if we treated lightly, and as a matter of no consequence, the astounding change of votes, and open violation of pledges to constituencies, which have marked the present Session of Parliament; and I am very much mistaken if a short trial of Free Trade will not produce consequences which will lead to such a reaction in the public mind as to render it very unadvisable to succumb to it as to an inevitable destiny, without a serious struggle at a General Election. I have always thought that event a necessary preliminary to any reconstruction of the Conservative Party; before it, the two sections must have opposite views and aims ; after it, the judgment of the country may be said to have been pronounced one way or another, and those who desire to unite will have less difficulty in shaping their course. In the meantime I cannot but think that any hasty attempt to re-unite the scattered elements, more especially while Peel maintains his present position, is more likely to do harm than good; and that all that can be done is to abstain, in and out of Parliament, from unnecessary recurrence to what is past, and from multiplying topics of irritation.

But I am afraid we have no leaders in the House of Commons with enough of *sang froid* to act upon this cautious

and, I must admit, difficult line of policy, or with enough
of influence over their more hot-headed followers to induce
them to acquiesce in it.   I therefore long to see the prorogation of the present Parliament; and on the balance of
inconveniences, I think an early dissolution desirable.   I write
in haste, and hardly know whether I have made my views
intelligible; but if a line can be taken which shall at the same
time point out the common dangers against which all Conservatives may, and probably will have to guard, and the
necessity of union for the attainment of great political objects,
—shall hold out the olive-branch to those who may desire to
unite for such a purpose, and shall nevertheless refuse to bow
down to the newly-set-up idol of Free Trade, and leave to the
just resentment of the several constituencies those who may
not only have changed their opinions or their votes, but also
broken their solemn pledges;—I think such an article as you
could write, conceived in such a spirit, and adopting such a
line, might do great good, and smooth the way for future
reconciliation.   In the mean time, what I can do I will do, to
prevent new sources of irritation from arising; but it is very
difficult, not being on the spot, to foresee when and how they
are likely to spring up, so as to interpose effectually.   Again I
say, we want a prorogation, *pour calmer les esprits,* and to leave
the Government at leisure to take such steps as may array a
Conservative Opposition against them.

Believe me, my dear Sir,

Yours sincerely,

STANLEY.

Lord Ashburton to Mr. Croker.   Extract.

Stokes Bay, August 20th, 1846.

MY DEAR CROKER,

I wish I could see much chance of our great party rallying
after its marvellous betrayal; our best hopes are with Stanley,
but we must have a commoner, and though a leader generally comes when wanted, I do not see him through my
telescope.

Before next session I hope we shall get licked into some
shape, but the elements are as yet very chaotic, and if the

Whigs are wise they will get their new Parliament during the confusion, and I think they will. If they do not, they will find their deathbed session next year wholly unmanage-able, even without any split among themselves, which, with so restless and unyielding a companion as Grey, can hardly fail. I wish some good Samaritan of a Conservative with sufficient authority could heal the feuds among our friends I think all this might be quieted and settled, but the only man capable of this is the good and great Duke, and I hardly know whether he would undertake it. Ere dismissing bygones, it is indispensable that some guide for the future should be clearly traced, and in the state of things and of the country party, this can only be done by distinctly giving up Peel as leader. Whatever may be his merits or demerits, he can clearly not be a Tory leader. Could not you promote this good work ? We must have a captain before we can take the field of a General Election. Cobden's speech to the French economists showed great tact and ability. That is a very clever Cottonian, and his character puzzles me, but he will not move the French one inch beyond toasting and praising him, while they avail themselves of our follies. If I had half your talent and industry I think I could destroy his very shallow, plausible theories, which are our ruin.

A.

Mr. Lockhart to Mr. Croker. Extract.

I fancy the certainty of Peel's determination must disem-barrass your pen a good deal on the present occasion. Pro-bably, it will be from you that the public will first learn that his retirement is *bonâ fide;* and that being granted, it seems that your disposition to treat him and his later acts with all possible leniency, will not now give offence to any of his late opponents—but the contrary. I know you feel even more—a hundred times more than I do—reluctant to say a hard word unnecessarily of him, and I seriously believe that he was for his last year of power *not* in full possession of his faculties When he cut his foot, Brodie found it bleeding buckets full, yet he *instantly* cupped him on the temples, for he at once inferred that the accident had resulted from great disorder of the whole system, nerves included. This I know to be the case ; and my own doctor (Ferguson), who occasionally visits

Lady Peel and the girls, has at this moment a strong impression that Sir Robert is in a dangerous state. The *Elbing* letter *sent furieusement l'apoplexie.**

Ever yours,

J. L.

Mr. Croker to Lord Stanley.

390, High Street, Cheltenham, August 21st, 1846.

MY DEAR LORD,

I must begin by thanking you for my papers and your observations, all of which shall be duly attended to; I only wish there had been more. In the next place, as an apology for again troubling you, I must tell you that having, the day before I left town, called upon the Duke of Wellington—my oldest, indeed, I might say, my only *political connexion*—we fell into a confidential talk on the state of affairs. You, I suppose, may not know that his Grace has always been very kind and confidential with me, and that last Christmas he talked and wrote a good deal to me on the then recent events. I, during the crisis, urged him with great earnestness to follow *your* course, and not resume the Cabinet key; and I foretold him everything that has since come to pass.

This he now cannot but confess, and painfully feel the mischief that his countenance enabled his colleagues to do; but in the course of our conversation, I said something as to the line that the Conservative party might or might not adopt, on which he said " that my Lord Stanley must decide —he is now the person to be looked to," with some expressions of confidence in your views.

I mention this as my justification for troubling you, on the new *phase* which this unlucky outbreak of Lord G. Bentinck against Lyndhurst gives to our affairs.† Lyndhurst's answer

---

* [The Prussian seaport town of Elbing had forwarded an address to Sir R. Peel, congratulating him upon the repeal of the Corn Laws. He wrote a reply on August 6, advocating the principles of Free Trade and direct taxation.]

† [The story of this "outbreak" is told by Sir Theodore Martin in his ' Life of Lord Lyndhurst,' pp. 421–426. Lord Lyndhurst caused overtures to be made to Lord George Bentinck, with a view of reconciling all differences within the Tory party; they were misunderstood and resented by

must still further widen the breach. The haste and indiscretion of Lord George seems unpardonable, and the attack on Lyndhurst seems to me to have been not merely unjust, but in the highest degree impolitic, and I suppose really all hope of an early reunion of the Conservative party, either in Parliament or the *Press*, hopeless. I underline the *Press*, for though I know nothing of the newspapers' allies, I have heard that the editors (for these are *now* distinct hands, I am told) of the *Standard* and the *Herald* are personally hostile to Lyndhurst. In fact, I have only just now heard this and many details on the subject from Mr. Charles Phillips, one of the parties in the late affair, whom I met in the street, and who, on a very slight acquaintance, volunteered to tell me a very long and not uninteresting story, the main point of which, as regards my present purpose, is the hostility of those two papers, and the position of the party whose sentiments they speak, towards Lyndhurst. All this seems to me to render it the more advisable that the *Quarterly Review* should take a higher and more conciliatory tone ; but it renders the execution of such a purpose much more difficult. In the present state of affairs, I know no other organ that the moderate Conservatives have but the *Quarterly*. I say moderate, in contradistinction to those who wish to proscribe *every one*, high and low, that support Peel in any degree—a line of conduct that I fear would completely ruin the party themselves as well as us. I therefore ask you, in confidence, how you think we ought to proceed. You have already seen my own general opinion, which I am very glad to find yours ; but this event will, I fear, call for some more pressing and practical exhortation to reunion and reconstruction. I need hardly tell you that I am a mere volunteer in this matter. I have quitted public life, and personally have no political object whatsoever, but I am anxious to lend my poor aid to avert, or, at least, delay, the revolution with which we are threatened. As to the Irish Church, I have already embarked the *Quarterly* in an unhesitating support of that—the outwork

Lord George, who accused Lord Lyndhurst of having been a party to a "nefarious job" in public life. This charge was thoroughly unjust, as Mr. Disraeli and others admitted at the time. It does not appear that a reconciliation was ever arrived at between Lord Lyndhurst and Lord George Bentinck.]

of the Church of England, and, as I almost believe, Christianity in these nations; but I have also (with some difficulty) pledged it to a State provision for the Catholic Clergy. This has been always my opinion, which is every day strengthened.

I am satisfied there is no other security, or even chance of security, for the Protestant interest and English connexion.

I tell you honestly I feel towards Peel more of sorrow, and I am reluctant to confess, more of resentment, than becomes my age and position; but I really cannot, even now, believe the extent of his aberrations. The facts, to be sure, are there—lamentable, disastrous, and unquestionable; but the motives and objects I cannot comprehend. All that I see with any degree of certainty is that he has ruined himself and us—and all for what?

Excuse this rambling essay, which, however, it seems to me necessary that I should submit for your consideration and further advice.

Ever, my dear Lord,

Yours sincerely,

J. W. CROKER.

Lord Lyndhurst to Mr. Croker.

George Street. [No date.]

MY DEAR CROKER,

I return the enclosed, as you requested, and with many thanks, as well as for your obliging letter to me. If the councils of the party were to be directed by Lord G. Bentinck, there would soon be an end of the Conservatives. This species of controversy is very painful to me, and I feel that I would submit to almost any imputation rather than to be dragged into a defence, of the sufficiency and fulness of which the newspapers of a party are to be the judges.

Ever, my dear Croker, yours faithfully,

LYNDHURST.

As to Lady L., she is in a perfect fury, and only wishes she were a member of the House. *She* would give it him! She desires to be kindly remembered.

Mr. Croker to Dr. Giffard, Editor of the ' Standard.'

390, High Street, Cheltenham, August 22nd, 1846.

MY DEAR SIR,

I hope I need not tell you how great an interest I take in the *Standard*, not merely as the organ of the party to which (as far as I can be considered a public man) I belong, but, if you will allow me to say so, for your sake also ; and I trust you will forgive me for expressing my regret at the line it has taken in this last affair about Lord Lyndhurst, which will be, I fear, of the greatest injury to the cause that you, I am sure, have at heart in common with myself—the reconstruction of the great Tory party, which has been so incomprehensibly betrayed and scattered.   I must premise by saying that the *only* exact knowledge that I have of Lord Lyndhurst's disposal of his patronage arose from his kindness to your nephew William ; and in that case he combined a lively desire to show his regard for poor Sir William, with, I must say, a due inquiry as to character and fitness ; and in some collateral moves that came to my knowledge in the course of this affair, I saw great kindness to individuals mixed with a conscientious desire to execute a great public duty to the public advantage.   As this was the only case in which I was personally interested, I can speak as to no other, but I feel that I ought to bear that witness as far as it goes.   But a more serious question is the general use of the Chancellor's patronage, which you think should be given to the bishops. Surely, my dear sir, this proposition must have escaped you under a too hasty impression, both as to chancellors and, I am sorry to add, bishops ; and it seems to me quite contrary to all the principles that you have so long taught the world.

In the first place, this Crown patronage is the real bond between *Church and State;* if *that* were severed, there would no longer be a " Church of England " (as we understand the term), and the election of bishops by the clergy would soon follow the nomination of the clergy by the bishops.   A volume would not suffice to expose the political and social consequences of this awful revolution ; but, even if this power were taken from the Crown, the bishops are the *very last* people to whom I would give it.   I speak not of the present Bench, nor of individuals ; but historically of man ; and I think I may safely say that the disposal of church preferment by the bishops has always been, and must always be, liable to

great abuse and scandal. The first, and often the *only*, care of
a bishop is to provide for his own family ; and there is not
(at least there has not been to my knowledge) any single
case in which the promotion to the Bench has not been
preceded or followed by circumstances connected with
patronage which would look very unseemly to the public
eye.   I remember to have heard that old Bishop Law of
Elphin saluted a newly-mitred brother with this congratula-
tion, " My dear Lord, I give you joy; you will now be able
to provide for your large family ; you will unite all your
sons to the Church, and the Church to all your daughters."
Of the last bishop who died, and of the last bishop who has
been made, I could tell you stories that would amuse you
more than a farce, and I verily believe that Newmarket does
not afford more, or more ludicrous, instances of jockeyship
than could be found in the secret history of episcopal promotion and patronage.   For my own part, I am satisfied that
of the *two* it would be infinitely better that they should
have *no* patronage than *all*.

But to return to Lord Lyndhurst, the individual case has
been triumphantly explained ; but what can be more proper,
as a general rule, than to allow a proportionate, though not
predominant, weight to the wishes of a great landowner in
appointing clergymen to parishes ? It is of the greatest advantage to all parties, and particularly to the poorer parishioners,
for whom the parson is an *ex officio* mediator.   When, the
other day, Lord Lyndhurst had two livings to give away—
one in Surrey and one in Lincolnshire—was there anything
blameable in his allotting Weybridge to our William, because
it happened to be the most desirable place in England to him
and his family ? It is equally fortunate for Weybridge, which
has thus got a minister young, active, zealous, and able, who
has already done more good and made himself more popular
in the parish than any of his predecessors (at least in modern
times) were able to do. If Lord Lyndhurst had, as the
Standard seems to say he ought to have done, looked all
through England for the greatest claims, he could not have
made a better choice, though our young man had little
chance ; and my firm belief is that promotions for supposed
merit, without the guarantee of personal interest and recommendation, are nine times in ten the very worst promotions
that can be made.

Ever yours,

J. W. CROKER.

P.S.—This was written yesterday, but there was no post out. I hear this morning of the new incident between Lord L. and Lord George, which increases my anxiety and alarm. I am confident that it will be found that Lord George is again under some misinformation ; but, although this affair aggravates the difficulties and dangers of the Conservative party, it does not, I think, make any essential difference in the *principles* advanced in my letter, and I therefore think that I may as well send it to you.

Lord Lyndhurst to Mr. Croker.

Turville Park, Henley-on-Thames,
Monday, September 14th, 1846.

MY DEAR CROKER,

You ask me as to the prospects of the party. "Lost and obscured in *Turville's* humble bower," &c., how can I know anything that party does or party intends ? " No candidate for power " is, as you know, the rhyme for " bower " in the passage to which I have referred, and a being in that situation is generally left to know nothing ; but I shall receive with delight every information that you will give me.

Now, as to the Small Debts Bill. It had been so frequently before Parliament that it did not become the subject of consideration in the Cabinet this year. The measure was prepared by Drinkwater (Bethune), under the sole direction of Graham. I was suprised at the device to conciliate Whiggery. I should not have consented to the proposition, nor would any of the Whigs themselves, as I know from conversation with them. The absurdity was too glaring. But in fact it was never, I believe, intended to proceed with the Bill. This and several other measures were brought forward, I suppose, merely to make a show when it was known that our fate was determined. It was thought desirable to manifest our good intentions—an article with which it is said hell is paved.

I am sure I cannot say with any certainty what passed between Peel and the Queen ; he never told the Cabinet nor me in particular. But I think it highly probable that something of the kind passed, as it corresponds exactly with his conversation with her. He enlarged upon the pains in his head, his dimness of sight, &c. I have now answered your questions, and you must do in return a favour to Lady L. and

myself, by paying a visit to us at this place when you can
afford a day or so for that purpose.   You will receive a most
hearty welcome.   We can talk about rural affairs, and you
will find—as indeed I am sure you know—that a Sabine
farm is not a hum.

Ever yours most truly,

LYNDHURST.

As to my appointments, to which I am told the *Examiner*
refers, they are about as follows :—

12 Commissioners of Bankruptcy.
24 Registrars of ditto.
30 Official Assignees.
2 Masters in Lunacy.
6 Commissioners of ditto.*
4 Taxing Masters in Equity.
1 ditto in Bankruptcy.
1 Accountant in Bankruptcy.
Total, 80.

Out of these I appointed a first and a second cousin, and
two much more distant connections—altogether, four; and I
further appointed an old secretary who had been with me
from the first, and another gentlemen who had held an
inferior appointment under me to two other of these offices
(and more shame for him if he had not ! G. L.).† This is all
that can in any way be referred to self.

The Duke of Wellington to Mr. Croker.

Walmer Castle, September 12th, 1846.

MY DEAR CROKER,

I have this morning received your letter of the 10th inst.
I have not received from any quarter, much less from either
of the parties, any information respecting the conversation
supposed to have passed between her Majesty and Sir Robert
Peel.

I am certain that he has announced now publicly that he
does not intend to return to office.   I have been certain that
for many years, at least since 1819, it was not wise to be in

---

* [With reference to the spirit in which these appointments were filled,
see Lord Shaftesbury's letter to Lady Lyndhurst, 26th July, 1871, in Sir
Theodore Martin's *Life of Lyndhurst*, p. 521.]

[† An interpolation by Lady Lyndhurst.]

office, even at the head of the Administration.   I know that
lately he had been most desirous of quitting office, and that
he would not have accepted office in 1841–1842 if he could
have avoided it.   I am not with you in thinking that the
example of the loss of preceding Ministers, and the state of
the House has had some effect in producing this feeling; and
that Lady Peel has been very much affected by the personal
danger, as well as by the state of irritation in which the
business of his office, and particularly that of Parliament, kept
him.

I have heard nothing of the animosities with his former
supporters.   But I am quite certain that he is not sensible of
the advantage which the public interest or the Queen's service
would derive from the establishment of a Conservative
Government under the lead and guidance of any other individual.   Right or wrong, I think that he was quite in earnest
in respect to the abstract commercial and financial policy of
the measures of the last session of Parliament.

Believe me, ever yours, most sincerely,

WELLINGTON.

Lord Stanley to Mr. Croker.   Extract.

Knowsley, September 27th, 1846.

MY DEAR SIR,

There seems now no prospect of a dissolution this year;*
but I expect an early meeting of Parliament, which I shall
regret on every account, but chiefly because I fear an early
renewal, in the House of Commons, of discussions between
the Protectionists and the Peelites.   I presume you do not
really anticipate, as in the least degree probable, Sir Robert
Peel's retirement from Parliament.   On the contrary, I am
satisfied that he intends to attend regularly, take a leading
part on most great questions, and act, with a small body
of adherents, the part of an arbiter between the Government and the Protectionists, a position productive of the
greatest embarrassment to all parties, and one which, I fear,
will perpetuate the present dissensions, render the re-construc-
tion of a Conservative party all but impossible, and smooth
the way for those measures of gradual downward progress
which Lord John Russell must introduce, but which I think

* [Parliament was not dissolved till July 23rd, 1847.]

he will introduce as gradually as he can. Peel will oftener be
found voting with the Government than against them; and I
am afraid he will be found full as often urging them onward
as restraining them.   I hope I do him injustice; but I think
I saw unmistakeable symptoms of his determination to be at
the head of *a* party, and that his release of his former friends
from their allegiance to him was meant to leave himself quite
free to form any connection, independent of them, which
might enable him again to take a prominent part, and guide
the progress of social changes which he thinks cannot be
averted.

> Believe me, my dear Sir, yours very truly,
>
> STANLEY.

Lord Stanley to Mr. Croker.   Extract.

Worsley, October 6th, 1846.

MY DEAR SIR,

I return you, according to your request, Arbuthnot's letter,*
and I quite concur in the view he takes of your article,† both
as to its truth, its severity (*because* of its truth), and at the
same time its freedom from anything which can be considered
personally offensive, or calculated to widen the unfortunate
breach in the Conservative Party.   That the Duke of Wellington should cordially approve is singular enough; but it is
an additional proof of that extraordinary candour with which
he can judge his own past course, as if it were that of another
man, and see dispassionately where it has been erroneous;
and on this occasion it has been fatally so for the country.

I do not understand the distinction Arbuthnot draws
between being in office and in Cabinet, as regards Peel.   I
cannot conceive his being one without the other.   As an
illustration of the rate of wages directly springing from railway schemes, and its effect upon consumption, I was assured
the other day that the railway navigators (of whom there are
employed above 200,000) consume on an average two pounds
of meat daily, of which they require that one-fourth part
shall be *fat!*   I should think the actual rate of wages now in
course of payment to railway labourers and those connected
with them does not fall short of a million a week!   I heard
of iron-workers earning 15s. a *day;* almost the whole of
which is consumed in meat and drink—the practice being for

* [This letter is missing.]
† ["Close of Peel's Administration," Q. R., No. 156.]

the gangs to have constantly by them a *pail* of ale, with a
bottle of gin in it, from which every man takes a swill, at the
completion of a certain number of bars of iron ; and one case
was named to me in which a lad of sixteen, receiving 13*s.* a
day, struck for 15*s.*, and the employers were obliged to give it
him.   This is not a wholesome state of things, far from it, but
for the present it must have a powerful effect in keeping up
the prices of agricultural produce, and blinding the farmers to
the ultimate effect of the late measures.

I am, dear Sir, yours faithfully,

STANLEY.

Mr. Charles Arbuthnot to Mr. Croker.

Walmer Castle, October 10th, 1846.

MY DEAR CROKER,

It is just possible that I may have been dreaming when I
wrote to you ; for I am sure that if awake, and in my right
senses, I could not have hinted that Peel would be willing to
become a member of a Cabinet though not the chief of it.

Last year he declared to me, that if he could have a good
and valid reason for retiring, he would not only quit his then
situation, but that, as I understood him, he would never
consent to be again in any Cabinet.   I refrained, in writing
to you, from putting the case so strongly, because I thought
that he might be speaking under some temporary irritation,
or that he might have said hastily what he would not afterwards adhere to.

But let his conduct hereafter be whatever it may, I should
have led you into error if I had hinted that I was aware of
his having the design to resume office in some shape or other.
I have always believed that he had taken leave of office
altogether and for ever.   I have been apprehensive that he
might support (but without office) the present Whig Government; and that apprehension was increased by what the
Duke of Bedford told me.   He said, that Peel had manifested
a kindly disposition to their Government by going up to
E. Ellice and telling him that he was obliged to leave London,
but that he had desired all those whom he could influence to
support their Sugar Bill.

Ever affectionately yours,

CHARLES ARBUTHNOT.

Mr. Lockhart to Mr. Croker.   Extract.

December 16th, 1846.

DEAR CROKER,

I aggravated my cold so much by the railway travel that I was not able to dine with H. B[rougham] yesterday, nor am to leave my room to-day. He and A. [Ashburton?] and I, however, walked and talked together all Sunday afternoon, so that I fancy I may safely say that neither one nor other of them sees his way in the least. H. B. spoke just as you would do about Stanley, and the absurdities by which Lord George has so shattered his hastily built reputation. H. B. and A. also both concurred that Gladstone is incapacitated for a leading place by his zeal in Ultra-Œconomics and by his Puseyite mania—but even more by the Jesuitical structure of his mind. In a word, there is no leader, and therefore as yet no hope for the Protectionists, who must await the results of experience on the sense of the country at large. Not a whisper for [from ?] H. B. on the merits of the Peel measures, but much bitter eloquence on the way in which he carried them. He said, " *he is done*—he has for him no support either in the gentry or in the Church or *among political men of any class*, except his few underlings. He fancies that he is to regain the position of 1835—that of great power without responsibility—but he is mistaken, for he has now been tried. By-and-bye he will perceive this and, giving up all hope of a legitimate sort, will try to construct a new party on the mere cotton-spinning principle, but he is too old to see the success of that attempt." H. B. spoke with bitterness too of Lord John—he said he had read his preface to Bedford letters, vol. iii., and thought it very poor—but I found he had *not* read it to the end, for he knew nothing of the only remarkable part of it, the little disquisition on *party*. I think he has merely read the *note* about one of his own productions; and I doubt if he ever reads anything but what is written by or about himself! Both A. and B. thought Government would rub on with this Parliament till August or so, but Ashley, who has just been here, and who knows a great deal of the Whig plans, says he is satisfied that there is no idea of deferring the dissolution beyond Easter. He, too, now speaks with great scorn of Peel, and pronounces him politically dead.

From Mr. Croker's Note Book.

Strathfieldsaye, December 16th, 1846.

I have had a great deal of confidential talk with the Duke on late and future political events. He had no reason to think that Peel had any *arrière pensée*, but was really alarmed at the failure of the Irish potato crop, and wished towards the end of October to have suspended the Corn Laws by proclamation, but was overruled, and when Lord J. Russell's letter came out was very much piqued that he had been thus forestalled; and then he pressed it again without effect, and at last had some scheme by which the Corn Laws were to be successively changed, in three periods of seven years each, till totally reduced.* It would seem as if he had had no one with him in the Cabinet but Sidney Herbert and perhaps Aberdeen, but he (the D.) was not at all in the secret of this change of opinion, and knew very little of what was going on or intended. He was much surprised to hear that I had long suspected that Peel had modified his opinion on *his own* Corn Law. My suspicion—I might indeed say my proofs—were long anterior to the alarm about the potato crop, but the Duke had no suspicion of any other motive at the time. I mentioned to him that before the potato failure was known, some time in August or very early in September, I had been surprised at hearing from Sidney Herbert some free trade observations, which confirmed my previous suspicions about Peel's change. "Well," said he, "it is odd that the first inkling I had of what was intended was also from Sidney Herbert. We had been attending a Cabinet at Peel's house, where he was confined by the gout, and as we were walking the short step between that and our offices (he was then Secretary at War) he dropped a few words which gave me the first hint that any one was dreaming of such a thing. That fit of the gout depressed Peel exceedingly—to a greater degree than was suspected, and I think it had its influence on his mind and on his measures. But as to the wheel about on the Corn Laws, I was no more prepared for it than any gentleman who was walking in Whitehall the day I crossed it with Sidney Herbert. It looks to me like what Sheridan

---

* [The word is "reduced" in the original; "abolished" was doubtless meant.]

said of the Whigs, ' building up a wall to knock their own heads against.' Nor do I comprehend how the repeal of the Corn Laws can remedy the potato famine in Ireland, where the want is not of food, but of money to buy it."

As I had come down by his invitation on purpose to talk with him on these matters, I urged him with all the earnestness that I could, not to associate himself to so great a shock on confidence and character as this would be—that he might remain at the head of the army, though not in the Cabinet, but that it would never come to that point, for his opposition would assuredly stop it for the present ; or at all events, that if it were carried, it would be without any loss of character to him, which I dreaded more even than the measure itself. He took all I said in very good part, fully agreed in all I said about the measure itself, but could not persuade himself to break up the Government which would fall into the hands of the Radicals. I said that really if Radical *measures* were to be carried, I thought it fairer, and in fact better, for the country that they should be carried by Radical *men*. Admitting as he did that these measures were dangerous in their principle and even more so in their detail, did he not see the vast difference that must result from the ministers being halloo'd on and stimulated by the charge of their political opponents, instead of being restrained and checked by a *bonâ fide* and sincere opposition, with whom they would naturally endeavour to keep some measure. He agreed in all I said, and in as strong terms, but he could not persuade himself to go into opposition.

CHAPTER XXV.

1847.

WE have seen that one of the closest and most valued of all the friendships of Mr. Croker's life was sundered in 1846. He had been on terms of the most affectionate intimacy with Peel for nearly forty years, and the final separation cost him a deep and bitter pang. Peel had been faithless to his party, but Mr. Croker felt that he had been specially un-faithful to him; for many of the articles which had appeared in the *Quarterly Review* on Protection had been written "under the eye," and at the suggestion of Peel himself. In deserting his followers, Peel had not only left them without a leader, but had divided them into irreconcileable sections. There was no longer a Conservative party at the opening of the Session of 1847. Some of its members still followed Peel, and were called after his name; others owned no allegiance to any leader; a third section looked for a rallying point to Lord John Manners, Mr. Disraeli, or Lord George Bentinck. But the historic Tory party was dissolved.

Whether it was wise or unwise to abolish the Corn Laws, it has since been acknowledged that Sir Robert Peel betrayed his followers pitilessly when he made himself the means of accomplishing the work. He was pledged to the support of the principles of Protection, and never gave the slightest ground for the supposition that he had changed his opinions until he was ready to produce the measure which violated all his promises, and left his supporters humiliated and crushed. No writer of any authority has attempted to defend this want of good faith. "As the leader of a party," writes a Liberal historian,* Peel "was unfaithful and disloyal." Sir Erskine May goes on to lay down principles which would perhaps scarcely be received in the present day by Liberal politicians without material qualifications:—

"The relations between a leader and his followers are those of mutual confidence. His talents give them union and force; their numbers invest him with political power. They tender, and he accepts the trust, because he shares and represents their sentiments. Viewing affairs from higher ground, he may persuade them to modify or renounce their opinions in the interests of the state; but, without their concurrence, he has no right to use for one purpose that power which they have entrusted to him for another. He has received a limited authority, which he may not exceed

---

* Sir Erskine May, 'History of England,' chapter viii.

without further instructions. If, contrary to the judgment of his party, he believes the public welfare to demand an entire change of policy, it is not for him to carry it out. He cannot, indeed, be called upon to cancel or disavow his own opinions; but he is no longer entitled to lead the forces entrusted to his command—still less to seek the aid of the enemy. Elected chief of a free republic—not its dictator— it becomes his duty, honourably and in good faith, to retire from his position, with as little injury as may be to the cause he abandons, and to leave to others a task which his own party allegiance forbids him to attempt."

These were the very opinions which were expressed by Mr. Croker after Sir Robert Peel's "apostacy," but he expressed them without personal bitterness towards the friend of former days. The world has, indeed, received from Miss Martineau a different account.* " When he had been staying at Drayton Manor," so ran her story, " not long before Sir R. Peel's death, had been not only hospitably entertained, but kindly ministered to under his infirmities of deafness and bad health, and went home to cut up his host in a political article for the forthcoming *Quarterly*—his fellow guests at Drayton refused as long as possible to believe the article to be his." There is not a word of truth in this statement from beginning to end. Any one who was likely to be a guest at Drayton Manor knew perfectly well who wrote the articles in the *Quarterly Review;* Peel himself knew; and Mr. Croker was not at Drayton Manor for several years prior to Peel's death. The following letters—melancholy enough, considering the affectionate intimacy which had existed between the writers for so many years—are conclusive on these points; they show that Miss Martineau, like some

---

* The account published in the *Daily News* (afterwards copied into the *Gentleman's Magazine*) the day after Mr. Croker's death, in which he was spoken of as the "unhappy old man who has just departed," with " a malignant ulcer " in his mind, &c.

others who have sought to wreak revenge on Mr. Croker, paid little regard to truth or justice.

Mr. Croker to Sir Robert Peel.   Extract.

West Moulsey, January 12th, 1847.

I cannot write to you without expressing my deep regret at having been placed, by my zeal for and confidence in your former measures, in a position which has forced me into so decided a difference of political opinions as must render any personal intercourse between us awkward and painful. Thus closes, with this note, a correspondence of seven and thirty years; but it does not alter my—I believe—unalterable affection for yourself, and my regard for Lady Peel and your family, which are as lively and sincere as my wishes for the failure, as I understand them, of all your political views.

If we should happen to meet (which is not very likely, as I go very little from home), I hope it may be with such civil forms and as much personal kindness as may very well coexist with strong political differences.

I am, my dear Peel,

Very sincerely and affectionately yours,

Up to the Altar,

J. W. CROKER.

Sir Robert Peel to Mr. Croker.

Drayton Manor, January 15th, 1847.

SIR,

As I am confirmed by your letter in my previous impressions, that you are the author of certain articles which have appeared in recent numbers of the *Quarterly Review,* I concur entirely in the opinion you express, that any personal intercourse between us would be awkward and painful.

There are no doubt many cases in which personal good-will may co-exist with strong political differences, but personal good-will cannot co-exist with the spirit in which those articles are written, or with the feelings they must naturally have excited.

I trust there is nothing inconsistent with perfect civility in the expression of an earnest wish that the same principle

which suggests to you the propriety of closing a written correspondence of seven and thirty years, may be extended to
every other species of intercourse.

I have the honour to be, Sir,

Your obedient servant,

ROBERT PEEL.

Mr. Croker to Sir Robert Peel.

West Moulsey, January 17th, 1847.

I think it proper to acknowledge the receipt of your letter
of the 15th inst., concurring in my view of the expediency of
closing all intercourse written or personal between us.   I
have no objection to make to the terms, nor, of course, to the
conclusions of that letter; but I cannot admit—and indeed
feel myself bound to deny—the personal feelings by which it
supposes me to have been actuated.

J. W. CROKER.

It does not appear that these once firm friends ever met
again.   After Peel's death, Mr. Croker wrote to an acquaintance:—"The death of Sir Robert Peel, so strangely accidental, affected me much; for thirty years I loved him as a
brother, and no mere change of opinions would have separated
me from him.   My complaint was his concealing the change,
and betraying the trust reposed in him as well by private
friendship as by public confidence.   If his candour had been
equal to his judgment, and his courage commensurate to his
capacity, he would have been a great man; as it was, he was
only a great misfortune, and perhaps his death may turn out
to be as great a misfortune as the last portion of his life had
been."   Mr. Croker's just complaint and chief grievance was
that after having been encouraged by Sir Robert Peel to
write articles in the *Quarterly Review* in support of Protection, he was kept entirely in the dark with regard to the
Minister's intention to make a sudden change in his policy.

The articles to which reference has been made did not

exceed the fair bounds of political discussion. They disputed
Sir Robert Peel's right to betray his party—everybody has
done that; but there was nothing in them which was aimed
at the *man* as distinguished from the statesman. Some proof
of this may, perhaps, be required, considering the specific
accusations of personal malice which have so often been
levelled at Mr. Croker on account of his treatment of Peel.
Here, then, is the proof.

Mr. Croker on Sir Robert Peel's Policy.
(*From the 'Quarterly Review' of September* 1846.)

We speak of Sir Robert Peel's share in the whole of this
unhappy affair with the deepest pain, and with a reluctance
which nothing but a sense of public duty could overcome.
We had given him throughout his administration a cordial,
disinterested, and, to the best of our power, efficient support ;
we adopted from his own lips his profession of faith, both
commercial and political ; and our readers will not have forgotten that in several successive articles on the Whig budget
of 1841—on his own financial legislation of 1842—and on
the Anti-Corn-Law League, in January, 1843—we recorded
our own confidence, and solicited that of our readers, in his
principles and his measures. He has changed his opinions—
we have not—he has even run into the adverse extreme, and
we must oppose him. But differing, as we have the misfortune to do, from every opinion that he has recently delivered
on these subjects—disapproving all his measures, and deplor-
ing both the form and the substance of his whole course of
proceeding—it is the more due to his character, and to our
own feelings, to declare our entire conviction of the purity of
his intentions—nay, of his goodwill to the very interests
which he seems to have sacrificed.

*   *   *   *   *

We must take this opportunity of expressing our more than
regret at some imputations which have been made in private
and in print, of his having some low personal motive in the
depreciation of the landed interest. The accusation is not
merely wholly groundless—it is absurd. Sir Robert Peel's
interests—as we stated in defence of his Corn Law of 1842—

are essentially identified with the land; and his measure is
the more anomalous and alarming from its being contrary to
those personal interests. But we take higher ground. Sir
Robert Peel is infinitely superior to any influence of that low
nature. His heart, if not as stout, is as pure as Mr. Pitt's.
He may be deficient in official candour and frankness—in
fidelity to political friendships—in firmness against political
adversaries—in contempt of the *civium ardor prava jubentium*
—in the wise courage that prefers to meet the storm in the
deep waters rather than in shoals and straits—these defects,
we say, may be imputed to him, and they are probably in
some degree constitutional; but his mind was never sullied by
even the passing cloud of any sordid or unworthy thought.
It is an over-cautious and over-sensitive ratiocination that
reduces him to the level—below his spirit and alien from his
taste—of a temporizing Utilitarian. If his heart were as
firm as it is pure—if he were as inaccessible to the delusions
and plausibilities of theorists, the hypocritical applause of
adversaries, the insidious and interested flatteries of the foreign
press, and the menaces of popular agitation, as he is to either
passion, corruption, or any other ignoble motive—if he could
trust himself as he requires others to trust him—he might, as
we once hoped he was destined to do, have stayed the revolution, instead of, as we now fear, rapidly accelerating it. And
this fear—very strong and very sincere—must be our justification, for the frank severity with which, while doing justice to
his private virtues and splendid talents, we must question and
even censure so many circumstances of his public conduct.

These quotations are in themselves sufficient to dispose of
the charge that Mr. Croker assailed Sir Robert Peel in an unjustifiable and unbecoming manner. He was not guilty of
betraying Peel, or of any disloyalty to him; nor could Peel
accuse him of any such offence. He felt, however, that he
had a right to complain of having been betrayed by Peel,
who had led him to support Protectionist principles *after* he
had made up his own mind to abandon them.

On the general question of Free Trade Mr. Croker contended for these opinions :—

"We will not stop to debate whether there can be, under any circumstances, such a thing as *Free Trade* in the abstract; it is enough for our immediate purpose to say that, in the present condition of mankind, it is utterly unattainable as regards the intercourse of independent states. In countries united under the same sovereign and identified in national feeling and commercial and financial interests, it may be possible indeed, but it is rarely carried out. Between England, Scotland, Ireland, and the Channel Islands you might have perfect free trade—but you have not; you might collect in each a like rate and species of revenue—but you do not;—which might be applied—though it is not—without distinction of local interests, to the common expenses of the empire. In such a case, we say, a very near approach to free trade is possible, and may perhaps (though with many exceptions) be said practically to exist. But how can any such community of interests or concert of measures be expected from independent countries? Is there any man so Utopian as to believe that the nations of the world can ever concur in a general abrogation of all custom-duties? Some countries, particularly America, have hardly any other permanent source of revenue, and as long as there are custom-duties there can be no free trade, even in the loosest meaning of the term. Each nation will lay on such duties as will be most profitable to its exchequer with the least disadvantage to its own subjects, or, in other words, as will ensure the greatest favour to its native industry and the greatest discouragement of foreign rivalry. This is common sense, and the first and most obvious duty of a statesman ; and it would be thought the silliest, if it were not the most mischievous, of delusions to expect that, because *we* are mad enough to sacrifice our national exchequer or our native industries, other nations will follow the suicidal example."

" On the whole, then, we are more and more convinced by all we read, and see, and hear from all quarters, that the promise that our free-trade mania is likely to meet with anything like reciprocity from any foreign powers of the New World or the Old, will turn out to be a lamentable deception. . . . They will not be the dupes of such a juggle—they will send us their corn, first laying on it, for their own use, the duties which we have sacrificed, and—awakened still more sharply to their own interest by this gross attempt to deceive them—

they will, with greater vigilance than ever, recur to the old
Continental text—

————" timeo Danaos et dona ferentes."

If these predictions are placed side by side with those of
Sir Robert Peel and of Mr. Cobden, and compared with the
attitude at the present time of foreign powers on the Free
Trade question, it is not upon Mr. Croker's memory that the
reproach of want of foresight will rest.

When Lord John Russell met the House in January, 1847,
he found himself obliged to confess that the state of Ireland
was getting worse and worse every day. The repressive
measures asked for by Sir Robert Peel were refused, but it
was evident that the Whig Government would be reduced
to follow the course which the defeated Minister had indicated. In the previous year there had been a complete
failure of the potato crop in Ireland, and now began the great
famine which sent thousands to the grave, and thousands
more to seek homes in distant lands. " Ten thousand persons,
at the meeting of Parliament, had died in the union of Skib-
bereen, which numbered one hundred thousand souls." * The
Government measures of relief appeared to do little good ; in
the autumn there was another bad harvest, and before the
second week in October a commercial panic took place which
shook every branch of trade, and sent the rate of interest to
60 per cent. per annum. The bank rate of discount was
from 8 to 12 per cent. Consols touched 79¼. In the city of
London alone there were eighty-five failures. Lord George
Bentinck had urgently advised the Government in the spring
of the year to suspend the operation of the Bank Restriction
Act, but it was declared that this would be a dangerous step
to take. In October Lord John Russell found that the
" dangerous step " was the only thing which could save the

---

* Mr. Disraeli's ' Life of Lord George Bentinck,' orig. ed. 1852, p. 351.

commercial system of the country from utter ruin; the Bank
Charter Act was suspended, and the panic stopped as if by
magic. Throughout the discussions on this subject, and upon
the general measures brought forward, the "Peelites" usually
supported the Government, while the Protectionists devoted
themselves to the task of preventing the return of Sir Robert
Peel to power. In July there was a dissolution, Parliament
having lived out its full period; and when the contest was
over, it was seen that the relative strength of parties remained pretty much as it had been before.

Mr. Croker to Lord Brougham.

West Moulsey, Kingston, February 5th, 1847.

My dear Brougham,

You ask me what I think; I will tell you:—

1. All Lord John's Irish measures, except the soup kettles,
are visions and humbugs, and (which is very proper for Irish
legislation) would, if practicable, double the original mischief.

2. It follows that I am astonished at Lord George's calling
them "*beautiful*" and Lord Stanley "*satisfactory*" unless
these epithets apply to the prospect of the Ministry's utter
failure, for which purpose they are "*beautiful* and *satisfactory*."

3. I am still more astonished at the impolicy—I might
say insanity—of an Opposition taking upon itself the responsibility of administration, and associating itself with the
odium and risk of a crisis which their antagonists have
created. It is like a solvent man forcing himself into
partnership with a bankrupt.

4. If I were in Parliament, I should endeavour to hold on
by Stanley as the best chance of doing any good, and should
try to induce him to act the part of his ancestor at the battle
of Bosworth, waiting the movements of the other two parties.
Your position is not so clear. It is embarrassed by your
having changed your original opinions on the corn laws (the
Duke, Lyndhurst, &c., have changed, not their *opinions*, but
only their *votes*, and that on a compulsion that no longer
binds them). You will be, as far as I see, the only anti-

Protectionist at your side of the House. For that I see no remedy at present; by-and-bye, when we come to general legislation, to further democratic reforms, and to direct taxation and so forth, you will be in your place and have room and solid ground for all your exertions.

Ever sincerely yours,

J. W. CROKER.

Mr. Croker to Colonel Wood. *

West Moulsey, February 3rd, 1847.

MY DEAR WOOD,

I was very glad to find that you remembered me when you thought of your friends in England; and I should have immediately thanked you for your letter and pamphlet, but that I expected that you would have come over to the meeting of Parliament. As I find that has not been the case, I no longer delay my acknowledgment.

You say very truly that I am not a *free trader.* First, I don't believe that there ever was, or will, or *can* be any such thing as perfect free trade ; and, secondly, that any approach to free trade should always be measured by the great scale of public safety; and, thirdly, I do not think it wise to over-throw and destroy, on mere theoretic prospects, a system under which a nation has risen to a state of grandeur, power, and happiness unparalleled in the world. But if what has been done were ever so right—indisputably expedient, it ought to have been done by *other hands.* A power created and con-fided for a distinct and specified purpose, ought never surely to be employed to destroy those who had confided that trust. This last consideration, and the consequent damage to public character, is my main objection to last year's work, for, as to the measures themselves, they are still within the power of the legislature, and may be replaced, or altered, or continued as they may be found to work. But what cannot be repaired is the breach by which they were let in. I never expected that you and I should have differed in politics, and I cannot refrain, in consequence of your allusion to our present divergence, from letting you see thus shortly my reasons for standing on our old ground.

I am afraid that I should differ from you as much about

---

* [Col. Wood, of Littleton, near Sunbury ; M.P. for Middlesex.]

your poor laws scheme. It is a subject that I do not pretend to understand, and which you do, and I certainly should have deferred to your opinion in preference to that of almost any one I could name; but again I confess my fear of sweeping changes in general, and in this particular instance I see, or fancy that I see, the not distant ruin of the landed interest in the scheme which you propose. I think well of the principle of acquiring a new settlement by work and labour in a new locality. It is clearly right, both in principle and practice, that the place which has benefited by the labour of the young and strong, should have the burden of maintaining him when he becomes old and feeble : 'tis almost, I should say, the law of nature. Why should your estate at Littleton be burdened with the old age of a runaway boy, who left it fifty years ago, and has spent all that time in helping to raise a gigantic fortune for some cotton lord at Manchester. I observe that you set out by quoting a text, as if of Scriptural authority : " Where the tree falls there let it lie." * I believe there is no such text in Scripture, and that the text most like it has quite a different meaning ; but, however that may be, your project seems to me to be at variance with your quotation, for you propose that the weight shall *not* fall and lie where the tree does, but *anywhere and everywhere else.* But the grand objection is that which you admit, but which I think you have not in any degree answered, the *moral* and financial checks and control which *district* reliefs must always afford more effectually than any *national* system, however well planned. I quote yourself against yourself. Can you imagine any Government officer that could possess the same information and interest, or exercise the same blended influences of charity and economy, that you brought to the administration of your own parish and union ? Your system, or any system which shall make the poor law a branch of *national finance,* would, I am satisfied, combine the two grand contradictory mischiefs of severity to the poor and prodigality of public expense.

J. W. C.

The following letter is one of many which show the estimation in which the Peelites generally then held Lord George Bentinck and Mr. Disraeli.

---

* [" In the place where the tree falleth, there shall it be."—Ecclesiastes xi. 3.]

Mr. W. B. Baring * *to Mr. Croker.*

House of Commons, January 25th.

MY DEAR CROKER,

There was a *blow up*—I use the term of my informant—at the Stanley dinner, between the two leaders in Lords and Commons. Stanley made a nice speech, recommended forbearance from strong language and agitation. Lord G. took it as a rebuke to himself, and spoke angrily. D'Israeli poured oil and calmed the waves; but this looks like a want of cordiality. It is better, however, that it should be so than that the reports spread by your opponents should be true. I do not wish to see the weaker nature of Stanley moulded by Lord G. and his Jew.

Yours truly,

W. B. BARING.

Mr. J. G. Lockhart to Mr. Croker.   Extract.

I hear there was a very hot little *scena* at a late Carlton Club dinner between Stanley and Lord George Bentinck; but they were pacified ere they parted. Still, the Jockey's complaint was of *dictation*, and that word indicates, I should think, a course of thought.

Lord John's Irish plans appear to me to be mere moonshine but I shall be curious to learn whether you think you can see anything solid in them.

Ever yours,

J. G. LOCKHART.

Mr. Croker to Lord Stanley.

February 20th, 1847.

MY DEAR LORD,

I know not how you feel on the great subject of *paying the Irish priests,*† but I dare say you are aware that *I* have

---

* [Second Baron Ashburton; succeeded his father in 1848.]

† [At the outset of his political career, again in 1821, and again in 1825, Mr. Croker earnestly pressed the proposal to make payments to the Irish priests; it is needless to say, in vain.]

thought for these fifty years (and every year with more and more conviction) that it was not merely the first, but the *only* measure that could pacify and civilise Ireland ; but though in my opinion more politic than it ever was, it seems to have become as a general scheme every day less practicable ; but if you approved the principle, I think the present state of Ireland affords an opportunity of getting in the small end of the wedge, and of sounding and perhaps preparing the public mind here for the permanent measure.

The Irish priests must, I suppose, be starving ; the Protestant clergy are, no doubt, distressed also by the wants of their parishioners when not by their own ; but *they* have resources—their rent charge, their glebe, their connections,—they at least are not starving ; but the Roman Catholic priest is altogether dependent on the victims of the famine, and must be therefore wholly destitute. We voted a million to the Protestant clergy some years ago. The present occasion is much more awful and more urgent. Why not vote 100,000*l.* for the Roman Catholic Clergy, who are suffering the same calamity as their flocks, but who cannot *work*, and therefore cannot be provided for as their flocks may be. The money to be voted to, and distributed by Peel's mixed Board of Charitable Bequests. It seems to me that, if this were done, the famine (like all dispensations) might in the end be a blessing.

Yours, &c.,

J. W. CROKER.

Lord Stanley to Mr. Croker.

St. James's Square, February 21st, 1847.

MY DEAR SIR,

Though my opinions on the subject of the provision for the Irish priests has not been formed *more* than *twenty-five* years, I have never varied on the question, and am as much persuaded as you can be, that *if* it were practicable, it would be a most useful measure ; and I do not feel the same scruples on the score of principle, which I do not think involved, as are felt by many of our friends. But I fear it is a proposition which would raise up as one man against its authors the nearly unanimous voice of the clergy of England and Ireland, the absolutely unanimous voice of the clergy and people of

Scotland, and the great mass of the English Protestant Dissenters ; and I should fear that the modified suggestion in
your letter that a sum of 100,000*l.* should be voted for the
relief of the Roman Catholic clergy, would meet, in itself,
with great hostility, and might even operate to check the sub-
scriptions which are now in progress for the relief of Irish
distress.   It might perhaps diminish the weight of objection
if the sum were voted under the restriction of being allotted
among those priests who should engage, for a specified period,
not to receive any dues or other payments from the members
of their flock ; but I doubt whether even this would reconcile
the people of England to it, and I doubt almost equally
whether it would be accepted by many of the clergy. I think,
however, that this is the light in which it might be presented
to the public with the least chance of doing mischief ; though
I should not be very sanguine as to its effecting much good.

Believe me, my dear Sir,

Yours very sincerely,

STANLEY.

Lady Ashburton to Mr. Croker.   Extract.

Thursday, April 29th, 1847.

MY DEAR MR. CROKER,

The Whigs are puzzled as to the distribution of the places
which are to be filled. No one likes Ireland. Clarendon
wants Paris, and so does Clanricarde. Normanby must have
something, and is fit for nothing in these days. Labouchere
can't remain where he is; they say that he looks so frightened.   The last reports were that Auckland was to govern
the Emerald Isle, or perhaps Morpeth, although his prologue
was not successful. We don't understand the old Duke. He
is repeating the same error which cost us so dear, by misleading his followers, with the consciousness of doing wrong.
We have good hope of bringing in Portal for Winton. Two
yeomen who were violent Rads., and who command thirty
votes, have given in their adhesion to the Protectionists.
Fleming has just announced his intention to come forward in
opposition to Pelham, and we think he will succeed. I must
tell you an anecdote of Sir Bobby. If you read the list
of people congregated to see his pictures, you will have seen

there, not only all the artists, drawing-masters, men of science, but reporters and writers for journals. Thackeray, who furnishes the wit for 'Punch,' told Milnes * that the ex-Minister came up to him and said, with the blandest smile: "Mr. Thackeray, I am rejoiced to see you. I have read with delight *every line* you ever wrote." Thackeray would have been better pleased if the compliment had not included all his works; so, to turn the subject, he observed that it must be a great gratification to live surrounded by such interesting objects of art. Sir R. replied: "I can assure you that it does not afford me the same satisfaction as finding myself in such society as yours!!!" This seeking popularity by fulsome praise will not succeed. We are invited to the royal concert, albeit I have not appeared at the drawing-room for two years. Adieu.

Mr. J. G. Lockhart to Mr. Croker.

Mitre Place, May 11th, 1847.

MY DEAR CROKER,

I have finally settled all our Sir Walter's affairs. There remained: debt secured on his lands, 8500*l.*; to Cadell, 16,000*l.*; and sundries, 1000*l.* I have taken the 1000*l.* on myself, and Cadell obliterates the 24,500*l.*, on condition of getting the whole remaining copyrights of Scott's works, and also of the Life. In a year or so thus my son gets Abbotsford, burthened only with his aunt's jointure—the surplus income, unless things improve, about 400*l.* a year.

I am now ready for the *Quarterly Review* again, and glad to hear you are looking that way. The Grand Jurors will be very good materials for *you*, and Murray gladdens me with the hope of a political article for a close.

Now he says I am to have the offer of an Anti-Peel Currency article from a very able hand, and supervised by Mr. Fullarton,† whose book is, I believe, in high esteem. We must settle what is to be our line on that head. The *Quarterly Review* had a series of articles against the Bill of 1819, but nothing about the later Act, except, perhaps, some brief remarks of your own. I have no opinion. Messrs.

---

* [Richard Monckton Milnes, Lord Houghton.]

† [Mr. Fullarton was a retired East India banker, author of a work on Currency, and of several articles in the *Quarterly Review*.]

Fullarton and Co. say this is to be *the* question at the hustings
of 1847. What say you? Is it worth while to consider
their article at all? If you have a clear opinion in favour of
Peel's Currency plans, I think better tell them now not to
send it in at all. I have no notion what Lord Ashburton
thinks of the concern, but probably you know.

Ever yours truly,

J. G. L.

Lord Stanley to Mr. Croker.

St. James's Square, June 7th, 1847.

MY DEAR SIR,

Not only is there no subject at this moment prominently
occupying the public mind, but there seems to be a general
confusion of parties, persons, and principles. Thus we find
Lord John Russell at the head of a Whig Government, and
supported by Radical followers, adopting, for the present, a
strictly Conservative line of policy, courting the alliance and
support of the Church, and braving the hostility of the Dissenters; Sir Robert Peel, the apostle of expediency, professing
entire abstinence from party, yet perpetually closeted with
his under-strappers, interfering with every borough in the
kingdom, through his agents, and bent on keeping together a
party whose bond of union shall be personal subservience to
Sir Robert Peel. Lastly, I find myself in the position of
watching, rather than opposing, a Government which I cannot
trust, yet aware that on some points on which they are most
likely to be attacked by those with whom I am acting—as
for example on the question of Education—I am unable to go
the lengths of my supporters; and to add to all this personal
confusion, we have the effects of the Free Trade policy completely obscured by the deficiencies of last year's harvest, and
the consequent high price of grain, the result of which is,
that the farmers, who never look a yard beyond their noses,
are completely apathetic, and begin to think that there is not
so much harm in Free Trade after all. That they will ultimately find out their mistake, I do not doubt; but for the
purpose of the present election, it is vain to shut our eyes to
the fact that Protection as a cry is dead. I think, however,
it would do good service if, in a well-written article, it were
shown, first, why the effect of the recent measures *upon the*

Agriculturists has not been felt, owing to the disturbing causes which have intervened; next, how fallacious were the expectations held out *to the Manufacturers* of a large export of goods, and consequent ample employment at high wages, following necessarily on a larger import of corn; and how correct were the anticipations of those who held that such a large import could only be met by a larger drain of bullion; and lastly, that such a drain can only be stopped by an universal lowering of prices here, by which our manufactured articles may be forced into consumption in foreign markets; an operation the success of which is dependent on many causes over which we have no control, but which, if successful, must be purchased by great sacrifices on the part of manufacturers, both masters and operatives.

You know my sentiments on the subject of the Roman Catholic Priesthood; but this is a question not to be touched. The Protestant fever runs high, and the utmost that can be done at the elections is to induce one's friends to abstain from pledging themselves up to the ears by anti-Popery declarations, which will be exacted by a vast majority of the constituents.

The first question which will arise on which this feeling will be evoked will be that of Education, on which subject I think the safe line to hold is the reasonableness of aiding Roman Catholic schools in the great towns where there is a large Roman Catholic population, on the principle of their submitting generally to Government inspection and control, and introducing the Scriptures. If these terms are refused, I think support ought not to be given; but if the only objection be that they be allowed their own version of the Scriptures, I do not think that condition ought to be an insuperable obstacle, though on this point there will be a strong feeling both among Conservatives and among the Protestant Dissenters, especially the Wesleyans. The question will be equally embarrassing to us and to the Government.

I am, dear Sir,

Yours sincerely,

STANLEY.

Mr. Croker to Lord Stanley.

West Moulsey, June 4th [14th?], 1847.

MY DEAR LORD,

I have had communicated to me the pages of a pamphlet,* which is in the press, and about to be published in defence of the policy, and still more of the fairness and consistency of Sir R. Peel's conduct. The main argument is that his proceedings were absolutely and to the end approved of by the Duke of Wellington, and, in principle, and to a great degree by you.

When you come to see the pamphlet, you will find on p. 45, &c., your personal accordance with Sir Robert's free trade measures, and particularly your Canada Corn Bill produced in his behalf.

The pamphlet is well written, and in rather a conciliatory tone, and certainly looks like a move towards re-uniting the party under Sir R. Peel; but there is no argument for, and indeed hardly any palliation of, the particular steps of his proceeding in 1845-6. It *assumes* that the Irish famine has proved, and that the state of England by and by will further prove, that all he did was *right*, as the writer thinks that he has shown that it was all *fair*.

I shall take an opportunity of hearing what the Duke of Wellington says about it; though I think I can anticipate pretty certainly that he will not confirm the writer's view of his cordial concurrence in all Sir Robert's measures; in fact, no one seems to me to lament them, I might almost say to *resent* them, more than he does, whenever the subject is mentioned.

Believe me, &c.,

J. W. CROKER.

One point established by this pamphlet (though incidentally only) is, that there is no approximation between

---

* [A pamphlet in defence of Sir R. Peel, entitled 'The Commercial Policy of Pitt and Peel.' The Duke of Wellington evidently shared the belief, then prevalent, that it was written by Peel, or under his direction. The main object of the pamphlet is clearly stated in Lord Stanley's letter of the 20th June, p. 114. It was written by Colonel William Mure (1799-1860), M.P. for Renfrewshire 1846-55, author of a 'Critical History of the Language and Literature of Ancient Greece.' He afterwards wrote another pamphlet in reply to the *Quarterly Review* article on Peel.]

Sir Robert and Lord John. I have no idea who the author is—Gladstone was hinted at, but it is too clear and simple for him, and too much directed to the single defence of Peel.

Cardwell has also been mentioned, but I do not know him at all, and therefore cannot give any opinion as to him ; but it is in that *measured* tone both of language and thought which might be expected from a person in his position.

The Duke of Wellington to Mr. Croker.

London, June 19th, 1847.   At Night.

MY DEAR CROKER,

I enclose the pamphlet which I received this night upon my return home. It is quite obvious that it must have been written by him to whom it relates, or by one closely connected with him in politics and friendly relations.

I have not seen the words in relation to me which you [here follow a few words utterly unintelligible] ; and I don't think that I have much reason to complain of what is said of me where my name and conduct are referred to. I think that if I had made the reference I should on each of those occasions [have] referred more fully to the record, which would have shown more accurately how I stood on each of the occasions mentioned.

But I don't think I have much reason to complain ; and do not and will not complain.

, It appears to me that the object of this pamphlet is to hold out the olive branch, which I confess that I was glad to see, however useless it may prove.

Ever yours most sincerely,

WELLINGTON.

Mr. Croker to the Duke of Wellington.

West Moulsey, June 21st, 1847.

MY DEAR DUKE,

They have published the Peel pamphlet, and I hope they have, as I desired, sent you a copy. You will see that the authors have had, on revision, the good sense to omit the impertinent observations on your grace from page 11 of the pamphlet—they have done wisely—but I am very glad that we have happened accidentally to see what their real feeling towards you actually was.

They still, you see, persist in seeking the shelter of your countenance and sanction to their treachery, though they know, as every one does, that you acted on entirely different principles.

>   Believe me to be, my dear Duke,
>   Your most attached,
>   J. W. CROKER.

The Duke of Wellington to Mr. Croker.

>   London, June 22nd, 1847.

MY DEAR CROKER,

I returned the pamphlet, as soon as I received it. Great use is made of my name. But I believe that the record would show that the view taken is not very correct. Having in 1834 brought Sir Robert Peel from Rome, and handed over to him the government of the country, and having once found that he possessed the confidence of the sovereign, of Parliament, and of the country, and thinking that a *government* is of more importance than any measure or particular law, since the passing of the Reform Act—I have been most anxious that Sir Robert Peel shall retain power in his hands; and I did everything in my power on the one hand to induce him to modify his proposed measures, and to take time for carrying them into execution, in order that they might satisfy those who supported his Government, and on the other to persuade his colleagues in office to go on.

I failed in attaining either object. But seeing the existing state of things, and considering the pamphlet as a sort of olive branch and feeler in the right direction, I am anxious that it should be fairly considered.

>   Believe me, ever yours most sincerely
>   WELLINGTON.

Mr. Croker to the Duke of Wellington.

>   West Moulsey, June 29th, 1847.

MY DEAR DUKE,

My answer to the Peel pamphlet* was printed before I had your note about it, but as Lord Stanley went over it very

---

* ["Peel Policy"—*Quarterly Review*, June 1847.]

carefully I hope you may, on the whole, approve of it, though it certainly does not treat the pamphlet as an olive-branch. That it was not so intended is clear from the two impertinent passages about your grace, which were originally inserted with the object of putting your grace aside, and the omission of which is the only alteration that has been made; it therefore follows that the pamphlet could never have been originally intended as an olive-branch. I have no doubt that Mr. Cardwell and the rest of Peel's followers are very uneasy at their position; but you may depend upon it Peel himself does not mean to give up the principles advanced in the Cobden panegyric and the Elbing Letter,* and he means to hold out no olive-branch to the aristocracy of England, either territorial or commercial. His last appearance was in hostility to the Navigation Laws; and I myself am satisfied that he is much nearer to the Radicals than to any other party in the State; and if he can get an opportunity, you will see that he will disclaim the pamphlet as not speaking his sentiments in the sense of reconciliation and recon-struction. I have no doubt that he is sore vexed, but I doubt whether he even confesses to his own heart that he has been wrong; the mischief he has done I do not believe that he or any one else can now repair.

Ever, &c.,

J. W. CROKER.

Lord Stanley to Mr. Croker.

St. James's Square, June 20th, 1847.

MY DEAR SIR,

The main object of it [the pamphlet] is to prove that Sir Robert Peel always held Free Trade opinions, that the Whig Government, though ultimately turned out upon their Budget, had long lost public confidence, and that by their fall the issue of Free Trade was not raised; that Sir Robert Peel never pledged himself to the agriculturists to the maintenance of protection; that in the measures of 1842 I concurred; that I was prepared for further change in 1845,

---

* [This was a letter written by Sir R. Peel in reply to an address from the town of Elbing, in Prussia, in which, as before explained, he advocated the principles of Free Trade and direct taxation.]

having previously, in 1843, by the Canada Corn Bill, made a
great inroad on the existing law; that the opening of the
ports was required in 1845, and that if they had been
opened, it would have followed as a necessary consequence,
and not by any act of Sir Robert Peel's, that the law itself
must have come under consideration; and that, all things
considered, Sir Robert Peel's followers were not entitled
either to be surprised at or to condemn his course.

Such I think is a fair outline of the argument. As to the
principle of the increase or the relaxation of protective
duties on articles of commerce, it is quite beside the question
to enquire whether the policy of Whigs or Tories twenty
years ago were the more *Liberal.* It is quite clear that no
party contemplated Free Trade in the sense in which it is
spoken of, and least of all, Free Trade in corn; and no one
was more strong in his expressions on this subject than
Mr. Huskisson. It is equally true that the question of Free
Trade was not that on which Lord Grey's Government, and
subsequently Lord Melbourne's, were broken up. There are
some inaccuracies in the statements of the pamphlet, but in
the main it is undoubted that the Whig Governments fell,
and the Conservative party was formed, upon questions
affecting the maintenance of the Established Church, and the
integrity of the institutions of the country, the House of
Lords included.

It is also true that before the discussion of the Budget
in 1841, the Whig Government had lost the confidence
of the country; and they were justly charged with having
adopted the principles of Free Trade at the last moment,
in the hopes of regaining popularity, and that their measures
for sugar, timber, and corn, were really directed to the
purpose of making up a deficient revenue. It is quite
true that these charges were made against the ministry
before, and at, and after the election of August 1841, by
Sir Robert Peel, by me, and by others; but I think it is too
much to say that in the questions which formed the subject
of debate on the Budget, and which finally overthrew the
Government, the principle of Free Trade was not deeply
involved, and prominently put forward by the Conservative
leaders. On the Corn Law especially, Sir Robert Peel, while
he declined to pledge himself to all the details of the existing
law, referred, as the correct representation of his opinions,
to a speech delivered by himself on the 3rd of April, 1840.

If you will turn to the closing paragraphs of that speech you will find, I think, a tolerably strong, and, *for the Speaker*, an unusually explicit declaration of principle.

Again, in 1842, in introducing his modified Corn Bill, he entered into an elaborate argument, first against absolute repeal, and next in favour of the principle of the sliding scale against that of a fixed duty. In all the discussions which followed on that subject and on the tariff, removal of prohibition and maintenance of protection were avowed and contended for as the principles of the Government; and I cordially concurred in measures which I thought fairly effected both those objects. If my wishes had prevailed, we should then have had a free admission of colonial corn, from which I never apprehended any danger, and which I believed to be a measure wise and sound in policy, and likely to afford us an increased supply and a firmer ground for resisting the introduction of foreign corn. I was overruled, and yielded; the duty on colonial corn was fixed at from 5s. to 1s. Then followed the Canada Corn Bill, the principle, object, and effect of which I explained to you fully the other day. So stood matters up to the potato failure of 1845, when, to meet a temporary emergency, the opening of the ports was recommended, to be followed by a revision of the Corn Laws with a view to their extensive modification.

Now the pamphlet is in error in stating, p. 60, that a temporary suspension involved necessarily a reconsideration of the law. If the law had been merely suspended to a given date, it would have revived at that date as a matter of course, without the necessity for any legislation or discussion; and I will take upon me to say, that, if such had been, as is stated, the course proposed by Sir R. Peel, though some of us might have doubted the wisdom of the course, there would probably have been no division, and certainly no resignation among us. But I separated from my colleagues because, from the first, it was avowed that the opening of the ports was intended as the prelude, if not to the total repeal, at least to an extensive permanent alteration of the Corn Laws. A memorandum which I made shortly after, and on which I put my hand to-day by mere accident, will prove my statement. I must ask of you to send this memorandum back, and to make no use of it. But it is said, p. 48, that I "was not averse to some modification of the Corn Law," and that in my presence the Duke of Wellington stated that "every-

body admitted that some alteration was *necessary.*" Now
I had at that time a very anxious wish not to appear at
variance with the Duke of Wellington; and I consequently
abstained from noticing several inaccuracies in his statement
to the House of Lords. This one indeed is but slight, because
looking to the state of Ireland, though I did not think *any*
alteration *necessary*, yet I should have thought that a reduction of the duty on Indian corn would for many reasons
have been both unobjectionable and even wise. This opinion
I stated; but I was prepared to stand by the existing law,
without alteration, as to wheat, barley, and oats, the only
grain which affected our home growers, and I have seen no
reason to alter my opinion that as a permanent measure the
scale of 1842 was a satisfactory one for all parties. I
certainly did also say that I was not, in December 1845,
prepared to attempt the formation of an administration, all
my colleagues having ultimately followed Sir Robert Peel.

I have thus given you my view of the case as put forward
by the pamphlet; and looking back at the whole transaction,
I retain the impression that the Conservative party had been
led to believe in Sir R. Peel's maintenance of the *principle of
effective protection;* and that they had a right to complain of,
and to resent, the course which he took in making a temporary
calamity subservient to the object of a total abandonment of
a principle which he had led them to believe he would
maintain, and in which belief he had accepted, and availed
himself of, their Parliamentary support.

Believe me, my dear Sir, yours sincerely,

STANLEY.

Major Beresford to Mr. Croker..

Thursday Night [July ?].

MY DEAR CROKER,

I got your letter to-night when I came home late. I am
going to-morrow morning to canvass my constituents that (I
trust) are to be. I have not time therefore to reply in detail
to your enquiries. I have not the tables drawn out. The
result is not *certain* of course at this time, and I doubt any
one even making an accurate and just calculation. I will,
however, try my hand at it on my return from Essex on
Sunday, and I hope on Monday to present you with some

details. I believe that there never was so blind an election. The very fact of Peel's apostacy has not only paralysed our party, but it has made all calculation abortive. Supineness is the order of the day among most Conservatives. Spite animates many, whether to keep out Peel or to kick Stanley and Bentinck. Again, the only real cry in the country is the proper and just old No Popery cry. That is in opposition to Peel, Russell, and Bentinck. I say just, because it is no longer the same cry which refused the Catholics equal rights, it is a cry against their attempt at domination. They are no longer content with fair equality, they aim at supremacy. How difficult it is to act and regulate this general feeling of the country when all the leaders of the several parties are tainted with the prevailing *heresy.*

Yours ever truly,

Wm. Beresford.

While this correspondence was going on with Lord Stanley, Mr. Croker was in constant communication with Lord George Bentinck, who had made great and unexpected progress in winning the confidence of his party, and in commanding the attention of the House of Commons. Unfortunately, all Mr. Croker's letters to Lord George, save one or two of no great importance, are missing;* but the letters from Lord George to Mr. Croker have been preserved, and they will be found to help much in the elucidation of a character which, in spite of Mr. Disraeli's book, has often been misunderstood.

Lord George Bentinck is, indeed, a unique figure in our history. No one, before or since, has entered political life under circumstances so remarkable, or made such rapid strides towards distinction in an equal period of time, or vanished so suddenly from the view of men. All his parliamentary reputation was achieved in about two years. It is true that

---

* The editor has made diligent enquiry for them, with no other result than to elicit the information that " all Lord George Bentinck's political correspondence was probably destroyed by the Duke of Portland, his father." (Letter from Lady Ossington, Fcb. 27th, 1884.)

he had been a long time in the House, but he had taken
scarcely any part in the debates, and no one knew anything
about him, except that he was the son of the Duke of Portland,
and that he owned one of the finest racing studs in England.
Most people supposed that he cared for nothing in the world
but horses, and for some years he did not; no dream seems
ever to have passed through his mind of becoming the leader
of a political party. Yet he was not wholly without political
training. For three years he had acted as the private secretary of Mr. Canning, and in the course of that novitiate he
must have gained a certain degree of insight into the secrets
of public life. That a power of mastering facts and of ac-
cumulating information was among his natural gifts, the
letters below amply attest. He had been in the army, but
the fortunes of the turf, as Mr. Disraeli has stated, engrossed
his whole being, and he pursued them "on a scale that
perhaps has never been equalled." When he went to the
House, he seldom remained long, and appeared to take very
little interest in the discussions which happened to be going
on. He spoke unwillingly, and with difficulty. Such was
the man to whom the Protectionists looked for guidance
when they found themselves cast off by Sir Robert Peel.

It was not till the beginning of the session of 1846 that
Lord George Bentinck was impelled by his strong feeling
in favour of the agricultural interest to take an active part
in the debates. Before the close of that session, he had
accomplished wonders. "He had," Mr. Disraeli asserts—and
the statement is confirmed by other testimony—"rallied a
great party which seemed hopelessly routed; he had established a parliamentary discipline in their ranks which old
political connections led by experienced statesmen have
seldom surpassed; he had proved himself a master in detail
and in argument of all the great questions arising out of the

reconstruction of our commercial system."   In the autumn of
the same year, the public was astonished to hear that Lord
George Bentinck had sold off all his racing stud, although his
horses had been very successful that season.   He saw that if
he was to do anything in the political world, he must make
sacrifices, and he began by making one of the greatest which
could have been required of him.   Among the horses thus
disposed of, at any price they would fetch, was "Surplice,"
which won the Derby—the object of Lord George Bentinck's
greatest ambition—in 1848.   When he heard the news he
gave, as his biographer says, "a sort of superb groan."   No
doubt he was still sometimes spoken of as "the jockey" by
men who did not know the ability which was in him, and
jokes about his "stable mind" have lingered down to our
own day.   But the country read his speeches with attention,
and great commercial bodies gave him proofs of their
sympathy.   The Protectionists, let it not be forgotten, were
still a powerful body in 1846-48; Lord Stanley estimated
their numbers in the House of Commons at 230.   There
seemed still to be a future before the party, and it was
long before its new leaders despaired even of the broken
and discredited cause which was identified with it.

In 1847, Lord George Bentinck was prevailed upon to take
his seat on the front Opposition bench in the House. It appears
to have required much wary management to get him into
this position.   Repeatedly he had told his followers that they
must not look to him as their head—that he would do what
he could for a time, but it would be only for a time.   But
apparently Mr. Disraeli—although he does not expressly say
so—helped to persuade him to take the usual place assigned
to the Opposition leader.   "This was the origin," Mr. Disraeli
writes,* "of his taking a position which he assumed with

* 'Life of Lord George Bentinck,' p. 372.

great reluctance, and of his appearing as the chief opponent of a Ministry which he was anxious to uphold." Throughout that session he worked on with great steadfastness and courage. "He was not the man," remarks another observer,[*] "to know despair or discouragement. He seemed cast to storm in a breach. He had, in rare perfection, the unconsciousness of defeat assigned by Napoleon to the English character." As an orator, he might never have made a brilliant reputation; but if no dazzling flights of eloquence marked his brief career, he greatly stirred curiosity, delivered many effective speeches, and sometimes roused his followers to genuine enthusiasm. It was said at the time that he kept Mr. Disraeli in the background; but if he had ever tried to do so, Mr. Disraeli, it may safely be taken for granted, would not have become his biographer and panegyrist. Mr. Disraeli did not readily forgive any one who, by purpose or accident, interfered with his success in life. What Lord George Bentinck thought of Mr. Disraeli will be seen from one of his own letters, written a few months before his death. He boldly predicted that, in spite of them all, Mr. Disraeli would become the Conservative leader; and this prediction was made at a time when even the late Lord Derby looked askance at the author of *Vivian Grey.*

The first of Lord George Bentinck's letters, in the order of dates, was written in reference to a project, much discussed in 1846–47, for the removal of the Duke of Wellington's statue from the arch at Hyde Park Corner. The Duke himself seems to have been much mortified and hurt by this proposition, and some portions of his letters on the subject with the correspondence which grew out of them, must now be given.

---

[*] Mr. Albany Fonblanque, 'Life and Labours,' p. 99.

The Duke of Wellington to Mr. Croker.   Extracts.

Walmer Castle, May 18th, 1846.

My dear Croker,

I have received your letter of the 17th.

I think that I never did anything in better taste; or one that was more consistent with good sense, than the act of constituting myself a *caput mortuum* in all matters relating to the statue, from the moment at which in this house I expressed to the Duke of Rutland and the deputation of subscribers to the work who accompanied his grace, my gratitude and thanks for their kindness to me, and the notice which they were disposed to take of the services on which I had been employed, and which I had endeavoured to render to the public.

I stand at this moment on the same ground; I was informed, some days ago, in the House of Lords, by the Earl of Clare, of the disapprobation of himself, and other men of note, of the intention to place the statue on the archway as proposed. He stated that it was the intention to notice the subject in both Houses of Parliament, and to ask a question; and he inquired about Lord Canning. I told him that that was a subject on which I was, and always had been, a *caput mortuum*. That I could say nothing about it. I told him that the Duke of Rutland, who took the greatest interest, was coming to London, if he had not arrived, and that he had better converse with him.

The result of my reflections upon it is, increased respect for the taste and wisdom of my original decision that I was to be a *caput mortuum* upon this subject.

Believe me, ever yours most sincerely,

WELLINGTON.

Walmer Castle, October 31st, 1846.

My dear Croker,

I am much obliged to you for your letter,* and the inspection of the engraving of the statue.

I saw the statue very well from my windows when I was in London a week ago, but there was still a forest of scaffold-

---

* [The letter referred to is not among Mr. Croker's papers.]

ing to the eastward of the statue, which prevented my forming a judgment of the general effect of the whole, and my seeing the statue at all from the lower part of the hill called Constitution Hill, or at all from Piccadilly. It has, therefore, been most *unfair* in Lord Morpeth to ask at all a few artists to form an opinion upon it, and to report the same to him, and particularly to have done so before the forest of scaffolding should have been cleared away. Lord Morpeth is upon this question the Government. It was he that endeavoured to swamp the statue in Parliament, of which I read the discussion, and the Duke of Rutland got the better of Lord Morpeth in it. If he think proper to consult the members of the Royal Academy at all for an opinion, which it is very proper that he should, it should be done individually, in private, by word of mouth, and after the statue and its general effect are generally exposed to view!

But instead of that he thereupon writes a circular letter to the members of the Royal Academy before the statue can be seen at all; and requires each of them to assist him with their opinions of it. What is the meaning of this? It is a Minister offering a reward for opinions against the work; which, it is well known, has been placed where it is not only against, but in despite of his, the Minister's, opinion! Will ever any member of the Academy, looking to the Court for favour—and which of them does not?—give a fair or independent opinion upon the subject?

Ever yours, my dear Croker, most sincerely,

WELLINGTON.

London, November 19th, 1846.   (At Night.)

MY DEAR CROKER,

It appears that the Queen and Prince Albert came to London from Windsor on Saturday morning, the 7th, and her Majesty ordered that it should be removed.

Lord Morpeth wrote to me to Walmer Castle a letter dated the 9th, and which I received on the 10th, in which he informed me that the Government had felt themselves called upon to recommend that the statue, &c., should be removed from the top of the arch on Constitution Hill; and that they had received her Majesty's permission to signify this decision to the Sub-Committee.

I adverted to his lordship's statement that the sole foundation for the decision which he had announced to me had been in reference to views of art and architectural effects.

I observed that it has happened to many men to have their statues removed from the pedestals on which [they were] placed while still alive, and that I had heard of one such instance in modern times.

But that I should be the first instance of the statue of a man removed in his life time from the pedestal on which [it was] placed, before it could well be seen. I added that I was sensible that a statue to commemorate the acts of a man in bygone transactions was quite distinct from the acts themselves. And that excepting on account of the feelings of many to whom I was grateful for the honour in which they intended to manifest that they held me, I should be indifferent as to the fate of the statue in question.

Ever, my dear Croker, yours most sincerely,

WELLINGTON.

London, November 21st, 1846.

My DEAR CROKER,

I have received your letter of the 20th Nov. I have heard of, and I perceive no change in the state of the statue.

It is said that it is to be moved to the Parade opposite the Horse Guards. But if I am not much mistaken, and my recollection does not fail me, I think that the Committee on the Duke of York's column tried that ground, having thought of placing there that column, but found that they could not lay a foundation on it.

On the other hand, some say that the statue will never be moved. God knows!

I think that you are mistaken in respect to the date of the verbal communication between the Committee and me. It was, and a recollection of the circumstances will prove to you that it must have been, long before the Queen's reign, and even before that of King William. I don't think that the gateway into the Park was constructed when the idea of the statue was first mentioned to me by the Duke of Rutland. The intention to have it in sight of my house was mentioned. It was upon that occasion that I desired to be considered as *dead* upon all matters relating to the statue, excepting to give sittings to the artist, whether for a bust or on horseback.

I think, indeed I am certain, that it was King William who first mentioned the archway as the pedestal. Indeed, his Majesty offered to place it on the marble archway in front of Buckingham Palace.

I think that from the first there was great opposition among the Whig officials to the statue being placed upon the Green Park Archway. I recollect a caricature wooden equestrian statue of an enormous size being placed on the spot on which the statue now stands, purposely to beget opinions against the adoption of that situation.

It is quite true that when the Queen came to the throne she consented that the statue should be placed on the arch as indicated by King William.

This is what I recollect! But if I am again to write officially, or to speak in public on the subject, I will take care to consult documents.

It is certainly true that the Queen and Prince Albert quitted Windsor Castle at nine o'clock in the morning on Saturday, the 7th of November, and came to London by rail, to express the desire that the statue should be removed from its pedestal on the arch.

The order was given by the Commissioners of Woods and Forests on Monday, the 9th.

I think that the interference of her Majesty in the case makes a remarkable difference in my position ; I can be dead upon the affair, as long as it is a mere party business; and it is best possibly that I should. But when the Sovereign, having acquiesced in the selection of the arch for the pedestal orders that the statue placed on its pedestal should be removed therefrom, I think that it would be scarcely respectful for me to continue to say I am dead. Do as you please !

Ever yours most sincerely, my dear Croker,

WELLINGTON.

Arundel Castle, December 3rd, 1846.

MY DEAR CROKER,

I have only this morning received your note of the 1st inst. I have been here since the 1st inst., and I have not heard one word about the statue from anybody; notwithstanding that besides the Queen and Prince Albert, Lord Morpeth and Lord John Russell are here. I return the excellent paper which you have sent me, which I would recommend to have published, as taken from the *Literary Gazette*, in some of our daily papers.

I could not send this note to the post yesterday; I wanted to add a postscript to it, and kept it open for that purpose till the last moment. But Prince Albert came to my house and stayed nearly 2½ hours, till the time being eight, it was absolutely necessary that both should go to dress.

He talked upon every subject excepting the statue; but did not allude to that in the most distant manner. Of course I could not mention it.

I entertain no doubt, however, that there exists at Court an earnest desire to avoid to appear to aid to persecute me, and that your paper will have an immense effect.

Ever yours most sincerely,

WELLINGTON.

Strathfieldsaye, December 19th, 1846.

MY DEAR CROKER,

It appears to me that I stand now very much as I did in 1808, when I was persecuted by all factions, out of doors as well as in Parliament; and the Lord Mayor and the City of London, wishing to treat a general officer, according to the precedent of Admiral Byng, petitioned the King George III., in my own presence, to bring me by name to trial before a general court-martial. I faced all; then went abroad and took the command of the army, and never returned, or even quitted the field, till the nations of the Peninsula, Portugal and Spain, were delivered from the French armies; till I had invaded France, won the battle of Toulouse; established the British Army within the French Territory; of which I governed several departments; till the general peace was signed at Paris; and the British cavalry sent by sea to Portugal, Spain, and the South of France; marched home across France; and embarked for England in the ports of France in the British Channel!

If the Almighty favours me with a continuance of health and strength, I think it most probable that in the same Christian spirit I shall again perform my duty by endeavouring to serve and protect those who persecute me! This is the way in which I desire to meet this affair.

I should desire never to move from my principle of indifference and non-interference on the subject of a statue of myself to commemorate my own actions.

As for the rest, I can only perform my duty !

Ever yours most sincerely,

WELLINGTON.

Mr. C. Arbuthnot to Mr. Croker.

Woodford, November 12th, 1846.

MY DEAR CROKER,

Your letter has followed me, and I should have written as soon as I received it had I not been unwell.

I heard, and I thought from good authority, that the Queen had been in London for the purpose of looking at the statue, and that she, disapproving of it on the arch, had decided that it should be removed. I heard this in London from Lord Mahon, who came to see me, and I know that her Majesty did come up on the day mentioned, and that she returned on the same day to Windsor.

I believe it to be true that she objected to the position of the statue.

I could not write to the Duke of Bedford. I should not like to ask any favour, besides which I feel that my interfering (as I was in the Duke's house) will look like the Duke's interference.

I am sure that this would annoy him greatly.

I have this morning a letter from Lord Brougham, in answer to one which I had written to him after he had been at Walmer.

He has had much conversation with Louis Philippe on the Spanish marriage. He says that the King is very angry with Lord Palmerston, but he remarked that, if what had been done had made him unpopular in England, it had at least had the effect of making him adored in France.

Ever, my dear Croker,

Yours most sincerely,

CH. ARBUTHNOT.

The Duke of Wellington to Mr. Croker.

London, June 14th, 1847.

MY DEAR CROKER,

It has always been my practice, and is my invariable habit, to say nothing about myself or my own actions.

More than forty years ago Mr. Pitt observed that I talked as little of myself or of my own acts as if I had been an assistant-surgeon of the army ; and from the year 1838 to the present moment I have considered it most becoming to avoid to interfere respecting a statue, of which the professed object is to commemorate bygone transactions in which I had borne a part.

I follow the habit of avoiding to talk of myself and of what I have done, with the exception only of occasions when I am urging upon modern contemporaries measures which they don't like, and when I tell them I have some experience and have had some success in these affairs, and feel they would experience the benefit of attending to my advice. I never talk of myself.

These are the reasons for which they think that I don't care what they do with the statue.

But they must be idiots to suppose it possible that a man who is working day and night, without any object in view excepting the public benefit, will not be sensible of a disgrace inflicted upon him by the sovereign and Government whom he is serving.   The ridicule will be felt if nothing else is !

This last would have been vastly aggravated if I had not cautiously avoided to take any part in the affair since the year 1838.

Ever, my dear Croker, yours most sincerely,

WELLINGTON.

Lord Strangford to Mr. Croker.

Harley Street, July 8th, 1847.

MY DEAR CROKER,

I frankly avow to you that I am a vehement anti-arch man, and that I even go so far as to think that a much better site for the statue might be found in the bed of the Serpentine.

This is all (I dare say) rank heresy and schism, but *de gustibus*, &c., &c.

I cannot believe that it will be acceptable to the Duke

(who, at the outset of the business, was so cautious and reserved in the expression of his opinion as to the site) that his name should thus be dragged forward at the eleventh hour in opposition to what is always a matter of religion with him—the wishes of the Queen. I cannot think that he would greatly relish a Parliamentary triumph over them, achieved under his supposed sanction.

Ever most sincerely yours

(non obstantibus Frederico et Wyatto),

STRANGFORD.

Lord George Bentinck to Mr. Croker.

Harcourt House, June 30th, 1847.

MY DEAR MR. CROKER,

You will see by the papers that a most important skirmish took place at the close of yesterday's proceedings in the House of Commons. The report is not very accurately given, but you will observe that a most vital question as to date is involved, which, if you are positive that your communication of the Duke of Wellington's letter to Lord John Russell took place "*within ten days*" of *last Monday*, would clearly convict Lord John not merely of shuffling but of wilful untruth, for Lord Morpeth's communication to the House of Commons was made on Friday the 4th of June—ten days back from last Monday would only bring us back to the 18th of June. It is therefore of all importance to fix beyond all dispute the exact day when your interview with Lord John in Downing Street took place. With Hume, Wakley, Tom Duncombe, and Bernal Osborne all on our side, on the ground that the people of England will hold the Duke's wishes on the subject conclusive, we have the Government dead beat.

Anyhow, Lord John shuffled, inasmuch as he gave the House to understand that you had only reported the contents of the Duke of Wellington's letter, whilst you laid the original itself before him.

When Wakley and Hume take the high ground, I think there can be no doubt that it would ill become me to walk below them.

Do what they will, I think we have the Government upon the hip now.

If our people make anything like a muster, the statue is safe to stand for ever on its present pedestal.

I have read your article in the *Quarterly* and think it quite admirable—a complete stunner for the Peel party. You are quite right about me as regards a State provision for the Irish Roman Catholic Church; but for that accursed National Club we should have had both members for Liverpool; as it is we may save one, but are more likely to lose both.

Believe me, always very sincerely yours,

G. BENTINCK.

Lord George Bentinck to Mr. Croker.

Harcourt House, July 10th, 1847.

MY DEAR MR. CROKER,

You will see what passed last night in the House of Commons.

A private communication and negotiation had previously taken place between Lord John and me, the result of which was that Lord John engaged "that the equestrian statue of the Duke of Wellington should remain where it is unless the Duke should intimate to Lord John that its removal to some other site would give him more pleasure;" and that *"the Duke's declining to give any opinion is to be construed as dissent."*

This of course concludes the business. I have written to the Duke of Wellington acquainting him with this, and likewise, at the desire of my supporters in the House of Commons, telling the Duke that they all came up manfully; sixteen, I believe, who had left London for the season, came up from the country, and, from the appearance of the House, I have no doubt whatever that I should have beat them two to one if the artistical gentlemen had persevered.

My idea is that the discussion would have damaged Lord John Russell and Lord Morpeth more than anything that has occurred, either during this or any preceding Whig Government. I believe we should have raised the blood of the whole country against them.

But I am a jockey, and it is the first principle of our craft to be satisfied with winning the race, if it is only by a head, and never to risk losing by showing off how much farther it might have been won.

Always yours most sincerely,

G. BENTINCK.

My people were very anxious I should wait upon the Duke and tell him how cheerfully they had responded to the call to protect him from any slight; but I hate ceremony, and never call upon anybody; so I have written to him to satisfy my people, who have been disappointed of the blood of the Whigs they calculated upon tasting.—G. B.

Lord George Bentinck to Mr. Croker.

Harcourt House, September 8th, 1847.

My dear Mr. Croker,

I have got no copy of my address to my constituents except the *Morning Post*, which I will send you to-morrow, together with a copy of my speech in answer to the Tamworth manifesto, and a pamphlet out last week under the most inapposite title of 'Plain Facts,' no doubt written by Goulburn; to this pamphlet I will take the liberty of affixing a few marginal comments, and I will accompany it by certain returns which will warrant my comments, and pretty satisfactorily refute his arguments.

If we could have had the General Election next month we should have met a very different feeling, not only in the counties but in many of the commercial boroughs. Wheat tumbling down to 45s. is beginning, just too late, to make the farmers open their dull eyes, and the failures of the corn merchants, and those coming among the sugar traders, have palled and will pall the taste of these gentlemen for unreciprocated free imports.

There is no doubt that Peel's friends are in high spirits and expect soon to be in power again. The return of all his official men is looked upon as a great triumph; but seeing that they have all crawled into the House of Commons under the gabardine of the Whigs, I cannot understand, if they were to recover office, how they could get their seats in the teeth of the angry Whigs.

Goulburn got in for Cambridge University through the assistance of 300 Whig votes, with the Speaker at their head.

Gladstone came in for the University of Oxford by like means. Cardwell, at Liverpool, succeeded through 4100 Whigs and Roman Catholics splitting. Sir George Clerk and Lord Lincoln, I apprehend, equally got in through the help of the Whigs.

Smythe was brought in upon Albert Conyngham's back ;
I do not suppose he got 250 votes of his old party.

So with my colleague, he came in triumphantly, and would
have been at the head of the poll by an open coalition between
all the Whigs, Radicals, and Dissenters, and about 100 or 150
of his old party.

If these men were to conspire to turn the Whigs out of
office, the Whig electors would speedily avenge their chiefs by
conspiring to defeat them at their elections.

I cannot therefore conceive how it can be possible for Peel
to recover power, and I incline to think it must end in such
men as Graham, Cardwell, Sidney Herbert, Lincoln, and Sir
George Clerk being amalgamated with the Whig Government.

That Lord John Russell is ready to take them cannot be
doubted, as he offered to take in Dalhousie, Lincoln, and
Sidney Herbert upon the first formation of his Government,
Peel giving him leave to do so, and merely hinting that so
early a fusion with a Whig Government might be indelicate.

This must happen, or else Lord John must go to the House
of Lords, making way for Peel to take his place in the House
of Commons.

> Believe me, always most sincerely yours,
>
> G. BENTINCK.

Lord George Bentinck to Mr. Croker.

Welbeck, near Worksop, Notts, September, 1847.

MY DEAR MR. CROKER,

I am delighted with your article, and am working away to
answer all your queries as well as I can, with such documents
as I have at hand, and hoped to have got all done by return
of post, but the early exit of the post here has not left me
time.

There are a few mistakes, which do not affect the argument,
which I have put right.

The question of duties on certain raw materials, such as
timber, cotton, and wool, is a very large one, and deserves
very serious consideration.

Practically Norway, Sweden, Russia, and Prussia have a
monopoly of the timber trade at Sir Robert Peel's differential
duty of 14s. per load, the freight to the Baltic being 18s.

against 38s. to the St. Lawrence, and the timber of the Baltic
being of finer quality.   The result of Peel's alterations consequently has been that the Baltic growers have been enabled
to maintain their prices on the other side to very nearly two-
thirds the amount of duty reduced.

The cotton question must grow into a very big question.

Is the United States to be fully installed in a monopoly ? or
are we, as Huskisson once hinted, to cherish the cultivation
of cotton in our own East India possessions by a protective
duty ?   A duty of 1d. per lb. on foreign cotton would give
us a revenue one year with another of 1,800,000l., whilst
Huskisson declared that our own East Indies might be encouraged to grow cotton sufficient to supply cotton for all the
world.

Three-farthings per lb. would supply a revenue sufficient to
enable the window-tax to be abolished.   A tax of 2d. per lb.
on foreign wool, admitting Colonial, to wit Australian and
New Zealand, wool free, would encourage the Colonies and
give a tax annually of near 300,000l.   My own idea is, that
we shall eventually come back to the principle of raising
revenues from all foreign produce and manufactures, as
the Americans do.   With these views, I venture to counsel
nothing being said about the policy of taking off duties on raw
materials.   I think I can prove that in most cases—in all
cases where you can call the untaxed produce of your own
colonies or country into competition—the grower pays nearly
the whole duty, though I herein mightily offend against
Macgregor, Porter, and modern economists.

I think next to corn, Peel's greatest blunders have been his
abolition of the American cotton tax, and his impolitic reduction of the timber duties.

Believe me always, yours most sincerely,

G. BENTINCK.

Lord George Bentinck to Mr. Croker.

Harcourt House, September 11th, 1847.

MY DEAR MR. CROKER,

I send you some more rough memoranda, but they are very
imperfect; they will suffice, however, to prove how 'Plain
Facts' has garbled his statement.   The comparative statement

of exports and imports to the United States is the most remarkable, as contradicting his argument that imports govern exports. You will observe that in 1815 we exported to the United States 13,255,374*l.* worth of manufactures, &c. We only imported 2,891,748*l.* worth of United States produce. Unhappily I have not been able to continue that column down to the years 1835, 1836, and 1845, or the circumstances would show a wonderful contrast.

In 1845 the official value of the cotton imported from all the world was 23,950,189*l.* I should say that 18,000,000*l.* of this would be imported from the United States; the official value of cotton is 7$\frac{3}{4}$*d.*; its sterling value in 1845 may be taken as about 4*d.*; this alone would give upwards of 9,000,000*l.* sterling. In the same year we imported from the United States 32,000,000 lbs. of tobacco; this at 2$\frac{1}{2}$*d.* per lb. would give nearly three millions and a half, so that on these two heads alone we imported in 1845 twelve and a half million sterling worth of produce, whilst by his own showing we exported but 7,142,839*l.* What a contrast to 1815, and indeed I doubt not to 1836, if I had the data to give you.

I am going to Welbeck on Monday, or I would complete these statistics.

Always yours sincerely,

G. BENTINCK.

Lord Stanley to Mr. Croker.

Knowsley, September 12th, 1847.

MY DEAR SIR,

I agree with you that there never was a Parliament, the probable working of which was so much a matter of entire uncertainty as the present. I own that I do not augur well of our prospects. We have, it is true, a nominal party of something like 230; but there is not a large amount of debating power among them; and, unfortunately, the strongest bond of union among them is an apprehension of Popery, which I think exaggerated, and in which Lord George Bentinck is so entirely at variance with them, that he is certain to make some strong declarations which will still farther weaken the imperfect hold he has of them in the House of Commons. The result of the late elections proves, I think, that the game of Free Trade must be played out, and its effects, which the late crisis has served to disguise, must be tested by actual experience before the experiment can be retracted, or it would be wise in us to press for its retractation.

As far as the Corn Laws are concerned, I am convinced that all our predictions will be more than verified. Already we have a fall of price of more than 20s. a quarter in the last six weeks; and so far from there being any corresponding improvement in the condition of the manufacturing classes, or any extension of our foreign or home trade in manufactured goods, the labouring classes are literally addressing the masters, praying them to provide against the evils of over-production by an early closing of mills and working short time, in order to avoid the more fatal consequences which would result from taking these steps at a later and more unfavourable period of the year. Facts like these must tell in the long run; but some time, I know not how long, may be required for their development.

Meantime our course, as a party, must be guided by that adopted by the two others in Parliament—I mean the Government and that of Sir Robert Peel, for I suppose even he will hardly now deny himself to be at the head of a party, ostensibly as well as in truth. But the elements of party must be changed, and whatever be the immediate course adopted by the leaders on any side, I think I see that the time is coming when there will be a struggle between the Democratic and Aristocratic (and Monarchical) principles, in which I should reckon with much more confidence on the support of some of the old Whigs than on some of the supporters of Sir Robert Peel; and many things would surprise me more than to find him going in this direction far ahead of Lord John Russell. Still we are at present in the dark as to the course which is likely to be taken by the latter; and until we are more enlightened on this point, it seems to be very hazardous to decide absolutely as to the tone to be adopted towards him and the Peelite party respectively.

I agree with you in thinking that Lord G. Bentinck has the best of the argument in the manifesto, and that Peel obtained far more credit than he deserved for his commercial policy. That, in truth, the improvement which took place in the finances was mainly owing to good harvests increasing our real capital, and railway enterprise stimulating its active diffusion. The arguments on this head, drawn from the effects produced respectively on articles touched and articles left untouched, appear to me very strong. I have no doubt you would find in Peel's and Lord George's statements materials for a very useful article, and I am very clearly of opinion that the policy which we are most likely to be called on to resist, and which we are most in danger of seeing adopted, whether by Peel or Lord John, is that of reducing customs duties to the minimum, and supplying their place by direct or purely internal taxation. I think an article pointing out this danger, and its effects on various classes in the country, might do good, and rouse some of the real Conservatives, whether nominal Tories or nominal Whigs, from a state of apathy in which they appear to be at present, and in which, if they continue, the tide will be too strong for them, and carry them on to a point which at present they very little contemplate.

Believe me, my dear Sir, yours sincerely,

STANLEY.

Lord George Bentinck to Mr. Croker.

Welbeck, near Worksop, Notts, September 27th, 1847.

MY DEAR MR. CROKER,

I was so pressed for time yesterday that I was obliged to cram the papers I sent you together anyhow and without sufficient explanation.

I send you more papers to-day, which further prove that Peel's Free Trade policy, the spirit of which is "Take care of your imports, and the exports will take care of themselves," is the greatest absurdity and fallacy that ever was yet put forward.

The whole history of our foreign trade disproves the doctrine.

At the conclusion of the war we had almost the entire export trade of the world. From Russia, Holland, France, and the United States, our imports were comparatively light compared to our exports, but those countries set about fostering their own manufactures and industry, and the effect has been that from every one of those countries our imports have largely increased, and our exports to them, if not absolutely, have in all cases by comparison with our imports greatly fallen off.

Our great export trade is to Cuba, Chili, Peru, Columbia, China, and our own colonies; but Cuba, Chili, Peru, and Columbia prove that if countries want your manufactures they will have them, whether you take their produce from them or not, and if they have no mind to have your manufactures, but desire to encourage their own, you may take as much as you like from them, and they will not take your goods in return.

The United States is a most striking proof of this; she is every day stealing from us our capital and wealth, by which alone we have hitherto been enabled to compete with and beat foreign manufactures. Already our money is cheaper in New York, in Berlin, and at St. Petersburgh, than at Manchester, Birmingham, or London; 4 and 4½ per cent. are the current rates of discount in Russia, Prussia, and the United States, for bills of the same stamp that would not here be discounted under 5½ per cent.! Thus our overgrown purse-proud cotton lords are already beat at their own game; and unless we repent our evil free-trade ways, and insist upon reciprocity or retaliate where we fail to obtain it, our manufacturing and commercial greatness must begin to go down hill.

I see Peel stated the loss of revenue on cotton alone at 680,000*l.* when he repealed the duties in March, 1845; he said that was the duty received in 1844.

Peel's reductions have been most clumsy and injudicious in every case; he has put the duty, or a large part of it, into the pocket of the foreign producer; neither timber, cotton, or corn have been reduced (corn perhaps now) to the consumers; the timber growers and cotton growers have certainly got all the duty, or the greater part.

So it was when Peel reduced the sugar duties; the West Indians and East Indians got the duty.

Charles Wood, on the contrary, by setting up a competition, has reduced the price of sugar full 10*l.* a ton to the consumer. True he has ruined the West Indies and the Mauritius and the East Indies; but at least he has wonderfully cheapened sugar, and greatly increased the revenue; but Peel by his reductions practically gives a monopoly to the foreigners; he ruins the Canadian colonist and the East Indian cotton grower, and will ruin the English agriculturist, but he gets neither timber or cotton cheaper, and throws away entirely an enormous revenue.

The contrast between this country and Belgium is very remarkable.

Believe me always most sincerely yours,

G. Bentinck.

The return of Baron Rothschild for the city of London, at the general election of 1847, revived that question of the removal of Jewish Disabilities, which had been frequently discussed ever since 1830, when Mr. Robert Grant first brought forward a Bill to enable a Jew to exercise the most highly-prized prerogatives of citizenship. The state of the law at that time rendered a Jew a sort of pariah in the community ; he was tolerated on terms which inflicted upon him almost every species of humiliation. He was not allowed to vote if he refused to take the elector's oath, which might at that time be administered ; he could not practise at the bar, or be an attorney, or find employment in a school. He was not liable to receive the treatment which was inflicted on Isaac of York ; he could not, for instance, have his property confiscated, or his teeth drawn one by one until he had paid a ransom. But he was conspicuous in a free community as a man under a social and a political ban. And even when the Catholics were relieved from their civil disabilities, the Legislature refused to extend any toleration to the Jews.

Mr. Grant's Bill failed in 1830, and again in two subsequent sessions ; but concessions were gradually made, until in 1847 there was no privilege of a citizen from which the Jew was excluded, except the right to sit in Parliament.

Baron Lionel Rothschild was the first Jew ever returned to the House of Commons in this country. Lord John Russell brought in a Bill to enable him to take his seat, and the Conservative party, as a whole, opposed it. Lord George Bentinck had on previous occasions voted for the Bill,

and this, as Mr. Disraeli admits,* " occasioned great dissatisfaction among a very respectable though limited section" of
his followers. They conveyed to him "their keen sense of
disapprobation," and, in consequence of this, at the end of
the year he resigned a position which he had never sought,
and which undoubtedly was irksome to him. It is evident,
however, from his letters to Mr. Croker that he felt his
" dismissal " more keenly than Mr. Disraeli allowed the
readers of his ' Life' to suppose.

At the opening of the following session (1848) he " walked
up to the head of the second bench below the gangway on the
Opposition side, and thus significantly announced that he was
no longer the responsible leader of the Protectionist party."
Mr. Disraeli, who generally sat by the side of Lord George
Bentinck, was thus left to occupy the usual place of the
Opposition leader. He states † that it was his desire to have
abdicated the prominent seat " in which he had been unwillingly and fortuitously placed ; but by the advice, or rather
at the earnest request, of Lord George Bentinck, this course
was relinquished as indicative of schism."

With this brief recapitulation of the facts, the remainder
of the Bentinck correspondence may be given without further
interruption.

Lord George Bentinck to Mr. Croker.

> Welbeck, near Worksop, Notts,
> September 29th (Wednesday), 1847.

My dear Mr. Croker,

I have only this morning received the proofs, and I see
time presses. By rights they should have met you on your
return to town this evening. Thus circumstanced, I have
hurriedly gone through them, making flying comments as I
went on.

---

* ' Life of Lord George Bentinck,' p. 513.   † *Ibid.* p. 523.

I have always, I believe, voted in favour of the Jews. I say I believe, because I never could work myself up into caring two straws about the question one way or the other, and scarcely know how I may have voted, viewing it quite differently from the Roman Catholic question, which I have ever considered a great national concernment, and from the first, in point of fact, adopted your opinions almost more than Mr. Canning's—your opinions and Mr. Pitt's, because, with you and with Mr. Pitt, I attach the greatest importance to getting the Roman Catholic Priests and hierarchy into the pay of the State.

The Jew question I look upon as a personal matter, as I would a great private estate or Divorce Bill.

I think the subject amazingly well handled in this article,* but I think, like the questions affecting the Roman Catholics, with the Protectionist party it should remain an open question. I shall probably give a silent vote, maintaining my own consistency in favour of the Jews, but not offending the larger portion of the party, who, I presume, will be the other way.

Disraeli, of course, will warmly support the Jews, first from hereditary prepossession in their favour, and next because he and the Rothschilds are great allies; and, in addition to this, there is every probability that Baron Rothschild will be Lord of Stowe † with all its Parliamentary influence.

The Rothschilds all stand high in private character, and the city of London having elected Lionel Rothschild one of her representatives, it is such a pronunciation of public opinion that I do not think the party, as a party, would do themselves any good by taking up the question against the Jews.

It is like Clare electing O'Connell, Yorkshire Wilberforce. Clare settled the Catholic question, Yorkshire the slave trade, and now the city of London has settled the Jew question, and I hear a rumour that South Lancashire is to follow the example of the city of London, and to choose the other brother for her representative.

At Liverpool those same bigots who kept John Manners out of the representation, seemed quite indifferent about the Jews.

---

* [An article on "Jewish Disabilities," by Mr. Croker, in the *Quarterly Review* for September, 1847, p. 526.]

† [Owing to the bankruptcy of the Duke of Buckingham, the bailiffs were put in possession of Stowe on Sept. 29, and the estates were subsequently sold.]

I am sure Peel is, and so was Lord Lyndhurst, in favour of the Jews. No doubt it was this knowledge made Lord John identify himself with Rothschild.

I quite concur in your fears that the tendency of Peel's measures is driving towards a confiscation of real property. I had not seen the *Daily News;* that is a paper very much inclined to Peel. The active proprietor is the Duke of Devonshire's celebrated gardener. I have quoted the exact words of Peel's speech, and noted them on the margin of the proof.

I now see for the first time that he meant to draw a subtle distinction between property and income tax. I am sure no one so understood him at the time, so that he will now say he always told us "that at the end of three years we should be able to dispense with the income as distinguished from the property tax." What a juggler the man is !

You have worked that matter admirably, and I heartily enter into the entire article on the navigation laws, which is most powerfully put.

I can tell you exactly about the operation of the navigation laws as regards corn.

They were suspended in February, exactly when the need for suspension—if there ever was any need of suspending them—had ceased.

The famine came of a sudden, and the demand for shipping at such short notice, that everybody's ships were under contracts and charters, from which they could not break to go and fetch corn at Christmas. Thus at Christmas the seaboard of the United States was crammed with corn, and there were not ships enough to bring it away. Freight went up to 14*s*. 6*d*. per barrel for flour, and to 25*s*. at one time per quarter for wheat. In September the Queen's ships were lying in the Tagus, seventeen of them taking care of her Majesty's cousin ; four of these measured 12,000 tons, equal to carrying 60,000 quarters of grain ; they should have been sent to New York to have brought corn to Ireland, but, instead of this, when the necessity had ceased at the end of February, the navigation laws were suspended, by which time ships, enticed by the high freight, had crowded into all the grain ports, and by the month of May there were at New York 34,000 tons more of ships than there was corn to bring away.

Everything the Government did was just too late.

I shall be too late for my post, and must conclude. I have more to say on this subject.

In great haste, yours most sincerely,

G. BENTINCK.

Lord George Bentinck to Mr. Croker. Extract.

Welbeck, near Worksop, Notts, September 30th, 1847.

MY DEAR MR. CROKER,

I will now go on to other subjects. You will have seen that I noted down 116 Peelites ready to descend *usque ad inferos* with the arch-traitor—in my inward thoughts I put them at 130—who would be glad to make friends with him and see him in power again. I could tell you a strange story about the Duke of Buckingham and his nine members in connection with the Coercion Bill. Such men, too, as Mr. Ker Seymour never meant that Sir Robert Peel should be turned out. I myself publicly put the question point blank to him: "Will you rather kiss and make it up with Sir Robert Peel, or would you rather submit to have Lord John Russell Prime Minister?" Mr. Ker Seymour frankly replied, "I would rather, as you put it, kiss and make it up with Sir Robert Peel." This was at the meeting where it was discussed whether or not we would turn out Sir Robert Peel on the Coercion Bill, and my then colloquist was the man who had but just stepped into Lord Ashley's abdicated office. Depend upon it, half at least of the two hundred and forty have never, and will never, forgive me the earnestness and sincerity of my opposition. They prefer to be kicked and fed, feed and fattened, and kicked again, to the false pride of poverty with unsullied honour.

I broke off yesterday in the middle of my story about the suspension of the navigation laws, and the effect of that suspension upon the Irish famine.

I believe it was on the 7th of August that the first intelligence was given of the potato blight, which in forty-eight hours withered the tops, and of course stopped the further growth of the potatoes in Ireland. At that time the highest price of "Best Brands" flour at New York was 4 dollars and 25 cents (*i. e.* 17*s.* 8½*d.*) per barrel of 196 lbs., and Indian corn was 22*s.* 4*d.*, and wheat 33*s.* 4*d.* per quarter, and freights were 2s. 6d. per barrel to England and 4s. 10d. per quarter for wheat. On the 4th of September, the *Britannia* arrived at New York with the news of the potato failure, but the price of flour only went up fifty cents (*i. e.* 2s. 1d.) per barrel, and freights to 3s., to England for flour. The Yankees and the corn trade generally had so burnt their fingers meddling with and believing the enormous lie of Peel's famine, that they would not believe the real cry of famine when it came in earnest. The consequence was no ships went for corn. The famine was not believed at New York even so late as the 11th of December, when 20,000 barrels of flour, Gennessee best brands, were sold at 5 dollars 6 cents to 5 dollars 12½ cents (*i. e.* 21s. 4¼d., the highest price), and freights had only risen to 4s. 9d. to Liverpool, making 26s. 1¼d. the highest price, freight included, of the finest flour to Liverpool.

Still, the Government at home sat with its arms folded; no steps were taken till towards the end of January, by which time the corn trade awakened from its sleep. Flour had jumped up to 7 dollars a barrel, and freights to 12s. 6d.; and Indian corn, which on the 11th of December was selling at New York and Philadelphia at 20s. 4d. per quarter, suddenly rose in Liverpool Market to 70s., and at last I believe to 80s., a quarter.

At this time there were seventeen ships of war lying in the Tagus and cruising off the coast of Portugal, seven or eight of these averaging 3000 tons a piece. Lord Hardwicke, the first seaman in the British navy, declared his readiness, with forty-eight hours' notice, to get the guns out of seven of these, to have their portholes battened down, and I think he said to have their top-gallant masts taken out, and be away for New York, and he said in eight weeks back again on the coast of Ireland with 80,000 quarters of corn. I made this statement in the House of Commons, and Lord Hardwicke said something of the kind in the House of Lords the first night of the session.

The Government laughed at the proposition, and brought in a Bill for the suspension of the navigation laws; but at that time all the merchant service ships of foreign nations were either under contract and tied fast, or else they were locked up by the ice and laid up in the different rivers and seas of Northern Europe.

I then told the Government that their suspension of the navigation laws would be of no avail, that there would be plenty of ships before it could come into effect. However, we let the suspension of the corn laws and navigation laws pass in February, after my urging what should have been done was to have sent seven or eight line-of-battle-ships in September, October, November, and December, to have brought the corn to Ireland and prevented the people from starving.

Lord John Russell, however, had pledged himself to the mercantile interest—that is, to the corn speculators and corn merchants of the city of London—" that the supply of the people of Ireland should be left to private enterprise," and "that private enterprise and free trade should not be interfered with."

But the famine had come on so suddenly, private enterprise was taken by surprise, and was quite unprepared. The Irish people were like an army on a desert island, like the Israelites in the wilderness, only, happily for them, the God of Israel was not a Whig, or a Free Trader, or a political economist, or a Scotch philosopher; and thus I really believe a well-counted million of Irish perished of famine, and of fever consequent upon famine, before assistance reached them. The Irish were starved all December, January, February, and March; in April they began to be glutted; in May there were 34,000 tons of shipping at New York unable to obtain freights. I believe at one moment freights which had got up to 14s. 6d. a barrel for flour, and to 25s. for wheat in bulk, had dropped so low that one cargo was actually freighted at 2s. a barrel for flour.

And, as you have probably observed, a fortnight ago Indian meal actually sold in Belfast 1l. per ton cheaper than guano! Indian meal selling for 7l. 10s. and guano for 8l. 10s. per ton. Such was the improvidence of the Whig Government that for three months they allowed the opportunity to pass of laying in stores at two-fifths of the price at which the great mass of the food for Ireland was eventually purchased : they allowed one million of people to perish, and the Irish people to draw the odious comparison and contrast between the English Government, which preferred keeping seventeen ships of war idle in the Tagus nursing a Coburg, and the Congress of the United States, which sent two ships of war—one, the *Macedonian* (they took from us)—loaded from stem to stern-post, and from her keel to her gunwale, with 1800 tons of breadstuffs. And I verily believe there is not an Irishman in Ireland who has not marked the contrast.

But this was not all; there was a fleet of 800 grain-laden ships from the Black Sea lying wind-bound for seven weeks in the gat of Gibraltar. Of these the greater part were bound for England, the rest for the French Atlantic ports. Louis Philippe sent all his war steamers to tug the French ships through the gat of Gibraltar. We had five war steamers lying in the Tagus and Douro; our ships were left to wait the change of wind, and when at last they arrived in the Thames in May, the grain, from being so long on board, had in many—I believe in most—cases become so heated that I am assured you might wind the stinking corn nearly a quarter of a mile to leeward of the fleet.

Well, in the month of May or June, Lord John Russell brought in a fresh Bill to renew till next March (the first suspension was only till September) the suspension of the corn and navigation laws. I permitted the corn law suspension to pass after midnight, acquiescing in that; but I demurred to the further suspension of the navigation laws until the Government were enabled to make a case. Weeks passed, no case was made. John Russell laughed; he knew (Charles Wood told me privately) they had no case. However, at last, at the end of June, they produced a return by which they showed that between 200,000 and 300,000 quarters of grain had been imported under virtue of the suspension of the navigation laws, and I think that 220,000 quarters had been thus imported into Ireland. I doubted and demurred to the truth of the return, and openly challenged it as being contrary to notorious facts, and, though 180 or 200 ships, mostly lighters and barges, averaging fifty tons, had come into the port of London, it eventually turned out that four I think, but certainly half a dozen, line-of-battle-ships would have sufficed in one voyage to have brought to England more than all that was imported under favour of the Whig suspension of the navigation laws up to the 5th of June last!

Almost the whole Scotch and Irish return was false. I think the whole importation into Ireland, instead of being 220,000 quarters, was only 20,000 quarters!

Always yours most sincerely,

G. BENTINCK.

Lord George Bentinck to Mr. Croker.   Extract.

Welbeck, near Worksop, Notts, October 5th, 1847.

MY DEAR MR. CROKER,

My services, such as they are, shall always be at the command of anyone who, like yourself, can put the facts which I am able to collect with more force and in a more striking light before the world.

Virtually an uneducated man, never intended or attracted by taste for political life, in the House of Commons only by a pure accident, indeed by an inevitable and undesired chance, I am well aware of my own incapacity properly to fill the station I have been thrust into. My sole ambition was to rally the broken and dispirited forces of a betrayed and insulted party, and to avenge the country gentlemen and landed aristocracy of England upon the Minister who, presuming upon their weakness, falsely flattered himself that they could be trampled upon with impunity.

I did deceive myself with false hopes that the old English spirit would have been roused, and that it was only necessary to keep the dismantled ship floating and fighting under jury-masts till she went through the thorough repair of a new election, and then that scores of better men would have come to her rescue.

I own I am bitterly disappointed and broken-hearted that England has proved to be so degenerate that, in face of an emergency, she has produced, as far as I can see, no new leaders to take my place.

When their rents are not paid and their mortgages are called in, then the country gentlemen will exert themselves, and so will the farmers when wheat falls under 45s. per qr., but not before.

They actually won't go to the poll unless they are carried and have refreshment tickets! I understand that in North Essex we were beat by two entire parishes not sending up a single vote to poll for the Protectionist candidate, because he had not personally canvassed them, and trusted to their going up to the poll.

Nothing but pinching adversity will bring such men to a proper sense of their duty.

And as regards the gentlemen, the entire fund subscribed

for the election did not exceed 8000*l.* (I believe), and of this King Hudson subscribed 2000*l.*

Till the landed interest, and the Colonial and shipping interests, all together feel intolerable distress we shall do no good, but in my conscience I believe (if the navigation laws are repealed, which I scarcely doubt) this will happen within two years.

Always yours most sincerely,

G. BENTINCK.

Lord George Bentinck to Mr. Croker.

Welbeck, near Worksop, Notts, October 6th, 1847.

MY DEAR MR. CROKER,

I have got the *Quarterly* and am highly delighted with your contribution to it,* which I esteem most admirable, and I feel confident that in the way you have put the statistics they cannot be disputed ; indeed, in my conscience I believe them to be substantially correct.

Pray keep Marshall and Burn. You will find them very handy on many occasions. The cotton trade will occupy a good deal of attention, and there is a good deal to be learnt from Burn,† who is a very handy and civil fellow, always ready to obtain and give any information in his power.

Ferguson and Taylor's ' Manchester Monthly Trade Circular,' which I have received to-day, after generally observing " that at no former period in the course of a long experience had they ever known the business of that market so embarrassed as at this moment," note in their postcript that for money the " Terms are : One and a quarter per cent. for cash in ten days ! " 45*l.* 12*s.* 6*d.* per cent. per annum !

I gave your message to my father, who has not forgotten that you and he were fellow-labourers in the House of Commons nearly fifty years ago.

Always yours most sincerely,

G. BENTINCK.

---

* [" Peel Policy," *Quarterly Review*, Sept. 1847.]

† [Burn was the editor of a paper called the *Commercial Glance.* Some correspondence with him is published in Disraeli's ' Life of Lord George Bentinck.']

I think on a pinch my father could still walk ten miles in a day.*

Mr. Croker to Lord Brougham.

Alverbank Gosport, October 10th, 1847.

My dear B.,

You have indeed the pen of a ready writer, and what is better, the energy of a young mind, and the sagacity of an old one. I need not say how much I am obliged to you in your being so kind as to write to me so frequently and so fully—*inter peregrinandum*—most other men would have been overlooking the packing of their trunks and locking up their writing case instead of using it.

You will by this time have seen the *Quarterly*. I hope you will think that what I have said of Lord George, and what I really believe to be nothing but the truth, is likely to do no harm. If he had obtruded himself into leadership, I should have judged him differently—but he came forth in our hour of need and we should be grateful—and at least stick by our adoption till circumstances can produce us a better. No one ever felt more than I did at his most absurd and unfounded attack upon Lyndhurst and Ripon,† the greatest mistake as well as the greatest calumny that ever was made; and some later things have, not equally, but very much vexed me; but poor Lord George was rather the victim, than the offender. He was prompted by Dr. Giffard and Mr. D'Israeli, who are two as bad guides as any man can have. If Lord George were free of them, or rather if he had been from the first unconnected with them, all would have been well—not as well as if you or Lyndhurst were young, and able to thunder in the House of Commons, but very well for these degenerate and untalented (forgive the word—it suits the age) times. And O, my dear Brougham, if the House of Commons had in it one man, only one man such as we have seen, then the

---

* [The Duke of Portland was born in June, 1768, and was therefore in his eightieth year. He survived Lord George Bentinck.]

† [See note, *supra*, pp. 78–79. It is clear that Mr. Croker was mistaken in supposing that Mr. Disraeli had instigated the attack, for he expressly defended Lord Lyndhurst, and declared that if the question "were investigated, the conduct of the noble and learned lord would come out perfectly immaculate." Mr. Croker must have totally forgotten this speech.]

country might still be saved! Have you still any dream
about Peel? I don't think he can stop. I don't doubt that
he repents bitterly, keenly, but for that very reason, he will
dash on. I address this *au risque*, to Walmer. If it finds
you there remember me to the Duke and Lyndhurst, both of
whom I think must now deplore, as I did at the time, their
reunion with Peel in '45.

Yours,

J. W. C,

Mr. Croker to Lord George Bentinck.

Alverbank, Gosport, November 2nd, 1847.

My dear Lord,

I am anxious to hear what you think of the Government
measure, and in order to obtain your opinion will venture to
give you my own.

Imprimis, I have never been of the *Morning Post* school;
but though a fast friend to the principle of a metallic currency, and so far to Peel's Charter Bill, I always suspected
that it was a piece of machinery of no great use in fair
weather, and which would and must break down under any
serious pressure; for suppose any panic affecting the bank
itself (and we saw such a one in 1825), how was it possible
that they could stand a run of depositors as well as of note-
holders? I must further say that, in my own secret mind, I
differ from my great friend and authority, Lord Ashburton, in
thinking that Peel's Act had little or nothing to do with this
crisis, his Act only rendering imperative what the Bank
Directors ought to have, and probably would have, done in
their own discretion.

With this preliminary explanation, you will not be surprised at my disapproving the Government measure, which is
a mere timid compliance, which ought to afford no relief, and
I should not be surprised if Peel himself had consented to the
experiment in the hope that it would turn out inoperative,
and so vindicate his bill and himself. I cannot imagine any
other motive for his acquiescence, and from all appearances
I should guess that the Ministers have had some kind of
sanction from him. I recollect in one of my papers, on mentioning Arnold's opinion that Peel would probably stick to his
currency opinions, I said that I would not guarantee his consistency even on currency if the adverse pressure were to be strong

enough. It would be curious if this prophetic doubt were to be fulfilled; but Peel is a different man in and out of place. In office he has no resolution; out of office he is a kind of lion—as brave as Bully Bottom; and if he has, as I believe he has, sanctioned the Government measure, it is because he is not sorry to transfer all the responsibility of his bill to them. But he may have two other motives: first, he may anticipate, as I do, the failure of the suspension, as a measure of relief, and will then be cock-a-hoop on the proof that his bill had had nothing to do with the crisis; or if it succeeds in any degree he may say, as I am told he does, that his act originally provided for such an emergency, and that he was over persuaded to leave it out. I do not recollect the debates on the bill, but this latter hypothesis seems to me very doubtful. If the Government were to interfere at all, I think they have done it wisely, and they will certainly test the causes of the crisis, for I confidently believe not two millions of Exchequer Bills will be deposited with the Bank—it will be clear that people are stopping payment, not from want of credit, but of means, and that Peel's bill is innocent of the catastrophes with which it is charged.

These are my very crude notions, and at best I am a wretched financier; but whether I look at the Government measure as a party or a public question, I equally fear that it will do no good, and have no other effect than to give Peel's bill a kind of triumph, which it really does not deserve. By charging so much upon it, we shall have given to the verdict of "not proven," to which it is entitled, all the air of an entire and glorious acquittal. You, I dare say, are well informed as to what has passed, and what the wise ones expect, and I shall be thankful if you will condescend to enlighten my ignorance.

Ever, &c.,
J. W. C.

Lord George Bentinck to Mr. Croker.

Harcourt House, November 3rd, 1847.

MY DEAR MR. CROKER,

Had the Government moved in time and gone far enough, I should have warmly approved their conduct in setting aside the Bank Charter Act of 1844; but they have come full three

months too late with a homœopathic cure, when the whole
trade and commerce of the country has fallen into a state of
collapse.

Brandy won't save now what broth would have cured in
May, when I called upon the Government to repeal the
Bank Charter Act. A panic may easily be averted, but
once in operation is hard to stay. Mr. Pitt is the great
magician to whose financial policy I pin my entire faith; next
and nearest to him I place my faith in the old Sir Robert
Peel; his letter addressed to the two Houses of Parliament in
1826 contains my creed. I would set all things to rights by
authorising the railway companies to issue railway debentures
as low as 5*l.*, and receiving them in payment for taxes, bearing
5 per cent. interest.

Lord Stanley did not profess to understand the subject, and
Tom Baring at that time was unwilling to meddle with the
currency beyond a repeal of the Bank Charter Act, which he
dawdled about till we lost the opportunity; so I let the first
matter drop, and never mooted it, and between us the motion
for the repeal of the Bank Charter Act missed fire.

The present difficulties, in my humble judgment, arise in no
degree from railways in England; they arise a good deal from
English money (13,000,000*l.*) gone to construct foreign railways, from the money taken out of the country, and from the
balance of trade being against us, owing to the enormous imports
of provisions, and 800,000*l.* worth of slave-grown sugar, un-
compensated by a corresponding exportation of manufactures.
If England exports 15,000,000*l.* of manufactures to the United
States in exchange for 15,000,000*l.* of provisions and cotton she
buys of the United States, not a sovereign or a dollar will
cross the Atlantic, or be required in the transaction; Bills of
Exchange will do it all; but if she imports 15,000,000*l.* and
exports but 7,000,000*l.*, the difference must be paid in gold or
in dollars, and once the gold is gone it is hard to get it back
again; and on this occasion 7,000,000*l.* of English gold has
gone to pay for the Mexican war.

In the spring, the Bank of England, with nearly nine
millions of bullion in the Issue Department, was within
an ace of stopping payment in the Banking Department.
Happily, she was saved by borrowing money of private banking houses. A South American merchant with 60,000*l.* in
silver bullion was unable to raise either sovereigns or bank
notes upon it. The North of Ireland Bank was actually in

the same position with 40,000*l.* in silver coin of the realm, the Bank Charter Act only allowing one-fourth the amount of gold to stand represented by silver ; for example, if there are three millions of gold in the bank cellars and one million of silver, the bank may issue four millions of notes against the aggregate amount of bullion ; but if the gold falls to one million, 666,666*l.* of the silver bullion is rendered useless, and 2,666,666*l.* of notes must be withdrawn from · public circulation.   Nothing could be more absurd.

In 1844 no less than forty-four of the principal banking houses in London memorialised Sir Robert Peel (they did not petition Parliament, they memorialised the Ministerial Dictator) against the restrictions of the Bank Charter Act, predicting every single inconvenience that has arisen from them ; but Sir Robert Peel, adopting the counsels of Samuel Jones Loyd,* turned a deaf ear to the remonstrances of all these practical men.

Sir Robert Peel, no doubt, sees his error now, and I am convinced not only consented, but advised this miserable " half-and-half," " too late " relaxation.   There is no doubt when he passed the Act he had a mental reservation to the effect that he should be Minister for life, and whenever such an emergency as this arose, he would come forward himself and relax the restrictions.   Indeed, the Bank of England directors of 1844 affirmed that in the original manuscript of the bill a power was reserved to the First Lord of the Treasury, the Chancellor of the Exchequer, and Master of the Mint to relax to the extent of two millions those restrictions which confined the Bank to an issue of only 14,000,000*l.* of notes unrepresented by bullion.

However, when the matter came to be discussed in Parliament, Sir Robert Peel denied that any such elasticity was ever intended to be given to the Act, and divided against an amendment to that effect.   He declared that all the latitude he had proposed to give to the Ministers was to consent to a further issue against Public Securities of 2,000,000*l.* unrepresented by gold in the event of the issues of country bankers being reduced to the amount of two millions.   This was quite a different matter.

Peel's Act of 1844 provides that *pari passu* with the perma-

* [The celebrated banker, afterwards Lord Overstone ; born in 1796 ; died in 1883.]

nent withdrawal of three country notes the Bank of England may issue two additional notes unrepresented by gold. From this it follows, of course, that whilst the trade and commerce of the country are daily growing in magnitude, or ought to be daily growing in size, the shoes that are to carry them are by law daily diminishing in number and size. Imagine if a law were passed taking the average number of merchant ships employed for the last three years, and ordaining that the number of those ships should never be increased, but on the contrary for every three ships which decayed or were shipwrecked, only two new ones should be permitted to be built, though the commerce of the country should multiply tenfold. It seems too absurd for belief; but this is Peel's Bill. Bank notes are the grease that enable the wheels of the Bills of Exchange, which are the carriages on which commerce is borne, to work; nothing certain is known, but it is generally supposed that 300 millions of Bills of Exchange are daily constituting the circulating medium of the country, bank notes, gold and silver being the small change which facilitate, whilst they are indispensable to, their working.

Had the Bank Charter Act not been suspended when it was, there must have been a run upon the Banking Department of the Bank of England, for she showed in notes but 1,500,000*l.*, and in coin 500,000*l.*—total 2,000,000*l.*—in the Banking Department to meet 8,500,000*l.* of liabilities, which is a proportion out of all rule of safety. The least public alarm would have caused her to suspend payment in the Banking Department, all the while that (I believe only a green door separates the Banking from the Issue Department) on the other side the green door there was lying a heap of 8,000,000*l.* of bullion unemployed and useless, which Peel's Bill forbade the Banking Department to touch.

In this crisis nobody wanted gold; the cry was for bank notes; but Peel's Bill forbad the issue of bank notes unless covered by gold.

Peel's Bill is the bill of the usurer. It has caused already in Scotland notice to be given of a rise of one and a half per cent. in the interest on all mortgages—half per cent. now and one per cent. more in April next. It is causing, or will cause, a similar rise in the interest upon all mortgages in England and Wales. See what this will effect: the income of the landed property of Great Britain (exclusive of houses, &c.) is little short of 60,000,000*l.* a year—the capital

1,800,000,000*l.* ; it is not too much to say that the land
mortgaged represents 600,000,000*l.*, and the interest on mortgages consumes 21,000,000*l.* a year of this—say at 3½ per cent.
last year. Suppose six months hence the interest is raised
1½ per cent.—that is to 5 per cent.—this would incur an additional charge of no less than nine millions a year upon the
land in Great Britain. The charge upon the land of Ireland
is usually said to be 9,000,000*l.* annually. Say at 4 per cent.,
an addition of 1½ per cent. here would give 3,375,000*l.* as the
increased charge upon Ireland.

Here you have at once, in the shape of increased charges
upon the land through dearness of money created by Peel's
Bank Charter Act, and other money laws, a tax of between
twelve and thirteen millions a year, and if the money lent on
mortgage upon mines, houses, mills, collieries, ships, harbours,
docks, railways, and sugar, coffee, and indigo plantations,
amount to as much more, a rise of 1½ per cent. in the price of
money would practically impose whilst it lasted an annually
tax of twenty-five millions a year upon the property (not
funded) of the country, to the advantage of the Jews and
mortgagees.

No country ever prospered under a high rate of interest.
The commerce of this would not live two years under 8 per
cent. Hitherto we have beat the world because our merchants
and manufacturers were trading on cheap capital, but [with]
discounts at 4 per cent. in France, and generally over the
world discounts ranging between 4 and 6 per cent., how is it
possible our trade can be carried on ?

But I will give you two or three practical examples of the
working of Peel's Bank Charter Act.

The Act was conditionally suspended last Monday week.
The week previous a manufacturer holding 100,000*l.*—North-
Western Railway Debentures (guaranteed 5 per cent. for
five years)—required bank notes to meet his liabilities. He
went to Samuel Jones Loyd and desired to have his debentures discounted ; Samuel Jones Loyd refused ; the manufacturer replied, " I must have money." The banker rejoined,
" I can't do it. But stay ; strike off 25 per cent. and I will,
but I give but five minutes to consider." The wretched manufacturer had no choice but to submit to the extortion or to
suspend payments. Samuel Jones Loyd gave 75,000*l.* Bank of
England notes and became possessed of 100,000*l.* North-
Western Railway Debentures. On the Monday following, the

restrictions of the Bank Charter Act being suspended, the Bank of England was set at liberty to discount such a security at 8 per cent. for three months.   Jones Loyd consequently on the Monday could have gone to the Bank of England and have re-discounted for 2000*l.* what he himself four days before extorted 25,000*l.* for discounting.   Is not usury like this enough to make one's blood boil ?

Take Sir Robert Peel's case.   He holds 900,000*l.*—3¼ Reduced Consols—the annual interest or income on which is 29,250*l.*   In 1844 the 3¼ per cent. Reduced were at par. London and Birmingham Railway Shares (now North-Western), paying 10*l.* per original 100*l.* share dividend, were at 250*l.*   Had Sir Robert Peel sold out at par, he might have purchased, in 1844, 3600 London and Birmingham Shares, returning at 10*l.* per share 36,000*l.* a year income ; but though 3¼ per cent. Reduced have fallen from par to 80*l.* in 1847, if he were now to sell out of the funds and buy North-Western shares, which are down at 150*l.*, he would be enabled to possess himself of 4800 shares in lieu of 3600 ; and though the dividend has fallen from 10*l.* to 9*l.* a share, he would improve his income to 43,200*l.* a year !

Believe me always very sincerely yours,

G. BENTINCK.

Lord George Bentinck to Mr. Croker.   Extract.

Harcourt House, November 8th, 1847.

MY DEAR MR. CROKER,

Peel's monetary laws must be broken down, or the landed property of the country, burdened with encumbrances, will pass into the hands of the Christian Jews.

I hold this pressure to be the joint effect of free imports, and a currency restricted by Peel's Bank Charter Act.

I believe we never have had a famine, or a succession of short harvests, without a money pressure.

We have never had a great expenditure in foreign wars without a money pressure following, except when that pressure has been countervailed by a bank restriction.

We never have had a mania exist to invest in foreign loans, in foreign canals and railways, or in foreign mines, that a pressure for money has not ensued ; but [we] went on

spending half a million a week on railways at home up to
October, 1846, and, nevertheless, there never was known a
period when credit was so high or money so plentiful. The
Bank of England had 15,000,000*l.* in her coffers in August,
1846. Unable to get rid of her bullion, she was actually
obliged to reduce the maximum price of her discounts to
3 per cent., and did discount good bills at 2½ per cent. But,
as you will remember, I showed that in Peel's famine year,
ending the 26th of June, 1846, Great Britain and Ireland
were (with the exception of 1,300,000 quarters of foreign
grain, of all sorts, chiefly barley and oats, *i.e.* low-priced
grain) fed exclusively on grain of home-growth. Up to the
autumn of 1846 we lived upon colonial sugar, we did not
admit slave-grown sugar.

Between the 26th of June, 1846, and this time we have had
to pay for 12,000,000 quarters of foreign corn, say at 35*s.* per
quarter on an average of all sorts, 21,000,000*l.* sterling, in the
entire four years which preceded the severe distress in 1840–41.
It is estimated that we paid 35,000,000*l.* sterling for foreign
grain.

But, to aggravate matters, in the last twelve months we
have imported 800,000*l.* worth of slave-grown sugar paid
for in gold. These extraordinary importations it was which
did not exist in 1846, coming on the back of the enormous
importations of foreign timber, in substitution for English
timber, occasioned by Peel's reduction of the timber duties;
the large importations of American cotton, to the exclusion
of Indian cotton, all to be paid for in gold—this threw the
balance of trade against us, and began to drain the bank of
its specie; and then it was that, in obedience to Peel's Bank
Charter Bill, the bank was obliged to pull short up, and
refuse to discount the best bills, silver bullion, and even her
Majesty's silver coin; though there were still lying between
nine and ten millions of silver and gold in her coffers. In
old times, before Peel's Bank Charter Act existed, the Bank
of England would have fearlessly gone on discounting, so long
as it had 4,000,000*l.* in its coffers; and then there would
have been no pressure and no panic. At this time the
discounts of the Bank of England, and the country banks
together, have been curtailed to such an extent that the notes
in circulation are nearly 7,000,000*l.* under what they were in
the corresponding month of last year. The entire note circulation is reduced to about 29,000,000*l.*; so here is a reduction

of no less than 20 per cent. in the note currency of the country.

Always very sincerely yours,

G. Bentinck.

Lord George Bentinck to Mr. Croker.   Extract.

Harcourt House, November 9th, 1847.

My dear Mr. Croker,

I think I have shown you ample cause why the balance of trade occasioned by too free imports and the non-discouragement of foreign investments, should have suddenly drained the money market, and have produced the current disasters. But you will ask, How does all this prove your case against the Bank Charter Act as an accomplice in the money pressure ? Because the Bank Charter Act forced the Bank of England, for every sovereign that went out to draw in a bank note, and accordingly when dearth was making everything naturally dear, and consequently requiring more money to carry on the same amount of " goods transactions," the Bank of England and the country banks (coerced to follow suit) were hard at work making everything artificially cheap by drawing in 7,000,000*l.* Bank of England and country bank notes, and thus enhancing the value of money in England by making it scarce ; the Bank of England all the while hoarding not less than from 8,000,000*l.* to 9,000,000*l.* of bullion in its cellars. But for Peel's Bank Charter Act the bullion might have been reduced with perfect safety to 4,000,000*l.* and with very little risk to 2,000,000*l.*, and that increased quantity of notes of course kept out. Had the Bank of England been at liberty to take so much latitude it is needless to say that they never would have been required, in order to bring back gold, to raise the rate of their interest on discounts above 4½ or at most 5 per cent.

It is this panic, so unnecessarily forced on, that is causing the absorption, the hoarding of gold, in the country. In the last fortnight 1,200,000*l.* of gold has flowed into the country, but the bank coffers only show an influx of 127,000*l.* ; the rest is all hoarded, lying useless and profitless, in the drawert of country bankers, starving the industry of the country ; bus till the panic was so artificially created by the bank first

raising, and at last refusing discounts altogether, nobody
wanted gold for domestic purposes; people were quite content
with, nay preferred, bank notes.

Always yours most sincerely,

G. BENTINCK.

Lord George Bentinck to Mr. Croker.

Harcourt House, December 26th, 1847.

MY DEAR MR. CROKER,

I got your proofs yesterday morning,* but was so busy with
my own affairs I was quite unable to look at them till after
post-time. I have now done so, and have taken you at your
word, and made very free with my comments.

I am very anxious you should distinguish between the
Dr. Ryans and McEnerys and the really mischievous priests.
Depend upon it, a priest who relies for his very subsistence
upon the multitude cannot altogether spare the misdeeds of
the upper classes, if he means to denounce in earnest and with
effect those of the many. And you may rest assured that
one-hundredth part of the suffering which Ireland has met
with in the last twelve months would have raised in England
a servile war from the Tweed-side to the Land's End. I had
no idea that any nation was so without "devil" in it as to
have laid down and died as tamely as the Irish have. Perhaps
the rice-fed coolies in India might.

With regard to the Coercion Bill, I think you all wrong;
my Hansard's Debates are all gone to be bound, or I
would have sent you the debates of 1846, and would have
referred you to Graham's speech, my own, and Henley's.
Henley tore the bill to shreds, and proved it to be utterly
worthless and ridiculous. Peel never meant to carry it.
I really forget whether it was the first or second reading
of the bill—I suppose it must have been the second reading
of it?—which we rejected on the 26th of June, having
been announced in January! Peel never dared have talked
of "parleying with assassins or of reparation" had I been in
the House; but I have been a miserable creature, prostrated
by the influenza all this session, in bed when I ought to
have been in the House of Commons.

You will think my free criticisms the more "free and easy"

* ["Ministerial Measures," *Quarterly Review*, No. 163.]

when I tell you that I have ceased to be the leader of the
House of Commons "Opposition!" My vote and speech on
the Jew Bill gave dire offence to the party, and on the Monday
morning I got a long letter from Beresford, who, as you know,
is the whipper-in of the party, the long and short of which was
an intimation that for daring to make that speech I must be
prepared to receive my dismissal. I need not tell you that a
hint that any considerable portion of the party were dissatisfied with and wearied of me, was quite enough for me to
proffer a resignation with a good grace, without waiting to be
" cashiered."

Appointed on account of my uncompromising spirit, I
am dismissed for the same reason; that which was my
principal virtue in 1846 is my damning vice in 1847. In
April, 1846, they would have me, *nolens volens*, for their leader.
I in vain warned them that my religious differences from
them, as well as my want of capacity to lead a party, alike
disqualified me for the office. I foretold all that has since
come to pass—all in vain; they would not listen to me; and
now, when standing as true as the needle to the North Pole, I
get my *congé* from the whipper-in, and read in their ' Morning
Herald,' that "Lord George Bentinck has thrown over his
party!"

However, the great Protectionist Party having degenerated
into a "No Popery" "No Jew" Party, I am still more
unfit now than I was in 1846 to lead it. A party that can
muster 140 on a Jew Bill, and cannot muster much above
half those numbers on any question essentially connected with
the great interests of the empire, can only be led by their
antipathies, their hatreds, and their prejudices; and I am the
unfittest man in the world to lead them. Beresford, Newdegate, and Mr. Phillips, of the *Morning Herald* have raised
all this artificial zeal in the cause of religion, and fanned the
flickering embers of bigotry, till they have raised a flame,
of which, as a matter of course, I am necessarily the first
victim.

I think it very unfortunate, but things have been brought to
that pass that I see no chance of the party being kept from
melting away, except by the choice of a new leader, and he a
" No Popery " man. I wrote this to Stanley long ago. I have
put my resignation into the hands of Bankes, from whom,
and through whose enthusiastic feelings and good offices, I
originally received my appointment.

I have resigned with a good grace and in a tone of good feeling, and I hope that the result will be that the party will henceforth act with more concord and zest, and may thus, on the only subjects which concern the empire, be led by their prejudices to muster more strongly than they could be by argument or reason, so long as they were led by a man who endeavoured to lead them by their understandings, but knew not how to sympathise in, or to pander to, their religious prejudices.

Always yours most sincerely,

G. BENTINCK.

Mr. Croker to Lord George Bentinck.

West Moulsey, December 27th, 1847.

MY DEAR LORD,

I have received your criticisms with great gratitude, and your intelligence with great regret. I, as you know, lamented your pledge on the Jew question, and should have been glad if there had been any way of extrication, but nobody could, or at least ought to have expected that you were to have forfeited pledges or deserted opinions from so accidental and unforeseen a circumstance as this Jew Bill happening to co-incide with your leadership. Allow me to assure you of my sincere regret at the loss our party will sustain by your secession from our head. I have admired the zeal and ability and courage with which you accepted and conducted the command of a scattered and dispirited army, which nobody else would undertake, and which no one that I know would have executed half as well. I have been exceedingly helped and obliged by your most valuable assistance, and I wish I might be allowed to hope that you would still favour me with your advice for the short time that I shall probably take any part in politics. I have just turned my sixty-seventh year, and even if I were not otherwise growing unequal to, and displeased with, the task, which has somehow fallen to my lot, years begin to whisper the *solve senescentem*. Will you forgive me for venturing to offer one piece of humble advice? Don't quit the field, though you give up the lead; many occasions will necessarily arise in which your talents and firmness may be of great use to the public, and I am not sure that you may not speak with more effect in your in-

dividual capacity, than as spokesman of a party that is
distracted with such a diversity of petty differences.

Ever, my dear Lord, most faithfully yours,

J. W. CROKER. •

Lord George Bentinck to Mr. Croker.

Harcourt House, December 27th, 1847.

MY DEAR MR. CROKER,

You are an historian, and I cannot refrain from again
writing to implore you not to treat Peel's concession of the
Roman Catholic claims in 1829 as a " compact." You have
not a foot of ground to stand upon. It was an unconditional
surrender, a surrender at discretion.

I have not time to look back to the debates, but I well
remember them. The Duke of Wellington grounded his
concession on his dread of " civil war in Ireland," Peel his
on the majorities in the Commons, and more especially upon
the fact of the popular constituencies having turned against
him. With whom was the compact? I know of no compact
except that between Peel and George IV., that Daniel
O'Connell should be personally excluded from sitting in
Parliament in virtue of his election for Clare.

Compact with the great Whig party certainly there was
none; I was a member of it, and never heard a whisper of it.

Our whipper-in, the late Lord Bessborough, actually moved
the rejection of the 40s. Freeholders Disfranchisement Bill; I
supported him. Lord Stanley opposed in committee, and so
did Lord Sandon, these very enactments which it is part of
the object of Anstey's bill to repeal.

Whom, then, was the compact with? Not with the Tory
party; they were kept in the dark till the Queen's Speech
announced the tergiversation of their leaders; the Duke of
Rutland presented a petition signed by 7000 of the gentry
and yeomanry of Leicestershire against Catholic emancipation.
" Rutland " stood at the head of the signatures.

Lord Lowther, at the head of nine of his father's members,
marched out with the minority, setting the Government at
defiance.

Lord Winchilsea and Sir Edward Knatchbull in November
called 20,000 persons together on Pennenden Heath (I was

present) to petition and remonstrance against Catholic emancipation, and to uphold the Government in their supposed Protestant ascendancy views.

The Duke of Richmond at Christmas entertained the Duke of Wellington and a large Orange party (of which I was the solitary exception); we had orange cards in compliment to the Duke of Wellington and the old Dowager Duchess; the old Lord Lieutenantcy "Pious and glorious memory tablecloth" was called into service, and Lady Jersey publicly insulted common decency and me by expressing "her great rejoicing at Mr. Canning's death." All this in honour of and to promote Protestant ascendancy! The befooled Duke of Richmond accepted the garter, which, when he discovered how he had been deceived, so annoyed him that before he had been invested he went down almost on his knees to George IV., and obtained the intercession of the Duke of Cumberland with the King, but all in vain, to have the letters withdrawn, and himself divested of his new but loathed honours.

The surrender of Catholic emancipation, as it appears from a declaration of Peel's in either 1835 or 1839, was agreed upon exclusively between the Duke of Wellington and Peel in the summer of 1828, immediately upon the close of the session, and antecedently to Peel's triumphant Protestant progress through Lancashire to Liverpool and Manchester, when he planted the celebrated "Protestant oak" with great ceremony and parade upon the occasion of a grand public breakfast given him as the champion of Protestant ascendency.

Then with whom was the compact? Not with the Canningites; Huskisson, Palmerston, and the Grants had been ignominiously kicked out of office on the East Retford Bill in 1828; not with poor old Lord Eldon, he was totally neglected and disregarded. I don't believe there is a line or a letter in any speech delivered at the time or since, until the assertion became a convenient tool against Walton's bill, which justified, nay which does not utterly refute, the allegation of a compact in 1829. It was an unconditional, cowardly, treacherous surrender at discretion.

There was a compact in 1842 on the Corn Bill. The agricultural interests were called together and consulted, and the great majority agreed to the bill of 1842, and again to the Canada Corn Bill. Peel and Gladstone both treated the

Corn Bill of 1842 as a compact reluctantly agreed to by the
agricultural interests.

But sure I am if, as an historian of your own time, you try
to stamp the Act of 1829 as a compact, there is not a penny-
a-liner who will not be able to turn you heels over head. I
hope to God you will not commit such a mistake.

In 1825, the carrying the Roman Catholic Emancipation
Bill by its warm friends and advocates would have been a
clear, distinct, and manifest "compact."

Ever, my dear Mr. Croker,

Yours most sincerely,

G. BENTINCK.

Lord George Bentinck to Mr. Croker.   Extract.

Harcourt House, December 28th, 1847.

MY DEAR MR. CROKER,

I have only got Hansard to-day; I have marked the
particular passages in the Coercion Bill debate, and send
them to you.

Remember Lord John has pledged himself to ask for
stronger measures if required, or to go beyond the law, to
put down outrage in Ireland; this pledge he gave at the Lord
Mayor's dinner.

The step to trial by court-martial would be a mighty short
one; proclaim a district, the Roman Catholic soldiery and
police, as a matter of course attending chapel and mass with
their small arms by their sides, would furnish fearless, ready,
and willing witnesses before a court-martial; and then with
Baines' Clause I would not give much for the chance of an
altar-denunciating priest escaping a conviction and a visit to
the penal settlements.

The military, police, and veterans scattered over Ireland
muster at this moment very little short of 60,000, nearly 30
in every parish upon the average, probably many more in
the disturbed districts.

The Government last year instituted an inquiry into the
subject of the number of guns imported into Ireland; the
report was never published; but I understood that they
amounted in the whole to 3000, which appears to be a very
small consumption for 8,000,000 of people; that consumption,

however small as it was, was accounted for in this way, that
the purchases were chiefly made by the farmers wishing to
protect their corn stacks and potato pits against the depreda-
tions of a famished people.

I saw a statement the other day that in the whole of Cork
and Kerry only one murder had been committed in this
year; the population exceeds 800,000. That one murder was
the murder of Lord Shannon's under-bailiff, which was no
doubt executed by one or other of two tenants, one of whom
held a farm of 40 acres let at 29*l.* 14*s.*, the other the holder of
a farm of 93 acres, the rent 59*l.* 8*s.*, the Poor Law valuation
of it 65*l.*, his own valuation of his house 600*l.*, the award of
the arbitrators 200*l.*, and yet the under-bailiff was shot, I
believe in broad day, by one if not by both of these respectable
tenants acting in concert.

Of what good would Peel's Curfew Act and registration of
Arms Bill have been as a protection against this county Cork
murder?

When people rave about the arming of 8,000,000 of people
through the purchase of 3000 guns, I should like to ask how
many guns they think are in the possession of English
farmers for the mere purpose of bird-tenting, and how many
farmers in England there are who for sporting, bird-tenting,
or self-defence are without a gun.

I very much think with you in the last paragraph of
your very kind and flattering letter; I have no thoughts of
deserting or "sulking" as my late party have done; on the
contrary, I do not yet despair of putting them to shame by
my example.

I find all the leading men of the party are indignant; it is
the bigoted rump that has created the dissension. The true-
hearted of the party feel that without dishonour I could not
have voted with them, or in my position contented myself
with a silent sneaking vote.

I cannot imagine what Stanley is to do; I think if he goes
in the face of all his previous votes he will be covered with
confusion and shame, and if he adopts the sentiment of
"unchristianizing the country," that his opponents cannot
fail to brand him as a "canting hypocrite."

In 1830 he was one of those who conspired to make the
Jew question the great trial of strength of the session against
the Wellington-Peel Administration. In 1833 he voted for
the same measure, and was one of the Government in 1843

who removed those disabilities, far more general and important than this petty and trivial question, for he admitted them to every office in the State; and it only requires that a Jew should be forthcoming, of sufficient ability to entitle him to hold these offices, for a Jew to be Chief Justice of England, a Cabinet Minister, Chancellor of Ireland, Keeper of the Great Seal, and of the Queen's conscience, with 800 Protestant livings in his gift! As I think I wrote to you, I could not have looked the House of Commons, and certainly not Peel, in the face if I had turned my back upon all my former votes, and had joined in 1847 in the cry of "Unchristianizing the Parliament."

As for the question itself, I look upon it just of about as much national importance as Lord Ellenborough's Divorce Bill, or the Duke of Beaufort's, or the late Lord Donegal's Marriage Bill; indeed, I am here over-estimating the importance of the Jew Bill; and as for the Jews themselves, I don't care two straws about them, and heartily wish they were all back in the Holy Land.

Happy to say that I cannot discover in your writings any of those "whisperings" to which you allude, and flattering myself that for the sake of this great empire it will please Providence to hush any such "whisperings" for many a long year to come.

> Believe me always yours most sincerely,
>
> G. Bentinck.

*Bishop Wilberforce to Mr. Croker.**

Cuddesdon Palace, Dec. 29, 1847.

My dear Mr. Croker,

The influenza which still keeps hold of me, and the turn Dr. H[ampden's] business has taken, have so entirely occupied me that I have been unable hitherto to thank you for your kind letter. I hope to-morrow to have your account of Dr. Rundle, and am looking for it with great interest. But I believe no opposition is now possible at Bow Church except on the ground of a wrong election. The Clergy Discipline quite unintentionally shuts out from the Vicar-General all

---

* [This letter relates to the celebrated Hampden controversy, and is interesting for the explanation which it contains of the Bishop's position and views. Opposition had been offered to the confirmation of Dr. Hampden in Bow Church.]

power of entering on anything but mere technical facts as to the election. This led the warm opposers to wish for a suit under the Clergy Discipline Act through my court : I sending it to the Arches. I granted them letters of request. Then the promoters asked me to try to bring Dr. H. privately to the same explanations which would be required. I assented, and thus was drawn unawares into a judicial position. This required a conscientious study of the works : and this has ended in my conviction that no articles can· be made good against him : in my withdrawing the letters of requesting and sending to the *Times* a letter to Dr. H., which I hope will hold him to such explanations I have got, and does him the substantial justice I think due to him. The extracts made in 1834 to show his unsoundness by Newman, and from which I chiefly drew my opinion of the work, are most Jesuitically unfair. If I had not withdrawn the "letters," and the Articles had not broken down, still Dr. H. would have been out of the jurisdiction of the Court before any sentence can be given. All this does not touch Lord John's wantonness in making such an appointment. Will you send me your views on it when you see my letter. I wish you heartily, my dear Mr. Croker, every blessing in the New Year of life to which God has so graciously brought you, and am, my dear Mr. Croker, with very affectionate remembrances to your ladies,

Ever most truly yours,

Oxon.

As there is but one more letter of Lord George Bentinck's to add to this correspondence, it is desirable to place it here, although it belongs to a later date. It was written in the month of March, 1848, in the midst of a great pressure of business ; for in addition to his usual parliamentary duties, Lord George Bentinck was serving on two important committees—on the committee to inquire into the state of the sugar and coffee industries, and on that which was seeking to ascertain the causes of the prevailing commercial distress. The industry and zeal which he brought to his new avocations have never been exceeded by any man in Parliament. He attended his committee meetings, and went from them to the

House of Commons, where he remained till the close of the
sitting. "This was the period of his life," says Mr. Disraeli,
"when he was frequently in the habit of working eighteen
hours a day." According to the same authority, he had
made great progress towards acquiring the habit of living
without food, for he "breakfasted on dry toast," and "took
no sustenance" all day, or all night, until Parliament was up,
"dining at White's half-past two o'clock in the morning."

Lord George Bentinck to Mr. Croker.

Harcourt House, March 2nd, 1848.

My DEAR MR. CROKER,

I have been so busy, sitting long days, and six days a
week, on two committees, that I forgot to write to you.

You ask me of Disraeli's manner of speaking and effectiveness in debate? I will answer you by giving you my brother
Henry's observations on the various speakers in the House.
Henry is rather a cynical critic. He expressed himself greatly
disappointed with Sir Robert Peel and Lord John Russell,
and concluded by saying that Disraeli was the only man he
had heard who at all came up to his ideas of an orator.

His speeches this session have been first-rate. His last
speech, altogether burked in the *Times*, but .pretty well
given in the 'Post,' [was] admirable. He cuts Cobden to
ribbons; and Cobden writhes and quails under him just as
Peel did in 1846. And mark my words, spite of Lord
Stanley, Major Beresford, and Mr. Phillips and the *Herald*,
it will end before two sessions are out in Disraeli being the
chosen leader of the party; but I think it will not be under
Lord Stanley's banner, whether he turns his coat on the Jew
Bill or not.

The Budget has damned the Whig Government in the
country. The Bank Charter Act, to which they and Peel
have linked their political existence, has been smashed to
atoms in the Secret Committee by witnesses whose dicta will
pass for gospel with the commercial world. Railways have had
little or nothing to do with the monetary difficulties, which,
but for the restrictions of the Bank Charter Act, would have
passed by without observation, and certainly without a panic.
The Bank Charter Act restrains gold from going out of

the country. "Gold shall not go out, means food shall not come in." These are the words of the most striking witness I ever listened to; they were spoken by old Sam Gurney. Neither the Bank of England nor the railways are to blame, it was all the Act of 1844. Peel's Bank Charter Act "has done it all."

Nothing but the pitiful disunion of the Protectionist party could prevent the Whig Government and the entire Free-trade policy from being overthrown; the country are sick of both.*

Always most sincerely yours,

G. Bentinck.

At the end of the Session, Lord George Bentinck went to Welbeck, and set out one morning in September to walk to Thoresby, the second of the three famous "Dukeries" which comprise within their domains the scenes of Robin Hood's most popular exploits, and some of the grandest forest-trees and avenues now remaining in England. From Welbeck to Thoresby the path lies chiefly through glades of unrivalled beauty and verdure, shaded by oaks, beeches, and yews of unknown antiquity. So much sylvan beauty is scarcely to be found elsewhere in these islands. A walk such as this might well bring rest to the jaded mind; to Lord George Bentinck it brought everlasting rest. He was found lying face downwards upon the ground, quite dead; more than that no one has ever known. Some hours before, he had been seen leaning against a gate, with his head bent down. It was conjectured that he had at that time been struck with a fatal attack of heart disease; but all is mere conjecture. Thus brief and strange was the career of a man who, had he lived, would undoubtedly have made a great name in the political annals of his country.

* ["It was as much for the sake of trade and manufactures as of agriculture that they opposed free trade; and I remember that Lord George Bentinck said that the first who would wish again for protection would be the manufacturing interest of Great Britain."—*Letter of the Duke of Rutland to the ' Times,' March 29th,* 1883.]

General Correspondence of these and preceding Years — Death of Sir William Follett in 1845—His Early Success at the Bar—Great and Peculiar Reputation—His Politics—His Letter on his Illness—Correspondence between Mr. Croker, Lord Lyndhurst, and Sir James Graham — Letter from the Duke of Wellington on the Battle of Quatre Bras—Anecdotes of Mr. Pitt and Lord Grenville—Charges against Mr. Huskisson of Dabbling in the Funds—Lord Liverpool's Family and Character—Bishop Phillpotts on Forms of " Grace before Meat "—Lord Aberdeen on the Homeric Poems—Sir P. Francis and Junius—A Letter of Advice to Sir G. Sinclair—Pitt and the " Doctor " —Reminiscences of the Duke of Wellington—Division of Land into Small Holdings—Mr. Henry Drummond's Opinion—The Bishop of Oxford on the Conservative Leaders—" Blundering Feebleness and Dishonest Audacity "—Lord Lonsdale on French Affairs—Notes on Pope by Mr. Hallam and Samuel Rogers—The Duke of Wellington and French Politics—Proposed Statue to Lord George Bentinck—The Duke's Recollections of Lord Castlereagh—Letters from Mr. Charles Arbuthnot—And from Mr. Lockhart—Macaulay's History—Bishop Phillpotts' Criticisms—Remarks of the Duke of Rutland—M. Guizot on the Corn Laws—Letters from Mr. J. C. Herries—Lord Lonsdale and Arthur Young's Travels—Notes on Difficult Passages in Pope by Lord Mahon.

THE correspondence of these two years is of a very miscellaneous character,* and before entering upon it, it will be necessary to introduce a few letters relating to the general events of the three preceding years. The political letters

---

* There is a total and unaccountable absence of letters on political affairs.

from 1845 to 1847 are so important, that it seemed advisable
to break their sequence as little as possible, and therefore no
reference has yet been made to an event which was a great
affliction to Mr. Croker personally, and a loss to the whole
country—the death of Sir William Follett, Attorney-General
in the second Administration of Sir Robert Peel. He had
long been an intimate friend of Mr. Croker, and, in fact, was
Mrs. Croker's cousin. Moreover, he had married a ward of
Mr. Croker's, Miss Giffard, daughter of Sir Hardinge Giffard,
formerly Chief Justice of Ceylon, who had been at Dublin
University with Mr. Croker.* Sir William Follett was
Solicitor-General in Sir Robert Peel's first Administration, in
1835, and took the same post on Peel's return to office. He
afterwards became Attorney-General, and at the time of
his death, in 1845, he was only forty-seven. Few men have
ever risen to eminence at the bar at so early a period of
life, and few have been so universally popular, with the
public as well as with the profession. The *Times*,† in reviewing his career, remarked that he was " not only the most
eminent lawyer of the present day, but a man who had
acquired a much higher reputation than usually belongs even
to the first member of the bar. He had surpassed his contemporaries in so extraordinary a degree, that his merits,
power, and authority, as an adviser and an advocate, were
never estimated by ordinary rules, or rewarded in the proportion and manner of other men." The writer went on to
state that Follett had been a Whig at Cambridge, and only
adopted Tory principles as he grew older, but against this
passage Mr. Croker made the following memorandum :—

" I cannot say anything about Follett's politics at Cam-

* Sir Hardinge Giffard was a brother of Dr. Stanley Giffard, for some years
editor of the *Standard*, and father of the present Sir Hardinge Giffard.
† Monday, June 30th, 1845.

‚bridge, but I can say that from the moment he came to London, long before he was called to the bar, he was a Tory. He was domesticated in a great measure in my house. When he began to study the law, I made him a present of my law books, of which I had a tolerable collection. He made a very different use of them from what I could have done. I mention all this to show that he kept Tory company. But the story contradicts itself, and cannot be true, for he contested Exeter on Tory principles three years before he got into Parliament, and he actually came into Parliament and office in the overthrow of the Whigs in 1835."

Sir William Follett was only the second Attorney-General who had died while still in office. His health declined rapidly just as he was reaching the summit of his profession, and he was well aware some months before his death that his day was nearly done. Lady Follett survived him little more than two years.

Sir William Follett to Mr. Croker.

Park Street, May 31st, 1845.

DEAR MR. CROKER,

Dr. Chambers and Dr. Bennet, who both examined me very minutely on Monday, said that there was a substantial improvement in me, and that the complaint in the throat was much better. Dr. B., who sees me every day, says that I have been going on well since ; my own feelings, however, do not go along with this account. I feel much weaker, and the sensation of illness and depression increases rather than otherwise. I feel it difficult to look hopefully on the future ; but it is very possible that the long confinement and the remedies I am taking may produce these sensations, although in reality I may be substantially better.

Thanks for your offer of the Constantia.* I wish I could venture on it, but I cannot at present; at some future time, if I get well enough, I may, perhaps, ask you for some of it.

My kindest regards to Mrs. Croker. I am afraid I cannot

---

* [A Cape wine.]

ask her to come and see me now. I must venture to look forward to better times as the summer comes on.

And believe me, dear Mr. Croker,

Yours sincerely,

W. W. F.

Mr. Croker to Lord Lyndhurst.

West Moulsey, June 29th, 1845.

My dear Lyndhurst,

You will have heard that our dear Follett expired yesterday afternoon at five minutes after three. I was at his bedside for the last four hours, and it is a melancholy consolation that the transit was as easy as possible, so easy, indeed, that the moment was scarce perceptible. Till near two, he knew those around him, took occasional medicine or refreshment with his own hand, and desired one or two things to be done. From two, his state was a short-breathed but not unquiet sleep—or what appeared so—which passed gradually into a silent one. He certainly suffered nothing like pain, and that bright intellect was eclipsed in a gentle and gradual mist.

You know better than any other man what a public loss he is, and no one can express what a loss he is to us, his family and private friends.

It is a satisfaction to me, and I am sure it will be to you, that I was able to communicate your kindness and sympathy.

He was very sensible, as long as his mind was unclouded, to the anxiety of his friends. *Quando ullum inveniemus parem?*

Ever, my dear Lyndhurst,

Sincerely yours,

J. W. Croker.

Sir James Graham to Mr. Croker.

Netherby, September 18th, 1847.

My dear Croker,

I have read in the newspapers with great regret, but without surprise, the report of the death of Lady Follett. An event, so sad and so deeply affecting the welfare of the family of our departed friend, could not fail to excite in my mind many mingled emotions. I thought of poor Follett's fate, most fortunate in many respects, yet so solemn as a warning. I remembered that he had lived long enough for fame, that he had climbed the rugged path, that his success in Parliament was complete, that he had just touched the summit of his profession, and that he was called away to a better world while his friends, who lamented over him, were many, and his enemies were few.

You cannot forget the day when we followed him to his long home; and you, who know Tacitus so well, will agree with me in thinking, that what is said of Agricola may be justly applied in this case: "festinatæ mortis grande solatium tulit, evasisse postremum illud tempus; potest videri etiam beatus, incolumi dignitate, florente famâ, salvis affinitatibus et amicitiis, futura effugisse." * I cannot think of him without unavailing sorrow, except that the sad reflection is useful, "what shadows we are and what shadows we pursue"! The widow of such a man might well droop and wish to follow him. I had always understood that this was Lady Follett's feeling, and I could not wonder. Duty to her children might detain her here, but her heart was in her husband's grave. I do not remember to have read or heard of the sensation of instant death in its final struggle so vividly described as in the words, which you tell me were her last.† To her, with that last gasp, life's idle business is now over; and those two, who living were so united, in death will not be divided; and together, we hope, they will receive their great reward. It is fortunate that poverty is not added to the sorrows of their children: none ever owed more to their parents; and the sense of their obligation, early inculcated, will lead them, I trust, in the paths of virtue and of happiness.

I am, yours sincerely,

J. R. G. GRAHAM.

Mr. Croker to Sir J. Graham.

Alverbank, September 23rd, 1847.

MY DEAR GRAHAM,

Your excellent and affecting quotation from Tacitus induces me, in the same kindly spirit in which you wrote it, to remind

---

* [Tacitus, 'Agricola,' XLIV.] .
† [The letter here referred to is missing.]

you of a circumstance which I should be sorry that you had
not sometimes in your memory. It regards only you and me
and one other person. Do you recollect that in the autumn
of 1842 I met you at Drayton, and that you came into my
room one morning, and proposed to me to write an article
in the *Quarterly Review* against the Corn Law Association?
I told you that you had come *just too late*, for that I had only
the day before resigned my *Quarterly* pen. You pressed
upon me to undertake what you thought a public duty. Lockhart happened at the same time to write to request me to
suspend, at least, my resignation. I consented to the double
request, bargaining with Lockhart, as my price, that he was
to admit my intended Corn Law article, the *Quarterly* not
having yet taken any line on that subject. Towards the close
of 1845, the editor and proprietor of the *Review* summoned
me, as a man of honour, to keep the engagement, and to maintain the principle to which I had, in December 1842, pledged
the *Review*.

I could not but do so, more especially as it became more
and more strongly my own individual conviction, for I had
never looked closely into the matter till I did so in the
autumn of 1842; but I did so with reluctance, and was not
wanting in endeavours to avert the necessity. I hope you
will believe that in retracing this fact, I have no other object
or wish than to remind you, that I am not voluntarily
responsible for estrangements which I felt like losing a limb,
and shall deplore as long as I live. This, I need hardly
add, requires no answer, but think of it whenever you think
of me.

Ever very sincerely yours,

J. W. C.

The following letters bring the correspondence down to
1848. The first is an answer to a request from Mr. Croker
for information concerning a conversation alleged to have
taken place between M. Walewski and the Duke of Wellington on the battle of Quatre Bras.

The Duke of Wellington to Mr. Croker.

London, January 28th, 1845.

MY DEAR CROKER,

I received a letter from you two or three days ago, enclosing one from Mr. Tracey on a conversation in your presence between Count Walewski and me at the Grange, some years ago, in which I am stated to have talked of the battle of Quatre Bras. I have been at the Grange, and have met you there more than once, but I don't recollect to have met there the Comte de Walewski ; still less do I recollect conversing about the battle of Quatre Bras. I know that gentleman perfectly, and have met him elsewhere : in London, at Hatfield, &c. I knew his mother at Paris, and at Liège. But I don't recollect the supposed conversation about the battle of Quatre Bras ; and I don't think that I could have expressed myself as is supposed, because the statement is not consistent with the facts as I recollect them. I reached the field of Quatre Bras twice on the day in question, the first time at about ten o'clock in the morning, having quitted Bruxelles before daylight. I found there the Prince of Orange with a small body of Belgian troops, two or three battalions of infantry, a squadron of Belgian dragoons, and two or three pieces of cannon which had been at the Quatre Bras—the four roads—since the preceding evening.

It appeared that the picquet of this detachment had been touched by a French patrol, and there was some firing, but very little ; and of so little importance that, after seeing what was doing, I went on to the Prussian army, which I saw from the ground, was assembling upon the field of St. Amand and Ligny, about eight miles distant.

I reached the Prussian army ; was at their head-quarters ; stayed there a considerable time ; saw the army formed ; the commencement of the battle ; and returned to join my own army assembled and assembling at the Quatre Bras.

I arrived then at Quatre Bras a second time on that day, as well as I recollect, at about two or three o'clock in the afternoon.

The straggling fire there had continued from morning ; the Prince of Orange was with the line troops still in the same position. I was informed that the army was collecting in a wood in front. I rode forward and reconnoitred or examined their position according to my usual practice.

I saw clearly a very large body of men assembled, and a Maréchal reviewing them, according to their usual practice, preparatory to an attack.

I heard distinctly the usual cries : " En avant ! en avant ! L'Empereur récompensera celui qui s'avancera !

Before I quitted the Prince of Orange, some of the officers standing about had doubted whether we should be attacked at this point.

I sent to the Prince of Orange from the ground on which I was standing, to tell him that he might rely upon it that we should be attacked in five minutes, and that he had better order the retreat towards the main position of the light troops and guns which were in front, and which could make no resistance to the fierce attack about to be made upon us.

These were accordingly withdrawn, and in less than five minutes we were attacked by the whole French army under Maréchal Ney. There was in fact no delay nor cessation from attack from that time till night.

The reserves of the British army from Brussels had arrived at the Quatre Bras at this time ; and the corps of Brunswick troops from the head-quarters, and a division of Belgian troops from Nivelles, Braine, &c.

There were originally on the ground two corps of the French army, or forty thousand men.

But of these, at least one half moved off to their own right, that is, towards the left of the French army engaged with the Prussians, under the direction of the Emperor himself.

I saw this movement, but could not easily comprehend its meaning.

I was enabled from the first to defend our position.

We were receiving reinforcements constantly, and at last were stronger than the enemy.

These are the facts which I recollect. I could not have said that there was any delay or slackness in the French attack. It was as fierce as I ever witnessed.

Ever yours most sincerely,

WELLINGTON.

Mr. Charles Arbuthnot to Mr. Croker.

London, February 22nd, 1845.

MY DEAR CROKER,

· In Lord Malmesbury's house in Spring Gardens, Lord Dover afterwards lived. I dined with Lord Malmesbury in that house in November or December, 1803, where I met Mr. Pitt, and scarcely anybody else. That dinner remains in my memory from the circumstance of the great appre hension expressed by Mr. Pitt, lest Buonaparte should invade England in some dark night, we being then in a very defence-less state.

Great differences were perpetually occurring between Mr. Pitt and Lord Grenville. Lord Grenville did not approve of supplicating Prussia to take part in the war against France, at the expense of a large subsidy; and Mr. Dundas (Lord Melville) acted for a short time as the Secretary of State for foreign Affairs, and sent the instructions to Berlin. I re-member that Huskisson, then the Secretary to Mr. Dundas, drew up those instructions; Lord Grenville, in the meanwhile, going to sulk at Dropmore, from whence Lord Wellesley, as his old friend, went to bring him back. But he could not elicit a single word from Lord Grenville, and returned to London *re infectâ.*

The reading Lord Malmesbury's diary was very interesting to me, as at that time I knew all that passed.

Ever most sincerely yours,

CHARLES ARBUTHNOT.

*Mr. Croker to the Earl of Ripon.**

Wést Moulsey, February 25th, 1845.

MY DEAR RIPON,

I know not to whom I can address myself so properly as to you, on a point that affects the character of a common friend, who has left no personal representative that I could appeal to on such a subject. You have seen, no doubt, the passage in Lord Malmesbury's diary in which poor Huskisson is accused of gambling in the funds while he was in office. I am reviewing

* [The Earl of Ripon, it will be remembered, preceded Mr. Huskisson as President of the Board of Trade under Lord Liverpool's Administration.]

the work, and find this passage in a part which I am obliged
to notice. Is it possible to say anything about it ? *   I have
ascertained that Huskisson's personal property was *under*
60,000*l.*, and I know not that he had bought any land but
the estate of Eartham,† which was not, I believe, considerable.
I have also heard that his wife had a good fortune, and that
his old Jacobin uncle, Dr. Gem, left him a large sum of money.
With these helps, a man who had been near forty years in
high and lucrative office, might have left 60,000*l.* without
being suspected of dishonesty ; and he himself has often in
conversation complained to me how ill office and public life
had remunerated him. I should be glad, if I could, to say
something kind and respectful to his memory, and I *believe*
him wholly innocent, but my knowledge of the matter is so
very slight, that I fear I may do more harm than good if I
act on my own vague impressions. What think you ?

Ever, my dear Ripon,

Sincerely yours,

J. W. Croker.

Lord Ripon to Mr. Croker.

1, Carlton Gardens, February 28th, 1845.

My dear Croker,

I certainly have at times heard stories of our friend
Huskisson having dabbled in the funds ; but I never heard
upon what foundation these stories rested, nor to what period
of his life they referred ; and I have [not] had any reason to
give the slightest credit to them. I know that Mrs. Huskisson
was an heiress and had a very good fortune : and I have
always understood that Dr. Gem left Huskisson the bulk of
his property. In addition to this, it is to be recollected that
he had no children, that he was in office, with good salaries,
for a great number of years, and that he was (to my certain
knowledge) a very careful manager of his affairs. It is

[The subject referred to in these letters was not touched upon by
Mr. Croker in his review of the Malmesbury Diary—*Quarterly Review*,
No. 150, 1845.]

† [Eartham, in Sussex, six miles from Chichester. The estate once
belonged to William Hayley, a well known " patron " of arts and letters.
Mr. Huskisson is said to have added much to the house and estate.]

[not *] surprising, therefore, that he should have left the sum
which you mention.

Most truly yours,

RIPON.

The Earl of Liverpool † to Mr. Croker.

Pitchford Hall, December 7th, 1845.

MY DEAR CROKER,

I ought to apologise for not answering your letter sooner,
but it reached me just as I was leaving Sussex to come here.

My father has often told me that George III. and Lord
Bute differed upon some point; that they had a meeting in
Kew Gardens; that at that meeting the King urged Lord
Bute upon this point, and that the King then told him, "If
you do not carry this matter out as I wish, we must part."
Lord Bute did not acquiesce, and Lord Bute left his place;
that after that George III. never had any private communi-
cation with Lord Bute, either personally or by letter.

My father was, I am sure, never the channel of communication between Lord Bute and George III. after the fall of
Lord Bute.

I have no vanity about my family, but I know from Lord
Fitzwilliam that the Rockingham party, who hated my father,
put about stories of his low condition and low position,
which had to us, who really knew the facts, no sense whatever. Perhaps it may not be uninteresting to you if I state
some circumstances respecting the Jenkinson family, and in
doing so I shall answer your questions about the position my
father held with Lord Bute. My grandfather Col. Jenkinson,
commanded the Blues, and was remarked by George II. at
Dettingen. Some time after this my grandfather solicited
a pageship of honour for my uncle, John Jenkinson, the father
of the late Bishop of St. Davids. It was competed for by
some one else; and the Minister, probably the Duke of
Newcastle, was against Jenkinson; but the King, George II.,
said: "Col. Jenkinson's son shall have it. Col. Jenkinson is
a brave man." I should here observe that Col. Jenkinson's
father, Sir Robert Jenkinson, had all his life been Tory

---

* [The word "not" is omitted in two places from the original letter,
clearly by accident.]

† [Half-brother of the Prime Minister.]

Member for Oxfordshire, and that his elder brother was so at this time. My father, Col. Jenkinson's eldest son, was bred for the Church. He was first at the Charterhouse, and then at University College at Oxford, where he took his Master of Arts degree. A living belonging to his uncle, Sir Jonathan Cope, of Brewern, in Oxfordshire, was destined for my father, and was held, in my recollection, by a clergyman of the name of Lockwood, to whom it was given to hold for my father; but my father got connected when at Oxford with Charles Duke of Marlborough and the then Lord Macclesfield, adopted their politics (they were Whigs), and took an active part in the famous Oxford town election of Parker and Turner, who were Whigs, against Wenman and Dashwood, Tories. It is curious that my father wrote the electioneering verses and squibs for the Whigs at this election, and Sir W. Blackstone for the Tories. There are two copies of verses, each celebrating their rival colours (blue and green). Blackstone's are far the best, but my father's not amiss. All this matter made my father give up his clerical pursuits; and he must have published about this time one, if not both, his political pamphlets, viz., the one on a national militia, and the other on neutral rights. My father has often told me that he was sent up to London by the then Duke of Marlborough and Lord Macclesfield, before the death of George II., with a strong recommendation to Lord Holdernesse; that he was introduced at the Riding School to George III., then Prince of Wales, or, I believe, only called Prince George, by John Jenkinson, who, as I said before, was page of honour, and was a remarkably fine horseman. This was very shortly before George III.'s accession, when my father became confidential secretary of Lord Bute, if you can call secretary a man who all through his life was so bad a penman that he always dictated everything, and of whom, although I have a house full of papers, I have scarcely any in his own hand. The truth is he was highly esteemed and trusted by Lord Bute, as he was afterwards by Mr. Grenville, the Duke of Grafton, Lord North, &c.; but I do not believe, nay, I am certain, that he did not carry on any correspondence between the King and Lord Bute, for never such existed, although on many critical occasions the King consulted him privately, of which I have the proofs, though here again I really believe that it was with the approbation, or at least the acquiescence, of the Minister for the time being. I should also add that my father was in the service also—I think they called him Treasurer—of the Princess Dowager of Wales till her death. He was very much in her confidence.

Ever sincerely yours,

LIVERPOOL.

The Bishop of Exeter to Mr. Croker.*

Bishopstowe, Torquay, August 3rd, 1846.

MY DEAR SIR,

There is no accounting for fancies. When one of them gets possession, even of a very powerful mind, it commonly obtains complete mastery.

Your sensitiveness to the supposed danger of anything like change in the line of increased strictness in religious matters is a phenomenon, considering your intellectual eminence, which astonishes me. How is it possible that the addition of the words cited by you from Eph. v. 20 is always "heard by you with a certain degree of pain"? What say you of 1 Tim. iv. 4 in conjunction with Col. iii. 17? Why, you will find some small hole to creep out. Your objection about knives and forks is an objection to every form of saying grace, not to an apostolic form solely or mainly.

If the addition were indeed as novel as you imagine, I should have thought that you would rejoice in it, as a manifest indication of a more truly evangelical feeling than prevailed in our youth.

But the truth is, that the practice is not novel. More than forty years ago I became chaplain to Bishop Barrington, saying grace daily at his table, as well as my own ; and I am confident that I was during that time in the habit of saying a grace with St. Paul's conclusion.

My grace, indeed, was not the very meagre form which you say you always heard, and which I believe to have been the fruit of modern fastidiousness in its transition state—between saying grace and omitting it altogether.

I must possibly own that I never hear that brief form, or any other, unsanctified by the name of Christ, without the feeling which you say is excited in you by the adoption of the apostolic conclusion.

* [No communication from Mr. Croker explanatory of this letter is to be found.]

N 2

I entered at Oxford in 1791, and being in the habit of dining not only in the hall of my own college, but also in the halls of most other colleges in that University, I can vouch for the practice being universal (though the formularies of saying grace differed) of concluding always *per Jesum Christum Dominum nostrum.*

I am not sure that there is within my reach, certainly there is not within my easy reach, any clergyman considerably older than myself, who am in my sixty-ninth year :—I, therefore, do not delay my answer, in order that I may institute the enquiry which you wish, as to the experience of one of my reverend seniors.

I wish I differed from you on the other points mentioned by you, as I differ on this. When I think of politics, I turn from the subject as absolutely sickening, and a little feeling of (I fear uncharitable) satisfaction, that Sir R. Peel will never again have an opportunity of betraying (with however honest intention) the interests confided to him. Our Church is, I trust in God, safe. Our Establishment, I fear, is in danger.

Yours, my dear Sir,

Most faithfully,

H. EXETER.

The Earl of Aberdeen to Mr. Croker.

Haddo House, September 1st, 1846.

MY DEAR CROKER,

You may easily imagine that for some years I have thought very little of the text of Homer, or the productions of the Rhapsodists ; but I dare say you will also believe that it is not without pleasure that I return to such subjects.

I should have answered your letter sooner, but I had not a copy of the Life of Johnson at hand ; and before writing to you, I wished to see the passage to which you refer.

From the expressions of Johnson, it would appear that he thought the lines quoted by Thucydides were from the Iliad or Odyssey, in which case they certainly would not be found in any of our copies. But the quotation is from the hymn to Apollo. It is in the third book of his history, and in that part of it in which he gives an account of the extraordinary and barbarous proceeding, called by the Athenians the purification of Delos.

I need not observe to you that these hymns, which figure in the list of eighteen or twenty different works, attributed by the ancients to Homer, are universally admitted by modern critics to be spurious, and of a date long posterior to the Iliad and Odyssey.

It is remarkable that the most judicious of Greek historians should have quoted the hymn to Apollo without expressing any doubt of its authenticity, more especially as in the first book of his history there is great evidence of a real spirit of inquiry, and of something like the philosophical criticism of modern times. It is a proof of the manner in which the Greeks of every class blindly received the current reports and popular traditions of the country; although it may not be improbable that everything delivered in the name of Homer became in some degree connected with their religion, which, at Athens at least, could not safely be treated as it deserved.

The belief which you profess in your letter, so much at variance with my own opinions respecting the origin of the Homeric poems, offers a tempting opportunity for me to enlarge upon the subject; but I will refrain from doing so at present. I will only repeat, that continued reflection and inquiry have more fully convinced me that the views of the German critics upon this matter are correct, and that when we divest ourselves of the effects of early prejudice and habit, we shall find them to be entirely consistent with reason and common sense.

Believe me, my dear Croker,

Ever truly yours,

ABERDEEN.

Mr. C. W. Williams Wynn to Mr. Croker.

Grafton Street, February 11th, 1847.

MY DEAR CROKER,

I am sorry that I have not the means of at all enlightening you on the subject of your letter.

Lord Grenville always declared to me, as to others, that he knew nothing about Junius; that he had only conjectures, the grounds of which he did not intend to disclose. These, I think, were not founded on any papers at Stowe.

Lord Nugent believes that he has there found some which

throw light on the subject, but did not inform me what was the result.

The external evidence applying to Sir Philip Francis is so strong as would to my mind establish any other fact, and I should have but little difficulty in believing him equal to having produced it ; but what I cannot credit is that he whose most conspicuous characteristic was extreme vanity, accompanied by moral as well as personal courage, could for so many years have continued to conceal it.

I have not seen Dean Pellew's Life of Lord Sidmouth, but cannot believe that Lord Grenville held to him language so opposite to what he used to all his family.

I remain, dear Croker,

Ever most faithfully yours,

C. W. WILLIAMS WYNN.

*Mr. Croker to Sir George Sinclair.**

West Moulsey, Kingston, Surrey, February 27th, 1847.

MY DEAR SINCLAIR,

I have been very much touched with your interesting but painful account of yourself. You need no advice, I see, as to the true source of consolation ; but I think there are minor helps which you seem to neglect too much. You should join your family in Edinburgh, and mix with the morning and evening thoughts of the world to come, the daily duties, avocations, and even amusements of the world in which we live. This you will find indicated in the Lord's Prayer which, beginning with prayer and ending with praise, points out the intermediate course of worldly duties, in which it supplicates our Father to assist us. Leave then, my dear Sinclair, the hyperborean gloom of your castle near the pole, and follow Lady G. Sinclair to Edinburgh, where old and new friends will convince you that, as long as Heaven is pleased to leave us in this world, it provides us with the *pabulum vitæ*—something worth living for. I return you the inclosures of both your letters. I am ashamed to own that I look upon the gentlemen you mention as a knot of dreamers, and Mr. —— as something even beyond a visionary ; but as you, who know

---

* [Written in reply to a very melancholy and complaining letter.]

more of them (which, indeed, is very easy) than I do, think otherwise, I suppose I am wrong.

I agree with them that the times are out of joint, but they are not, I think, the more [the men ?] to reduce the dislocation.

Ever sincerely yours,

J. W. CROKER.

The Duke of Rutland to Mr. Croker.

Belvoir Castle, March 2nd, 1847.

MY DEAR CROKER,

Although I have in my mind's eye an accurate view of Mr. Pitt coming in during the second course, and rubbing his hands with delight at having escaped home to his company, yet my recollection of the accompaniments of the story which I told you is imperfect. I think it must have been late in the spring of the year after Mr. Pitt had placed Addington in his position as Prime Minister; Lady Hester Stanhope was at the head of his table on that day, and it was in Downing Street, at his official residence that he lived. He came joyfully in exclaiming, " I am delighted to have got amongst you, for we have had the doctor travelling with his own horses for the last hour and a half, and we thought he would never arrive at the end of the stage." In those days gentlemen's postilions used to drive with long whips and velvet caps with silver tassels to them, which played up and down in conformity with the measured and slow action of the postillions on their horses. And one can conceive Addington's pompous delivery, measured phraseology, and monotonous intonation, affording a . capital likeness of a gentleman's own horses during a long stage.

Ever, my dear Croker, yours most truly,

RUTLAND.

Mr. Henry Drummond to Mr. Croker.

April 23rd, 1847.

MY DEAR CROKER,

You are quite right about the unavoidable consequences of *morcellement.* The system of a people is a unity : when landlords were few and powerful, it was difficult to procure dwellings, and population did not advance beyond the

demand of agriculture, which alone could feed it; but so soon
as cotton lords grew, the population grew, and since there is
no check to the procreation of children, and their support
is thrown upon the land, infinitesimal *morcellement* is the
necessary result.

I have followed the allotment system here* ever since I
came, now nearly thirty years ago; every labourer on the
estate has as much land as he pleases, from ¼ to 5 acres or
more. As a practical thing it is good, like charity; but as a
national system it is again infinitesimal *morcellement.* I wish
you would come and spend a few days here that you might
examine it for yourself; it is as perfect a specimen both from
extent and variety as can be seen.

As for *realities,* they no longer exist in the world; all men
and things are become personæ, masks, shams or shapes as
Carlisle [Carlyle] calls them.

Always yours faithfully,
HENRY DRUMMOND.

The Bishop of Oxford (Wilberforce) to Mr. Croker.   Extract.

February 19th, 1848.

MY DEAR MR. CROKER,

I quite agree with you as to the prospect of affairs. But I
am far more dispirited by either the apathy, or want of intellectual power, or mad hostility of the Conservative party,
whichever it be, which leads them quietly to leave all our
interests in hands in which a blundering feebleness and a dishonest audacity are almost equally united, than by any one
other evil aspect of the times. Either they ought to restore
Peel, or to supply his place. But to let things go to ruin as
they now do is fatality.

S. OXON.

The Earl of Lonsdale to Mr. Croker.

[Without date.]

DEAR CROKER,

I shall see Mr. Hudson † to-morrow evening. I will ask
him the questions you put. He is in his bluff exterior the

* [At Albury in Surrey.]
† [The "Railway King"—then Member for Sunderland.]

most remarkable man I have ever known.   It is not fortune
that raises a man from a shop-boy to be a large landed proprietor, but he is also a most influential political character, and
[has] a most effective, common-sense sort of way of treating
questions in the House of Commons that enables him to carry
and defeat measures, and turns the scale of many elections.

I generally agree with you on political matters, but I cannot offer my adhesion to the last political article of the
*Quarterly,** from impressions made upon me, in my short
visits a few years since.   In my last visit I recollect a person,
in whom I had some confidence, telling me that the state of
corruption was so great, it endangered the reign of Louis
Philippe, that in no period was corruption of all descriptions
so flagrant.   But what I attribute blame to Guizot for is, that
though perfectly pure himself he took no decided and active
step himself to check the system.

I am quite at issue with you about Louis Philippe.   I
think he frittered away his crown, and lost it at the last
moment by cowardice; in fact, he thought of nothing else for
the last three years but marrying his family.   His attention
was directed to his family, and not to the State.

Faithfully yours,

LONSDALE.

Mr. Hallam to Mr. Croker.†

Cardiff, August 20th.

DEAR CROKER,

You will guess by the date of this that I have no means of
assisting your inquiry by help of books.   But I own that I
doubt whether we should not overshoot the mark in seeking
any deep allusion in Pope's couplet.   He is often obscure by
excessive effort at a pregnant brevity.   "Which made old
Ben," &c.,‡ I take to mean, which might have made, or was
enough to make, them swear the King has no more taste than
a bear.   If you choose to suppose that Dennis had really said

* [An article by Mr. Croker on the French Revolution of 1848,
Quarterly Review, March, 1848.]

† [Mr. Croker was still making notes for the proposed new edition of
Pope.]

‡ [See the next letter.]

something like this about William, it would be easy to apply
the same, by poetical analogy, to old Ben. I do not think
more can be made of it than this.

I passed three days with Guizot at Sir John Boileau's, near
Norwich, in the first week of August. He was then proceeding to St. Andrew's with all his family, and meant to pay
some visits in the Highlands.

The position of France is certainly a strange one; and it
seems as if no Government but that of the sword will be
practicable, at least for the present. It is impossible for
a regular monarchy to exercise this power, and therefore I do
not see how its restoration is to be looked for, though it may
be the wish of three-parts of France. The supremacy is
better in the hands of Cavaignac, whom Guizot thinks an
honest man, and who seems to be acting well, than of such
political intriguers as Thiers.

I am, yours truly,

H. HALLAM.

Samuel Rogers [*] *to Mr. Croker.*

St. James's Place, August 19th, 1848.

MY DEAR SIR,

Happy indeed should I be to throw any light on the
passage. I can, however, suggest an interpretation, and a
friend of mine, the Rev. Mr. Mitford, Gray's editor, concurs
with me in my reading.

What he says explains it so much better than I could do,
that I have enclosed it. You need not return it.

Yours sincerely,

S. ROGERS.

You and I have suffered a great loss this year in Lord
Ashburton.

[*Enclosure in the above.*]

The hero William and the martyr Charles,
    One knighted Blackmore, and one pensioned Quarles;
Which made old Ben and surly Dennis swear,
    "No Lord's anointed, but a Russian bear."

---

[*] [Then in his 85th year.]

Ben Jonson and Francis Quarles were contemporary, and I think had some dispute about patronage bestowed on one of them. Dennis and Blackmore were contemporaries also.

Both B. Jonson and Dennis were noted for their railing against an age, which they considered did not sufficiently value their talents, and preferred other writers to them. See B. Jonson's well-known lines on " The Stage."

When Charles pensioned Quarles, and William knighted Blackmore, Jonson and Dennis are supposed to say, in contempt of the royal patronage being bestowed on a couple of blockheads or dunces (as they esteemed them), while their own merits were overlooked: * " It is not an enlightened monarch on the throne, an Augustus—the judge and rewarder of genius, but one as ignorant and brutal as a Russian bear, a savage, a Czar."

The last line in inverted commas is not a quotation, but a speech. " Old Ben," I take it, uses the term Russian bear, without giving any further meaning to " Russian " than as the *natale solum* of the bears : but if we suppose " Russian " not to be without its meaning, then we must recollect that *Peter* himself was a gentleman compared to those who preceded him, as the one who nailed the Ambassador's hat on his head. The difficulty certainly would be increased by supposing the last line to be a quotation from Dennis. But I have his poems at home, and will look when I return.

J. M[ITFORD].

Mr. Croker to Samuel Rogers.

Alverbank, Gosport, August 21st, 1848.
MY DEAR SIR,

Thank you very much for your letter, and for Mr. Mitford's memorandum ; but the latter does not, to my mind, clear up the difficulty in any degree. It says only what we are all agreed upon, that Pope meant to represent Jonson and Dennis as dissatisfied at the patronage shown to Quarles and Blackmore, and that he (Pope) partook of their feelings ; but why he should have coupled a " dunce " like Dennis with Ben Jonson's opinion and his own—how Dennis and Ben could have " sworn " the *same* oath or made the *same* speech —why a " Russian bear " should be the type of ill-judging

* [" Dryden alone escaped his judging eye."]

patronage—and what antithesis the poet, generally so exact and even nice in his phrases, would see between the "Lord's anointed" and a "Russian bear," Mr. Mitford's observations do not explain, any more than how, or when, or where, Dennis and Jonson expressed any opinion at all on the subject. I myself have little doubt that Pope had distinct anecdotes, or passages, of Jonson and Dennis in his eye, and when we can discover them we shall see how he came to combine them into one oath. Alas! my dear Sir, we have, in common with all his friends and the country, suffered an irreparable loss in dear Lord Ashburton. I had the melancholy satisfaction of having passed his last week with him. *His* departure was sudden and surprising. *She* is here near me, and as well as could be expected.

Yours sincerely,

J. W. CROKER.

The Duke of Wellington to Mr. Croker.

Walmer Castle, October 19th, 1848.

MY DEAR CROKER,

When I passed through London on Tuesday I signed my name on the engraving which I had kept for you, and gave it to the artist whom I employ to frame and glaze my engravings; and it shall be sent to you as soon as he will return it framed and glazed.

It is difficult to see what will happen in France. This single Chamber will be a despotism; if they can only get an officer of some reputation to command their army, they will govern France with a rod of iron. They will probably not leave in the hands of the officer in command sufficient power to enable him to do all that they will require from him.

It is impossible to conjecture what will be the result of the existing chaos in the world. It must first explode a little. But I see no man anywhere capable of conducting any great affairs, or even of understanding the position in which he is placed.

I can't tell what Lord Palmerston has done; but nobody is satisfied with or has confidence in him. Everybody complains of him. I believe that he and Lord Minto encouraged the foolish Pope; and that the mischief in Italy, which has caused the whole, was done by them. I detest this French Convention. But I confess that I should be sorry to see it broken off under existing circumstances.

I perfectly recollect my views for the defence and security of Ireland. But one might as well propose to recommence to build there the Tower of Babel as to act upon such a system. Everything of that kind is out of the question.

Believe me, ever yours most sincerely,

WELLINGTON.

The Earl of Hardwicke to Mr. Croker.

Wimpole, October 28th, 1848.

MY DEAR CROKER,

D'Israeli thinks with you that Wyatt is an impudent charlatan, and he takes no part with him.

Stanley, D'Israeli, and I are agreed on the question of a statue to G. B. [Lord George Bentinck].

As to his deserving so great an honour, we need not discuss it; but if the merchants, farmers, shop-owners, and ship-owners meet for the purpose of raising funds, and the meeting be brought about by spontaneous feelings on their part, not being urged on by G. B.'s friends or political followers, why then we will give our *mite* towards carrying out *their plans*, and show ourselves desirous to go with them in honouring the departed senator.

Ever most affectionately yours,

HARDWICKE.

Mr. Charles Arbuthnot to Mr. Croker.

Woodford, Kettering, December 7th, 1848.

MY DEAR CROKER,

That I had the greatest regard and affection for my departed friend Lord Castlereagh is most true. But I have not read his brother's memoirs * of him, though I happened to see the two first volumes; but I did no more than just look at them.

Had I read the work, many things might have occurred to me; but, on the spur of the moment, I can only say that

* [Correspondence, Dispatches, and other papers of Viscount Castlereagh," edited by his brother, C. W. Vane, Marquis of Londonderry, 12 vols. 1848–50.]

in private life his kindness and good temper were exemplary and never failing, and that in his public capacity truth and honesty of purpose were at all times his invariable characteristics, his colleagues well knowing that on him the most perfect reliance might be placed, as he had no other feeling than to act cordially with them, his mind being totally free from all sinister and selfish feelings.

Of this I can give one striking instance. Lord Liverpool was the Prime Minister, but he was not a favourite of George IV. His Majesty always preferred having confidential communications with Lord Castlereagh, in which Lord Liverpool not only acquiesced, but was also glad that his colleague should relieve him from personal discussions with the sovereign, which were ever painful and distressing.

This was particularly the case about the time that the King went to Hanover and took Lord Castlereagh with him.

On their return Lord Castlereagh said to me that he wished I would tell Lord Liverpool that he had been able, when at Hanover, to remove from the King's mind the erroneous impressions which had been in it; that now he must press upon Lord Liverpool the propriety of his always communicating freely and openly with his Majesty; that he certainly had never used his influence with the King but for the purpose of putting them well together; but that this being effected, he must entreat and urge Lord Liverpool to do his own business, and never to trust any one to do it for him, adding that, as Prime Minister, Lord Liverpool should never run the risk of allowing any one to gain influence which he ought to possess himself.

Upon one occasion, after the death of his first wife, Lord Liverpool begged that I would see Lord Castlereagh and let him know that, after the close of the session, he was resolved to retire, and that, considering him as the proper person in their Cabinet to succeed him, he wished to have a communication with him upon the subject. He named the day when Lord Castlereagh should call on him, in order that they might talk the whole thing over, and fix the particular time when the change should take place.

Lord Castlereagh desired that I would be in my room, as, after seeing Lord Liverpool, he should wish to see and talk with me. They had their meeting, after which Lord Castlereagh came to me as he had said he would. He asked me to go with him into St. James's Park that he might tell me what had passed, and that he might discuss with me the various arrangements to be made.

He first asked me whether I thought that the Duke of Wellington would consent to be Lord Liverpool's successor, as under him he would most willingly and cordially serve.

I answered that, to the best of my belief, it had never occurred to the Duke to wish to be the Minister of the country, his object ever appearing to be to adhere to his own profession.

Lord Castlereagh then told me what his arrangements would be on the retirement of Lord Liverpool, and that there was but one difficulty that he apprehended, and that difficulty was the Church. 'He feared that at first there might be apprehension of his leaning towards the Presbyterians, but that, if he had only time, he thought that his conduct would be seen to be most fair, as the Church should always have all the support and aid in his power to give.

Our conversation ended, each of us feeling certain that Lord Liverpool would retire, he having told Lord Castlereagh, as he had previously told me, that the state of his health made his retirement necessary.

But not only did he not act upon his then declared determination, but never afterwards did he allude to it.

This, however, had not the slightest effect upon the conduct of Lord Castlereagh. He had never sought to be Prime Minister; his ambition ever was to act with his colleagues most fairly and cordially, and Lord Liverpool, choosing to remain as Prime Minister, to give him all the support and aid in his power.

You know that in 1814 he went to the Continent to reside at the headquarters of the allies, and to be ready to act as negotiator for peace should the occasion offer. It did offer at Châtillon, but there failed. He returned to the headquarters of the allies, where he was the chief instrument in prevailing upon them, after some disaster, not to fall back upon the Rhine, as had been almost resolved upon. One day at dinner, where were the Emperor Alexander, the chief among the generals, and various Prime Ministers, it was observed by some one that the only person without order or decoration was Lord Castlereagh, on which Prince Metternich exclaimed, "C'est bien distingué!" And in truth absence of all vanity and perfect simplicity of mind always characterised him.

In debate the language of Lord Castlereagh was not always

equal to his other great qualities, but occasionally he very much surpassed what the House expected from him. One instance I well remember; it was on the last day nearly of the session previous to the trial of Queen Caroline.

Brougham unexpectedly rose and made a furious philippic against Sir Charles Stewart, the brother of Lord Castlereagh, and our ambassador at Vienna, accusing him of employing spies to ferret out and to fabricate stories against the Queen. Lord Castlereagh instantaneously refuted all the charges against his brother, and answered Brougham's speech in the most powerful and eloquent language.

I was sitting next to Canning. He said to me that he had never heard Lord Castlereagh speak half so well; that he could not by any possibility know that his brother would be attacked; but that on all occasions when quite unprepared he spoke brilliantly, and in a style far superior to his general speaking, whereas he must own, for his part, that he liked to know beforehand what he would have to speak upon.

Ever affectionately yours,

CH. ARBUTHNOT.

Mr. Lockhart to Mr. Croker.　Extract.

January 12th, 1849.

If you could do it * pure justice, nothing more is wanted to give the author sufficient pain. He has written some very brilliant essays—very transparent in artifice, and I suspect not over honest in scope and management, but he has written *no history;* and he has, I believe, committed himself ingeniously in two or three points, which, fitly exposed, would confound him a good deal, and check his breeze from El Dorado. Chiefly, his bitter hatred of the Church of England all through is evident; it is, I think, the only very strong feeling in the book; and his depreciation of the station and character of the clergy of Charles II. and James II. to-day is but a symptom.

Then his treatment of the Whig criminals Sidney and Russell, is very shabby, and might be awfully shown up by merely a few quotations from the State trials and Barillon.

---

* [Macaulay's 'History of England.' The two first volumes had then been recently published.]

You will tell me by-and-bye what you think of this. I own that I read the book with breathless interest, in spite of occasional indignations, but I am now reading Grote's new volume of his ' History of Greece,' and, upon my word, I find the contrast of his calm, stately, tranquil narrative very soothing. In short, I doubt if Macaulay's book will go down as a standard addition to our *historical* library, though it must always keep a high place among the specimens of English rhetoric.

Ever yours,

J. G. L.

The Bishop of Exeter to Mr. Croker.

Bishopstowe, April 13th, 1849.

My dear Sir,

I have been very tardy in writing to you; but I have had much of special business, which could not be easily laid aside. Moreover, I was not satisfied with one reading of your article.

The repetition has more than doubled my gratification, and my sense of the effectiveness of your chastisement.*

The great point of all is that you have decidedly fixed Mr. Macaulay's position in the literary republic. He is a great—a very great—historical novelist, and can never more be regarded in the severe character of an historian.

In connection with this matter, I may tell you *confidentially* that one of my great inducements to communicate with Sir J. Stephen, and, at his request, with Mr. Macaulay, was that Sir James told me that *he* had undertaken to review the work in the *Edinburgh*. I therefore fully hoped that between the author, whose " eagerness to be set right if he had in anything fallen into error " was strongly—most strongly—and repeatedly vouched, and the friendly reviewer, who would be eager to get his client easily through any little difficulty in which he might be involved, I should obtain for the Church some important admissions. That I failed with the principal,

---

* [Referring to an article on Macaulay's ' History of England ' by Mr. Croker in the *Quarterly Review* (vol. lxxxiv., March, 1849). In this article Mr. Croker insisted that Macaulay's work must be regarded chiefly as an historical romance. He declared that the book would " never be quoted as authority on any question or point of the history of England."]

and how completely I failed, I need not again tell you. But I have not yet told you that I failed with his second, nor the reason. This is a curious little anecdote of an *Edinburgh* reviewer.

Sir James, to my astonishment, two or three weeks after our first conversation, told me that he had abandoned all intention of reviewing the book, because it was, in truth, not what it professed to be—a history, but an historical novel.

Now, you will see the fitness of not recollecting that I ever told you this coincidence of opinion avowed by his intending panegyrist with that of his actual flagellant.

Will he correct his misstatements respecting the Church? No; he is too small-minded, and his ambition is of too low an order. If he does not, I hope that Harington* will punish him more sharply than he has yet had spirit to do, for the excellent Chancellor has a spice of cowardice in his composition.

But for your review. Where all is so good, it is not easy to specify what seems best; yet there are two or three particulars which I specially delight in.

First, your rubbing off the varnish which Macaulay had so shamefully thrown over Cromwell. What you say of the necessity of the murder of Charles, and afterwards of Louis, to consolidate the parties respectively by the bond of a common crime of the highest malignity, is a truth which cannot be too deeply fixed in the minds of Englishmen.

The Liberal Committee for building and decorating the Houses of Parliament thought fit to insult their loyal and honest countrymen, be they few or many, by placing a statue of the arch-regicide among the monuments of our national gratitude to departed merit. The people of St. Ives are, I see, about to collect a subscription for another monument to him in his native place. Your little caution is well timed, but may be less successful than it ought to be in checking the rage of Liberalism in this its most extravagant act of foolery.

Your exposure of William's faithless conduct to his father-in-law, so far as the *wish* for his throne and long ruminating over his chances can be called conduct, was another of my favourite bits.

Of the minor matters, your setting in its true light the

---

* [The Rev. E. C. Harington, Chancellor of the Diocese of Exeter.]

self-devotion of the Bridgewater heroine in her visit to the Royalist camp is perfect.

I am called away; farewell. I shall be anxious to hear how the world is affected by the dose of truth which you have administered in a manner as taking as is the falsehood which you correct.

Yours most faithfully,

H. EXETER.

The Duke of Rutland to Mr. Croker.

11, Dover Street, May 7th, 1849.

MY DEAR CROKER,

We have, indeed, been long without any communication with or sight of each other, much longer I assure you than is satisfactory or agreeable to my feelings. I look back to the quiet days which we passed together at the Woodhouse with unmingled pleasure, and with regret only at their having been so fleeting. I have been out of health almost ever since that time, and I am even now under the medical hands.

I read with much interest your review of Macaulay's book. I cannot deny that I read the book itself with much amusement and gratification. But there are very many parts of it which I could not read without pain, and for the very reason which you give in the criticisms you have made upon it. Of course I have heard Mr. Macaulay's friends very abusive of your review. I fear that I cannot give you much information, but if I can pick up any from more experienced persons than myself I will do so. I can remember Madame Recamier reclined in her bed, receiving her morning visitors while in it, with pillow-cases edged with lace, and a whole sheet of mirror at her head, in which she could see herself and be seen.

I have a miniature by Cosway of a famous lady of the year 1798, in bed, and if you will call upon me some day when you are in London, I will show it to you. The pillow in that case is of large dimensions, and I apprehend that for night use they were large, and were replaced by small ones for *show* during the day.

Ever, my dear Croker,

Yours most truly,

RUTLAND.

o 2

Mr. Croker to M. Guizot.*

West Moulsey, Surrey, June 11th, 1849.

MY DEAR SIR,

I have to-day received a letter from a friend, telling me that at the great agricultural meeting, held the day before yesterday at Gloucester, Lord Ducie, in a speech against the protective object of the meeting, quoted you as having told him that " you considered our Corn Laws as a *monster* grievance, and that if we had not got rid of them, we should have been in the same anarchy as the rest of Europe," and my friend asks me if this be possible. It seems to me very improbable, seeing that you had and have in France laws on the same principle, of which the only complaint I ever heard of in France was from some agriculturists, that they were not protective enough. But I should not have troubled you with this inquiry about it, to gratify my country friend's curiosity, but I have another reason; in reviewing the state of France and England, I have had occasion to take your essay on 'Democracy' for my text,† and to quote, with the applause it deserves, your defence and explanation of the superiority of the landed interest as a basis of government, and of the natural feeling that all mankind seem to have for that species of property. Now it is quite true that one may be of opinion that land is the most solid species of property and yet that it requires no protection ; but with our English feelings, such an opinion would appear somewhat inconsistent, and would require a long explanation which I could not give; and I should be afraid of so much as quoting the passage if we were to be liable to have Lord Ducie's report of your opinion confirmed. If you have given that opinion, I shall either not quote the passage or add some explanation; and therefore I ask you to tell me, in one word, *oui ou non*, Did Lord Ducie express the substance of your opinion? I hope not for another reason—it is this, that, be assured *your* political party has no sympathy in England but from the Protectionists, who are

---

* [M. Guizot was living in London at this time, and corresponded frequently with Mr. Croker, each in his own language as a rule, although sometimes Mr. Croker wrote in French. The letters generally related to some book or article on which M. Guizot was engaged. He became an occasional contributor to the *Quarterly Review.*]

† [*Quarterly Review*, vol. lxxxv., No. 169.]

the real Conservatives. There are a few men like Aberdeen,
who from confidence in Peel, or some private reasoning in
their own mind, are at once Free Traders and Conservatives;
but they are a very small party, and the general rule is as I
tell you, all Free Traders are not Democrats; but there is no
Democrat who is not a Free Trader.

Ever yours,

J. W. CROKER.

M. Guizot to Mr. Croker.

Brompton, 13 juin 1849.

MON CHER AMI,

Je n'ai jamais dit à personne que les *Corn Laws* fussent
a monster grievance. Je ne l'ai jamais dit, parce que je ne l'ai
jamais pensé. J'ai plus d'une fois, depuis quinze mois, en-
tendu dire à des conservateurs anglais très décidés, et j'ai
reconnu et dit moi-même, qu'au milieu de l'explosion révolutionnaire de l'Europe, il étoit heureux pour l'Angleterre que
toute question irritante, tout prétexte populaire de révolution,
eussent été supprimés dans son sein, et que l'abolition des
Corn Laws avoit eu cet avantage-là. C'est là ce qui a pu
devenir le texte des commentaires dont vous parle votre
correspondant du Gloucestershire. Mais vous n'avez pas
besoin que je vous explique comment on peut dire aujourd'hui cela, et être cependant profondément convaincu,
comme je le suis de plus en plus, que le *landed interest, landed
influence,* est le fond même de la société, la source de sa
grandeur comme de sa sécurité, de sa moralité comme de sa
force, et qu'il faut maintenir, soigner, protéger les intérêts
agricoles, les influences agricoles, si on veut protéger et
maintenir *efficacement* la société elle-même. Bien loin, donc, de
rien retrancher aux paroles que j'ai dites à ce sujet dans ma
Démocratie en France, j'y ajouterois plutôt si j'en parlois de
nouveau, et je vous prie formellement de citer ces paroles en
les donnant comme l'expression de ma bien réelle et ferme
opinion. La question du *free trade,* soit sous le point de vue
économique, soit sous le point de vue de l'organisation politique de la société, est trop compliquée pour que j'essaye
seulement de vous dire aujourd'hui ce que j'en pense. Mais,
tenez pour certain que mes idées à ce sujet n'altèrent en rien
ma conviction générale et dominante, que la propriété foncière

est, et doit rester, la base première de la société et de sa constitution, si on veut que la société et sa constitution subsistent elles-mêmes.

J'ajoute que, plus d'une fois depuis que je suis ici, j'ai soutenu la sagesse et l'utilité de notre loi française sur les céréales. J'ai dit qu'elle étoit populaire en France, et que c'étoit là un des bons résultats de cette grande division de la propriété foncière qui donnoit, à notre peuple des campagnes, les mêmes intérêts, les mêmes sentimens à cet égard, qu'aux grands propriétaires eux-mêmes.

Vous pouvez donc, en parlant de ma *Démocratie en France*, maintenir, sur ce point, tout ce que vous étiez disposé à en dire, et je vous en remercie d'avance. Vous le ferez, j'en suis sûr, avec la réserve convenable, et de manière à ne point m'engager personnellement dans des querelles de partis, ou de personnes, auxquelles je désire et je dois rester étranger. Vous le pensez certainement comme moi.

Je regrette bien de ne pas vous avoir vu depuis quelque tems. J'aurois eu bien des lettres à vous montrer et bien des choses à vous dire.

Tout à vous, my dear Sir,

Guizot.

M. Guizot to Mr. Croker.

Val Richer (par Lisieux, Calvados), 28 juillet 1849.

Mon cher Ami,

Je suis rétabli chez moi. Au moment même où j'ai remis le pied en France, j'ai reconnu que ni la situation générale, ni ma propre situation n'étoient, au fond, changées. Ni les honnêtes gens, ni les drôles ne m'ont oublié. Les honnêtes gens selon leur coutume, se sont levés plus tard que les drôles Pendant que je dînois au Havre, il s'est formé, sous les fenêtres de mon auberge, un rassemblement de 50 ou 60 gamins, entourés de 50 ou 60 curieux ou curieuses, sifflant et criant : *à bas Guizot.* J'ai dîné fort tranquillement, et quand je suis descendu dans la rue pour retourner à la maison où je devois coucher, j'ai trouvé autour de ma voiture une vingtaine de *gentlemen* qui écartoient assez rudement les gamins. Ils m'ont entouré, m'ont serré la main, et l'un d'eux m'a dit avec effusion : " M. Guizot, nous serions désolés que vous prissiez les cris de quelques polissons, ameutés par quelques coquins, pour les sentimens de la population de notre ville ; nous vous respectons tous ; nous sommes tous charmés de vous voir de retour," et autres paroles qui portoient l'empreinte d'une bonne politique très prononcée.   Je les ai remerciés et je suis rentré chez moi.   Une demi-heure après, j'ai vu arriver une députation de ces mêmes *gentlemen,* le commandant de la garde nationale du Havre, le capitaine des sapeurs pompiers, et deux ou trois négocians, officiers de police municipale, etc., qui venoient me renouveler leurs excuses et leurs protestations de bon vouloir et de respect.   Le lendemain matin, je me suis embarqué, pour passer du Havre à Honfleur, au milieu d'une foule silencieuse et respectueuse.   Je n'ai trouvé sur le bateau que des personnes bienveillantes.   On a parlé du tapage de la veille.   J'ai dit que j'avois rencontré au Havre des gamins et des amis.   "C'est comme partout, Monsieur," m'a dit un homme de fort bonne mine ; "mais soyez sûr qu'ici les amis dominent."   En débarquant à Honfleur, plus de partage ; j'ai été également bien accueilli par les *gentlemen* dans le salon de l'auberge où je me suis arrêté un quart d'heure, et par la foule dans la rue.   On a même un peu crié : *Vive Guizot.*   Et depuis que je suis ici, on s'empresse très amicalement chez moi, des environs et de Paris.

Ce petit incident de mon arrivée n'avoit pas, en soi, la moindre gravité.   Mais c'est un symptôme exact de l'état du pays et de mon état dans mon pays.   Toujours la lutte des vestes contre les habits, des casquettes contre les chapeaux, des mauvais sujets contre les honnêtes gens, de la multitude, folle ou perverse, contre les classes aisées et bien établies. Et quoique étranger depuis près de 17 mois, aux batailles quotidiennes, je suis encore, dans cette lutte, pour les uns et pour les autres, ce que j'étois il y a dix-sept mois, un drapeau qu'on attaque ou qu'on défend, avec ardeur.   Je ne m'en plains point.   Quoiqu'il doive arriver un jour, cela me convient aujourd'hui.   En attendant, je resterai fort tranquille dans mon nid, disant mon avis quand je le croirai utile pour mon pays ou convenable pour moi-même, et ne me mêlant activement de rien tant que je n'y serai pas hautement et forcément appelé, si je dois jamais l'être encore, par un sentiment public très clair et par l'espoir d'un succès sérieux.

Pour le moment, tous les partis sont stationnaires.   Le Président seul gagne du terrain.   Phénomène singulier !   Il avance sans grandir.   Et il avance sans qu'on sache vers quel but, car personne ne sait s'il veut réellement devenir

Empereur. Est-il plus modeste qu'ambitieux ou plus ambitieux que modeste ? C'est une question qui se débat auprès
de · lui comme loin de lui. Il est réservé, taciturne, décidé
dans ses actes, sournois dans ses manières et son langage, un
vrai Hollandais. D'autres disent un prince allemand sensé
et dépaysé. Qu'il le veuille ou non, je ne crois pas qu'il reste
où il est et comme il est. Il faudra qu'il monte, comme s'il
étoit grand.

Adieu, mon cher ami. Donnez-moi de vos nouvelles.
Est-ce qu'il n'y a vraiment pas moyen d'avoir, dans le *Quarterly Review*, un article sur les deux premiers volumes de
Madame de Maintenon du duc de Noailles ? Il le désire bien
vivement. Les derniers volumes tarderont peut-être beaucoup à paroître, et les premiers ont en France un vrai succès.
On en publie la seconde édition. Laissez-vous ébranler dans
votre rigorisme. Je m'occuperai bientôt de l'article que j'ai
promis à M. Murray sur Cromwell et Carlyle. Je veux
rester fidèle au *Quarterly Review*, et ce sujet me plaît.
Faites, je vous prie, mes complimens à Mr. Murray. Pré-
sentez mes respects à Madame Croker et à Lady Barrow, et
croyez-moi bien sincèrement tout à vous.

GUIZOT.

Right Hon. J. C. Herries to Mr. Croker.

July 6th, 1849.

MY DEAR CROKER,

It would seem as if I had always a scrap ready for you.
I enclose one which will show, as late as the year 1846,
the number of servants (taxed as domestic in-door) kept in
Great Britain, divided into classes, and the number of persons
keeping them.

You will not fail to remark how few the persons are who
keep (what appears to be a very general scale of establishment, viz.) four men-servants, in the upper classes—only
1785 persons in Great Britain ! The whole number of
persons keeping four *and upwards* is only 4437.

This is a good illustration of the error into which all men
are disposed to fall in estimating the numbers of the wealthy
classes as compared with the middle and lower orders, and
the absurdity of their expectations of deriving large national
resources from graduated taxation.

Truly yours,
J. C. HERRIES.

I doubt whether you would get the names of the persons keeping the highest number of servants. You will see that there are sixty-eight who keep ten. I am more surprised by the number who keep eleven and upwards than by any other part of the return. I think it may be an error. The number of servants kept by those who pay the highest duty (beyond which there is no scale) is, no doubt, correct: but the division of that number by eleven is obviously liable to objection. Some may keep fifteen, some twenty servants.

September 2nd, 1849.

MY DEAR CROKER,

With reference to our party proceedings (about which you and I are of the same opinion in the main), I hope you are aware that I have steadfastly declined, in opposition to the application and remonstrance made to me from the highest quarter, to undertake any responsibility as a leader in the House of Commons; while I, at the same time, asserted my perfect freedom from any obligation to follow the lead of any other individual in *our House.*

You and Lockhart must not abandon the good cause, and the very large party well disposed, for the most part, to support it honestly. We may yet achieve much good, or at least, avert much evil.

Yours truly,
J. C. HERRIES.

The Earl of Lonsdale to Mr. Croker.

Lowther, September 4th, 1849.

DEAR CROKER,

I am a *worshipper* of Arthur Young's, and from me you will hear only his praises. I think him the most truthful writer and fuller of information upon any subject than any other author. In his 150 volumes that he wrote and edited, like Shakespeare, and *another book,** you find everything, or something *à propos* to every subject. He is the only man of eminence of my time that I unfortunately was not acquainted with; I did not then appreciate his merits. Since I have turned my attention to agriculture, I look upon him as the

---

* [Meaning, perhaps, the Bible.]

real source of information upon all matters ; his correctness, his accuracy, has never been impugned. I have a duplicate of his works, one at Lowther and another in London, and some odd ones both at Barnes and Whitehaven. His agricultural tours in France and Italy I consider the only works that give an intelligible account of those countries.

His tour in Ireland has given me the idea that his views of Ireland were nearer the truth than any other work. When I received your letter yesterday, I was just starting to make a journey with Mr. Parker to look at some land that he had recommended in his northern tour seventy years ago to be cultivated, and drained, and which is now in the same state as it was at the time he wrote. We found it as he described it ; no one but an enthusiast in agriculture would have made such researches or taken such trouble at that time. We determined to-day to set about executing what he recommended seventy years ago. Mr. Parker tells me his accuracy and correctness as to all statements of prices and of all things of his day are respected and considered as matters of fact by all the leading agriculturists. I have read everything as regards agriculture, from Xenophon and Virgil, to Mechi and Huxtable. There is everything in Arthur Young, and I believe that a good farmer in those days knew quite as much as the writers and farmers or men of *science* of the present day. There is a great parade made upon systems of management, and the growth of various vegetables, but there is not one in which Arthur Young has not noticed the experiments of his own day or those of others. In the present day there are more good farmers, and measures are carried out better. Implements are better made ; but it seems to me, there is nothing Arthur Young did not know. He did not pretend or affect any knowledge of chemistry, and I have yet to be persuaded that any discovery has been made for general practical use. There are volumes of dissertations and many artificial manures, but as far as my experience goes, they are dear at the money. His ' Farmer's Calendar,' which is for the management [of a farm] advising what to do each month by month, is the standard book of all farmers at present, and has gone through many editions. I have three different editions of it.

He was spoilt by the success of his early works, and became a bookmaker, and in all his histories of the agriculture of the different counties he occupies twenty pages at a time in the description of the pictures. statues, architecture of different gentlemen's seats to fill up the volume. He obtained an immediate gain, but his general reputation ceased.

Faithfully yours,

LONSDALE.

Lord Mahon to Mr. Croker.

Oakley Park, Scole, December 26th, 1849.

MY DEAR MR. CROKER,

I am well acquainted with the lines you mention and have got them in my collection of *Chesterfieldiana*, although my version, which is as follows, differs, as you will see, a little from yours :—

> "Say, lovely traitor, where's the jest
> Of wearing Orange on thy breast,
> While that breast upheaving, shows
> The whiteness of the rebel rose?"

But I am not able to say where, if anywhere, they are to be found in print.

You have some hard nuts before you to crack in your edition of Pope. I have never found any one, even amongst those best read in the days of Anne and the two first Georges, able to explain who or what is meant in the passage beginning—

> "And pray how did the florid youth,"

and ending—

> "Where not his lust offended, but his pride."

Believe me, ever yours sincerely,

MAHON.

Grosvenor Place, December 31st, 1849.

MY DEAR MR. CROKER,

I must beg leave to intrude upon you with a few lines in explanation of my former note, since, writing as I did from memory in a country house, where there are very few books, I find that I have blended two passages into one and mentioned two "nuts to be cracked" instead of one as I intended.

The passage as to the "florid youth" seems, to me at least,

a puzzling one, for I am not acquainted with the anecdote to which it may relate.

But much greater is the difficulty of the other passage, beginning, " What pushed poor Ellis," and ending, " not his pride." I have found the men most conversant with our literature and history, as Mr. Hallam, when these lines happened to be mentioned, not at all able to explain them. If, therefore, you should in your new edition [of Pope] have discovered and show forth the key it will do you great credit.

I ask your pardon for the trouble of this second letter, which is caused by the foolish slip of memory in my first, but which, at least, need not put you to the further trouble of any reply ; and I remain,

Very sincerely yours,

MAHON.

(207)

CHAPTER XXVII.

1850–1851.

AFTER the French Revolution of 1848, the exiled King,
Louis Philippe, took up his residence at Claremont, where
Mr. Croker occasionally visited him, and where they conversed much together on the events which brought about
the expulsion of the Royal family. In the *Quarterly Review*
for March, 1850, there appeared an article by Mr. Croker
relating all the incidents of the King's escape from France,
and to this article Louis Philippe contributed several passages,

" which are not," as Mr. Croker afterwards wrote, " in point of Anglicism, distinguishable from the rest." It was partly his facility in the use of English that enabled him to effect his escape as " Mr. Smith," for on his way to the steamer he conversed so freely with his English companions that the French officials who were on the watch for him were completely thrown off the scent. He passed as the uncle of the English consul at Havre. The following is one of the King's letters to Mr. Croker, written in a bold and clear hand :—

Claremont, June 16th, 1850.

Dear Sir,

Accept my best thanks for the trouble you took of transcribing for me the very interesting passage of M. Guizot's letter. He is at the fountain head, and well situated to know what may be the disposition of parties; but nevertheless, futurity is darkness, and more impenetrable in my unfortunate country than anywhere else.

The steps of my misfortune, which your kind interest have (*sic*) led you to follow on your Cassini maps, were from Dreux through the forest part of my sequestered property, to Anet. Hence, crossing the river Eure through the forest of Ivry (also my sequestered property) to La Roche St. André, and hence by the road to Evreux, and very near that town, close to the road on the western side to Melleville farm and petit château.

Cassini's maps are now ancient, and a few years ago I might have supplied you with a copy of the very superior map which is published by Government; but those days are now past for me.

I thank you also for your kind offer of resorting to your collection of almanacks and other publications of my time, when I may want it, and probably I will avail myself of it.

I am, with great regard, dear Sir, your affectionate,

Louis Philippe.

(*From Mr. Croker's Note Books.*)

March 18*th*, 1850.—Dined with Louis Philippe. Before dinner and after he told me several anecdotes. I wish I could remember all, and especially that I could repeat them anything like as well as he tells them.

"I once dined in company with Robespierre, but his whole conversation was these words, 'Je ne me marierai jamais.' There was a M. Decritot, a great cloth manufacturer at Louviers, who had a charming villa near Poissy, which all the world went to see. He was of the *gauche;* and meeting me one day on horseback, he asked me to dine with him that I might see the villa and meet some members of the Assembly; so I went, and there amongst others were Pétion and Robespierre. Pétion was '*grand et gros*,' good-humoured and talkative, but heavy (lourd) withal. He talked away, Robespierre said not a word, and I took little notice of him, he looked as *   * said, like a cat lapping vinegar. Pétion was rallying him on being so taciturn and *farouche*, and said they must find him a wife to *apprivoiser* him; upon which Robespierre opened his mouth for the first and last time with a kind of scream, '*Je ne me marierai jamais*.' I heard him in the Tribune; he was exceedingly tedious and confused.

"When Louis XVIII. got to Paris in 1814 I was in Italy, and wishing to get to Paris, I asked Lord Wm. Bentinck to let me have an English officer under whose cover, as *porteur de dépêches*, I might get along safely. So he gave me M. Campbell (I think he said), with whom I came from Genoa to Marseilles, and thence to Paris. I put up at *an inn*, and went next day to pay my respects to the King. He received me very well, and after some general conversation, he said to me, 'Duc d'Orléans, vous étiez lieutenant-général avant la Révolution; vous l'êtes encore.' I made him my humble acknowledgments. He added, 'Vous étiez Chevalier du Saint-Esprit; vous l'êtes encore, et je vous fais colonel général des hussards.' I renewed my bows and thanks, and retired highly pleased, and expecting to see my name and my reception and appointments in next day's 'Moniteur,' but the 'Moniteur' took no notice whatsoever of me. I immediately sent for ——,† the tailor, and ordered the uniform of a Lieutenant-General, which I had in time for the King's reception next day, whither I wore it, and over it the cordon and star of the St. Esprit. When I went into the room, the Salle des Maréchaux, where the company was waiting, there was a great assemblage, but nobody knew me

---

* [Blank in the original notes.]
† [Blank in Mr. Croker's notes.]

personally, nor knew that I was in Paris, and I knew nobody; but I saw that the appearance of a personage of a certain figure in the uniform of a Lieutenant-General and with the St. Esprit, whom no one knew, excited a great deal of curiosity and stir in the room. At last I saw in the embrasure of a window Marshal Macdonald, who had served with me in Dumouriez's army, and whom I recognized. I went up to him and offered him my hand. He looked surprised, could not make out who it was, and at last confessed that he did not recollect me. When I named myself, he actually took me in his arms and hugged me, and in a moment there was a great hubbub in the room, every one crowding about me, and all manner of felicitations, &c. It was quite a scene. which did not please the King when he heard it, but which would not have happened had he permitted my previous visit to him to have appeared in the 'Moniteur,' for then every one would have expected me.

"Talking of this reception of me, puts me in mind of the cause of the great animosity between Louis XVIII. and Dumouriez. The Emperor Paul had great notions of Dumouriez, and invited him to St. Petersburg to consult him on plans of campaigns and what not. Dumouriez was to pass through Mittau, where Louis XVIII. then was, and Dumouriez went to pay his respects to him *en passant.* The interview was very gracious and friendly for some time; at last, as a mark of his great favour, the King said to the General, as he did afterwards to me, 'Général Dumouriez, vous étiez maréchal de camp avant la Révolution; vous l'êtes encore!' 'Comment,' says the other starting up, 'je le suis encore! Maréchal de camp! Moi! Quand on a commandé des armées en chef et gagné des batailles, on ne redevient pas maréchal de camp.' Still warmer and even offensive words ensued, and Dumouriez flung out of the room, and Louis XVIII. never forgave him. He would not permit his name to appear at all in the Army List, and when it was represented to him that he ought not to suffer such a man to be subsisting on a small pension from England he would not listen. Once Macdonald, who felt this strongly, took an opportunity, as Chancellor of the Legion of Honour, to insert Dumouriez's name as a Grand Cross (which would have given him the pension of the rank) on a list which he had submitted to the King; who, when he saw this name, said 'Ah çà; donnez-moi une plume et de l'encre,' and very quietly effaced Dumouriez's name, and said, 'Qu'on ne m'en parle plus.'

"I liked Charles X. much better than Louis XVIII. Charles X. was frank, good-natured, and very much of a gentleman, he always treated me well." [I could not help thinking that he had shown no great sense of that kindness. There was an article in the *Quarterly Review* (vol. lii. p. 550), I remember, that explained his treatment by the two brothers.—J. W. C.]

May 19*th*, 1850.—The King said that legitimacy was what everybody would agree to in the abstract, but was it now a possible basis?—were not all the ideas of mankind on the subject of government *bouleversées?* Then he began, with wonderful volubility and graphic power, a compendious history of the Revolution, from the selfish profligacy of Louis XV. to the well-meaning imbecility of Louis XVI.—the factions of the Parliament—the English revolutions—the American independence—the anarchy of the Republic—the despotism of Buonaparte—the attempt at constitutional monarchy at the restoration—his own *avénement*—his struggle with La Fayette and Co. against a *republican* monarchy—he insisting on a *constitutional* monarchy—his resolution to stick by and preserve all he could of the old Charter—all forms of government, all sources of power, divine right, government by états provinciaux et généraux, constitutional monarchy, democracy, despotism, election, had been all tried in turn, and all in vain! What was to be tried next? He ran through the history of near one hundred years with wonderful conciseness and effect, and a vast number of striking and brilliant expressions. I wished for a *stenograph.* He even twice enlivened the narrative with verses of songs illustrative of the public opinion of the periods—one under Louis XV., and one under Louis XVI.—which he actually sang to their proper tunes. In the midst of this gush of talk (which was sometimes indistinct, both from my own deafness and the weakness of his voice, which became more observable as he spoke quicker and with more mental animation) I could see that the leading idea was to derive *his* legitimacy direct from *Henry IV.*, and to throw all the blame of the Revolution on the four last Louis, but only indirectly. He likened his own position *vis-à-vis* the Legitimists and the Republicans, to Henry IV. *vis-à-vis* the *Guises* and the *League*, and concluded the comparison with saying *they* had attempted the life of

Henry IV. — (I think he said twenty) times, but his only
ten or twelve. When he had arrived at present times and
future prospects, he said he knew not what to think, to hope,
or to fear—fear predominated. The Count de Chambord was
impossible; the Count de Paris seemed equally impossible—
a child, a regency, with a female regent and a *Protestant,* or
with one of the princes for regent. He doubted whether
either "*prince ou princesse s'en chargera.* Enfin, l'avenir est
un chaos pour moi." " I have shown you that the whole
progress of men's minds has been for a hundred years to faire
chapeau bas à l'opinion publique " (he took off his cap and
made a short, disdainful salute), " which is right and proper,
as long as public opinion will accept any rational government;
but when, as lately, and indeed for a hundred years, in France
public opinion is nothing but opposition to whatever *is,* I do
not see how mankind are to be governed. There must be,
according to modern policy, a popular representation : but
the problem is, how that popular representation can be made
manageable—how it can be prevented from becoming, like
the National Assemblies of now-a-days, the depositaries of
the sovereign power, which can only be anarchy. If it were
attempted to balance such an assembly by another chamber,
how could that second chamber acquire stability and influence ?
I give it up."

. One more point I this moment recollect, which was a sly
defence of his father's party's share in forming the first
National Assembly. *Dauphiné,* he said, had been a *pays
d'Etats,* but having lost them by long desuetude, had petitioned Louis XVI. for their restoration, which was granted,
but instead of each order being equal in number, the Noblesse
were allowed $\frac{7}{22}$, the clergy $\frac{4}{22}$, the Tiers Etat $\frac{11}{22}$, "which,
you see," said he, " was an exact and royal precedent for the
double number of the Tiers in the Assembly of 1789."

I feel quite ashamed at such a meagre report of this very
striking oration, for such it was, for I suppose forty minutes
long, without any interruption ; and he would have gone on
longer, but that I saw that he was weak, and took advantage
of a pause to remind him not to lose his drive. It had been
hinted to me before I went in not to let him fatigue himself,
but I really could not stop him. The vivacity of his language and *his eyes* contrasted strangely with the weakness of
his voice and the hollow *wanness,* or rather yellowness, of his
countenance. He seems to me as much changed within the
last fortnight as any one I ever saw, and I am, I confess,

alarmed about him, though they all say he is better, and that apparently he has no complaint but want of appetite and a kind of lassitude, which however does not seem to invade his mind in any degree.

The King died in August, and Mr. Croker prepared for the *Quarterly Review* (September, 1850) an interesting account of his last days, derived from facts contributed by the members of his family.

The Duke of Wellington to Mr. Croker.*

Walmer Castle, September 20th, 1850.

MY DEAR CROKER,

I don't recollect to have sent an officer to King Louis Philippe. I had a correspondence with him from Bruxelles, Paris, and the Battle of Waterloo, which was published by Gurwood.

And I recollect that in the course of the negotiations which I had with the representatives of the different parties of *faiseurs* at Paris on my march from the Netherlands to that city after the battle, it was proposed by some of them that instead of restoring Louis XVIII. to his throne, we should propose that the Duc d'Orléans, Louis Philippe, should be called to the throne. I answered positively, *No!* That such a proposition could not be considered. He would be an " Usurpateur, tout comme Napoléon est le Roi de Rome ! Usurpateur bien né peut-être, mais toujours usurpateur ! " and it is essential to the settlement of France and of Europe that the sovereign should not be such.

I have seen the report of the Convention in print in one of the pamphlets of the day. But at all events I perfectly recollect it.

* [The Duke was now in his eighty-first year, and his handwriting was almost illegible. Sometimes Mr. Croker sent his letters back to his private secretary, Mr. A. A. Greville, to be deciphered, and on one occasion Mr. Greville owned that he could not perform this task. " The Duke," he said, " always writes without spectacles; he fancies his eyes are much stronger and better than they were twenty years ago. He consequently often writes parts of words only, often omits them altogether. However, I have one consolation, and that is, that I am a much better hand at his own writing than he is himself." Mr. Greville wrote a hand which closely resembled the Duke of Wellington's, and sometimes was quite as bad, or even worse.]

I don't recollect to have sent an officer to Louis Philippe. It could not have been Gordon. He was mortally wounded in the Battle of Waterloo, and died in the night. It must have been Sir Colin Campbell if anybody was sent. But I have no recollection of having sent anybody.

Ever yours most affectionately,

WELLINGTON.

Mr. Croker to the Duke of Wellington.

Alverbank, Gosport, September 27th, 1850.

MY DEAR DUKE,

I am much obliged by your letter; but I find that I did not put my question with sufficient accuracy. The journey I meant to enquire about was in 1814 from the South of France, when the Duke of Orleans went to Paris to meet Louis XVIII. on the *first* Restoration. Louis Philippe was not at all at his ease, from the Buonapartists on one hand and from the Royalists on the other, and travelled *incog.*; and he told me how thankful he was to *you* for giving him an English officer, under whose protection he got to Paris, where he told me he was received by Louis XVIII.*

This story that he told me, just before his last journey to St. Leonards, was, I believe, the very anecdote which he was so anxious to finish on his death-bed. It was a portion of his general complaint against Louis XVIII., and was curious enough, but, as I thought when I heard it, of no great importance. The main object, I suppose, was to show that he owed no great obligation to the elder branch, though he admitted that Charles X. had always been kind and obliging to him.

Ever, my dear Duke, most sincerely yours,

J. W. CROKER.

The Duke of Wellington to Mr. Croker.

Walmer Castle, September 29th, 1850.

MY DEAR CROKER,

I have not a notion to what Louis Philippe could have referred.

---

* [In Mr. Croker's 'Note-book,' March 18th *supra*, p. 207, the king states that he applied to Lord William Bentinck for the officer in question. It appears probable that Mr. Croker afterwards confounded Lord William with the Duke of Wellington; and this would account for the Duke's ignorance of the circumstances.]

It must be obvious that I was not at my ease at all, nor could have sent an officer to look out for the Duke of Orleans till after the battle of Toulouse ; a few days after which I heard of the events at Paris of the end of March and beginning of April.   Some days elapsed after the Battle of Toulouse and the accounts received from Paris, before the armies of Soult and Suchet, both of which were in my front looking towards the Mediterranean, took their arms and submitted to the Provisional Government and the new order of things.   I was upon the point of attacking, which of course I wished to avoid.   After I had got things quiet, I went myself to Paris, where I saw Louis XVIII., and the Allied Sovereigns, Lord Castlereagh, &c. ; and on my way back to Toulouse I met Marshal Soult going to Paris.   I could have had no communication with Louis Philippe till after my return to Toulouse.

But I don't recollect any, and was then under the necessity of going into Spain and to Madrid, to see King Ferdinand VII., who had gone on there.

I was aware that King Louis Philippe had never been on such good terms with, and had never been so well treated by, Louis XVIII. as by Charles X.   Louis XVIII. suspected him, and pretended that *he knew him.*   I rather think that something not very pleasant between them had passed at Stowe.   The late Duke of Buckingham had some story about it.

Louis XVIII. would never style him Altesse Royale ; Charles X. did so immediately.

Ever yours most sincerely,

WELLINGTON.

*Mr. Croker to Mr. C. Phillips.**

West Moulsey, Surrey, June 22nd, 1850.

MY DEAR SIR,

I wish I could hope to be of any use to you, but old as I am (69½), I am too young to have known anything personally of Flood or Burke ; Yelverton and Scott (Clonmell) I have

---

* [Author of ' Recollections of Curran,' ' Specimens of Irish Eloquence,' and other works. He conducted the defence of Courvoisier, and was much censured for asserting the prisoner's innocence after he had privately admitted his guilt.]

been in company with. They were friends of my father, and
Clare I knew a little in private life through the Whalleys
and Beresfords; with Grattan and Plunkett I had more personal acquaintance, but not an *anecdotical* one.   Curran I
knew to the extent of meeting him in society, of having been
twice, I think, at a consultation with him, and meeting him
twice on circuit, where he had come down special, and of
course lived with the Circuit Bar. All I could say of him
would be that he was a wonderful orator—the greatest, I
think, for moving the passions that I ever heard—a wit, too,
of *both* the first and the worst water; and in his conversation
as disagreeable a person as ever I met. I remember on one
occasion when he was dining with the Bar mess, he was so
coarse, and even worse, that several of us left the table; but
when he kept within bounds, his wit was copious and spark-
ling, and he had a most effective style of *firing off* his joke.
It was like the electric spark, and one doubted almost whether
it came from his lips or his eye, which was as quick and
brilliant as the wit.

You will find a pleasant anecdote of Lord Avonmore (and
Plunkett) in a note to my preface to Boswell's ' Johnson.'

If we were conversing together, I have no doubt several
things would occur to my recollection, but I have never, even in
my youth, been able to *sit down to remember*. Conversation
breaks through the surface that time spreads over events, and
turns up anecdotes as the plough sometimes does old coins.

Ever sincerely yours,

J. W. CROKER.

*Memorandum by Mr. Croker.**

I have heard four orators—Pitt, Canning, Kirwan,† and
Curran. Pitt commanded. I never heard anything like his
dignity; his voice was like a silver bell, and when Fox rose
into a scream, his voice only sounded a diapason. Canning

* [Copied by Mr. Giffard, on a sheet of note-paper.]

† [Walter Blake Kirwan—1754–1805—was educated at the College of
the English Jesuits at St. Omer, but afterwards embraced the Protestant
faith, and attained an extraordinary popularity as a preacher. Some
time before his death he was said to have collected 60,000*l.* by his charity
sermons. Kirwan was appointed Dean of Killala in 1800. He was a man
of remarkable powers, although his name is now almost forgotten.]

amused. Kirwan, perhaps, was more extraordinary than either. He was able to prevent your laughing at his mountebank manner. He pretended not to know the Lord's Prayer, and after *reading* it with hesitation he launched into the most magnificent oratory. I have his orations, and have read over those that struck me most, and though they are very correctly reported, I cannot for the life of me discover what it was that carried me away. But perhaps Curran was the most striking, for you began by being prejudiced against him by his bad character and ill-looking appearance, like the devil with his tail cut off; and you were at last carried away by his splendid language, and by the power of his metaphors.

Bishop Wilberforce to Mr. Croker.   Extract.

Near Bakewell, October 21st, 1850.

MY DEAR MR. CROKER,

I had an exceedingly pleasant visit at Brougham's. I saw a great deal of him, and you know how well he can talk upon every subject-matter. He was very friendly, very communicative; but seemed to have no more guess than anybody else how the entangled skein of politics was likely to run itself out. I heartily wish you had been there too. But such *cænæ deorum* are seldom allowed us. I am now on my way to spend an evening with Denman, and to-morrow halt at Cuddesdon on my way to the Palace, Chichester. The *Pavilions* have disappeared from Drumlanrig,* but I saw them in an old print of the Castle which the Duke showed to me.

Manning is not yet gone abroad,† but he is going very speedily. Alas! that misgovernment should lose us such men.

With kindest remembrance to Mrs. Croker,

I am ever, my dear Mr. Croker,

Most sincerely yours,

S. OXON.

* [The seat of the Duke of Buccleuch in Dumfriesshire.]

† [Referring, of course, to his joining the Romish Church, which he did in 1851. At the date of this letter, Manning was Archdeacon of Chichester.]

Bishop Wilberforce to Mr. Croker.   Extract.

Little Green, October 30th, 1850.

· My dear Mr. Croker,

If Manning leaves us it will be because his trust in our being a true branch of the Church Catholic is killed; and this will mainly be the work of Lord John Russell.

I am, ever most sincerely yours,

My dear Mr. Croker,

S. Oxon.

Mr. Croker to Lord Stanley.

Alverbank, August 15th, 1850.

My dear Lord,

There has been no Parliamentary summary this year, nor indeed the two last, and they tell me that the Conservative party throughout the country are puzzled what to think or say. If my old stump of a pen could be of any use, it is much at the service of my friends, but I am so much out of the world that I should need your direction and assistance as to the line to be taken and the points to be urged. Mr. Stanley's assistance, in all that might relate to the House of Commons, would be most useful, and indeed it might be rather wished that he should try *his own pen* on the subject —it is fully equal to do it justice, as his pamphlet * on the West India question has shown; but at all events he could furnish us with some hints of the topics which struck him in the House of Commons as most deserving observation.

I am not one of those who reproach the House or Ministers with doing so little. They, I think, do a great deal too much; but they show their rashness and their weakness by attempting so much more than they are either able, or, I believe, *willing* to perform. I know very well that the natural or acquired turn of Lord John's mind is to disorganise, and that he contrives to unite an aristocratical confidence in himself and his connections with very democratic views for the rest of mankind. But still I cannot suppose that he can be ignorant of, or blind to, the rapid decay of the power of the Sovereign and the Government, which already makes us a

* ['The Claims and Resources of the West Indian Colonies,' by Mr. Stanley, the present (1884) Earl of Derby.]

monarchy little more than in name, and which if helped on by the *promised* or menaced extension of the suffrage in England, to keep peace with Ireland, will very soon carry us to direct government by the House of Commons, or perhaps by Committees of the House of Commons.

But where is the remedy ? I confess I see none, nay, less than none, when I find the *soi-disant* Conservatives forgetting their old principles and their future interests as a party, and supporting the democratical propositions of Bright and Cobden.

I confess that the conduct of some of my old friends in the Public Office Committee has filled me with disgust and alarm —not so much for what they propose as for the spirit that actuated them—the same spirit that prompted and supported Mr. Henley's * motion last year, and which was to my notion as Jacobinical as any that Hunt or Cobbett ever made.

Ever yours sincerely,

J. W. CROKER.

Lord Stanley to Mr. Croker.   Extract.

Longshawe Lodge, August 18th, 1850.

MY DEAR SIR,

I received your letter of the 15th yesterday, and had sat down to answer it, beginning by telling you that an opportunity was given me of doing so by a day very much in harmony with the tone of it—a steady downpour, without a ray of light in any quarter, and not a prospect of a break in the clouds ; when half-way through this simile I was agreeably interrupted by the rain suddenly ceasing, the clouds breaking in every direction, and a bright sunshine calling us out to shoot, and setting out at one o'clock I returned at six with fifteen brace of grouse.

I know not whether the analogy may hold good with our political horizon ; at present it certainly looks as threatening and as hopeless as the weather of yesterday morning. The session which has just passed was to my mind most unsatisfactory, not so much from the actual mischief done as from the obvious downward tendency of our course, and from the

---

* [Joseph Warner Henley, M.P. for Oxfordshire from 1841 to 1878. He was President of the Board of Trade in Lord Derby's second Administration in 1852, when he was made a Privy Councillor.]

apathy with which all, or nearly all, appear inclined to let themselves float helplessly down the stream. All the tendency of our legislation and of our proceedings in Parliament is towards the lowering of the weight, in the social scale, of the proprietors of the soil ; and while they, and those dependent upon them, are gradually sinking under the new pressure of their old burthens, the apparent success of the Free Trade policy, as exhibited by the state of the revenue and the amount of our foreign trade, furnishes a plausible argument in its favour, and blinds the eyes of the country to the real dangers we are incurring. The next election must be the turning point of our destiny ; but who shall say what we may witness before that time ? If the country has by that time seen its danger, *and felt it to be danger*, then there is some hope of a change for the better ; but if this or any Free Trade Government *then* acquire a majority, the game is up; and I firmly believe we shall be in rapid progress towards a republic in name as well as in reality. *Then* I believe the monied interest, which is now all in the ascendant, will have cause to tremble ; and the classes who have been hitherto the firmest supporters of public credit, will be found to hold the language, which indeed they are beginning to listen to already, that all must come down together ; that not only establishments, but money obligations must be placed upon a footing suited to the altered circumstances of the country, and in everything the lowest and the shortest-sighted utilitarianism will be the policy of England. Had Peel lived,* we should have seen him at the head of this new system, even currency notwithstanding. *Some* of the present Government will not go so far, and will be shelved; and Johnny, having pushed us to the brink of the precipice, will decline himself to conduct us over it. Meantime, the most dangerous men are at this moment the scattered remnant of the Peelites. I have in this session done everything in my power to conciliate them ; with Aberdeen personally I am on the most friendly terms ; but while they are themselves powerless for good, they have never failed to give the Government a helping hand, when, but for them, we could have neutralised, or mitigated, the mischief of their measures. I verily believe the Government would have been glad to have been forced to accept the 15*l.* franchise for Ireland, but almost every Peelite, even those who had voted

* [Sir R. Peel died on the 2nd of July, 1850, from the effects of a fall from his horse.]

for the 15*l.*, joined them in adopting the Commons' amendment of 12*l.*, and more than turned the scale against us. With a House of Commons ready to support the Government in *any* Radical measure, and even to drive them onward; with a body of professed neutrals in the Lords, always ready to impede our otherwise successful opposition; with a Court jealous of the power of the aristocracy, and ignorant that on that rests the safety of the Throne, we are hoping, and struggling against hope. I have never before taken so gloomy a view of our position; and, to make matters worse, I see few, if any, young men coming forward or taking an interest in public affairs imbued with *Conservative* principles and ready to stand by and with "their order."

For all this, I own, I see no remedy. If you take the field in the *Quarterly*, I am afraid it must be in a most Cassandra-like strain, endeavouring to rouse the *gentlemen* of the country from the apathy which is fast destroying them. But desertions and defeats have at once reduced their means and depressed their spirits; and they neither can, nor will, make the pecuniary sacrifices and exertions which might yet place them at the head of a powerful party. As it is, while they are seeking to relieve themselves by measures utterly insufficient, and in some cases not overwise, they are allowing their dependents to strike out a line for themselves, and to fall into the hands of leaders with whom they have no natural connection.

I have given you Jeremiad for Jeremiad, but I neither have given, nor can I give you, any advice or assistance. If the country could be roused, it might be well; but we are falling into the fatal sleep which precedes mortification and death.

> Believe me, sincerely yours,
>   STANLEY.

Mr. Croker to Lord Brougham.   Extracts.

West Moulsey, December 5th, 1850.

MY DEAR BROUGHAM,

I hardly know what to think or say about this "No Popery" paroxysm.* I do not believe that there is much

* [In September, 1850, the Pope issued a Bull establishing a Roman Catholic hierarchy in England. In Lord John Russell's letter to the

religious feeling at the bottom of it, for there is not, I think, much fear of any religious danger, and the most forward in the agitation have been your worthy friends, the Dissenters, who would have rather liked, as they did in James II.'s time, the encroachments of Popery on the Church ; but who, on this occasion, come forward as partisans to support Lord John, and who are glad of the plausible (and with many *the real*) ground of their old aversion to Popery. The Anglican clergy join more reservedly. The most zealous are the anti-Puseyites, who are glad of an occasion to *snub* the Tractarians, and the latter are willing (or, at least, most of them) to retreat back into a truer position. But I am, like you, totally unable to account for Lord John's letter, which seems to me to be at once rash and insidious—rash as against his friends the Romanists, insidious as against us ; and the attempt to lay the blame of the Popish attempt on the Tractarians is really the old story of the wolf and the lamb. Lord John and his allies frightened some weak-minded but sincere Churchmen into Puseyism, and then he turns round and accuses Puseyism of being the cause of the natural and inevitable results of his own prior policy. But all this explosion has been no novelty to me. In the *Quarterly Review* for December, 1847, p. 306, on the subject of Minto's mission, I distinctly and by name announced that the Pope was about to parcel out our territory into provinces and dioceses, and that we should soon see " an Archbishop of Westminster and a Bishop of Birmingham ! "   I dare say there is no copy within your reach, but the whole discussion there is very curious and prophetic. The only question now is, will Johnny stand to his gun ? I think not. I am really inclined to believe that the Queen herself felt the *insult* strongly, and that she prompted Johnny's resolution ; but why he chose to make his declaration so gratuitously and so grossly offensive, I cannot guess,

---

Bishop of Durham, which was written on the 4th of November, he said : " No foreign prince or potentate will be permitted to fasten his fetters upon a nation which has so long and so nobly vindicated its right to freedom of opinion, civil, political, and religious." The situation was described in the well-known picture in ' Punch,' of Lord John Russell as a little boy chalking up " No Popery " on Cardinal Wiseman's door, and then running way.]

unless there be some secret diplomatic cause. I see none either in reason or in policy.

Ever yours,

J. W. CROKER.

Sir George Sinclair to Mr. Croker.   Extract.

Thurso Castle, January 11th, 1851.

MY DEAR CROKER,

Many thanks for your kind and valuable letter. It is, in one sense, very gratifying to learn that our sentiments are so much in accordance as to the present position and future prospects of our country and of the world; but, on the other hand, it is to be lamented that we cannot take a more cheering view of the general aspect of public matters, either at home or abroad. There seems to be everywhere a conspiracy to annihilate and ruin the landed proprietors, and to bribe the working-classes into a concurrence in this project, by holding out to them fallacious hopes of the benefits which *they* are to derive from the downfall of the "privileged" order. Neither the Court nor the Whigs seem to dread or deprecate such a catastrophe. They are too intent in acquiring a spurious popularity by pandering to the passions of the multitude, and favouring the monied and *parvenu* interest at the expense of the ancient proprietors of the soil. In this country the public burdens (local and national) amount to about 25 per cent., and the poor law, inflicted in Scotland a few years ago, is doing the work of the revolutionists, by demoralising the minds of the poor and crippling the means of the wealthy, falling chiefly on the landlords and tenants, and increasing in every parish every year. Philanthropy seems to have gone mad everywhere, and to vent all its insane venom upon the unhappy proprietors, who are now expected not only to reduce their rents, but to sufficiently clothe, educate, and provide for the entire population on their estates, in every season of distress, and under every casualty arising from recklessness, guilt, or misfortune. I see that at the ragged school meetings it is proposed that all the children of the poor should be educated each for five years, at a cost of 5l. per annum, and the expense defrayed by the parishes, so that wherever an unprincipled drunkard lavishes all his means on gin and whisky, the industrious classes and all (especially) who have land or farms

must, if he has ten children, lay out 50*l*. per annum on that
family alone, and ten such families would cost the district 500*l*.
per annum. It is impossible that this system of extracting all
that is required by vice and folly out of the pockets of those
who have anything to lose can go on long.

> Ever, with great regard,
>> Most truly and faithfully yours,
>>> GEORGE SINCLAIR.

Mr. Croker to Lord Brougham.

And so you are reading my Bozzy—I presume in the
single volume edition; *if not* look at my notes there—p. 799[2],
p. 800[1] and [3]; * if so, I have nothing to add, except that we
all know that Johnson was once young, and in that perilous
state of poverty which, as Shakespeare says, "brings a
man acquainted with strange bed-fellows;" but beyond that
fact, and the inference that the general faculty of mankind
suggests, we have not a tittle of evidence that even then he
lived loosely. His acquaintance with Savage (on which so
much was said) I have shown to have been much shorter and
in every way more insignificant than was before supposed;
and as to what Boswell says, my notes, I think, afford a conclusive answer. I never heard any of those stories which
you think may have come from Beauclerk—from *Beauclerk
himself* I should have received them with suspicion, for many
reasons; but a hearsay, conjectured to have been a hearsay of
what Beauclerk might have said, I should dismiss without
ceremony. When I began my Johnsonian inquiries, I knew
several persons who had known Bozzy, and those that I consulted upon this very point (wondering why he should at the
very close of his book trump up these old and apocryphal
stories) explained it as one of Bozzy's crazy tricks, introduced to sanction his own practice. I am not concerned to
dispute the possible frailty in early life of Jeremy Taylor, or
Bishop Ken, or George Herbert, or Dr. Johnson, but I say
there is not a tittle of evidence against the last more than the
others, and that the pretended proofs alleged by Boswell I
have shown irrefragably, I think, to prove the very reverse.
We have evidence of such practices against Lord Somers and

* [Containing extracts from Dr. Johnson's 'Meditations and Prayers.']

Lord Cowper, but that would not justify an inferential condemnation of Lord Hardwicke or Lord Eldon.

Boswell's book is a most curious picture of the human mind in a vast variety of aspects, but there was one view of it which I was unwilling to open more largely, namely, the numberless little touches by which he exhibited, sometimes unconsciously and apologetically, his own follies and frailties, and in fact his own mental disorder. I have just hinted this, but I abstained from dilating upon it out of regard to his family, but it is a clue very essential to the right appreciation of his most extraordinary book. Have you ever read his letters to Malone while he was busy with it ? They are very curious.

Lord Aberdeen to Mr. Croker.

Argyll House, February 21st, 1851.

My dear Croker,

In reading Lord Holland's book,* which I did very cursorily, I was more struck by its dulness than by any other quality. A senseless hostility to all legitimate Kings and Queens, and a ludicrous exaltation of *"that great Prince,"* Bonaparte, might have been expected ; but it is wonderful how little the volume contains which has not either been long well known, or which is not worth knowing.

The calumny upon the Queen of France is scandalous, supported, too, by the pretended testimony of Madame Campan, notwithstanding the contents of her book, written under the government of Bonaparte, and by which the Queen is fully acquitted.

The omission in the narrative, relating to the marriage of the Duchess of York, gives rise to conjectures very unfavourable to the Duchess, and is surely a most unjustifiable mode of conveying such imputations. But for this the editor is probably responsible.

Lord Holland greatly undervalues Metternich, to whom even the present generation seems now disposed to do justice, and whose qualities will be fully appreciated by posterity. Any one who has witnessed the calm philosophy, the constant cheerfulness, and the absence of all resentment

---

* ['Foreign Reminiscences,' by Henry Richard, Lord Holland, reviewed by Mr. Croker in the *Quarterly Review*, March, 1851.]

and complaint with which he has endured his great change of fortune, must have seen much in him to admire and to love.

When Metternich was in London in 1814, for about three weeks, he resided with me in this house; and I think I made him acquainted with Lord Holland at that time. I do not well recollect the impression produced upon him by this introduction; but I rather believe it was not very favourable.

Lord Holland, however, was a delightful companion, and his conversation most instructive and agreeable. I think he was one of the best tempered men I ever knew. I do not say good-natured, by which I understand something different; and his party rancour often appeared scarcely consistent with this quality. I believe this was also very much the case with his uncle, whom he greatly resembled in character. The amount of Whig prejudice and bigotry in him was marvellous.

Ever, my dear Croker,

Most sincerely yours,

Aberdeen.

In the month of February, 1851, the Government of Lord John Russell sustained a double blow: once on a motion of Mr. Locke King's for an extension of the suffrage, when they were left in a minority; and once on a resolution of Mr. Disraeli's, demanding some measures of relief for the owners and occupiers of land, which was regarded as a step backwards in the direction of Protection. The resolution was defeated by only 14 votes—267 for, and 281 against; and this also was looked upon as very little better than a defeat of the Government. Mr. Disraeli's resolution came before the House on the 13th of February, and Mr. Locke King's on the 20th.

Lord John Russell, in consequence of these votes, resigned office, and Lord Stanley—who on the death of his father succeeded to the title of Earl of Derby in the month of June this year—made an attempt to form a Ministry. He failed and Lord John returned to power, though he succeeded in holding it for a few months only.   Lord Stanley's views concerning the general state of affairs, and the prospects of both parties, are set forth in his letters to Mr. Croker.

Mr. Croker to Lord Lonsdale.   Extract.

February 14th, 1851.

MY DEAR LONSDALE,

   The Ministry are weak and tottering, but any other Ministry will be infinitely worse; and indeed it is a kind of consolation to me that I do not think that any attempt at a Conservative Ministry *possible*.   The very attempt, I hope, is impossible, because the result, I am sure, would be fatal.   No man who judges merely from the state of affairs under a Whig Ministry and a Tory Opposition has any idea of what the altered state of affairs would be if, at this crisis, we were to have a Tory Government and a Whig, or, as it would really be, a Radical Opposition.   All the boasted prosperity and quiet would vanish like a sunset, and we should hear of nothing but the darkness of bigotry and the desolation of misery overshadowing and devastating the country, though in fact all our material condition should remain exactly what it was, or perhaps even better.   Nothing but such a man as the Pitt of 1783 could afford a chance of success.

J. W. CROKER.

Mr. Croker to Lord Brougham.

West Moulsey, Surrey, February 21st, 1851.

No, my dear Brougham, you do *not* like Lord Holland's book.   I wish you did, or could, for then there would be assuredly something good in it, enough to enable me to say something of it that would be agreeable to you, which I very much wish to do.   I really have not found one redeeming page, or half page, which I could venture to quote with approbation, nay, nothing showing trace of that good-natured amiability, which *all* who knew him intimately gave him credit for.   As to his general talents, I am an imperfect judge ; but you and I have heard both him and his

uncle, and surely the resemblance between them was that
between the wrong and the right sides of the tapestry. There
was the vehemence without the energy, the physical defects
without the moral illustration—as Burke said of some one, the
nodosities of the oak without its strength, the contortions of
the sibyl without the inspiration. I assure you all this
sincerely vexes me, for I would infinitely rather show my
regard to your wishes than write the most brilliant review
that ever was penned ; but the book attacks our whole party
and principles, and affects to do so on the *evidence of history,*
and that you yourself would not have us submit to. But I
shall keep your wishes in mind, and perform the operation as
leniently towards both your friends as the respective facts
will allow.

Why do you call me an anti-Reformer? I was indeed
an anti-Reform *Biller,* but you know, for I showed you
the original papers, that I was far in advance of all my party,
and of most of yours in my, not merely opinions, but efforts
towards the enfranchisement of the great towns at the cost
of delinquent boroughs. I wrote for Lord Liverpool, in 1820,
a scheme for the immediate enfranchisement of two of the
great towns by the supersession of Grampound and some
other place then in jeopardy. This paper went into all the
necessary details on the subject, and showed at once how
just and even necessary it was to enfranchise Manchester,
Birmingham, Sheffield, and Leeds, and how easily we might
draw the line and stop there. I reviewed this proposition in
two or three shapes on the occasion of Penryn and East
Retford. I pressed it even at a meeting of the party at Peel's,
and was answered by — whom think you ? — Huskisson!
His reasons, too long for this note, were plausible, but they did
not satisfy me, and I did not vote with the Government on
East Retford ; and to my utter astonishment found that
Huskisson had changed his views in the debate, from which
I had absented myself. Even after that, I did not give
up *my* scheme of reform, and proposed members for the
four great towns in a letter to Peel, 24th February, 1830,
in which I urged him to bring over our anti-Reform friends,
by this warning, that they would soon be overwhelmed by
the torrent, if they would not consent to open one or two
sluices.

As to the present or late no-Popery excitement, I think
that it was almost altogether factitious, and directed almost

as much against the Church of England as against the Pope. The Bill seems to me a miserable and insolent juggle.

Ever yours,

J. W. CROKER.

The Bishop of Exeter to Mr. Croker.

17, Albemarle Street, February 23rd, 1851.

On what a crisis we have fallen! Will Lord Stanley undertake the Government? I think he *must*. It has dropped unsought into his hands; and if he cannot accept it, who can?

Gladstone will be at home to-morrow. Mr. Walpole told me yesterday that he is confident Lord S. may stand if he has Gladstone with him. They have many principles in common, and only one, I think, on which they are adversely committed —*Free Trade*. But Free Trade seems *fait accompli*: and many of the Protectionists are said to have gulped it.

The recasting of taxation is, I hear, not unlikely to bring together the severed party. But what a difficult, if not dangerous, attempt!

Some think a 5s. duty on corn for *revenue*, not Protection, may be tried, and the Income Tax given up by instalments. I fear the League have been too successful, and that Lord John is too tricky, to admit of such an expedient.

The Duke of Wellington to Mr. Croker.

London, March 10th, 1851.

MY DEAR CROKER,

I have not read Lord Holland's Reminiscences. I know nothing of that publication excepting what I have read in the *Review*. I sent for it, and will look into it, and write to you afterwards.

I really cannot recollect that I ever saw Alava in the presence of King George IV. He must have been here occasionally after the battle of Waterloo, but not frequently, as he was Minister Plenipotentiary from Spain in the Netherlands, as well as at my headquarters, and he was always at his post at Bruxelles when not at my headquarters at Paris or at Cambray. After the termination of the occupation at the period of the Congress of Aix-la-Chapelle he returned to Spain and became involved in fresh constitutional and revolutionary discussions, in which he took a part so forward as to be one of the Commissioners appointed to treat with the King in relation to some points on his removal from Madrid to Cadiz.

As well as I recollect, Alava did not come to reside in England for any length of time till towards the end of the reign of King George IV., if at all, at which period his Majesty was scarcely in a state of health to receive anybody. I think that Alava's residence in England was principally during the life-time and reign of King William. He went away in 1835.

I could not venture to assert that the removal of Bonaparte to St. Helena was never mentioned by anybody at the Congress of Vienna. But the subject certainly was never mentioned as a subject for consideration, or taken into consideration at all. If ever mentioned as for consideration, it would have been noticed in the despatches to the Foreign Office.

Designs were entertained to depose Murat and to restore the former Government. These were occasioned principally by Murat's eccentricities and his tormenting the Pope.

The King of France, Louis XVIII., was very anxious upon this subject. Certain favourite regiments of the French army, those bearing the names and titles of the royal family, and commanded by men of family, were placed *en échelon* on the frontier, which was the cause of Bonaparte finding them there when he made his invasion in March.

Though there was no conspiracy in Vienna against Bonaparte, there was a good deal in his favour in France. As well as I recollect, there were not less than three military conspiracies to induce him to return, one at the head of which was General l'Allemand, another at the head of which was General d'Orsenne. These were independent of each other. He may have known of each and have communicated with each; but my belief is that he founded his plan upon his knowledge of the general state of France and of the Government of King Louis and of the army.

He could not have suspected that there was a design to carry him off to St. Helena. If he had, he would have avoided to expose himself to capture on his passage to the coast of France.

Ever yours most sincerely,

WELLINGTON.

*Lord Aberdeen to Mr. Croker.	Extract.*

Argyll House, March 10th, 1851.

MY DEAR CROKER,

There is nothing more unjust in the whole of Lord Holland's book than the character which he gives of the Emperor Francis. Few persons have had the means of knowing the character and disposition of a sovereign more intimately than I had of knowing him. For two or three months, after the advance from Leipsic, I had the opportunity of seeing him daily, and of living with him in his most private society, sometimes in circumstances of great difficulty and uncertainty. There never was a man whose whole conduct was more governed by a sense of duty. His principles were conscientious and upright, and his feelings most benevolent. His unbounded popularity amongst all ranks, and especially the lower orders, was sufficient to prove the excellence of his character. "*Our Father Francis*" was the only title by which he was known amongst the common people; and they felt all that the title conveyed. By the simple rectitude and honesty of his character, without any extraneous advantages, he preserved the lasting respect and deference of his allies, and I know made the most favourable impression upon Castlereagh and the Duke of Wellington.

The Emperor frequently spoke to me about the marriage of his daughter, which he always represented as a sacrifice made for the interests of his country. But he made a great distinction between an Imperial Princess marrying Bonaparte, and allowing an Archduke to marry one of Bonaparte's family. To this, although often suggested, he would never consent. He frequently said that he had no reason to complain of Bonaparte's treatment of his daughter.

Ever most sincerely yours,

ABERDEEN.

*Lord Stanley to Mr. Croker.	Extract.*

St. James's Square, March 14th, 1851.

MY DEAR SIR,

I need not say that I see, for I have given practical proof of my feeling, all the difficulties of forming a Government which can stand its ground under existing circumstances.

The Whigs are daily proving their utter extinction as a party, and are at our mercy at any moment. The Peelites (to use the ordinary phrase) have confessed their inability to form an Administration by themselves, and their unwillingness to join any other section. Indeed the declarations of Lord Aberdeen and Sir James Graham debar them from uniting with any party, except the extreme Radicals, from which the former, at least, would shrink; and between the latter and Lord John I do not believe, notwithstanding late expressions of esteem and friendship, there is at bottom any very kindly feeling.

In short, I believe that sooner or later *we must* make an attempt to govern the country, which will soon be impatient to be *governed*, and will not be left, as at present, at the mercy of any and every wind that blows. But the sooner or later is the matter of most vital importance. We must endeavour to keep the present ricketty Administration on its legs, at all events, till it has got through a considerable portion of the routine business of the session; and there is no danger in doing so as long as questions are open, such as the Papal Aggression, on which the Government dare not appeal to the country. But I am not so sure that it would be safe to allow them to go through the session, and then dissolve on the popular cry of a further extension of the suffrage. I think the indefinite promise of a measure on this subject, which certainly has been in no degree matured, is the worst thing John Russell has done, and it was done in the worst way; to buy off for the moment a troublesome motion on the part of his own supporters, and met with a well-deserved defeat. I do not believe it was preconcerted, but that it was a move, and a false one, made on the spur of the moment, like the letter to the Bishop of Durham, or, still more, the University Commission. Still it may be not the less mischievous, and I do not doubt he will use it in opposition. But if it must be met, it would be better that he should bring it forward as an Opposition motion than as a Government measure, either to be carried in the present House, or to be the subject of appeal to the country. If a measure be carried on the principle recommended, and for the purpose avowed, by Mr. Locke King, that old Church and King and territorial feeling, which with you, I believe, still subsists, though much weakened, will be rendered absolutely powerless, and the counties will be wholly swamped by the influence of the towns.

On the whole, I believe that amidst a choice of appalling difficulties, the least danger to the country will be found in that which I also believe to be almost inevitable, the assumption of office by our friends before the close of the present session; and, if so, the later the better. All will then depend on the election which must. follow; and though no doubt we shall have a powerful and unscrupulous Opposition to meet, if the country is sound (and I hear in general favourable reports), with temper and moderation I believe we may succeed in stemming the Democratic tide which has been flowing of late with formidable rapidity. If we fail, we must at all events go through the ordeal of Cobden and Co., if we escape a Republic. Till the inevitable time for the attempt arrives, I agree with you, that as far as possible we should keep to a defensive policy, not provoking unnecessarily a conflict with an Administration on sufferance, but not allowing them to pass measures, if they are disposed to do so, which may cause us fresh embarrassments for the future.

Believe me, my dear Sir,

Yours sincerely,

STANLEY.

Mr. Croker to Lord Londonderry.

West Moulsey, Surrey, March 20th, 1851.

MY DEAR LONDONDERRY,

I have received your letter from Bordeaux and its valuable inclosure.* I had not intended to give you the trouble of doing more than giving me *your own* recollections, as I had access to Prince Metternich myself, through the medium of Dr. Twiss, who sent me some observations of the Prince's on Lord Holland's book, which fully supported the views I had already taken of the whole case; but it was fortunate that you did write to Bruxelles, as it has produced you an answer, which affords, as you say, such a happy exhibition of the clear mind and admirable cleverness and energy of that great statesman.

I knew him a little when he was here at our grand jubilee;

---

* [The letter which follows this, from Prince Metternich, who at this time was in his seventy-eighth year.]

he, I have no doubt, had quite forgotten the Secretary of the Admiralty, but I had forgotten neither his agreeable manners nor his great talents, nor his brilliant services to the European world, and I looked upon myself as being fortunate in having an opportunity of exposing Lord Holland's posthumous libel.*

J. W. CROKER.

Prince Metternich to Lord Londonderry. [*Enclosure in the above Letter.*]

Bruxelles, 13 mars, 1851.

MON CHER LONDONDERRY,

J'ai reçu hier votre lettre d'Angoulême, et si elle m'a fait plaisir comme toute preuve de votre souvenir, j'ai appris avec peine que c'est un motif de santé qui est la cause de votre excursion dans le midi de la France.

Vous me dites que vous sentez les approches de l'âge. Que cela ne vous effraie pas! Il en est de l'âge comme de toutes les lois de la nature; il faut baisser pavillon devant elles et se soumettre, *sans plus*, à leurs irrémissibles conditions. Ce n'est que sous cette condition qu'il est possible de les rendre favorables.

Je vois avec une véritable satisfaction que l'honnête C[roker] partage mon sentiment sur le produit littéraire qu'il qualifie de *detestable book!* Je ne crois pas que son pendant ait jamais existé sous les conditions sous lesquelles a paru celui en question. Quelle valeur doit avoir eu *l'homme*, qui a ramassé en un tas, sans valeur possible, des récits d'écouteurs aux portes, et des bâilleurs d'antichambre, recueillis avec un manque d'esprit de critique sans pareil! Comment le fils, éditeur, n'a-t-il pas senti, ce que le père, rabâcheur, aurait dû sentir? L'œuvre, en tout état de cause, trouvera *des censeurs;* qualification trop haute pour une tâche qui n'est que celle de la *flagellation*.

Vous pouvez assurer, en toute et pleine conscience et sécurité, "que jamais au Congrès de Vienne, il n'a été, ni

---

* [In Lord Holland's 'Foreign Reminiscences,' reviewed by Mr. Croker in the *Quarterly* (vol. lxxxviii.; March, 1851), Prince Metternich was spoken of as a " tool of Napoleon's," and a supporter of the "system which succeeded him." He was also described as a man "little superior to the common run of continental politicians."]

officiellement, ni confidentiellement, ni dans une forme qui n'aurait eu une autre valeur, que celle de l'expression d'une pensée individuelle, question de la translation de Napoléon, ni à Sainte-Hélène, ni dans un lieu quelconque!" *

Voici, en grands traits, la somme entière de l'impression que la fuite de N. de l'Ile d'Elbe, où, à tort, sans doute, on le croyait bien gardé, a produit à Vienne, et cette impression avec ses produits prouve combien peu on s'y occupait de l'homme.

J'avais défendu à mon valet de chambre (vous voyez que le récit commence par le bas) de ne point m'éveiller s'il arrivait un courrier dans le courant de la nuit. Les Cabinets ayant été réunis à Vienne, rien de pressé à l'heure ne m'avait semblé devoir se présenter et me défendre de me reposer de la fatigue de longues journées de travail. Une réunion de Plénipotentiaires des cinq cours, avait eu lieu chez moi dans la soirée du 16 mars, et elle s'était prolongée jusqu'à trois heures du matin du 17. A 7 h. mon valet de chambre vint me porter *une dépêche.* Je le grondai d'avoir oublié ma. défense, et trouvant la dépêche cachetée du sceau *du Consulat Général impérial à Gênes,* je la plaçai à mes côtés et me rendormis, d'un sommeil toutefois troublé, qui m'engagea à prendre connaissance du contenu du rapport, conçu en quatre ou cinq lignes, et du contenu suivant: Le " Commandant de la station anglaise devant l'Ile d'Elbe vient d'entrer dans ce port, pour s'informer si Napoléon n'y était point entré. Ayant disparu de l'Ile d'Elbe, le Commandant est à sa recherche. C'est tout ce que l'on sait ici de l'événement."

Je me rendis, dans le plus bref délai possible, chez l'Empereur, après avoir fait prier le P. de Schwarzenberg, alors Président du Conseil de la guerre, de passer chez moi à neuf heures, et avoir adressé l'invitation d'une réunion à 10 heures, au Prince de Talleyrand, à Lord Castlereagh, au C. de Nesselrode et au Chancelier Hardenberg; *pour une affaire fort pressée.*

Je ne crois pas l'histoire offre le second exemple, d'une *grande affaire,* plus promptement et plus catégoriquement, arrêtée.

---

* [Lord Holland had stated in his book that the Emperor was virtually released from the " obligation of his treaty and abdication of Fontainebleau " by his discovering that the idea of transporting him to St. Helena was broached at the Congress of Vienna.]

Je me suis présenté chez l'Empereur François à 9 h. ¼ ; je lui ai donné connaissance du rapport du Consul à Gènes ; il me l'a rendu en me disant, avec son calme et sa décision habituelle : " Voilà un gros événement ; il faut le faire tourner au profit de la cause de l'ordre. Allez de ce pas trouver l'Empereur Alexandre et le Roi de Prusse, et dites leur que, pour ma part, je suis décidé à donner l'ordre à mon armée de reprendre, sans perte de temps, la direction d'où elle est venue ! "

Je me trouvai chez l'Empereur de Russie à 9 h. ½. Il me dit ce que m'avait dit l'Empereur François, et ce qu'à 9 h. ¾ me répéta le Roi de Prusse. Je me trouvai ainsi à 10 heures en mesure d'inviter le Maréchal P. de Schwarzenberg, de réunir sans perte de temps chez lui les Chefs d'Etat-Major des armées alliées. A midi, les ordres requis pour ces dernières étaient expédiés.

M^r le Prince de Talleyrand fut le premier Ministre qui arriva au rendez-vous que je leur avais donné pour 10 h. Voici le début de notre entretien. Après que le P. de Talleyrand ait pris lecture de la dépêche de Gènes, il m'adressa avec l'impassibilité qui régnait dans ses traits la demande :

" Savez-vous où est à l'heure qu'il est Napoléon ? "

Je lui fis la remarque que, la seule notion venue à notre connaissance ne portant que sur la fuite, j'ignorais forcément la direction du fuyard.

T. " Eh bien, je vous dis, que Napoléon est dans ce moment en Suisse ! "

Moi. " Le savez-vous, ou le croyez-vous ? "

T. " Je le crois, et je ne le mets même pas en doute ! "

Moi. " Comme il s'agit entre nous de croire et non de savoir, je vous dirai que je cherche N. dans la droite direction de quelque point du rivage de la Méditerranée à Paris."

L'événement a prouvé qu'entre les deux croyances, la mienne a été la plus juste.

Je vous fais cadeau, mon cher Marquis, de cette relation, et vous pourrez en disposer en faveur de Mr C. Vous avez été témoin et acteur du drame de 1815, et vos souvenirs marqueront par défaut les miens.

Nos souvenirs datent de loin, et ils nous permettent d'utiles rapprochements entre les situations d'alors et celles d'aujourd'hui. Ceux qui portent sur le passé prennent facilement la teinte de temps pleins de poésie, en les comparant aux misères fort prosaïques, qui composent l'histoire du jour.

Le gâchis n'est pas une forme admissible dans la vie sociale, et c'est lui qui ne. pèse pas moins sur le monde !

Mille hommages et amitiés pour vous, mon cher marquis, et respects pour la marquise. Laissez-moi savoir comment vous avez employé vos loisirs sous l'influence d'un ciel sous laquelle je voudrais me trouver placé avec vous.

METTERNICH.

Lord Stanley to Mr. Croker.   Extract.

St. James's Square, March 22nd, 1851.

MY DEAR SIR,

Your suggestion is most valuable, and I am ashamed of not having adverted to it in my last communication.   There is at this moment an utter break up of all parties, except the Protectionists, who are, I hope, notwithstanding their recent disappointment, gradually consolidating themselves, and as a party

> " Ab ipso
> Ducit opes animumque ferro."

If I can consolidate with them the now awakened spirit of Protestantism, and at the same time keep the latter within reasonable bounds, I can go to the country with a strong war-cry, with which, indeed, the *Times* furnished me the other day, " Protestantism, Protection, and down with the Income Tax."   But let our watchwords be what they may, the real struggle, the real battle of the Constitution which has to be fought, is whether the preponderance, in the legislative power, is to rest with the land and those connected with it, or with the manufacturing interests of the country.   If the former, the Throne is safe ; if the latter, in my deliberate judgment it is gone.   How are we then to bring the masses of the electors to the support of the former rather than the latter alternative ?

In my mind, among all its evils and all its dangers, the evocation of the Protestant spirit, which has been aroused, is not without its use.   Even the most Radical towns, but especially the constituencies in which Protestant Dissent has any power, are so furiously anti-Papal, that that feeling will neutralize the cheap bread cry, even in many quarters in which that cry has not been already proved, or suspected to be a humbug. As to Protection itself, the Whig landed proprietors are just as sensible as any others of the ruinous consequences to themselves of the present state and prospect of prices; and nothing would secretly gratify them more than our success in imposing a moderate duty on imports. The financial policy which I sketched out on the late occasion tends to the same result; and the two opposite schemes may be characterized as our opponents seeking temporarily to benefit the middle and lower classes *at the expense* of the higher, their employers; ours, permanently to benefit the same classes *through* their employers, which to me appears the more reasonable and the less revolutionary policy.

Now, in carrying out this view, I am of opinion that we are more likely to have the support of the *old* Whigs, few as they now are in numbers, especially in the House of Commons, than of the Peelite section, now headed by Graham; while these last, on the Popish question, have thrown themselves absolutely into the hands of the pro-Popery faction, and have thereby lost support even among the Liberals of the towns. On this question, too, I do not think the old Whig traditionary principle is altogether lost among them; and as far as John Russell is an exponent of their views, his leanings are all to the Protestant Dissenters, and against the Papists, with whom the Whigs of thirty and forty years ago were brought into an unnatural combination from being both for the time engaged in the general cause of " Civil and Religious Liberty," which is now, as many think, endangered by the Papal proceedings.

My opinion, therefore, is that on financial and Protectionist policy we are more likely to have Whig support than not: and that on the religious question we shall have large portions of the Dissenters in the towns, and a mixed feeling on the part of the old Whigs; on the part of the pure Radicals and the " Grahamites," unmitigated hostility. It is well you should know that old Lord Ponsonby has given in his adhesion to me, and Lord Fitzwilliam, who is very strong on the Papal question, announced his intention of supporting me had I formed a Government. I name these as two instances, and we should find many more. I think, therefore, it would be wise to hold out a friendly flag to this party, which will be still further weakened by its being accepted by some of its numbers, and to use the most conciliatory language towards them; but I do not think it will be possible to include any

of them in a Government to be formed, and I think the offer
to do so would rather repel than attract, and would, moreover,
be an indication of weakness. If I try the game at all,
which I shall have to do, I must try it with my own force ;
and having manued the ship, and got her fairly afloat, must
strengthen my crew as opportunities occur from other vessels
I may meet *en voyage.*

I am, dear Sir, yours sincerely,

STANLEY.

Lord Lonsdale to Mr. Croker.

London, March 23rd, 1851.

MY DEAR CROKER,

Though we generally take the same view of politics, upon
the late events we have differed. I think the country is ripe
for a Tory Government, even more so than when Peel came
into office. I lament the opportunity was lost, as it may
never occur again.* If I was Lord John and wished to go on,
I would make a bid against Stanley for the Budget, which he
could do, having so large a surplus. Then, as to the Ceylon
question, I think the Government could get their Radicals to
support them, treating it as a question of censure and change
of Ministry. I do not look upon anything in politics as permanent or fixed, but I think a Tory Government would have
lasted two or three years, which is a certain space of time to
get over. I saw Edward Ellice the other day ; he said the
present Government were dead but not buried ; but, as we
had lost the opportunity, he thought the Government would
go over the session. What he feared was that the next
Parliament would be too reactionary ; that they would undo
in too great a hurry all that had been done of late years ;
all seem to contemplate that on a dissolution there would
be a great majority of Conservatives and Protectionists, and
that farmers will be elected in some counties.

From the information I get, the landed Whigs would not
oppose the Stanley Government. They are all sighing for an
import duty, and wish some one to do it for them. However,
the offer of the Government I do not think will come so
soon as Stanley expects, and, besides, there is the chapter of

* [It occurred within a twelvemonth, Lord Derby entering upon his
first Administration in February, 1852.]

accidents—a new revolution in France, deposing the Pope, a popular Budget tiding over Easter. I wish for Stanley and his present views, as I have always been a consistent Tory; and in my present position I like draining, rail-roading, and hunting better than the confinement of office, and the most irksome part of it—the dinners; and I should join just to assist in setting the work going, and back out as soon as friendly candidates for office appeared.

I understand Stanley has recast his parts, and that now he is ready for anything.

I remain, truly yours,

LONSDALE.

Prince Metternich to Lord Londonderry.

Bruxelles, 8 avril 1851.

MON CHER MARQUIS,

Je réponds à votre lettre du 25 mars en suivant l'indication que vous m'avez donné pour vous faire arriver mes lignes.

Mr Croker est trop modeste, en admettant que je ne garderai de lui qu'un souvenir effacé par le temps.

Si *une* rencontre personnelle ne suffit pas en règle pour asseoir sur elle l'opinion que tout homme est en liberté de se former sur un contemporain, il en est autrement d'une suite d'impressions, que les individus, que, soit leurs actes, soit leurs écrits, mettent en évidence, créent dans ceux qui sont engagés dans les affaires publiques. Je n'ai eu avec Mr C. que des relations personnelles passagères; je l'ai suivi avec constance dans son utile et brillante carrière littéraire, et je regrette sincèrement qu'il ne se soit point mis en rapport avec moi lors de mon dernier séjour en Angleterre.

Il eût assurément dépendu de moi de chercher ce contact; de graves considérations m'en ont empêché.

J'ai passé ma vie au service de la cause de l'ordre, et je ne me suis retiré du champ de bataille que le jour où je me suis reconnu privé des moyens absolument nécessaires pour ne point fléchir dans la lutte, que dans mon pays était engagée entre l'ordre légalement existant et des utopies parées du nom de réformes et ne couvant que la révolution, qui le 14 mars, 1848, a jeté le masque. Ami de la cause que seule je me suis senti la faculté de servir; ami de mon pays, je me suis

retiré d'une arène sur laquelle je ne me suis point connu une
place, et qui a nécessairement dû tourner en un champ clos,
sur lequel les réformes prétendues ont dû se trouver engagées
dans une lutte à mort avec les bases de l'existence de l'Empire,
avec les conditions de cette existence dont la faction révolutionnaire a vainement espéré pouvoir amoindrir la valeur en
les couvrant du nom de *Système Metternich.*

Je me suis retiré loin de mon pays pour ne point prêter,
aux adversaires de la cause de l'ordre, une arme qu'ils n'eussent
point manqué de chercher dans des influences cachées de ma
part, et dont ma conscience a dû me tenir éloigné par suite
de mon dégoût inné pour les manœuvres sourdes, et de ma
confiance dans la force de la vitalité de l'Empire ! Placé en
face de ces sentiments, je n'ai cherché personne en Angleterre,
si ce n'est d'anciens amis ; j'ai évité avec soin tout ce qui
aurait pû me prêter une couleur qui ne me va pas, et ouvrir
la voie à la fausse supposition d'une activité qui est étrangère
à mon esprit et à mes habitudes ! C'est dans ce franc exposé
de la marche que vous m'avez vu suivre, que vous trouverez
également la raison qui m'a empêché d'appeler à moi une
notabilité aussi connue que l'est Mͬ C., dont personne plus que
moi ne sait apprécier les qualités de l'esprit et du caractère.
Je ne vous parlerai pas, mon cher Marquis, de la situation dans
laquelle se trouve aujourd'hui placé le monde ; une position
à l'égard de laquelle il ne saurait y avoir une différence dans
l'appréciation des esprits droits. Une lutte sévère n'est encore
engagée qu'entre les avant-gardes ; les corps de bataille devront
finir par se heurter. C'est le *quand* et le *comment* qui sont
écrits dans le livre fermé de sept sceaux !

Ne vous inquiétez pas plus que de juste de l'Allemagne ;
c'est sur la France que doivent, avant tout, être dirigé les
regards.

J'espère que votre excursion vous fera du bien. Si je
n'étais point arrivé à cette époque de la vie, où le mouvement
se trouve neutralisé par le mal qu'il place à côté de son
influence salutaire, je suivrais votre exemple, et j'ai la conviction que j'en tirerais du profit. J'ignore encore ce que je
ferai l'été prochain, et je vous le dirai quand je le saurai.

Veuillez me rappeler, ainsi que ma femme, au souvenir de la
marquise, et croire à ma vieille et constante amitié.

METTERNICH.

Mr. Justice Wightman to Mr. Croker.

Hampton (Saturday), April 19th, 1851.

My dear Croker,

Depend upon it, Pope had no stronger reason for speaking of Page as he has done than that he had no other instance at hand to suit his purpose. Horace's line,

" Servius iratus leges minitatur et urnam,"

was well paraphrased by the instance of a judge who was remarkable in his day for his coarse, unseemly manners and demeanour on the bench, and his brutal behaviour and severity towards prisoners. Savage was tried by him at the Old Bailey in December, 1728, and his mode of dealing with the case is commemorated by Johnson in his life of Savage. Pope's mention of him was not (I. think) until some years after, for the ' Imitation of Horace' was not published until 1734 or thereabouts, and Page, happily for the judicial character, was *the only instance* since Jeffries that could be cited to suit Pope's purpose. Fielding, who was a cotemporary, and had many opportunities of seeing Page upon the Bench, has given a very graphic and lively description of his manner of trying prisoners in Partridge's narrative of a trial for horse-stealing upon the Western Circuit, of which Fielding was a member.

When Pope in the lines,

" Each mortal has his pleasures, none deny
    Scarsdale his bottle, *Darty* his ham pie,"

refers to two instances by name, I do not suppose that he had any personal cause for disliking the individuals, but introduces them merely because they were well-known amateurs, the one of wine, and the other of good eating.

Fielding's account of the trial before Page is introduced as an episode in the account given by the Old Man of the Hill of his life and adventures to Tom Jones.

Yours very sincerely,

Wm. Wightman.

Lord Derby to Mr. Croker.

Knowsley, September 22nd, 1851.

MY DEAR SIR,

I have not the least idea what John Russell's intended Reform Bill may be,* and I doubt whether he knows himself; the pledge to bring it forward, one of his most unjustifiable acts, was, I believe, given without the knowledge of the Queen or of his colleagues, for the mere purpose of escaping an adverse division, in which, after all, he did not succeed. And now he is in the condition of a man in one of the old stories, who, having sold himself to the devil, is anxious to cheat the devil, and get out of his bargain. But I am afraid the devil will be too much for him, and that, anxious as he may be to do as little mischief as possible, consistently with keeping himself and his friends in office, he will be driven, in spite of himself, into a larger measure than he wishes for.

The object of the Radicals is very plain. It is to swamp the county representation by the influence of the towns; and the plausible ground they take is the injustice of withholding from a 10*l.* householder in the country, or in one of the non-borough towns, the franchise which the same qualification confers on him if he happens to reside within a borough. There are two ways in which they may effect their object—by *adding* to the county constituency all the 10*l.* householders without the boroughs; or, which would be worse still, by following the precedent of their recent Irish Bill, and introducing, for town and country alike, one dead level of constituency, founded upon a low scale of rating. The former, if I mistake not, was Mr. Locke King's proposition; and Lord John may have some difficulty in adopting after having negatived it; but, whatever he proposes, the argument is almost equally strong against a wholly uncalled-for disturbance of the existing system.

Yet I think we should be cautious of committing ourselves absolutely to resist *all* change, even though we may not see its necessity, first, because a change *may* have a really Conserva-

---

* [Mr. Locke King's Bill for the extension of the suffrage was again brought forward on Lord John Russell's return to power, but it was defeated on the strength of a Government promise to bring in a new Reform Bill the following session. The Administration brought in the Bill but did not live long enough to carry it.]

tive tendency,* but chiefly because an absolute and unflinching
adherence to the present system, without listening to what
may be said in favour of a change, would, I think, give the
Government an advantage which we can ill afford to give
them when they start with the prestige of "enlargement
of the franchise" in their favour. What I think we may do,
and ought to do, is to enter our protest in the strongest terms,
beforehand, against any measure calculated to increase the
democratic influence, and to extend the power of the towns
against that of the counties. To such a measure we should
be bound to offer every Parliamentary opposition in our power.
But we are fighting against fearful odds, when the advisers of
the Crown throw all the weight and influence of the Crown
into the democratic scale. I am afraid also that Graham and
his section of the Peelites will be ready to support a very
large measure, and, if it pass the Commons, I can place no
reliance on that party for opposing it in the Lords. I do not
think there is any real feeling in the country in favour of a
change ; but it is too much to hope that we shall be supported in resisting a "Reform" Bill, unless it is so insignificant as to be scouted by the real Progressionists ; so that
J. R. has put himself in a position in which he must upset
himself or ruin the country.

Yours sincerely,

DERBY.

Mr. Croker to Mr. Murray.

Bognor, October 24th, 1851.

MY DEAR MURRAY,

I know that you may very naturally suspect me of being
somewhat old-fashioned, if not obsolete, in my notions, but I
think I am not really more so than serves to steady my
opinions. I have never been a *retardataire*. I have always
advocated and *pro viribus* advanced, all progress that I thought
improvement, but I always wished *improvement* to be based
on *experiment*. When yet very young, I was almost at the
head of the design for the erection of the Nelson pillar in
Dublin ; the first, I believe, of that species of monument now
so frequent, and always, in spite of defective taste in the

---

* [It is needless to point out that this belief was always urged by
Mr. Disraeli as the justification of the Reform Bill of 1867.]

design and execution of some of the individual objects, great and appropriate ornaments. It was my idea, borrowed, of course, from the Roman columns, but three or four years before the column of the Place Vendôme. I had also an active share in the erection of the London column thirty years later. The Admiralty front to Whitehall was, under my influence, the first public building in London lighted with gas. It was through my special persuasion that steam packets were tried between Calais and Dover. I was, I believe, the first person who in parliament ventured to recommend a uniformity of weights and measures; and especially a decimal system of coinage, which produced eventually the adoption of the sovereign instead of the guinea. I was the mover of the new Board of Longitude, and of all the measures for the improvement of chronometers, as our old friend, Dr. Young, was always forward to acknowledge. I was for many years of the Council of the Royal Society, and forwarded, as far as my humble influence, and still humbler knowledge went, every experimental improvement.

One remarkable improvement I attempted, as long as I was at the Council, but never succeeded in inducing England, France, and the Northern powers to adopt—one common *thermometrical* scale. Is it not the greatest absurdity in the world, that the element of heat, common to all mankind, and of such a clear incessant and vital importance, not merely to science, but to everyday life, should be measured in the three great classes of the civilized world by three scales, Réaumur, the Centigrade and Fahrenheit—not merely different, but absolutely incommensurable—no integral number of any one being convertible into any integral of either of the two others, and this in a matter identical to all! I even went so far as to endeavour to have it talked about at the Congress of Vienna. I probably should have succeeded but for Buonaparte's return from Elba.

As to the great political questions, I need hardly remind you that I was an advocate of Catholic emancipation, while yet it might have done good, and only grieved that it was postponed till it had become capable of nothing but mischief. In 1820, I drew up for Lord Liverpool, and with his concurrence, a paper showing the justice, the necessity and the safety of transferring the franchises of delinquent boroughs (of which there were then two available) to Manchester, Birmingham, Leeds, and Sheffield. That scheme Lord Liver-

pool was disposed to adopt, but he was overruled, chiefly, I
believe, by the influence of Lord Wharncliffe, who afterwards
had a great hand in passing the more sweeping, and, as I
think, fatal Reform Bill.   In 1830 I again endeavoured to
obtain the East Retford and Penryn franchises for Manchester and Birmingham; and though in office, would not
vote for the foolish course that was adopted.   In short, I
never have been opposed to practical improvements and
gradual progress founded on experiment, and it was for the
sake of such improvements themselves that I was anxious
that they should be made slowly, that they might be made
safely and successfully.

I have been led away into saying all this because, as I say,
you are perhaps inclined to underrate the value of my advice,
from a suspicion of my being too much of the narrow old
school.

Now as to your railroad literature; since I wrote to you
last I have visited three principal, and one or two secondary,
stations, where I found a poor literature—nothing but a few
local guides, some small trash of novels, and of course the
newspapers, the radical ones predominant.   It is very right to
endeavour to diffuse good literature through every channel,
but I think that the article in the *Times* which seduced you,
very much exaggerated the influence of the railroads in these
points.   Nobody will buy for such occasional purposes anything but the lightest matter, in the lightest shape and at the
lightest price, and the newspapers are now so voluminous,
and the majority of journeys so short, that few think of
buying more than the newspapers.   Those that are going a
little farther than the *Times* will occupy them, will seldom,
I think, exceed 1s., or at most 2s. 6d., in literary expenditure.
Of this, however, experience must be the proof; but I shall
be very much surprised if your 4s. worth of extracts from the
Times * (which originally did not cost so much, and which
all had read, and probably not quite forgotten) should sell to
any remunerating extent.   *Nous verrons.*

Don't think that it was any *amour propre* that made me
allude to the Keats' essay.   I only happened to look at it for
the purpose of seeing what of public or general interest could
possibly be produced on such a subject, when I happened to
light on the phrase I quoted.   You were captivated, I dare

* ['Essays from the 'Times,' published by Mr. Murray in 1851.]

say, with the appeal made to YOU *nommément* by the *Times* in favour of cheap literature. I wonder you did not see that that mention of you was anything but complimentary or friendly. You are not, and cannot be, a cheap bookseller. Your father gave Lord Holland 2000*l.* for the Walpole. Lord Byron screwed 2500 guineas out of him for two fugitive poems. He gave me 1500*l.* for the Boswell. He, and you after him, have been the most liberal and bountiful of publishers. How could *you* sell cheap when you buy so dear? Accordingly, you are a dear publisher, and the *Times* meant to *attack* you as one of that class, and to drive you to sell your costly wares at prices that will not remunerate you. 'Tis just the same principle as its advice to the farmers to *farm high* and to *sell cheap.* I do not at all blame you for taking the hint, for (however meant) it so happened that you were in a position to do so with advantage. You were possessed of many works which had ceased to be called for in their old form, and which it would cost nothing but the materials to reproduce. You had also an inexhaustible store in your review of the kind of Essays which one might give a shilling for, and which would just fill up the time to Brighton or Birmingham. I enter not into the tradesmen's view of the question, but your father told me, I think, that the 'Family Library,' which was a bold attempt at cheap literature, had not been profitable. You know best whether your 'Colonial Library' has been so; but, at all events, it would require a large return of profit to reconcile me to your making your " venerable " establishment in Albemarle Street a kind of old clothes shop, in which old worn-out articles were furbished up for second-hand prices. Your *Review* articles would be liable to no such imputation; they would be like the reprint of rare volumes that cannot be otherwise had. The *Quarterly* and *Edinburgh* must, of course, contain a great deal of such inferior or, at all events, temporary matter as it would be absurd to republish, but they both contain a number of Essays of permanent interest which will always have a certain degree of freshness and vitality. The republication of these may be profitable, and would be respectable, but neither if it were introduced by a preliminary attack on the bull-dog ferocity of that venerable periodical from which they are derived. I will venture to repeat that the literary merit of the articles selected from the *Times*, though considerable for such a publication, and curious, and to a certain degree valuable from their relation to that powerful paper, are by no means of that intrinsic and permanent value to justify their selection and republication by a house of your position, character, and connection.

With regard to what you say of my own papers, there are not many of them that I should select for republication. Those that are least unworthy of it are some historical ones—four or five papers on the early French Revolution contain much fact and truth that is not elsewhere to be found; for I gleaned them from multitudes of contemporary, and now rare and recondite, materials. Two or three of my English biographies have something of the same historical character. Some also relating to the last two revolutions may be of use to future historians; but they are all in their present state sufficiently accessible to those who are curious in such matters, and I should by no means advise you, as a matter of profit, to attempt to make *cheap literature* of them. One article I have long thought of expanding and publishing in a separate form—that on Macaulay's romance. There is not a word,— or but a word, to retract or alter, and it ought to be put into a condition to supply a more ready antidote to that elaborate compound of falsehood and poison.

Ever yours,

J. W. Croker.

Mr. Murray to Mr. Croker.

Albemarle Street, October 25th.

My dear Sir,

I thank you for another most kind and interesting letter. I listen with pleasure and gratitude to the advice which it contains.

Your sagacity and penetration have led you to conclusions perfectly just as to cheap publications. The books you see covering the station stalls are cheap because, for the most part, worthless or stolen; books for which little or no copy-money has been paid to the author. Although I call my series Railway Readings, it would never pay to address it solely to travellers, and therefore I decided on a series of various prices. It is also to be borne in mind that at the best central stations there is a demand for books of a price above one shilling. I had long been meditating on a new series to succeed my Colonial Library when the article in the *Times* appeared. It made a sensation. Anxious to strike while the iron was hot, I took the *Times* essays, which were ready at hand, without having read the whole of them, *e. g.* that on Keats among others. Now, though I admit that the remarks on K.'s critics are impertinent, I cannot believe that such shafts will ever stick in the hide of the *Quarterly.* If I had been aware of their possibly annoying you, I would assuredly not have published them. I am loath to admit any defects in the *Quarterly,* but I cannot help thinking that there are many papers of yours which would answer better for republication than that on Macaulay ; that on Louis Philippe I am going to send to press.

I have read with the highest interest the brief enumeration of grand objects accomplished, and great ends aimed at, by you in your political and official career. They are not sufficiently known beyond the circle of your own friends, yet I should hope that posterity will do justice to them.

JOHN MURRAY.

Mr. Croker to Mr. Murray.

Bognor, October 28th, 1851.

DEAR MURRAY,

We intend to return to Alver to-morrow, and I shall be glad when Mrs. Croker allows me to get back to my den at Moulsey—a fearful den strewed with the limbs of mangled authors—Keatses, Tennysons, and Moxons, Armitages, Maurices, and Kingsleys, whom the cruel monster hath torn to pieces.

You may perhaps feel some compunction at having had even an involuntary accomplicity with such a hyæna, but console yourself with the thought that the time is at hand when he will cease to bark or bite.

On one point we must have some future discussion. I will say nothing for the talent, the taste, or the temper of my article on Macaulay ; they may all be poor, but its *truth* is certain. I read it over again lately, and I am more and more convinced of its importance, as I will not venture to call it a refutation, but as a buoy, a beacon to mark the dangers and shallows of that most mischievous parody of history, which would richly deserve another *Examen,* for assuredly old

North's Whiggery was much less deceptive and malignant than Mr. Macaulay's. I do not ask *you* to publish it; all I would ask is that you would allow *me* to do so *meo periculo.* I should like to leave behind me an antidote in the same shape as the poison which it is meant to counteract. I should prefer doing so by an amended reprint of the article, because that is a style introduced by Mr. Macaulay himself; but as I acknowledge the copyright to be in you, I shall, if you do not consent, recast my materials (and I have a great many by me which the limits of a review did not allow me to employ) into another and more book-like form. But of this we may talk by-and-by.

J. W. C.

Lord Derby to Mr. Croker.

Knowsley, December 22nd, 1851.

My dear Sir,

I have been grieved to hear both from Beresford and from the Duke of Rutland, with whom I have been staying for a few days, very indifferent accounts of your health, and that you yourself take a very unfavourable view of your own case,* though bodily infirmity does not seem to have impaired the activity and energy of your mind. Beresford tells me that you are desirous of knowing my views upon the subject of the last revolution in France, and the language which the *Quarterly* should hold upon it. While writing I have been interrupted by the receipt of a letter from the Duke, enclosing yours of the 18th, which arrived at the Woodhouse just as I left it on Saturday. I deeply regret to find that it confirms to the full the apprehensions I had entertained from former accounts, while I am deeply touched by your kind mention of me under such circumstances. It also repeats the wish which I was about to endeavour to meet, though the subject is far too wide to be dealt with in a letter, and the results defy calculation as to the future. One thing I think is abundantly plain, that France and Frenchmen are incapable of rational self-government, and that sooner or later they will give themselves a master. I do not think that we have anything to do with the morality of the transaction. It is certain that the President has openly violated the constitu-

---

* [Mr. Croker was now subject to fainting fits, and his pulse was sometimes as low as 30; but his general health was still good.]

tion which he had sworn to observe and maintain; but, on the other hand, I believe that he sincerely endeavoured to make the constitution work, and that his *coup d'état* was not resolved upon until the inherent weakness of the constitution itself had brought the machine of government to a dead lock, and the folly and unreasonableness of the contending factions by which he was surrounded had left no choice but anarchy or despotism.   The promptitude of his measures and the adherence of the army have saved France from a sanguinary civil war, and have perhaps for the present suppressed a general European outbreak, which would have followed upon the success of the Reds; but that this has been owing *to the army* is a fact calculated to excite no little anxiety for the future.

That Louis Napoleon should wish, having secured his term of ten years (which means life unless overthrown by another revolution), to establish himself as a constitutional sovereign is hardly to be supposed; and, if he had the wish, I doubt whether France possesses the materials for working a constitutional government; and I presume that he will frame, and they will accept, just such a scheme as shall give them the appearance of freedom, while he retains all the real power in his own hands.   But then he must retain it by the support and at the good pleasure of the army.   Will he, and can he, obtain this and still maintain a pacific policy?   If he can, and if he will; if he applies himself to increasing the physical comforts and promoting the material prosperity of his country, while he devotes his great military powers to the control of the turbulent spirits which infest it, his usurpation will have been a fortunate event for Europe, and he will merit the title of a general benefactor; and towards this course, so far as he can be in any way influenced by the language held on this side of the water, he should be in every way encouraged.   A friendly tone should be taken with respect to the part which has been forced upon him, and his government should be acquiesced in, not only on general principles of non-interference with the purely internal affairs of another country, but as the only escape for the time from evils and dangers which could not have been confined to France had they been permitted to explode.   But if, for the purpose of conciliating the army, he finds it necessary to adopt a warlike policy, I should look upon him as the most dangerous neighbour we could have—far more so than either the old French Republic or the Empire, because, though at the head of a nominal "republic," there would be nothing in his propagandism which could alarm or shock the absolute governments of Europe; and, confident in the support of Russia, who will see with pleasure his success in the cause of "order," he may turn his arms against countries on whose behalf we should certainly interfere, and we might find ourselves, especially under the present Government, involved in a war of principle, in which our allies, though against a *soi-disant* republic, would be looked for in the revolutionists of Europe.

I firmly believe that, with the great bulk of the French people, nothing would be so popular as a war with England; but the end of a war once kindled in Europe no man living can foresee. We must only hope that the President, or the Emperor, as I suppose he will be before long, who has hitherto played his cards with great prudence, though, in truth, his adversaries have played them for him, may have sense and firmness to see and act upon the real interests of his country, in which case I shall for one cordially rejoice in his success, and heartily wish him a continuance of his power; and I am quite sure that a hostile tone taken towards him now, such as the *Times* is taking, is more likely than anything else to drive him to lean yet more and more on the army and the Russian alliance, which I should think most dangerous to the peace of the world.

You must excuse this very crude and hasty expression of my feelings, written in a hurry to save the post, after a day's shooting, to which I was summoned shortly after beginning my letter. As I see by your letter to the Duke of Rutland that your appetite, though not very good, may be tempted by game, I send off by rail to-morrow four pheasants and three woodcocks, part of our chase of to-day. And, with every good wish,

Believe me, my dear Sir,

Yours sincerely,

DERBY.

Lord Lyndhurst to Mr. Croker.

George Street, December 1st, 1851.

MY DEAR CROKER,

Cheer up; you have fifteen good years yet; many more than I can look to. The low pulse, I am told, is really nothing, and a little freer living, which I do not think a punishment, whatever you may do, may set all right again. Work less and laugh more.   But I am afraid you cannot do without work, which I am glad to say I can.   Your second letter and the account which Strangford gave us of his visit, dissipated in some degree the sadness which came over us here at your first letter.   Though we see you seldom, there is nobody can spare you less than Lady L. and myself, to say nothing of what the good cause would suffer by the loss of so chivalrous a champion.

We are down very low here, in consequence of the protracted illness of our little girl, but our prospects in this respect are improving, though we shall still pass our Christmas in London.   Pray at your leisure dictate to us a little note to say how you are going on.

Lady L. desires to be most kindly remembered.

Yours very sincerely,

LYNDHURST.

CHAPTER XXVIII.

1852-53.

It seemed probable, in the early part of 1852, that the Conservative party was at length about to recover from the
paralysis which had smitten it on the desertion of its leader
in 1846; and, as a matter of fact, its recovery actually pro-

ceeded so far as to admit of its return to power under the leadership of Lord Derby. But the total disintegration which had been the fatal bequest of Peel was still going on; the old Tory party was practically dead; the new Conservative party had not yet been formed. It required a generation at least to restore the shattered remnants of the organization, and to impart confidence to the rank and file who knew that they had been betrayed, and who saw no hope of finding a leader in whose capacity and good faith they could repose confidence. Ever since 1846, their weapons had been turned against each other. The Protectionists were determined, at all hazards, to keep the Peelites out of office, and the Peelites were equally resolved to guard the door against the Protectionists. Each section acted with the Whigs whenever it was necessary to carry on its own private *vendetta*. But the Protectionists were at the greatest disadvantage immediately after the repeal of the Corn Laws, for they were left completely without a head, whereas Sir Robert Peel was still present to guide his followers. There ensued, as it has been shown, the brief interval of promise opened up by Lord George Bentinck, under whom there was again seen in the House a compact body worthy of being called the Conservative party. After his death there was no one to· look to but Lord Derby, for not even Lord Derby himself, at that time, seriously thought of Mr. Disraeli as a leader. But when Lord John Russell was overthrown by a clever move of Lord Palmerston's in February, 1852, and it was found that a coalition of the Whigs and Peelites could not possibly be formed, Lord Derby was required to form a Ministry, and to Mr. Disraeli, much to the surprise of many old members of the party, was assigned the office of Chancellor of the Exchequer.

Mr. Croker was among those who had no faith in Mr. Disraeli. But he trusted implicitly in Lord Derby, and he appears for a short period to have entertained the hope that it might be possible for the party to secure a long tenure of power. He was, of course, well aware that the Ministry were in a minority, but the country, he was inclined to believe, was still at heart Conservative. "We are satisfied," he wrote,[*] "that [the country] is substantially in favour of an anti-revolutionary Ministry, not only by an immense majority of all the more intelligent classes, which ought to direct public opinion, and which in the long run always do so, but also of the great mass of the people themselves." And this opinion he continued to express, even after the appeal to the constituencies which Lord Derby made in July, and which resulted in leaving the Ministry intrinsically as weak as it was before. Mr. Croker went so far as to assert, on the "authority of those who ought to be" well informed, "that on any question involving the immediate defeat of his Administration, Lord Derby may expect in the whole House a majority of 348 against 306."[†] We can only suppose that he reckoned the Peelites in the number of Lord Derby's friends.

There was one point on which Mr. Croker was particularly earnest in the advice which he gave to the Ministry. It was, that it should not rush upon the rocks and quicksands of a "Budget before Christmas." The new Parliament was not to meet till November; there could be no pressing necessity to introduce a financial statement at that late period of the year. "The Budget is a long way off," he wrote; "and neither friendly suggestions nor hostile taunts will, we apprehend, induce the Ministers to make premature revelations, or even to enter into unseasonable discussions." But Mr. Disraeli seems to have entertained no misgivings. On the 3rd of December he introduced a Budget in what was described

---

* *Quarterly Review*, Sept. 1852, article on "Parliamentary Prospects."
† *Ibid.* p. 542.

at the time as a "rattling speech." On the 16th, notwithstanding the "rattling speech," the Ministry was out, and all
was over. Once more the legacy of Sir Robert Peel had done
its work. The Peelites amalgamated with the Liberals, and
the Government, which existed upon sufferance, could not
stand against the combination. And under these conditions
with little variation, the contest was carried on for years; for
it was not until 1874 that the Conservative party gained a
majority in the country sufficient to enable it to stand alone,
and to defy all combinations of its antagonists. Not till
then—if then—was it possible to say that the deadly wounds
of 1846 were healed.

Mr. Croker undoubtedly held Mr. Disraeli primarily responsible for the overthrow of the Government, and he objected
strongly to his Budget, but he did not attack him on any
personal grounds. He simply disapproved of the policy of
rashly and needlessly challenging an opponent to combat
who was eagerly waiting for a chance of trying his strength.
It is difficult to see what any one can have found to complain
of in such comments as these :—

"No one, of whatever political creed, can now affect to
doubt or disparage the many high parliamentary qualities of
Mr. Disraeli. His resolute spirit has been conspicuously
displayed under very extraordinary difficulties. He has combined an indomitable perseverance with great fertility of
resource. In opposition he has been, and, if he does himself
justice, he must again be, most formidably influential. He
may yet acquire whatever he needs for the discharge of the
high functions of a Minister. He has shown himself at once a
brilliant orator, and, what is still rarer, a powerful debater,
but he has not, as yet, we think, earned the reputation of a
statesman." *

This is from the article which has been represented by

* [*Quarterly Review*, December 1852, pp. 230, 240.]

Mr. Croker's assailants as a fierce, desperate, and malignant attack on Mr. Disraeli, designed in retaliation for Mr. Disraeli's lampoons. There is not a sentence in the entire paper which exceeds the fair bounds of criticism.

The letters which relate to the political occurrences of these years are now, as in previous chapters, detached from the general correspondence, and placed together.

The Earl of Derby to Mr. Croker. Extract.

Downing Street, March 11th, 1852.

My raw troops are taking well to their work, and will, I think, acquit themselves creditably; but we are threatened with a virulent opposition.

Mr. Croker to the Earl of Derby. Extract.

West Moulsey, Surrey, August 11th, 1852.

You have an awful part to play, and you will play it honourably, and to the greatest possible degree successfully. You may postpone the catastrophe, and save us from immediate revolution, but you cannot save us from the ultimate and irresistible effects of the Reform Bill. Your own personal character, the homogeneity of the great Church-and-King party, the gravitation towards the soil, the innate aristocracy of all classes, may enable you to resist—if you will resist—for a while; and the harder we die the easier will be the resurrection; but, depend upon it, die this Constitution will and must. France may advance or retard our revolution, but it cannot prevent it. The Queen is already a puppet. The House of Commons is King, as the first attempt of any opposition to his popular Majesty will show. Our sole hope now is the, not " *dolce*," but " *difficile far niente*." You can stand, perhaps; but if you attempt to manœuvre, either by retreat or advance, we are all lost.

Mr. Croker to the Earl of Lonsdale.

3, Radnor Terrace, Folkestone, September 4th, 1852.

MY DEAR LONSDALE,

I have studied Ireland politically for near fifty years, and my "State of Ireland," concocted with Sir Arthur Wellesley in 1807, is, I believe, true in every point; as true now as it was then, except only that the payment of the priests is now, I fear, entirely impracticable. Sugar-plums would have made them loyal if given in time; you must now use measures of severity.

Bold and firm measures against all these refractory ecclesiastics—here and there—will not only make them quail, but will gain you a popularity and strength beyond what you can have any idea, from that most brave, loyal, and powerful body, the Protestants of Ireland—the finest race of men, I believe, in the world, and abundantly able to keep their country quiet if there were means of quieting and controlling their enthusiasm. They are the English garrison in Ireland; but practically I know you cannot employ them under present circumstances; but if you show firmness against the priestly insulters of the law, the Protestants will give you a support of public opinion, a moral and religious force, that will, I am confident, act in the most beneficial way. The law must be vindicated, both here and there; and if the law is found to be ineffective, your first step in November should be to make it what the Emancipationists in 1829, and Lord John Russell in 1851, declared to be their intention—fulfil their pledges!

These are high and delicate and difficult matters, but they are forced upon you, and if you deal honestly and boldly with them you may save the country, and probably lengthen your own tenure of power; but, at all events, though you should lose the latter, you will preserve your character, and you will knit in confidence and respect towards you the whole of the loyalty and Church of Englandism in the two countries, of the Scotch Church, and even the majority of the non-political Methodists and Dissenters. We are a great party, the only great party in the country, but broken and dispirited by the double treachery of Peel.

If you are to go out, let it not be on some paltry question of bribery, or on the choice of a Chairman, or any small

matter. Word, or at least propose to word, your Queen's
Speech so as to pledge yourselves to the Protestant Constitution, and let that be your stand-or-fall question. Nothing
else is broad and solid enough to stand on.

Ever yours sincerely,

J. W. Croker.

Recollect, I always was an Emancipationist, but not in the
cart-before-the-horse style in which Mr. Pitt in 1793, and
Peel in 1829, mismanaged and spoiled, nay poisoned, a thing
right in itself.

J. W. C.

Lord Lonsdale to Mr. Croker.

London, December 25th, 1852.

Disraeli has extraordinary confidence in his powers of
speech. He thinks always he is going to put the question,
and [that] he will carry the whole House with him. He has
been deceived so often that he ought to be wiser. As a party
leader he will be encouraged, but I doubt if there is a single
man that would be his follower. He is our best man, but we
have great difficulty in keeping our troops in discipline.

Truly yours,

Lonsdale.

The Earl of Hardwicke * to Mr. Croker.*

Wimpole, December 30th.

I think the game is up as regards the Conservative party
(so called). It is clear to me that the union of Whigs and
Peelites, with the side-door open to the Radicals, leads to these
consequences—that while our party will be thinned, so slow
and moderate will be the democratic downward tendency, that
as a party we shall be deprived of a link strong enough to
hold us together.

It is, moreover, now so clear that the power and preponderance are in the hands of, and turns to, the trade, moneyed, and

* [Lord Hardwicke held the office of Postmaster-General in Lord
Derby's Government.]

manufacturing classes, that the land will be governed by them, and obliged to submit to a state of things that will enhance the value of trade. The positive injustice lately shown in the determination of the House of Commons not to advance Free Trade, except in the direction of trade and manufactures, together with the evidence given that the 10*l.* householders are strong enough to resist with success any proposal to tax themselves, seems to me to settle so clearly the question of a Conservative Government, that I no longer think it possible.

We must now depend on the moderation of the movement party for the safety of our firesides. There are other features in the case. Although Derby and Disraeli in the two Houses did wonders, and the Government in our hands was steadily carried on in the offices, yet we were destitute of Parliamentary talent compared with the allies opposed to us. Had Lord Aberdeen acted on his declaration (by implication made), namely, that as there was nothing between us and him but the question of Free Trade, he would give us his support, all would have been well, and he and his party might have taken our places under Lord Derby. The conduct of Lord Aberdeen and his friends (having acted alone on personal pique and hatred) is, in my opinion, disgraceful to them.

Now you know my mind on this question. I do not know if you agree with me, but I think the Conservative party beaten out of the field.*

Sincerely yours,

HARDWICKE.

Mr. Croker to the Earl of Hardwicke. Extract.

December 31st, 1852.

As to the party, I cannot but feel with you that a party without a spokesman in the House of Commons is as nothing; but with such a spokesman as Disraeli, it is worse than nothing. In opposition, his talents of debate would be most valuable if there was any security for his principles or his judgment. I have no faith in either.

But, after all, nobody is so much to blame as Derby. Why did he not take higher and truer ground ? Why are you all turned out on—neither you nor any one else can say—*what ?*

---

* [It remained out of power about five years.]

You had not even hoisted a flag to rally round. You have
been like some poor people I have read of in the late storm,
buried under the ruins of your own edifice ; but whether you
were stifled or crushed—killed by a rafter or a brick—nobody
can tell. You have died a death so ignoble that it has no
name, and the coroner's verdict is *found dead !* Why did
you not die in the Protestant cause ?—on something that
some party could take an interest in.

Why did you spare Cardinal Wiseman ? Why butter
Louis Napoleon thicker than his own French cooks ?

Why did you lay the ground of the confiscation of landed
property by a differential income-tax, and by hinting at
taxing property by inheritance ? " You have left undone the
things you ought to have done, and you have done those
things which you ought not to have done ; and there is no "
—*help* for you.

My own guess is this, that Disraeli's vanity, or, as he
would say, his character, was committed by his electioneering
speeches and addresses, and that you all—half generosity and
half prudence—resolved to stand by him rather than break up
the Government, which his resignation would have done.
That is my solution of the greatest political riddle I ever
encountered.

Mr. S. H. Walpole * *to Mr. Croker. Extract.*

Cowdray, Petworth, January 13th, 1853.

The great mistake in our financial propositions consisted
principally in attempting too much. Taken by themselves
each of them was right. But doubling the house tax was
absolutely fatal. This I foresaw from the very commencement ; and I did not foresee without forewarning. We
were placed, however, in a most difficult position. We were
bound to act on the Free Trade principles which the country
had sanctioned. We were equally bound, consistently with
those principles, to relieve the agriculturists as far as we
could ; and the Chancellor of the Exchequer had held out
such enormous expectations, with so little in hand to make
them good, that a common Budget of ordinary prudence was
no longer practicable, however desirable. Hence our fall.

* [Mr. Walpole held office for the first time under Lord Derby in 1852,
as Home Secretary.]

And the misfortune is that in that fall Conservatism appears
to be dragged down with us.   Where it will all end, Heaven
only knows!   I tremble for the future.

Always yours, my dear Sir, very faithfully,

S. H. WALPOLE.

Mr. Croker to ——.

West Moulsey, February 11th [1853].

I would ask you to remember (for I daresay you read)
what I said of Lord Derby and his Government in the
Review for September.   I there gave, upon the same grounds
that the Ministry did, the whole question of Protection; I
endeavoured—and, as I am told, with some success, amongst
my ultra-Tory friends—to remove that stumbling-block out
of the way, and it was thought that I prepared my readers'
minds for what I saw was the inevitable policy of the
Ministry; and I think I may say without vanity that I
placed both the personal and political claims of Lord Derby's
Ministry on as solid and practical, and yet as high and
honourable, grounds as any one has done.   My chief fear
was an untimely and wild Budget, founded on the Buckingham
electioneering addresses and speeches.   Was it unfounded?
    Then as to the Budget speech.   If Mr. Cobden or Mr.
Bright had thought proper to attack the *Quarterly Review*,
the principle which it has always advocated and the statesmen
with whom it has been connected, they could not have done
so more offensively on every point than Mr. Disraeli did.
You ask me whether I can deny that the "tendencies" of the
age are more "humanising" than those of fifty or a hundred
years ago, and especially in the Navy.
    But *that* was not Mr. Disraeli's statement.   He not only
stated that the departure from this system of oppression and
injustice was recent, but he even specified the very exact
periods of that oppression and injustice to have been between
from twenty to forty years ago, namely, the precise time in
which I was Secretary of the Admiralty under Lord Mul-
grave, Mr. Yorke, and Lord Melville, Sir George Hope, Sir
Joseph Yorke, and Sir Graham Moore, &c.   Had he said, *as*

* [It is uncertain to whom this letter was written. The copy is not
complete, and there is no name or address upon it.]

you do, fifty or a hundred years, neither the *Quarterly* nor I, nor my surviving colleagues, need have said anything about it (though we might have thought that the charges were much exaggerated in point of *fact,* and quite obsolete and idle in point of *time*).   But the selecting so definitely for his animadversions the *exact period* in which my friends were in office, could it be expected that I, almost the only survivor, and a not inconsiderable colleague, was to submit in silent acquiescence under such imputations?   You appeal to me for instance, as to the corporal punishment of young gentlemen.*   You are not aware that it was *just* in the stigmatised period that this practice was forbidden, and that I, individually I, was the person who first proposed and induced the First Lord and the Board to order its abolition.   As to Mr. Disraeli's treatment of every maritime topic, I ask you only to look to his speech, and say whether there is any one of them introduced without some sneer or charge against the Admiralty of thirty years ago.   They are all untrue, and most of them have no more to do with the Admiralty than with the Royal Academy, though *it* is (to use a vulgar expression well suited to such low malice) lugged in on every occasion as the fountain of all the imputed mischief.

My own opinion is that all this was done (for the matters were as foreign from a Budget as landscape gardening would have been) in mere spite against *me* as the author of the September article, which deprecated (though in civil and even complimentary terms) the introduction of the Budget before Christmas.

Perhaps also there may have been some old *personal* grudge against *me,* for the *Times* has since told us that my last article was in revenge for an unfavourable portrait of me drawn by Mr. Disraeli many years ago in his novel of 'Coningsby.'   Now it happens that I never saw 'Coningsby,' nor,

---

* [The passage in Mr. Disraeli's speech here referred to is the following:—" I have no doubt myself, from all I can observe and learn from inquiry, that the conduct of the officers of the Royal Navy, especially of late years, is distinguished by a generous sympathy with all classes of their countrymen, which cannot be too highly praised.   I have no doubt that in the Navy, as well as in all departments of life, much more humanising tendencies are exerting their influence than there did twenty-five, or forty, or fifty years ago."   This was one of the statements which Mr. Croker called in question in his *Quarterly Review* article.]

till after the review was printed, ever, to my recollection, had heard that it alluded to me *en bien ni en mal*. I had heard indeed long ago that he had drawn a flattering picture of me in another novel called ' Vivian Grey '; I never saw that book either, and know not whether the fact is so or not. All I can say is in the most perfect sincerity that I had no personal feeling, nor a suspicion that I had any personal cause of complaint, against him. Quite the reverse. But *if* what the *Times* says be true, and *if* he attacked *me* in ' Coningsby ' nine years ago, it only corroborates the probability that, what a Latin author calls *odium in longum jacens*—his longhoarded malice—was glad to find a vent in his Budget speech.

But of all that I was as unconscious before I wrote my articles as I am now contemptuously indifferent. If any one does me the honour to enquire about my character he will not, I think, look for it in Mr. Disraeli's contribution to the circulating libraries.

I took up the whole matter on grounds of public justice and policy. I treated Mr. Disraeli in the first article with civility, and in the last I attacked only his public measures without any personal feeling, and I think without any offensive expression. Though certainly the opportunities were not wanting, and if my letter had not grown to such an unconscionable length, I could give you positive—nay, ocular—proof of how desirous I was to uphold Mr. Disraeli if he had not so wantonly and so unjustly attacked the Administrations with which I had been connected.

I concur in all you say of Lord Derby, and shall never cease to regret, not that he went out—for I agree with you that the coalition would have forced him out—but that he did not go out on some principle round which his friends and the country could have rallied. On this point, too, when we meet I can tell you circumstances which would show you my good will towards and confidence in *him;* but it was thought by others, in whose opinions I ultimately concurred, that the ' Quarterly Review ' could not, without losing all character and with it its power of doing any good, have blinked the great question of Popish aggression—the only one of all the questions afloat in which the country feels any deep or lasting interest.

One word more. Soon after he came into office, Lord Malmesbury in some public document called Louis Napoleon *Prince President.* On seeing this, having some private acquaintance with his lordship, and feeling strongly for both the

credit of the Administration and the dignity of the country, I
took the liberty of observing to him that this was an irregular
denomination which might lead to embarrassing consequences.
That the French President himself never called himself in any
public document *Prince* President; that his private society
called him *Monseigneur*; and that his newspapers affected to
call him *Prince President*; but that in all his public acts (and
I quoted recent instances) he called himself *President, tout
court*. To this Lord Malmesbury made me (as perhaps my
officiousness deserved) a very short, dry reply; but even *that*
did not prepare me for such a fulsome and undignified panegyric as he afterwards pronounced on the *parvenu!*

Thus you will see that I did not at least take my friends by
surprise, nor look out for holes to pick. I had the *temerity*,
perhaps, but at least the zeal and sincerity, to apprise them of
the danger that I foresaw; and I now think that if you will
place yourself in my position, you will not take a very different
view of my article from what I have done.

Mr. Croker to Lord Brougham.

West Moulsey, February 22nd, 1853.

MY DEAR BROUGHAM,

We are indeed in the strangest state of public affairs—
anomalous and perilous. I agree with you that there is
nothing positively unconstitutional in Lord John's leading
the House without active office, if the House chooses to be so
led.* The office of Privy Councillor is sufficient to establish
responsibility—for *that* is the real responsibility, except as to
the few offices into which one is specially sworn. But it is
unprecedented, and I always dread new precedents; not
being able to foresee how they may be hereafter applied. In
principle, however, I think it much the same, or perhaps a
little less objectionable, than being in the Cabinet without
office, but I think it hardly respectful to the House, and absolutely derogatory to the station of his *official* colleagues.

Lord John's public and private proceedings are comically at
variance. He does his public work without an office, and he

---

* [In Lord Aberdeen's Ministry, which succeeded Lord Derby's, Lord
John Russell was for a few weeks Foreign Secretary, and then retired to
make room for Lord Clarendon. He afterwards led the House for a time
without office.]

accepts the office of Moore's executor without doing the
work.   The truth is that he fell asleep over Moore's papers,
and never awoke till the clamour the publication created
startled him into a consciousness that he had overslept
himself.

Has he given up the Queen's Foreign Affairs that he might
have leisure for Moore's domestic concerns ?   Has he given
up his interest in the nuptials of Mdlle. Montijo for those of
" Lalla Rookh " ? and has the " Veiled Prophet " usurped the
place of the mysterious Czar ?

When he sees some of his friends shying off from a ticklish
division, will he not try to detain them with " Fly not yet,
'tis just the hour " ?

I fear that the Government of the country is likely to become from such a strange mixture of things at once odious
and ridiculous.   And where are we to look for another ?   I
despair, and have done so ever since I read Disraeli's Buck-
inghamshire speeches.   Nothing is so dangerous as those
sharp blades in adventurous hands.   A vain, giddy man may
be brilliant, but never can be safe, and I am alarmed at
fireworks when I know that there is a magazine in the
neighbourhood.

J. W. C.

The Earl of Lonsdale to Mr. Croker.

London, May 22nd, 1853.

DEAR CROKER,

From the accession of Lord Derby's Government, and
during its short continuance, his administration was a succession of blunders, mistakes, miscalculations, and ill-advised
measures.   There was a want of practical knowledge for the
working of the Government, which his new Ministers had not
experience or judgment to meet.   The first false step was
sanctioning and adopting the Corrupt Practices Bill, when an
opportunity occurred to drop it.   The working of it was mis-
represented, and it is only just now at Canterbury that its
powers are beginning to be developed.   A new Parliament
would never have passed such a bill.   I believe with ordinary
prudence we should have had a majority in the last House,
but the Budget was calculated to rob everybody and conciliate no one.   The prospect is gloomy.

Our men are deserting. We have now no rallying point
to keep our troops together. We are helpless as a party.
Something may turn up, but this is a remote expectation.
There are three parties that hate one another cordially. The
Whigs, I am inclined to think, hate the Peelites more than
they do us, and the Conservatives and Peelites hate each other,
so as not to leave a hope of reconciliation ; and yet there is
likely to be a difference, if not a split, upon reform between
them. However, this is adjourned to next year. The Ultra-
Liberals, or Rads, will never be content with any reform that
will not give them a majority in the Commons.

Truly yours,

LONSDALE.

December 22nd, 1853.

Dear Croker,

I have been living very much out of politics, and my
immediate friends with whom I communicate were out of
town. Malmesbury is keeping Christmas at his place in
Hampshire. I know lately our friends have thought our
prospects better. However, upon the receipt of your letter,
though of course I did not quote you, I went to call on Dizzy,
who happens to be in town, and wished to hear what he
thought of present matters and of prospects. We clubbed
our views together. All our party seems to have recovered to
a certain degree the shock and disappointment they experienced last year, and appear to be in good spirits, and ready
to co-operate and to act as circumstances require. We cal-
culate upon 260 upon whom we can depend. Last session we
were sadly depressed by the *faux pas* of some of our colleagues, but that has passed away. On the other hand, the
Coalition Government, who were thought to be so strong and
invincible, have now had a great shake ; all the illusion of
their being such a strong Government is gone. This will
animate our friends, and as we appear strong, it is to be hoped
we may have some adhesions. Disraeli tells me he will be
against the principle of further reform, and of changing the
representation from one constituency to another. Of course he
cannot refuse to deal with such places as are convicted of whole-
sale [bribery], as the old Tories did in respect to Grampound.

I do not think we are well informed of the immediate

grounds of Pam's* secession.   It is said he was not attended
to in the Cabinet, he had no influence, and was almost
snubbed.   I hear from an old Whig that he approved of
Clarendon's Eastern Policy, and that Clarendon has letters of
his to that effect.   I hear Pam is very angry with his former
colleagues, which he did not even disguise to Cecil Forester,
whom he met and walked with in the Park.   However, we
shall have this difficulty with him, he will be for a half
measure of reform, and our friends will be against all reform.
His retirement has weakened and given the Government a
shake, and every one now thinks it is on the eve of dissolution.

I remain, faithfully yours,

LONSDALE.

Mr. Henry Drummond to Mr. Croker.

December 19th, 1853.

MY DEAR CROKER,

What I want to know is who drew the Reform Bill?
Ellice told me that it was not that which was prepared in the
Cabinet, but Durham drew it altogether.

What was Brougham's bill?   You remember that they
made him Chancellor in order to prevent his bringing it
forward.

There is no Conservative party to arouse or to consolidate.
You have the most reckless man in the country at the head
of it, who is himself the model of a destructive.

When you granted Catholic Emancipation in order to avoid
a civil war, a permanent premium was given to monster meetings, and carrying [legislation] by bullying.   When the
Reform Bill took power from the land and gave it to trade,
you took it from those who have a permanent, and transferred
it to those who have only a temporary, interest in the country.
The manufacturer must say, why have we a King at a
million a year when a President at three hundred would do
as well ?

When the Corn Bill was repealed because, as Lord Haddington told me (this is confidential to you), "it was only
another wave of that great deluge of democracy which neither

---

* [Lord Palmerston resigned his office of Home Secretary on the 15th of
December, 1853, but resumed it on the 26th.]

that nor any other Government could withstand," it is manifest
that every Government must grant every successive democratic demand that is made.

When I canvass this county [Surrey], and talk to 4000
men, and cannot find 100 who care or know about any one
public question, but vote according to some fancy about putting
down expenses, disbanding armies, and getting rid of all
taxes except upon rich men, I say that Bright is right, and
we are on the eve of becoming a Republic.

A Conservative splash will only aggravate. There is not
among them all two men, except Walpole and Newdegate,
who understand the abstract principles on which monarchy
is founded, nor how to apply them in a crisis like this.

I have had twenty years of wrath bottled up, which I
shall let out at last, with what success will be as God shall
please ; but I expect none, except to be stoned by some of the
thousand roughs with which the accesses to Parliament will
be thronged.

I am glad to see you write so clear and well, and hope your
health is quite re-established.   Lady Harriet and I are getting
old, but I am always,

Yours very faithfully,

HENRY DRUMMOND.

December 23rd, 1853.

My dear Croker,

Many thanks for the extracts. I know that Brougham had
a fully prepared bill, which he expected the Government
would call on him to introduce, so both Denison and Ellice
told me. They made him Chancellor to prevent his bringing
it forward in opposition to theirs, and he burnt it.

All is up. The pass was sold when the Duke of Wellington yielded the Popish claims rather than have civil war,
whilst he retained just enough prohibition to keep up a per-
petual raw place. The Test Act followed ; then the Reform
Bill ; and now all the efforts of statesmen have been directed
to the one object of putting on the drag to the State coach,
running down the hill into the slough of democracy. The
sword won kingdoms originally, and the sword only can
maintain them.

It was the Speaker who suggested the Militia franchise,
and I to the Speaker. It seemed that the House was strong

at that time on Locke King's motion for extending the franchise, and it was thought advisable to make it at least be earned by personal service.

It was Lord Stanley's fault alone that he offered to form a Government when he knew he had no materials; he had nothing to lose, and might gain something, but he sacrificed Walpole, turned Pakington's head, made Dizzy a Privy Councillor, which he despises, and has no idea fixed but that of returning soon to the Holy Land.

The reversal of the judgment on the Braintree case * has finished the Church of England. It is quite true, because Dizzy stated it in the House, that he was going to bring in a Succession Bill.

Palmerston is gone out upon the Foreign Policy. It is monstrous to have a fleet there, and see our ally beaten and never stir.†

Always yours faithfully,

HENRY DRUMMOND.

The memorable event of 1852 in Mr. Croker's eyes, and indeed in the eyes of the nation, was not the downfall of Lord Derby's first Administration, but the death of the Duke of Wellington, which occurred on the 14th of September, at Walmer Castle. Twelve days previously, the Duke had gone over from Walmer to Folkestone for the special purpose of paying a visit to Mr. Croker, with whom he had been on terms of cordial friendship and confidence for upwards of six-and-forty years. Mr. Croker fortunately made a memorandum the same evening of what had taken place at the interview, chiefly, as he mentions in a letter, for his " wife and Lady Barrow, who were present the whole time, and

* [The Braintree Church Rate case was the cause of litigation for twelve years, and was finally decided by the House of Lords in August, 1853. The rate was originally opposed by the Dissenters, who were in a majority, and the Lords decided that the rate was unlawful, having been imposed by a minority of the parishioners.]

† [Alluding to the destruction of the Turkish fleet by the Russians, at Sinope, 30th November, 1853.]

wished to have a note of what they had heard." The Duke
was at this time 83, and Mr. Croker 72.

Memorandum by Mr. Croker.

Folkestone, September 4th, 1852.—The Duke of Wellington
had never expected to see me again, and I, a few months
since, had never expected to see him, but as soon as he
heard that I had come here, he immediately came over to
see me. Not having written to apprize me, I had unluckily
gone over to see him, but I waited at Dover for his return,
when he promised to come again to Folkestone on Saturday
(this was Thursday the 2nd), which he did, and has staid
three hours with us, chatting in the most agreeable manner
on all manners of subjects, with a vivacity and memory
worth noting of in a man in his 84th year. We are
both deaf, I worse than usual to-day, and he, though he
walks very well in fact, seems to totter; but this he has
done for some years. Both our minds, however seem as clear
as ever.

He talked of the length of our acquaintance, which began
in 1806, and reminded me of his having in 1808, when he first
went to Portugal, left the Parliamentary business of the Irish
office in my hands, which led me into political life. He
remembered much better than I did the names of some of
the bills that I had to manage, even down to some local
Dublin bills.

This brought out some allusion to our years. He said,
"Now that the Duke of Hamilton is gone, Anglesey* and I
are the seniors of the House of Lords; indeed, I believe I am
the father of the whole Parliament, for I came into the House
of Commons in Ireland before I was of age, and was soon
drawn on an Election Committee. It was on a College
Election, and the chief question was whether the scholars,
who were *minors,* had a right to vote. The first morning we
took our seats the scholars had placed on every member's
desk a paper with '*Minors have a right to vote*' written on it,
but on my paper there was written, 'YOU KNOW *that minors
have a right to vote.*'"

The post coming in brought me a letter from Lord
Lyndhurst. The Duke said he was glad to hear that his

* [Lord Anglesey was born in 1768, and succeeded to the title in 1812.]

sight was much improved, and that there was a prospect of a complete cure. This brought him to speak of the Baron de Bode's case,* on which he said Lyndhurst had made, as he always does, a capital speech. He did not know why Lyndhurst had taken the matter up. He had stated it very ably, but had not convinced the Duke, who thought that the Baron claimed as a British subject what, being a British subject, he could never have possessed. He then went on to say that he had originally become acquainted with this and hundreds of similar cases by an accident which he thought had never before happened to any man, and probably never would again; he had been the accredited arbitrator of all the Powers of Europe. " When the question of restitution or indemnity for the private losses of individual foreigners from the lawless measures of the Revolution, was advanced at the Treaty of Paris, it produced great excitement, and even stock-jobbing; claims were brought up and trafficked in to an alarming extent, and there were suitors of all nations and to all amounts—some for the loss of sovereignties, and some for statues and pictures. The case grew so considerable that the Duke of Richelieu proposed to me to be sole arbiter of *all* these claims; the other Powers joined in the request, and I consented, and I think in four or five months of hard judicial application, I settled the whole account to the general satisfaction."

Croker. Not to that, it seems, of Baron de Bode.

Duke. Why, I don't know; I heard nothing of his complaint at the time, and I really doubt, in spite of Lyndhurst's excellent speech, whether his claim is a just one. He seems to claim as a British subject what he did not lose as a British subject. He confounds two characters.

We talked of Lamartine's description of Buonaparte's weakness, and even cowardice, towards the close of Waterloo: he said, " Of course I could see nothing about it; but I can hardly believe it. I think that even with ordinary men a great interest would overcome personal fear."

Croker. Perhaps it is as true as your having had eight

---

* [The Baron de Bode had made a claim, as a British subject, on the indemnity fund paid by France to England at the close of the war. The case was first heard in the Court of Queen's Bench in 1845, and was kept going, in some form or other, for many years afterwards, the Baron being always unsuccessful.]

horses knocked up or killed under you ?　" *Copenhagen* " must have been a very old horse when I saw him last at Strath-fieldsaye, if you rode him at Copenhagen.

Duke. Oh, no.　He was not named from my having ridden him at Copenhagen ; his dam was a blood mare, which Tom Grosvenor had in the expedition to Copenhagen, and he called her foal by that name, so that he must have been foaled after 1806.　Grosvenor sold him to Charles Stewart, now Londonderry, of whom, when he left the Peninsula, I bought him and rode him throughout the rest of the war, and mounted no other horse at Waterloo.

He re-told me the anecdote of Louis XVIII. having offered him Grosbois,* and that nothing came of it ; but he added, what I forget whether he told me before, that the Duke of Richelieu explained to him why it was not done, which was that the King was afraid of the Marshals, who would have been furious at it.　Some time after, however, the King sent him a cross of the St. Esprit in very fine diamonds, which he afterwards heard indirectly was meant as a compensation for Grosbois.

I asked him how the difference of religion was got over in giving him the St. Esprit.　He said he did not know of any difficulty, but if there had been any, Monsieur, the strictest of the family on such points, was very good humoured about it, and would, no doubt, have arranged it.

But any religious question could only have arisen on the ceremony of *reception.*　The Prince Regent, the Duke of York, and the Duke of Clarence had all had it from the King before he left England.　But none of us were ever *reçus.* The Princes who had been *reçus* before the Revolution, we strangers, and the surviving *staff* of the order figured in the Almanack ; but it was not till four or five years later that the King ventured to re-establish the order, which had been abolished early in the Revolution by a creation of French Cordons Bleus of the old fashion.†

---

* [See vol. i., p. 332.]

† [On the 30th July, 1791, the National Assembly had abolished the Order of the St. Esprit, and Louis XVI. never wore it after, but all the other Princes continued to wear it during their emigration.　When Louis XVIII. was about to return to France he gave it to the Regent and the Dukes of York and Clarence, and subsequently in Paris to the King of Spain, Don Carlos, and the Duke of Wellington.　But though it and the

We talked of Cardinal Wiseman, who had just passed through here. He asked me what sort of a man he was; I said I had never seen him, but that I had heard he had the appearance of a jolly Irish priest, to which he had a right, as we say in Ireland, as his father, I had heard, was Irish, though his mother was a Spaniard, of Seville, where I believe Wiseman was born.

Duke. Some of those Irish Spaniards were very useful to me in the Peninsula; they were our best spies, the most trust-worthy and intelligent. Curtis was a useful, and really a good sort of man, though somewhat spoiled when he got to Ireland. I think he meant well, and I had a regard for him. He had been some time in secret communication with me before I saw him, and he had sent me numerous documents and papers, and I enquired how he could venture while the French were in possession of the town (Salamanca) to keep these papers. "Oh," said he, "I got a lady to conceal them in her clothes" (here the Duke paused as if observing that my ladies were present, and then added), "thinking the French not likely to rummage a lady's clothes. I saw the lady after, and thanked her for her zeal in the cause." There was evidently some little waggish circumstance which he could not mention before my ladies.

I reminded him that one day at Paris, when the Emperor of Russia and King of Prussia dined with him, something was suggested that might have been better done at Waterloo, and that he had said, "Yes, I should have done it if I had had 10,000 of *my old Spanish infantry.*" Castlereagh was by, sitting near me, and said, "What can he mean? He never said a word to us of those Spaniards during the whole Peninsular War but that they were worse than nothing."

Duke. Oh, yes, I remember. I had read in my youth of the "*old Spanish infantry*" as the finest soldiers in the world,

----

surviving members appeared in the Almanack, and the King, and I believe the Princes, continued to wear the decoration, the order seemed in abey-ance till 1818, when it was given alone, and perhaps as an experiment on public opinion, to the Duc de Richelieu, and in 1820 there was a regular creation of about twenty of the most illustrious of the old and the new nobility as Cordons Bleus. In 1830 they amounted to about seventy, of whom the Duc de Nemours was the junior, but they all disappeared before the July revolution.—J. W. C.]

till they were cut to pieces and destroyed at one, I think, of the great Condé's battles; and this name *old Spanish infantry* had taken hold of me, and I used to call my old English regiments who were serving with me in the Peninsula "*the old Spanish infantry.*" This gave rise to Castlereagh's mistake (who was very often absent), which I remember made us laugh.

[It was at this same dinner party that, talking of general tactics, the Emperor and the King insisted on the superiority of Buonaparte's system of attack by *columns.* The Duke took the other side, denied that it had ever been or could be successful against steady troops on a large scale, and he instanced Waterloo. The two sovereigns, who had not quite got out of their *engouement* about Buonaparte, and who attributed their own successive defeats to the column system, persisted; though the Duke's reasoning was most clear and convincing; but at last he said he requested permission to show their Majesties his principle by the actual exhibition of the two systems by his whole army next day on the Plaine St. Denis. This was the object of that great review.—J. W. C.]

Croker. Did you ever see Spanish troops really stand to their work and fight?

Duke. No; the best would fire a volley while the enemy was out of reach, and then all run away. They were, no doubt, individually as brave as other men. I am sure they were vain enough of their bravery, but I never could get them to stand their ground.

In coming to see me (as he had done the day but one before, Sept. 2nd) he had chosen to walk from the station to our house, and without even a guide. He said he had found it a rough walk, and the ground intersected in a way he had not expected; so I said to him, " It seems you forgot *to guess what was at the other side of the hill.*" This was in allusion to a circumstance which had occurred between him and me some thirty years before. When travelling on the north road, we amused ourselves by guessing what sort of a country we should find at the other side of the hills we drove up; and when I expressed surprise at some extraordinary good guesses he had made, he said. " Why, I have spent all my life in trying *to guess what was at the other side of the hill.*"

I had reminded him of this just as we were driving across the ravine that had impeded him, and he turned round to Mrs. Croker to explain it to her, adding, " All the business of war, and indeed all the business of life, is to endeavour to find out what you don't know by what you do; that's what I called 'guessing what was at the other side of the hill.'"

He said the perfection of practical war was to move troops as steadily and coolly on a field of battle as on a parade. "Soult's fault was that, though a great strategist, he never seemed to me to know how to handle the troops after the battle had begun."

I then told him what Guizot told me of Lannes having said that "le plus grand Général était celui que la canonnade faisait mieux entendre, et que la fumée faisait voir plus clair."

Duke. Humph! (a pause) That's only a cleverer phrase for what I have been just saying—*sang froid*—presence of mind; but that's not enough; the mind besides being cool must have the art of knowing what is to be done and how to do it. I, of course, never met Lannes; he was killed in Germany, but I have seen most of the other Marshals, and I have no doubt that, as a General, Buonaparte was the best of them. When I met all the great allied Generals at Paris in 1814, they were so good as to compliment me on my successes in Spain. I told them that I quite agreed in the estimate that I had heard made, that the *absence* of Buonaparte was as good as 40,000 men. As *I* had never met Buonaparte, and as *they* had all been beaten by him *in person,* my allusion to that estimate was received as a compliment to them, and modesty on my part; but I really believe that it was true as to the continental armies. Yes, Buonaparte was certainly the best of them all, and with his prestige worth 40,000 men.

Croker. 'Tis easy to be best when one is master of them all, sovereign dispenser of punishment and reward, and having no control to thwart, no scruple to stop, and no responsibility but to himself.

Duke. Yes, that's very true; but still I don't think any of them could, even in his circumstances, have done what he did. Much of my ultimate success in Spain was owing to my singular position. I was a [here he paused for a word] *conquérant sans ambition.* I had for a time a sovereign power there, but no one suspected me of any design to become King of Spain or Portugal, like Joseph, or Soult, or Junot. I *was* almost King of Spain, but I handled my power with the greatest moderation and abstinence, and avoided every unnecessary exhibition of it. All the world knew that I desired nothing but to beat the French out of Spain, and then go home to my own country, leaving them to manage theirs as they pleased. So I avoided offence and jealousy, and was obeyed as willingly as the nature of that people would admit of.

He said that he had met the Duchess de Montpensier at Windsor, and happened to be near her (she, it seems, did not know who he was), when some mention was made of *La Granja* (pronounced *Granha*), and he said something about the site and style of the palace, and especially about a court and a fountain that were there, which she overheard, and asked how Monsieur came to know anything of La Granja? The Duke smiled, and said that he believed he knew the Palace of La Granja, and that of Madrid too, almost as well as Her Royal Highness. The Queen, seeing that the Duchess looked surprised, came up and told her who he was.

Croker. Had you not your Golden Fleece on? She might have guessed by that that you were a *Grand d'Espagne.*

Duke. She did not observe it in the crowd, and was only struck by overhearing so accurate a description of La Granja from she did not know whom.

He told us also a curious anecdote of the Prince de Joinville, whose late publication I mentioned. The Duke said he had never seen him but twice, and never had spoken to him; but on one of those occasions he saw and heard him guilty of a piece of rudeness and bad taste to our Queen, which he said made him quite satisfied to have no further acquaintance with him. It was at Windsor. The Queen, desirous of amusing everybody, was busy getting up some round game, and proposed, amongst others, to the Prince de Joinville to join the circle; he replied, "*Madame, je ne joue qu'à la guerre.*"

[N.B.—I am told that Lord Aberdeen says that he also was present, but that the phrase was not used by the Prince de Joinville, but by the Duke d'Aumale, when he accompanied Louis Philippe on his visit to Windsor in 1844; but Lord Aberdeen *must* be mistaken. I need say nothing of the Duke of Wellington's accuracy; and as to my own, my wife and Sir George and Lady Barrow, who were present, heard the name as clearly as I did; and, moreover, it could have been no other than the Prince de Joinville that was meant, for we were talking of his pamphlet and of his voyage to fetch back Buonaparte's bones; and, finally, none of Louis Philippe's sons accompanied him to Windsor but the

Duke de Montpensier. So that Lord Aberdeen clearly mistakes the *person* and the *time.*]

Croker. Well, that is a degree of rudeness and *fanfaronnade* that I could not have believed of any man, and besides such a *strut!* for he never, I believe, saw any real war. His Morocco affair seems to have been nothing worth mentioning. His brothers had seen something that might be called service, but his "*guerre*" was a very small war indeed.

Duke. Quite true; but all this rendered the ill-manners the more offensive.

Partridge-shooting happened to be mentioned; he said, "Ah, 'twas only yesterday morning that I was thinking how often you and I used to meet at this season to shoot red-legged partridges." I said in a doubtful tone, "Do you venture to shoot now?" for really there seemed no kind of reason why he should not. He paused as if unwilling to say directly No; and then said, "Why, Charles is with me, and if he goes out perhaps I may go and look at him." I think he said something of having hunted last season; but it is unluckily one of my deaf days, and I missed several points of what he said, and some I have already forgotten, for he talked alternately to me and the ladies for three hours with very little pause.

He said our present Queen had resolved to prevent such an affair as had occurred between George III. and "*our friend*" when Prince of Wales, as to the revenues of the Duchy of Cornwall during the minority, by appointing a Commission to receive and accumulate the revenues. He was one, Lord Lyndhurst another (he mentioned two or three more). They had already accumulated 100,000*l.*, besides paying for the education and personal expenses of the boy; for instance, 5000*l.* had been given to his late tutor, Mr. Birch. The Prince seems a fine, well-disposed boy.

He said he had had a letter from London to-day to say that a Mr. Neild had died, leaving his executor 100*l.*, and the rest of his fortune to the Queen, estimated, it was said, at 400,000*l.**

An old soldier, with a medal or two and several bars on his ribbon, and with, as he said, a French bullet in his thigh from the siege of Badajos, came up to him on the railway platform. He had some employment in the neighbour-

---

* [The estate was sworn as being under 250,000*l.*]

hood as a drill-master at schools, and said *he was well off*, but wished the Duke would make him a warden of the Tower. "No, no," said the Duke, "I cannot do that." The Duke then said to me, "All I can *now* do must be done to reward current service—the Cape and India; every one must have his day." The Duke, however, gave him the *accustomed sovereign*, which, I believe, he always carries loose in his waistcoat pocket for these occasions, so frequent are they; but he, on this occasion, gave it with evident reluctance, as the man (*an Irishman*) was obtrusive, and inclined to be over-familiar, and, moreover, a little *tipsy*.

Lady Barrow's five little girls were with us, and he won their hearts by writing his name in their albums; in the signature of one, the best written of the five, he wrote his name with a single *l*. His good humour and kindness to the children, and indeed to everybody, was very pleasing. To *me* (evidently on account of my precarious health) he was peculiarly affectionate.

On going away he promised to see me again next week, but as he could not then fix the day he would write to let me know.

As we were getting into the carriage that was to take us to the station, he handed the ladies in, and placed them in the back seats, the Duke insisting on taking the front seat, saying, "I must sit opposite to Nony; yes, I must sit opposite to Nony," referring to Lady Barrow by her early familiar name. But she forced him to take the back seat, and then sat opposite to him.

Going down out of the house, there were two sets of steps, which he went down very leisurely with Mrs. Croker on his arm, and counting them 1, 2, 3, and 1, 2, 3 and 4, and then looked back and repeated the numbers, as if for my use, for he thought me feebler than I really am, thank God.

How characteristic this trifle is both of his precision and his kind attentions to others!

Mr. Croker to Mrs. Bedford.

West Moulsey, January 28th.

DEAR MRS. BEDFORD,

My story of the cloak is short and clear. The Duke of Wellington gave me the cloak he wore at Waterloo. I had it for two or three years.

When Sir Thomas Lawrence was painting the Duke's por-

trait for Sir Robert Peel, which was intended to represent
him exactly as he appeared the evening of Waterloo, they
asked me to lend my cloak to be copied. I was goose enough
to consent. As soon as the picture was finished, I sent to
Lawrence for my cloak. He then began to hum and haw
about it, and asked me whether it was not still the Duke's.
At last it came out that he had delivered it to a lady who
said she had the Duke's authority for it. I complained to
the Duke, who seemed a good deal vexed, but equally dis-
inclined to attack the lady, and, with a strange misunder-
standing of the real value of the cloak, he had another—a
perfect fac-simile — made, which he gave me, and which
Mrs. Croker still has. You may be sure that I was by no
means satisfied with this substitution. But the lady was in
possession, and the Duke said, "One cloak is as good as
another." So I had nothing to do but to submit.

I know nothing more about the cloak, but wonder how it
could get out of that lady's possession.

Ever, dear Mrs. Bedford, truly yours,

J. W. CROKER.

Mr. Croker to Mrs. Bedford.

West Moulsey, February 5th, 1853.

DEAR MRS. BEDFORD,

There is, I think, no more to be said about the cloak; that
which you describe was *certainly* NOT that which the Duke
wore *at Waterloo*, and in which he was painted by Sir
Thomas Lawrence, as you may see in the prints, and as I
myself saw when I lent the cloak for that purpose. You are
mistaken if you think that I did not know who the lady was
who possessed herself of my cloak, but having acquiesced by
my (forced) acceptance of the *fac-simile* cloak from the Duke,
I had no longer any claim on the original. That lady was
not Lady Caroline Lamb. I, of course, know nothing of any
cloak which her " capricious " Ladyship may have exhibited,
or what she or Sir A. Carlisle may have said about it: all I
can say with *positive certainty* is, that the cloak which you
describe is *not* the cloak which the Duke gave me as the only
cloak he wore at Waterloo—which, at his desire, I lent to
Sir Thomas Lawrence—in which the Duke was at least twice

painted, and which at his desire again I left in the possession of the lady to whom Sir Thomas had delivered it.

Yours, dear Mrs. Bedford, very faithfully,

J. W. CROKER.

Mr. Croker to Mr. A. Greville.

West Moulsey, Surrey, March 14th, 1852.

MY DEAR GREVILLE,

Ask the Duke, from me, to be so good as to answer this question :—

M. Lamartine, amongst other wonderful (as they seem to me) stories, says that at the last charge at Waterloo, the Duke himself drew his sabre, and putting himself at the head of the column of cavalry " charged like a common trooper." I don't think that the Duke ever forgot that he was a general and not a trooper. It would not surprise me to hear that he had not even drawn his sword that day. Perhaps also I might venture to ask his Grace whether he did say " Up Guards and at them." This also is very unlike him; but it was certainly a moment in which he might have departed from his usual style. Pray let me have your answer as soon as you can find an opportunity of speaking to the Duke. Give him my affectionate regards, and, I fear, farewells ! I write from bed, where I am confined by (we think) some disease of the heart, and can (though the danger may not be immediate) hardly hope that I shall ever again see my illustrious and dear friend.

Ever, my dear Greville, faithfully yours,

J. W. CROKER.

The Duke of Wellington to Mr. Croker.

[Without date.]

I certainly did not draw my sword. I may have ordered, and I dare say I did order, the charge of the cavalry, and pointed out its direction ; but I did not charge as a common trooper.

I have at all times been in the habit of covering as much as possible the troops exposed to the fire of cannon. I place them behind the top of the rising ground, and make them sit and lie down, the better to cover them from the fire.

After the fire of the enemy's cannon, the enemy's troops

may have advanced, or a favourable opportunity of attacking might have arrived. What I must have said and possibly did say was, Stand up, Guards! and then gave the commanding officers the order to attack.

My common practice in a defensive position was to attack the enemy at the very moment at which he was about to attack our troops.

I am very sorry, indeed, to hear that you are unwell. You must keep yourself quiet and take rest.

Lord Hardinge to Mr. Croker.

Great Stanhope Street (Monday), November 15th, 1852.

My DEAR CROKER,

Before I received your note of Saturday I had on the Friday selected twenty-four of the Duke's most celebrated victories to be inscribed in bronze letters, three victories on each of the eight panels. The car is of bronze, of most beautiful workmanship, and, like his fame, will endure for ever.*

It is a simple epitaph on the car which conveys his remains to the grave, and will be kept as a national monument of great interest, for the bronze car is a most beautiful specimen of art, got up in a dozen parts of the country, by the enthusiastic zeal of our best workmen, who are completing it night and day.

You may say, best add the flags; that question has been considered and decided in the negative, and after consideration by authority higher than mine; and, as the more enduring inscription on the car is adopted, I think the other inferior in appropriate value, and concur in that decision; although, in a matter of this sort, I can have no authority, and I should say the victories on the bronze will be very generally preferred by the army and the country.

Your quotations are eloquent, and the reasoning good, but, upon the whole, the course taken seems to me to be the best.

Yours very sincerely,

HARDINGE.

---

* [The car may perhaps endure for ever, but it is not easy to distinguish its beauties, whatever they may be, in the dark corner where it is " stored," in the crypt of St. Paul's Cathedral.]

The following letters are selected from the general correspondence of these two years.

Lord Londonderry to Mr. Croker.   Extract.

Homburg, June 26th, 1852.

The enclosed letter is from our great and interesting friend Metternich, who seems as alive to everything, and his great mind to be as keen, as ever. Keep the letter till I am at Holderness House next month, when I will write to you and ask for my volumes with your judgment.

[*Enclosure in the above.*]

Vienne, ce juin 23, 1852.

Mon cher Marquis,

Je ne vous ai point fait de réponse à vos dernières lettres, parce que je ne savais pas où vous trouver. Vous jouissez encore de la liberté du mouvement; j'ai depuis longtemps perdu l'habitude de ce bien, et ce ne sont que de forts graves événements qui m'ont mis en mouvement, tout en me rendant à une liberté dont chaque jour me fait apprécier le bienfait. Cinquante-cinq années de service public sont une lourde charge pour l'homme consciencieux; il m'est ainsi permis de me sentir soulagé d'un poids après ma descente des planches dans le rang des spectateurs du drame qui est loin encore de sa fin! La pièce toutefois est mieux placée qu'elle ne l'était avant les explosions de 1848. Tout mal est son propre et implacable ennemi, et la marche des événements dans le cours de cette année et leurs suites renferment une nouvelle et bien éclatante preuve que la vérité sait toujours rentrer dans son droit. Le premier élément de la vie sociale, le respect pour l'autorité, a été attaqué dans ses derniers retranchements; ce sont les armées, fortes de leur discipline, qui ont sauvées la société; elles se sont acquises une gloire immortelle. Ce ne sont pas elles qui peuvent gouverner, mais sans leur appui le gouvernement serait encore impossible. Cet empire-ci qui, dans les conditions de sa vie, ne ressemble à aucun autre corps politique, a su résister durant vingt-cinq ans à l'attaque de la révolution civile et militaire de la France, à l'aide de la forte organisation de son système militaire; c'est l'armée qui ne s'est point démentie quand un *interrègne* de 13 années avait affaibli l'autorité civile ; c'est aujourd'hui encore l'armée qui permet au jeune Empereur de reconstruire l'Empire. Où en serait aujourd'hui la France sans son armée ? Ce ne seront pas les Cobden et les Bright qui rendront la paix morale ni à l'Europe ni à leur patrie. Ce service est réservé à d'autres esprits. Ce n'est pas le despotisme que je prêche du fond de ma retraite ; c'est l'ordre sans lequel il n'y a point de société. Vous voyez que je reste fidèle à la pratique de ma vie toute entière.

Vous me dites qu'il ne reste que peu de nos collègues du Congrès de Vienne. C'est que 38 années se sont écoulées depuis cette ligne tirée entre le passé et un nouvel avenir. Vous connaissez la collection des portraits que possède ma femme ; dans le premier des volumes de la collection qui date de l'année 1836, et qui renferme cinquante portraits, se trouvent 24 morts ! Les hommes de 1814 et 1815 ont bien moins de droits à la vie en 1852.

Veuillez, mon cher ami, offrir mes respects à la Marquise et continuez à compter le ménage du Rennweg parmi vos plus fidèles amis. Venez nous voir.

Mille sincères hommages,

METTERNICH.

Miss Langton to Mr. Croker.

4, Royal Terrace, July 29th.

MY DEAR SIR,

You were so good as to accept of my offer to leave you the letter which I had the honour to receive from that great and good man Samuel Johnson, and I have accordingly bequeathed it to you in my will. Since, however, I have made this intention known, some of my nearest relations have expressed their regret that such a document should be lost for ever to the family. Under these circumstances, I venture to request that you would, in the event of your own demise, give a direction that this letter might be given to my great-nephew, George Bennet Langton, possessor of Langton. Begging you to pardon the trouble I am giving you,

I remain, my dear Sir,

Yours faithfully, &c.,

JANE LANGTON.

Mr. Croker to Miss Langton.

Alverbank, Gosport, August 8th, 1853.

MY DEAR MISS LANGTON,

I was very grateful for the kindness of your intended bequest, but for the last few years my state of health made it very unlikely that I should survive you; that improbability is now still stronger, and I therefore have no merit in releasing you from your promise, and in leaving you at liberty to dispose of your valuable *relique* as you may think proper. If I had had the pain of becoming its owner, it was my intention to have left it to the British Museum, but it will be better disposed of by your present design of leaving it to your own family; but I hope, as I did in my own case, that it may be long before it reaches their hands. I this day heard of a lady neighbour who is twenty years my senior, and who still enjoys her faculties and much of domestic happiness. I heartily wish you the continuance of life as long as it is not a burden to you; and when it shall please God to call you, I may, I hope, venture to wish you, what Dr. Johnson wished for himself, *sit anima tua cum Langtone.* May you rejoin your excellent father!

I am, my dear Miss Langton,

Your affectionate friend,

J. W. CROKER
(ætat. 73).

Mr. A. Panizzi to Mr. Croker. Extract.

British Museum, October 30th, 1852.

MY DEAR SIR,

As to the encouragement of readers, I should agree with you; but how can they be *discouraged?* or kept out? or classed? In 1836 I stated, in giving evidence before a Committee of the House of Commons, that two more libraries ought to be founded in London, and provided with works and editions on a different principle from ours—that is, for mere *readers.* As to *scholars,* I suggested (in a paper which was printed by order of the House of Commons, and in which I gave a history of our library, of its then condition, and of its deficiencies) that *duplicates* of our books of value to *scholars,* and not merely books for *readers*, should be lent out under certain regulations.

If both these suggestions, or, at all events, the first, had been acted upon, we should not be, I think, now pressed as we are by the influx of both *books* and *readers.*

From the comparison you used with me here respecting codification, and the printing a perfect catalogue of an increasing library, I guess who is the reviewer of Hardy's ' Life of Lord Langdale '—that comparison occurring in a note to that article in the last *Quarterly.* I am sorry poor Lord L. should suffer so much owing to his biographer.

I congratulate you on the state of your health, which must be excellent, judging from your letter and your undiminished energy.

Believe me, with many thanks and great truth,

Yours sincerely and obliged,

A. PANIZZI.

Mr. Henry Hallam to Mr. Croker.   Extract.

Pickhurst, Bromley, November 20th, 1852.

MY DEAR CROKER,

I have not the least recollection that I ever heard Heber mention the intended sale of the Royal Library to Prussia, though I was often with him, and have no doubt that we have talked about its 'transference to the Museum. When the article in the *Quarterly Review* appeared, I was struck by the anecdote as one perfectly new to me, and I entertained strong doubts as to its truth, which you have since confirmed. But I do remember to have heard at the time, that Nash had suggested it to George IV. (then, I think, only Regent), wanting the space to build an institution, or some other rooms that were more necessary for the body than the mind. At the same time, while I disbelieve that the report about a sale to Prussia ever reached my ears, I am too conscious of the increasing imperfection of my memory to assert any negative with confidence.

I hope we shall not long have to wait for your Pope. You will have been led to consider the foundation for the ' Elegy on an Unfortunate Lady.' Roscoe, whose edition alone I

have with me, does not advert to the story, which I have
read, perhaps in Bowles, and which seems to me the most
satisfactory explanation.   It is, that one of the French
princes, perhaps the Duc de Berri, made proposals to the
young lady, which she was inclined to accept, when her uncle
interfered and shut her up in a convent.   This alone, as it
seems to me, explains what perplexed Johnson, the ambitious
love ascribed to her, and the pride imputed to the uncle,
i.e. an English gentleman did not think his niece honoured
by being the mistress of a prince.   Slight evidence would
induce me to accept this solution.   Roscoe ought, at least, to
have mentioned it if it is in Bowles; but he has written on
Pope's life with great partiality.

You know how much Pope kept Horace in view.   Thus the
couplet on ' Avidien and his wife,' which to an English orator
seems both coarse and unmeaning, becomes witty as a translation.   In the famous couplet on Sappho, the gross expression is suggested by ' vehemens ' in the original.   He had
followed this already in the preceding line about Delia; but
he wanted four lines instead of two, and wished to bring in
his enemy Sappho.

Excuse my garrulity,

And believe me truly yours,

H. HALLAM.

Mr. Croker to a Drunken Servant.

West Moulsey, January 20th, 1853.

JAMES,

You must be aware that after what has passed you can no
longer remain in my service.

This gives me as much pain as it will do to you.   You
have lived with us five and twenty years ; you have been a
most faithful, honest, intelligent, and attached servant.   I
have never had cause to complain of you in all that time till
within these few years, when the irregularity, which has now
grown intolerable, began to show itself.   I need not, I hope,
remind you of our reluctance to believe, and our indulgence
in excusing, those irregularities.   I claim no merit for it,
because your own services deserved all possible kindness and
consideration, and I most anxiously hoped that the serious

crisis of this time twelve months, the indisputable proof of the cause of your irregularities, and the solemn engagement you then entered into, would have averted the distressing result which has at last arrived.

I am in great anxiety as to your future welfare; I know not what you may be able to do for yourself, for the circumstances under which you leave me will not recommend you to either service or employment. In consideration, however, of your faithful service to me, I hope, during my life, or till you can place yourself as well as you were with me, to be able to allow you twenty pounds a year towards your maintenance.

You will always have my good will and good wishes. I had hoped that death only would have separated us.

J. W. CROKER.

M. Guizot to Mr. Croker. Extract.

Paris, 9 mars 1853.

MON CHER AMI,

J'aurais bien des choses à vous dire; toujours les mêmes au fond, et pendant assez longtemps encore ce seront toujours les mêmes. Ni la France, ni l'Europe ne renverseront le nouvel empire; il faudra qu'il se renverse lui-même par ses fautes fatales; et quoique je le croie toujours prédestiné à les commettre, il n'en est point pressé. Il n'a pas, comme son oncle, des besoins passionnés d'esprit et d'action; il jouit mollement de sa fortune, et ne recherche point les occasions de la compromettre. C'est un fataliste qui croit à son étoile, mais qui en a peur, et quoiqu'il ne cesse pas de rêver les limites anciennes de l'Empire, il se contente volontiers d'être Empereur comme il l'est aujourd'hui. Je crois donc encore, et pour assez longtemps, à la paix, quoique la guerre, la guerre révolutionnaire, soit au fond de notre situation, et doive un jour en sortir.

Son mariage* lui a fait tort; mais personne n'y pense plus. Il en reste cependant une impression d'abaissement et d'instabilité; tout le monde se dit qu'il n'a pas pu épouser une princesse, et qu'il est capable de céder à toutes ses fantaisies. La confiance est donc moindre que jamais. Mais

---

* [The Emperor Napoleon III. was married on the 29th of January, 1853.]

quand on est décidé à vivre au jour le jour, on n'a pas besoin de confiance. La France en est là. La vie civile est tranquille, régulière, et active. Personne ne demande, quant à présent, rien de plus. La vie politique n'est point définitivement éteinte ; rien ne le prouve mieux que la persistance des classes supérieures à ne point se rallier à l'Empire. Elles attendent autre chose. Mais elles sont incertaines sur l'avenir, et fatiguées dans le présent. Elles dorment en attendant.

J'ai vu, par l'un des derniers numéros du *Quarterly Review*, que vous travaillez toujours. Est-ce que le travail ne vous fatigue pas trop ? Votre article sur M. d'Israeli et son budget m'a beaucoup intéressé. Je travaille aussi. J'achève mon histoire de votre république et de Cromwell. Je vous la donnerai probablement à lire vers la fin de cette année. Je suis, et serai toujours, de tout mon cœur,

Tout à vous,

GUIZOT.

Lord Raglan to Mr. Croker.

March 18th, 1853.

The loss of the three days, 16th, 17th, and 18th June [1815] was, to the best of my recollection, 13,000, exclusive of the Belgian loss, of which between 800 and 900 are stated to have been killed ; but then it must be borne in mind that in these, as in all other engagements, many who were returned wounded died of their wounds.

Our force at Talavera was 20,000. Lord Castlereagh showed me a return sent to him by his brother, who was then Adjutant-General, which I brought over. Victor had a very large army, something, I believe, like 50,000 men, but he was not attacked, except on his left flank, to a certain degree, and crowds of his people bolted the night before, alarmed by the firing of their front line, just after the close of day ; at what I never discovered, though I stood with the Duke abreast of it.

My impression certainly is that at Salamanca the numbers of the two armies were nearly equal.

I have omitted to say that at Talavera we had no Portuguese. Our army was exclusively British.

My notion about Waterloo is that the Duke had nearly

60,000, including the American* brigade, which arrived at the very moment that the attack began, under the command of Sir John Lambert.

I should not put Prince Frederick of Orange's troops at so high a figure as 20,000. Besides the Dutch troops, he had only a portion of Colville's division with him, one of Sir Charles's brigades, consisting of the 14th, 28th, and 51st, being on the field of battle with us.

A French officer of the staff, whose name I never knew, but he was not of high rank, came over to us at Quatre Bras. He put the French army at 110,000 infantry and 22,000 cavalry, and I think he was not far wrong. The attacks of Ligny and Quatre Bras must have occasioned them a heavy loss, but supposing it was 20,000 and that 25,000 followed Blücher, there would still remain above 80,000 to oppose the British army.

When the battle of Toulouse was fought, the allied army was divided into three parts. The Duke had with him Lord Hill's corps, the 3rd, 4th, 6th, and light divisions. Sir John Hope was employed in investing Bayonne with the 1st and 5th divisions and two Portuguese brigades not in division, and Lord Dalhousie was at Bordeaux with the 7th division. Thus dispersed, the troops with the Duke at Toulouse, including the cavalry, could not have been more than from 30,000 to 35,000 men.

There was, however, the Spanish corps, of some thousands, which gave way after having crossed the open ground and reached the foot of the heights on which the French were posted, and got an awful mauling; and Morillo's brigade with Lord Hill.

R.

Mr. Croker to Lord Palmerston.

West Moulsey, April 13th, 1853.

My dear Palmerston,

A new and terrible crime has grown up recently amongst us out of a pious and charitable principle—the murder of children by parents, of husbands by wives, and *vice versâ*, for the sake of the wretched profits on their funerals from the

---

* [The 6th Brigade, consisting of the 4th and 40th Regiment (which had just returned from America), and the 27th Regiment, reached Waterloo by forced marches from Ostend as the battle was beginning.]

burial societies. The extent to which this has gone is, I am told, frightful; but a single instance that proves the possibility of such a motive and such results would sufficiently justify some specific measure against a crime unimaginable till it has appeared.

There is, I believe, at this moment a case before you for your decision, on the recommendation to mercy by one of the circuit juries, of an accomplice in a murder of this class, the principal being also convicted. This brings the matter officially to your cognisance, and requires from you, I think, some immediate measure to arrest this hellish abomination; and I venture therefore to suggest to you one which I hope would be effectual without really impeding whatever there is of beneficial in the operation of these societies—I mean the passing an Act to restrict these societies from paying to any subscriber any greater sum than may have been actually expended for the burial of the deceased party. That single provision would suffice to stop the crime at once. Whether any additional clause as to any surplus to be produced from such restricted payments would be necessary, I am not sufficiently acquainted with the internal details of such societies to say; but, no doubt, it might be easily arranged. All that is essential is to take away this fearful temptation to, and premium on, murder. And if that could not be done without abolishing these societies, let them be abolished.

Yours, my dear Palmerston,

Very sincerely,

J. W. Croker.

Mr. Croker to Lord Palmerston.

West Moulsey, April 13th, 1853.

My dear Palmerston,

I have just written you a note from an impulse of humanity. I now add another on behalf of historical and Parliamentary literature, to which you cannot be personally indifferent, and which you have now a kind of official duty to promote.

There is a *lacuna* in our Parliamentary debates of one of the most, if not the very most, interesting period of our domestic history, viz., from 1768 to 1774. That Parliament is commonly called the " unreported Parliament," though it was, in truth, the best reported Parliament that ever sat, as appears by the MS. notes of Sir Henry Cavendish, which were made during the whole of it, with a degree both of assiduity and intelligence superior to any other portion of our Parliamentary reports.

The publication of these notes was commenced by the late Mr. Wright in the same form as the Hansard series, and was intended to comprise four volumes, each of six numbers ; but, strange enough to say, it excited so little general interest that it stopped at the seventh number (that, at least, is the last that reached me), and I believe its failure very much embarrassed the poor editor.   Lord Brougham, Sir Robert Peel, Sir Francis Baring, and some others, gave it their countenance.   But the public sale did not answer our expectations.   Surely this is one of the cases in which a Government ought to interfere.   We have been for these fifty years expending large sums in the publication, or, indeed, I should rather say the printing, of public documents, none of which are, in my opinion, more important to history, or of more general interest, than Cavendish's reports.

I have no doubt that a very trifling contribution on the part of the public would revive and complete this publication, and I cannot but think that, as it is somewhat disgraceful to us that the work should be left in such a state, it would be all the more creditable to you to distinguish your Administration of the Department to which it belongs by having it completed.

I know nothing about the papers, and have no private or personal interest in the affair; but the new controversy about Junius having led me to look back to the Parliamentary history of that period, I found it a blank, and was thereby reminded of the case of which I have thus reminded you.

I enclose you one of poor Wright's prospectuses.

Ever, my dear Palmerston,

Very sincerely yours,

J. W. Croker.

Lord Palmerston to Mr. Croker.

April 22nd, 1853.

My dear Croker,

Many thanks for your two letters.   Your suggestion about burial funds seems to me well adapted to cure the evil, and

U 2

I will see what can be done about it. I felt it right under all circumstances, and in deference to jury recommendations, to commute the capital punishment of the two women you mention into transportation for life.

I will communicate with my colleagues about Cavendish's debates, of which, like you, I have only a portion.

Yours sincerely,

PALMERSTON.

Mr. Croker to Lord Brougham.

Alverbank, Gosport, May 15th, 1853.

MY DEAR BROUGHAM,

Lord Derby's Administration was, after Mr. Disraeli's speech, more formidable than Cobden's would have been, and the (to me) most alarming measures of Aberdeen's * are but corollaries of Mr. Disraeli's propositions. The coalition that I most disapprove is not so much the coalition in office between Lord John and Aberdeen, as the coalition of principles between the two Budgets. I, as I think I have often told you, believe as firmly in the political as in the moral and physical providence of God, and I therefore trust that this great ship, the Britannia, that has weathered so many storms, is not destined to founder in her own seas. She will somehow, though Providence only knows how, right herself, and save her people ; but one thing I look upon as certain, that the constitutional frame of government, as it existed in our earlier days, exists only in name, and will in no distant time exist not even in name. It is under the process of Sir John Cutler's silk stockings, so incessantly darned with worsted that they came at last to be altogether of the inferior material.

I have read Moore's second and third volumes,† and I advise

* [Lord Aberdeen entered office at the head of the celebrated Coalition Ministry, under which the Crimean War broke out, on the 27th of December, 1852. Lord Palmerston was Home Secretary, Mr. Gladstone Chancellor of the Exchequer, the Duke of Newcastle Colonial Secretary, Mr. Sidney Herbert Secretary at War. Mr. Disraeli had proposed and his party generally had accepted : i. An income tax of 7d. for Schedule A, and 5d. for Schedule D ; ii. A succession duty. The Aberdeen Government adopted the second proposition, but rejected of the first.]

† [Lord John Russell's ' Memoirs of Thomas Moore.']

you to read them too. They are not dull, for there is, as Horace Walpole once said, "such a charm in proper names," that I find even the Court Guide more amusing than most of the disquisitions that pass now for history and philosophy. You may read them, I think, without any serious annoyance, certainly without any on your own account, though you will feel vexed for some of your old friends' sake, but especially for Lord John and Tommy Moore himself.

What could have induced the latter to write, and the former to publish, such a farrago of petty egotisms and worthless gossip (with a sprinkling of trick and spite which tell only against the writer and editor) I cannot guess; but you should I won't say read, but skim them, though you will get curds and whey instead of cream.

Ever yours,

J. W. CROKER.

*Mr. Lockhart to Mr. Croker.**

May 26th, 1853.

DEAR CROKER,

I have read some slips of Moore, and when I get a larger portion will send you a set with marginalia. Meantime, I think you speak rather too much, and not very consistently, about an editor's right to suppress. That cannot be doubtful. But for it, why an editor at all? On the other hand, there never can be a right to add to what is produced as the letter or diary of another. Even to dream that Lord John Russell could ever confound these questions is quite out of my line. I have no doubt that he has suppressed much, though not so much as he should have done, and can well believe, such are the evidences *passim* of careless haste, that in his account of the passage as to Sir R. Wilson he describes what happened in many other cases.

Moore's diary was suggested by Byron's; so was Scott's. Besides many other views, Scott clearly, and indeed avowedly, considered himself as writing what would one day be published. In his will he distinctly directs what shall be done with the money that his executors shall obtain in respect of this and other manuscripts. But he never could have

---

* [This letter refers to an article by Mr. Croker, reviewing Lord John Russell's 'Memoirs of Moore,' published in the *Quarterly Review* for June, 1853. The controversy which it occasioned receives some notice in the next chapter.]

considered himself as writing a diary that could be published *in extenso* during the life of any whom he cared for, or at least of any whom he had ever seen. Greatly feeling the responsibility imposed on me, in selecting for publication within a few years after his death, I had the whole diary set into type, in order that I might obtain the advice throughout of his most intimate friend Mr. Morritt, and another person who knew very little of him but a good deal of society, and all literary questions—Milman. Three copies were struck off, and I now have them all, and I have no doubt that in the course of time some heir of his will sell the complete diary for a larger sum than my book brought for the relief of his immediate representative, as succeeding to an overburdened estate ; nor have I the least doubt that Sir Walter foresaw this also. Moore, it is plain, had money in view from first to last ; but that money [was] to be realised, as respected his own wife and children, only through the medium of an editor. Trusting to such intervention, both diarists absolved themselves from any very strict watch over their pens—set down much which the whim, or very often the laziness, of the hour could alone account for. You knew both well ; in everything else so dissimilar, they were both imbued with the deep political prejudices of provincial origin and connexion. Posterity will know that I at least endeavoured to avoid the offending of Scott's surviving contemporaries, and you will not doubt that I had to spare Tories about as often as Whigs the castigation of diarizing Malagrowther. The grand blame in Lord John's case seems that he took little or no thought about the responsibility he had incurred, and lent his *imprimatur* with a levity which bespeaks, in fact, contempt for Moore. His aristocratic insolence is, I think, apparent all through his very small contributions to the book.

J. G. Lockhart.

Lord Strangford to Mr. Croker.

London (Saturday), July 30th, 1853.

My dear Croker,

You must think me an ungrateful brute not to have given you *signe de vie* on the subject of the last *Quarterly* beyond my brief acknowledgment of your kindness in sending me the revised sheets before its publication.

On Tuesday, the 19th inst., I was stuck on a confounded Railway Committee in the House of Lords, and I have been nailed to my green morocco chair at the rate of seven hours per diem ever since. It is a renewal of the old "battle of the gauges," and, with the exception of Saturdays and Sundays, the belligerents have, literally, not left me a moment for my own use or that of my friends.

The article * is quite admirable, and a model in the art of unmasking. It is grievous to think that a mask should have been so long and so successfully worn. I am glad, however, that you do not publish the supplemental pages. It is not at all necessary to your case, which, Heaven knows, is strong enough already ; and I will fairly own to you that I think it would have been scarcely compatible with your dignity. I do not know that I explain myself sufficiently, but it is one of those things that, if not comprehended *de prime abord*, all the explanation in the world will not suffice for the purpose.

I have met two or three bitter Whigs at dinner last week, and I was very much amused to find that they blame you for letting Johnny Russell off so easily, when you might have made mincemeat of him.

The Earl of Lonsdale † to Mr. Croker.

London, August 22nd, 1853.

My dear Croker,

As a party we are disorganized and scattered. I do not see how we can rally. I believe Dizzy means well, but he does not comprehend the feeling of his party, or aware (*sic*) of the danger of sanctioning and avowing certain principles. It is presumption in me to say so, but he looks too much to the debate of the evening.

Herries is completely worn out. He was constantly ill when in office, and I believe has been *hors de combat* almost ever since.

I have the most troublesome property in England to manage, consisting of odds and ends of mines ; and from doubts about boundaries, many of them I have to manage and work myself, which forces me to look into details as much as a manufacturer. The Parliamentary influence I have is preserved only at great trouble and expense. When I am in the north, it is harassing work instead of repose.

* [The article on Moore.]

† [Lord President of the Council in this first Administration of Lord Derby.]

The old Whigs are, or pretend to be, full of regrets about reform, and hope to give as little as will satisfy their reforming supporters ; but they will aim at the destruction of the country party, in flooding the county constituencies with 10*l.* householders, or some such scheme.

I remain, faithfully yours,

LONSDALE.

Sir James Graham * *to Mr. Croker.   Extract.*

Admiralty, October 20th, 1853.

MY DEAR CROKER,

When you tell me that you have a mortal disease, and that your pulse, however low, beats kindly towards me, I gladly embrace the opportunity of a return to former friendly relations ; and let us not dwell on our political differences, either past or present; but while we still "linger" on the stage, let us remember that here time is short, and the day near at hand when every unreconciled quarrel will be a sorrow to the survivor. I have committed many errors, and I am conscious of many faults. I hope to be forgiven, as I am ready to forgive ; and, on the whole, I have done my best.

I still hope to see you some day, and to shake you cordially by the hand.

I am, yours very sincerely,

JAS. GRAHAM.

Mr. Croker to Sir James Graham.   Extract.

Alverbank, Gosport, October 19th, 1853.

MY DEAR GRAHAM,

You do rather an injustice to my personal regard for you when you call it "lingering." In fact, it is and has been unaltered. I lamented, and still lament, the fatal, as I thought it, error into which you were all (the Duke included) drawn, but my feeling extended no more to you personally than to him, or to Aberdeen, or to Goulburn ; and even now in a political view I have a much stronger individual feeling towards a majority of the present Cabinet than towards (with two exceptions) your predecessors, and my most serious (and

* [First Lord of the Admiralty.]

very serious it is) dissent from your measures is that they seem too like an executorship, of the nuncupative, at least, if not written legacies of the last Administration. I lament some things, and particularly the Succession Tax, that you have done, but I have a strong feeling that the others were likely to have done that, and worse ; and I cannot doubt that in three essential Departments *—Foreign, Home, and Naval —we are safer in your hands than we were a year ago. When I was writing on these subjects last year, I had quoted with such approbation as I could give your avowed principle on the maintenance of our naval policy, which I thought seriously endangered by Mr. Disraeli's programme.   But *inter scribendum*, events happened which induced me to abstain from those details, and I have been since glad to see that you have done nothing, at least that I know of, derogatory from the great principle avowed in your speech on the Seaman's Bill when you were formerly at the Admiralty.   The real danger of the country, in my view, is the impossibility of making a strong Government—a Government that can dare to govern on its own principles.

Ever sincerely yours,

J. W. CROKER.

Lord Strangford to Mr. Croker.

London, June 15th, 1852.

MY DEAR CROKER,

Grant tells me that " Hat " Vaughan † (so called from the affected singularity of his *castor*) was a wealthy shipbroker, a great *bon-vivant* and dear friend of Sheridan's, who almost lived with him in Dover Street.   In later times he lost caste.

I really cannot recollect, do what I will, the circumstances of the 200*l.* to Sheridan.   All I can remember is, that on my return from Sweden, I was very ill at Gould's Hotel, in Jermyn Street, and that Sir Matthew Tierney called on me by the King's command (for I was a bit of a favourite), and that on the conversation being directed by me to the scandalous

---

* [Lord Derby's Foreign Secretary was Lord Malmesbury; Home Secretary, Mr. Walpole; First Lord of the Admiralty, the Duke of Northumberland.]

† [See the statement made by George IV. to Mr. Croker in ch. x. vol. i.]

imputations cast upon H.M., he, Tierney, told me that the King had placed 500*l.* at Sheridan's disposal the moment he was made acquainted with S.'s destitute condition; that Sheridan's friends did at first avail themselves of this piece of kindness (he did not say to what extent), and that subsequently they, most scornfully and with the utmost insolence, "flung it back in the King's face." This is all I recollect on the subject, and I am pretty sure that at the time I wrote it to Moore, who was then in Paris. I suppose my letter will turn up some day or other.

> Ever most affectionately yours,
>
> S.

London, December 5th, 1853.

My dear Croker,

Here is some gossip for you, and I believe it to be well founded.

1st. Of the Reform Bill. I am assured from an authority which I cannot doubt, that it is to be of a "most extensive" and hitherto unexpected nature; that John Russell has been obliged to give up his 5*l.* clause; that he alone of all the Liberals stood up for it; that in the new proposition (whatever it be), Lansdowne and Palmerston are the only *dissidents*; that no constituency under one thousand is to have two members; and that a partial disfranchisement of such boroughs, &c., as have been proved to be corrupt, is to take place.*

2nd. The Eastern Question. The French are not satisfied with us (whoever thought they would be?). No proposition has yet come from France to us which has been favourably received; a tortuous negative has been put upon all of them. Distrust is at work, and it dates from the time when France proposed that troops should be sent by her to Turkey. It was in the belief that that proposal would be accepted by us, that Baraguay d'Hilliers was sent to Constantinople.

Madame de Lieven says openly, that Nicolas has been drawn into a snare by the pacific assurances of Aberdeen, who wrote to him just at the time of the passage of the Pruth (and when all the world thought that it must lead to

---

* [In 1854 Lord John Russell introduced a Reform Bill, but the nation was on the brink of war, and the Bill was withdrawn. Reform did not again make an appearance in politics till 1857.]

war), that he, Aberdeen, "had once seen forty thousand men
dead or dying on the field of battle,* and that he had solemnly
vowed never to be connected with a Government engaged in
war!" This, of course, she communicated to Nicolas, and
hence he was encouraged to go on, step by step, in the conviction that, do what he might, pen and ink would have been
the extent of our opposition.

I look forward with delight to our meeting at Moulsey.
Why should I not pass your birthday with you, with a day or
two thrown into the bargain? I cannot undertake the Alverbank expedition in the present state of my precious liver;
but at Moulsey I see no difficulty in our playing old grass-
hoppers together.

Ever yours affectionately,

S.

Lord Lonsdale to Mr. Croker.

December 16th, 1853.

MY DEAR CROKER.

You submit to me a question that requires much consideration, and more information than I possess at present—that is,
the state of our party? Malmesbury is just come up from
Lord Derby's, where he had been to meet Dizzy and some
others. I believe they agreed to oppose the principle of
Reform. Dizzy, I understand, promises to be entirely Conservative; to have no flirtation with the Manchester men.
He is our only man. He has nerve to face the pelting from
the opposite benches. Pakington has also good pluck. I
hear from different sources that our party show a disposition
to unite and co-operate together.

* [Probably at the battle of Leipsig.]

CHAPTER XXIX.

1854.

The Controversy over Lord John Russell's 'Memoirs of Moore'—Mr. Croker's Challenge—His Policy of "Living Down" Slander—Mr. Disraeli's attacks upon him—Not a Reader of Novels—Never read 'Coningsby' or 'Vivian Grey,' or a volume of Dickens—Repudiates the Suggestion of "Retaliating" on Mr. Disraeli.—Hook's Novels—Mr. Croker and O'Connell—Letter from Lord Lyndhurst—The "Biography" of Mr. Disraeli—The Crimean War—Mr. Croker opposed to it, and agrees with Mr. Bright—His Reasons—Correspondence with Mr. Murray —Mr. Croker's attacks on Napoleon III.—Announces his Retirement from the *Quarterly Review*—Correspondence with Lord Lyndhurst— Mr. Croker denies being a "Russian"—His Views on the Eastern Question—And on the French Alliance—Lord Lonsdale's Opinions on Russia and America—Lord Raglan's thanks to Mr. Croker—Defeat of the Aberdeen Ministry—The "Raw Coffee" in the Crimea—Mr. Pitt and the Faro Bank at Goostree's—Was Pitt a gambler?—The Borough of Midhurst — Lord Brougham on the Fitzherbert Marriage — The Weakness of Government—Power of the Press—The Force which controls Public Opinion—Mr. Secretary Johnston—Last Letter from Mr. Lockhart—His Death.

IN the early part of 1854, a somewhat bitter controversy arose between Lord John Russell and Mr. Croker, with regard to certain entries in the Diary of Moore, which Lord John had seen fit to publish. Until the appearance of this Diary, Mr. Croker had no suspicion that Moore entertained any unfriendly feelings towards him. He knew that he had more than once been of service to the author of the 'Irish Melodies,' especially at the time of his Bermuda difficulties.

Moore had acknowledged these obligations somewhat pro-
fusely ; on one occasion he wrote :—"No one feels more high
respect for your talents, or bears more ready testimony to the
great good nature experienced from you and yours, than yours
sincerely, Thomas Moore." No doubt, therefore, it was a
disagreeable surprise to Mr. Croker when he found himself
spoken of by Moore in disparaging strains—for example, as
a "quick skirmisher of reviews," but "as to anything of a
higher order of talent, I am greatly mistaken if he has the
slightest claim to it." To this was afterwards added a note
by Lord John Russell to the effect that there were passages
still more offensive in the Diary, which the editor had suppressed—a note scarcely calculated to redress the injustice
done by Moore. Mr. Croker defied Lord John to produce
the passages referred to. He wrote :—

"There is another very serious consideration arising out of
this surprising confession, which is, that for the purpose, I
suppose, of attributing to yourself the *gloriole* of a generous
delicacy towards me, as well as others, you sacrifice not only
your argument, but the character of your poor friend, by
revealing, what I never suspected, that during the many
years in which he was living on apparently the most friendly
terms with me, and asking, and receiving, and acknowledging
such good offices, both consultative and practical, as my poor
judgment and interest were able to afford him, he was making
entries in his 'Diary' concerning me so 'offensive,' that even
the political and partisan zeal of Lord John Russell shrank
from reproducing them.

"I must be allowed to say, under such strange circumstances, that I reject your Lordship's indulgence with contempt, and despise the menace, if it be meant for one, that
you have such weapons in your sleeve ; I not only dare you,
but I condescend to entreat you to publish all about me that
you may have suppressed. Let me know the full extent of
your crooked indulgence, and of Moore's undeviating friendship. Let us have the truth, the whole truth, and nothing
but the truth, while I am still living to avail myself of it.
Let it not be said that 'poor dear Moore told such things of

Croker that even Lord John Russell would not publish them. I feel pretty confident that there will not be found any entry of Moore's derogatory of me against which I shall not be able to produce his own contemporaneous evidence of a contrary tendency."

The correspondence was first published in the *Times*, and afterwards reproduced by Mr. Croker in a pamphlet. To this pamphlet he refers in the following letter:—

Mr. Croker to M. Guizot.

West Moulsey, February 23rd, 1854.

I have postponed answering yours of the 13th for a few days that I might send you the accompanying little *brochure*, which perhaps may interest you on my account. I began very early in life, full fifty years ago, to be a dabbler in literary and political polemics, and had given and received a good many hard knocks in various encounters in Parliament and the Press. In Parliament I could take my own part, and in the Press that of my party, but I seldom (indeed I believe *never*) noticed the personal abuse of which I was the subject —I was content to *live it down!* But when just on the verge of the grave I found myself assailed both in moral character and personal honour by a person of Lord John Russell's rank and station, I thought it a case to justify, nay to require, a direct defence—and so I made one—first, against Lord John in the *Times* newspaper; and, as I wished to place it in a more permanent shape than the *feuilles volantes* of a newspaper, I have added to my correspondence with his Lordship some account of my acquaintance and connection with Mr. Moore, whom Lord John had made the *prête-nom* of his old political and personal malevolence against me. All the world here, "*of all parties,*" as Brougham writes to me, agree that I have had a complete victory; I hope you will think so too.

Mr. Croker here affirms that he had never before noticed any personal abuse of which he was made the subject, and undoubtedly this was the case. Whether it is always wise to allow personal attacks to pass unheeded, in reliance upon the

"living down " principle, is a very delicate question, turning
much upon circumstances which every man ought to be able
to judge best for himself.   The plan does not always answer ;
it can scarcely be said to have answered very well in Mr.
Croker's own case ; for calumnies which he could have disposed
of very easily while living, were repeated and renewed after
his death.   Sometimes the prudent course is to grapple boldly
with slander, and strangle it on the spot.   But however this
may be, Mr. Croker consistently followed the rule which he
prescribed for himself, and never replied to his assailants.
Some one remarked of him, in a magazine sketch, that he
had " embroiled himself rather frequently in literary feuds,"
and his note upon the margin of the paper was this : " I can
hardly be said to have ' embroiled myself' with either
Macaulay or Lord John.   They were both the aggressors, and
attacked me as a writer because they hated me as a political
antagonist."   A biographical sketch appeared about the same
time, in which he and Mr. Disraeli were described as enemies.
Mr. Croker returned an answer to the gentleman who had
forwarded him a copy of the sketch, and the correspondence
which ensued is given below.

Mr. Croker to Mr. Charles Phillips.*

West Moulsey, Surrey, December 29th, 1853.

I looked hastily into the work to see if I could guess why
it was sent to me, and I suppose it was because my name is
mentioned two or three times in reference to some supposed
hostility between me and Mr. Disraeli, which at least, as to
my supposed hostility, is a mistake.   I never, I think, met
Mr. Disraeli above twice—once, when he was very young, at
his father's, and once, many years later, at Lord Lyndhurst's
table, and nothing certainly happened to create any coolness
on my part ; on the contrary, my impressions, as far as I

* [Author, as it has been stated, of ' Recollections of Curran,' &c.]

recollect them, were agreeable, and I had a particular regard for his father. I again met him one day in the street with Lord George Bentinck, and I shook hands with him, without dreaming of any estrangement, or cause of estrangement, between us, who, though then of the same political party, had so little personal acquaintance. I was once again, about three years ago, at a public dinner in Merchant Taylors' Hall, where he was, but we did not happen to speak, and I can sincerely say that I never had the slightest personal coolness towards him, nor any political difference or distrust till his Budget, which I thought, and think, highly mischievous to the country and to the party.

When I published my review of the Budget speech I heard to my surprise that I was supposed to have given him tit for tat, for that Mr. Disraeli had attacked *me* in two novels, called 'Vivian Grey' and 'Coningsby.' Now, the fact is, I never read either. This may seem strange, but you will easily believe it when I add that I am not a novel-reader—that, for instance, I never read one of Theodore Hook's novels, though some of them were written in this house, and the characters sketched from the society he met here. I have never read a volume of Sir Edward Lytton, or even of Mr. Dickens. I know Messrs. James and Ainsworth only by name; I never saw one of their works. This is to be sadly behindhand in the popular literature of my times, but such is the fact. However, when I heard that I was retaliating on 'Vivian Grey' and 'Coningsby,' I recalled to mind that I had heard, I am almost sure from Mr. Murray, that there was in the former some compliment to me; whether it was a compliment, as Murray thought, or a censure, as this new work says, I know not, for I never from that day to this either saw the book or gave the matter a second thought—for me, it is as if it never had existed. I may say the exact same of 'Coningsby': I had never seen it nor heard of it in connection with myself till after the publication of the Budget review; and I can most sincerely affirm that I had not the slightest personal pique, or any motive to have any, towards Mr. Disraeli.

On the contrary, there were one or two circumstances, of which Mr. Murray was the channel, which led me to suppose that Mr. Disraeli looked towards me with a friendly and approving eye. If, therefore, I have given Mr. Disraeli tit for tat it has been quite unintentionally, and only by chance medley. Whether I may have unconsciously offended Mr. Disraeli's *amour propre* in any way—that is, whether he may have heard something that may have created such an impression on his mind—I cannot say ; but it is not likely, for we had no points of contact, nor, as far as I remember, a common acquaintance, but Murray, Lord Lyndhurst, and Lord George Bentinck. None of them were likely to have received, and still less so to have repeated, anything disagreeable ; and yet, on the other hand, it is hard to suppose that Mr. Disraeli should, without some such motive, have done so unusual a thing as to make me the subject of a satirical novel. In short, I cannot account for, nor in fact do I care enough about it to endeavour to account for, Mr. Disraeli's attacks upon me ; all I care about is, that my political views as to him should be rightly understood as altogether uninfluenced by any personal pique or morbid spirit of retaliation.

If I fancied that I had anything to retaliate or resent, it is pretty evident that I should not have wanted occasions from the publication of ' Vivian Grey ' down to last Christmas— the date of my Budget article—for I find from the volume you have sent me that Mr. Disraeli has been publishing a numerous succession of works, which, to say the truth, I never heard of, but in which, had I been looking with a jealous eye on Mr. Disraeli, I think it very likely that I might have found some opportunity of indulging my spleen.

As you have been the channel through which this volume reached me, and as you seem to have some communication with the author or publisher, I have thought that you would forgive my troubling you with this explanation, which I hope will satisfy, at least your own mind, as to the error of attributing my dissent from Mr. Disraeli's Budget speech to any personal pique or literary " rivalry " *quorum causas procul habeo.*

Ever, my dear Sir, very truly yours,

J. W. CROKER.

Mr. Croker to Mr. C. Phillips.

West Moulsey, Surrey, January 3rd, 1854.

ΛY DEAR SIR,

Be quite at your ease about the ' Biography ;' there is nothing in it, as far as I have seen, that could be in the least ·

offensive to me, except only the notion that I was actuated
to attack Mr. Disraeli by a previous attack on me. The supposition was natural enough; nor should I have had any
reason to complain of it; all I cared about was to let you
know that the inference was erroneous, because the alleged
fact itself was an error.

As to my novel reading I confess that in my younger days—
I used to read them all, from Charlotte Smith to Maria Edge-
worth; Scott I have by heart; but I so far differ from you
about Hook's that I date my later indifference to novels from
my disappointment at his.

'Gilbert Gurney' is something of an autobiography, as you
say, but the majority of the characters are persons he met in
this house. And the book might have been called a picture,
for which our society furnished the principal sitters; yet I
could not read it. I diligently tried to do so, but never
accomplished a volume, and I have often debated in my own
mind how I, who looked with admiration and wonder at
Hook's power of oral amusement, should be so repelled by his
novels. I had and have some theories, critical and moral, of
the cause of this apparent contradiction, which I need not
trouble you with; but it led me at first to read no novel, that
I might have a better excuse to my poor dear Hook for not
reading his; and insensibly I lost the taste for them altogether, partly from my mind's growing less impressionable,
but partly, or perhaps chiefly, from a very matter-of-fact cause,
that I happened never to have subscribed to a circulating
library, and since I left office I have had, I know not how,
less spare time than I had at the Admiralty in the height of
the war. I was greatly struck with some early detached-
tales of Mr. Dickens, and some stray *livraisons* of his longer
works, but I found I could not read them continuously; and
the short and long is, that I never read either 'Vivian Grey'
nor 'Coningsby,' nor even heard of any other of Mr. Disraeli's novels. The book you sent me is inflated by hostility
to D—— beyond all measure of either taste or judgment.
The author, I believe, is well known; at least it is attributed,
I am told, to the author of a pamphlet of the same tone
which appeared last year, and who makes no secret of the
authorship; but I never read it, any more than an article in
the *Edinburgh*, which I heard was very severe on Mr. D——.
So little had I of any personal resentment towards him!

I wonder at your citing O'Connell to me as an authority for

any matter of taste or literature. I knew him long, and
though little yet well. If, as you tell me, he read novels, I
believe he read little else, and least of all, law. O'Connell
and I had what by poetical license I may call "a sharp
encounter of our wits" the first hour I ever saw him, and on
the first day of my public life, when I joined the Munster
Bar at Ennis, and he happened to be in the chair, and thought
proper to try my metal, as he phrased it. After that we were
always on the most good-humoured terms; even in four
years, in which we sat in the House of Commons, and the
very last time I saw him, which was in Palace Yard, the year
before his death, he opened his arms and enveloped me in
a strict embrace *à la française,* to the astonishment of his own
tail, several joints of which were following him, and of the
cab-drivers on the stand, who could not comprehend such an
ostentatious salutation: so we parted as we had lived, after
our first wrestling match, in personal goodwill, and I might
say cordiality.

Ever sincerely yours,

J. W. CROKER.

Lord Strangford to Mr. Croker.

Friday evening. [No other date.]

MY DEAR FRIEND,

I sent your letter to Phillips (according to your kind permission) to Lyndhurst. Here is his answer. I have not yet
shewn him (Lyndhurst) your last letter to me, containing
that permission, because George Smythe begged me to let him
read a part of it to Dizzy (whose great crony he is), to which
I saw no objection, but rather the contrary, and [am] sorry he
has not yet returned it to me.

[*Enclosure in the above, from Lord Lyndhurst.*]

Turville (Thursday).

MY DEAR STRANGFORD,

I return Croker's letter, and the copy of the one to Phillips.
I never heard Disraeli speak in any way unfriendly of
Croker, and was very much surprised and annoyed when I
read 'Coningsby,' and was told that one of the characters was

X 2

meant to represent him. Disraeli never spoke to me upon the subject.

I think the biography * is a very blackguard publication, and written in a very blackguard style. I don't know who Mr. Vernon-Harcourt † is, though I read last year a pamphlet written by him, attacking Lord Derby, somewhat in a similar manner, but with more scanty materials. I am afraid we cannot hope to see you immediately, as Croker is about to intercept you. Pray remember us (both) very kindly to him. I can't say how happy his recovery has made us. I have not yet seen the *Quarterly*, but suppose he figures in it as usual.

Ever faithfully yours,

Lyndhurst.

I heard from Brougham yesterday. He has hurt his leg, and is repairing it, as he says, by the differential calculus.

L.

Sir George Sinclair to Mr. Croker.

Edinburgh, March 18th, 1854.

My dear Croker,

A thousand thanks for your great kindness in sending me a specimen of your unrivalled epistolary gladiatorship.‡ You should, even without obtaining the Royal licence, quarter upon your escutcheon a Conservative St. George transfixing a Whig-Radical dragon. Never was triumph more complete than yours—never did an adversary who had "written a book" limp away in such a state of discomfiture from the controversial arena. Would that, for the sake of your friends, who are, like myself, steady and admiring, and even for the sake of your enemies, who are so vindictive and ungenerous, your health of body were as unimpaired as the vigour of your mind.

Ever most cordially yours,

George Sinclair.

---

* ['Benjamin Disraeli: a Biography,' by Mr. Macknight. London, 1853.]

† [Sir W. Vernon-Harcourt, to whom the "biography" in question was generally attributed at the time.]

‡ [The letter to Lord John Russell, about the 'Memoirs of Moore.']

Mr. Croker found himself this year opposed to many of his friends on the great event of the time—the war with Russia. He was at issue with the conductors of the *Quarterly Review* who, without defending the weak and undecided policy which had rendered the war inevitable, were of opinion that the Government ought to be supported by both parties while it was contending with a foreign foe. This spirit, it may fairly be said, has always animated the Tory party, as well as the *Quarterly Review ;* and it was well expressed by Mr. Disraeli on the 17th of February, 1854, in the House of Commons. " I can answer for myself and my friends," he said, " that no future Wellesley on the banks of the Danube will have to make a bitter record of the exertions of an English Opposition that depreciated his efforts and ridiculed his talents." The *Quarterly Review* contended that it was an " instinct of self-preservation " which induced the English people to consent to the war. " The people have felt that this is a war in which all States that can boast to be civilized—all that desire fair expanse for internal energies, and complete independence of foreign obstacles in the way of domestic progress, have a vital and permanent interest." * In these expressions it undoubtedly reflected the opinions of the nation at large.

It must have surprised Mr. Croker's friends, and perhaps it surprised himself, to find that on this question he was substantially in accord, not with his old associates, but with Mr. Bright. In the following correspondence relating to the war, Mr. Croker's position will be found clearly explained. The letters are arranged in the order of dates, and brought down to the end of 1855, when the war practically came to an end although the treaty of peace was not signed until 1856.

* [*Quarterly Review*, June, 1854, p. 251.]

Mr. Murray to Mr. Croker.*

Albemarle Street, January 2nd, 1854.

MY DEAR SIR,

I now enclose the reply which I have received to my enquiry about the rayahs, from Sir Gardner Wilkinson.

Upon this question of their protection, which was an afterthought of the Czar's, the war would seem to take its rise. I entreat you not to commit yourself and me without thoroughly investigating the question and reading carefully all the papers relating to it.

If in a matter of such vital moment—upon which the eyes of the whole nation are turned—the *Quarterly Review* should not only take up the unpopular side, but should turn out to be in the wrong, it would inflict a heavy blow on the *Review.*

There is no greater admirer of your wonderful powers at your advanced age than I am, and it was with enthusiasm that I hailed your beautiful paper on the Dauphin in the last *Quarterly Review,*† as showing what you excel in and can do with greatest ease to yourself.

This makes me the more regret that in the paper on the Buonapartes, you have assumed an acrimony of feeling against them which will revolt the public taste of the present day, and prevent people reading the paper, while the space you have given to discussing dates will render it further distasteful to our readers.

The world (even the English part of it) will not listen to abuse of Buonaparte, and the result of abuse is to drive readers to take his side.

I remain, my dear Sir, yours very faithfully,

JOHN MURRAY.

Mr. Croker to Mr. Murray.

West Moulsey, April 13th, 1854.

MY DEAR MURRAY,

I lately hinted to you that I began to feel that my stated arrangement with the *Quarterly Review* was likely to become

---

* [To this letter no reply can be found.]
† ["The Dauphin in the Temple," *Q. R.,* No. 186.]

more onerous to me and less valuable to you than it has been.

I know not whether my pen, like the Archbishop of Granada's, " sent l'apopléxie," but it would be very odd if it did not, and I cannot but see that I am in other respects, also, less useful than I used to be thought. The political views of Burke, Pitt, Castlereagh, and even Canning, which I have followed for fifty years, seem going out of fashion, and somewhat to "pale their ineffectual fires," of which my poor glimmer was, at best, but a feeble reflection. I am well aware of your liberality and delicacy, and feel how reluctant you would be to propose my retirement, but it must come sooner or later—and the soon may be very soon, and the latest cannot be very late—and therefore I think it will be more satisfactory to both of us that I should take the occasion of placing—to use the ministerial phrase—my resignation in your hands.

I take this step with double regret : first, for severing so old a connection so cordially and closely maintained ; but also for losing what I am well aware has been a great stimulus, and I might almost say, as Watson does, medicinal resource to my mind and spirits for the last few years ; but this beneficial result would be destroyed by the idea that I was no longer able to bear my accustomed part in the great struggle that is, no doubt, opening upon us.

·Ever, my dear Murray, with much gratitude for your kindness, and strong wishes for your welfare,

Most sincerely yours,
J. W. CROKER.

Mr. Murray to Mr. Croker.

50, Albemarle Street, London, April 15th, 1854.

MY DEAR SIR,

I could not read without emotion your letter of the 13th, in which you inform me that you find it necessary to give up your engagement with the *Quarterly*, of which you have so long been a prop and mainstay. Your kind expressions towards myself are very gratifying, and it will always be matter of pride and pleasure to me to have been honoured by your friendship, and to have profited by your wisdom and judicious advice. It is no flattery to declare that I know not where to look for the man who is to replace you. We of the present day, it seems to me, are but pigmies, while you belong to a race of giants in intellect.

Although, however, you may not find yourself equal to the stated drain of the *Quarterly*, and the necessity of working up to a particular day, it is some consolation to me to know that our literary connection is not to be severed, and I hope "the blue ink" may long flow from your pen, with benefit both to yourself and me, and with less labour to yourself. I hope that the completion of Pope will now prove an easy task to you—though it is one from which I am convinced you will derive no little fame. When that is completed, is it too much to hope that (perhaps in combination with Mr. Lockhart) you may be induced to undertake an edition of Shakespeare? I feel strongly disposed to bring out your Boswell once more in 8vo., as a member of my British Classics (which have, as yet, proved so successful), and as the best refutation of Macaulay's malice.

The speedy publication of your Pope has now become an affair of urgency to me, and I greatly desire that it may not be long delayed, if your convenience allows you to proceed with it.

On one subject connected with the *Quarterly Review*, I feel some regret, viz., the difference on the subject of the French Alliance and the Russian War. We felt so strongly that the interests of the country, as well as of the *Review*, were deeply involved in this question, that we could perceive no other course open to us; and I can only hope that as regards you, our resistance did not give offence, and in other respects that events may not prove that we were mistaken in taking that line.

John Murray.

Mr. Croker to Mr. Murray.

West Moulsey, Surrey, April 17, 1854.

My dear Murray,

I thank you for your letter. I feel a great relief at thinking that you and the *Review* are independent of my sickness and my sensibilities. I know very well that there was a class of subjects for which near fifty years' experience in the school of politics, under great masters, made me of some value; but in the new aspect of affairs, and especially the "entente cordiale," established by the three great parties in

Parliament, Lord Derby, Lord John Russell, and Lord
Aberdeen, between Queen Victoria and the French Auto-
crat, I feel that I am out of date—at least out of season—for,
I confess, I have a strong conviction that the present folly, as
I think it, is likely to be short-lived, and to end in a terrible
crisis. The last words the Duke of Wellington said to me in
parting at Dover, just before his death (which we then
thought less distant than mine), were, that it was a consolation
to think that the course of nature would spare us the experience of the terrible events which the course of politics
was evidently preparing for this country.

J. W. C.

Mr. Murray to Mr. Croker.

50, Albemarle Street, London, April 21, 1854.

MY DEAR SIR,

I had forwarded to Mr. Elwin your notes containing your
resignation and the subsequent rider to it, and have delayed
answering the latter until I should hear from him, which I
have done to-day. He and I are quite of one mind in regard
to the value of your contributions to the *Quarterly Review*,
but we have also come to a unanimous decision, which it is
necessary to impart to you, in reference to the subject of
King Joseph's Memoirs, which you have chosen—that the
Quarterly Review shall on no account give admission to abuse
of Louis Napoleon directly, nor to indirect attacks conveyed
in condemnation of the first Emperor. The publication of
your former paper on King Joseph has elicited from so many
quarters unmitigated disapprobation on account of its tone
and character, as clearly to demonstrate that it is no longer
for the interest of the *Review* to persist in this strain.
Moreover, we deem it to be contrary to the interests of the
country to contribute to stir up feelings of animosity on the
part of the French, and we will persevere in this course so
long as the alliance lasts, and while the French continue to
act towards us with good faith and honesty.

We feel that this is the almost unanimous opinion of
Englishmen at present, and it is the more necessary to persist
in this determination to give the present French Government
a fair trial, because it cannot be unknown to you how many
engines are at work in this country and others to estrange the
two Western allies.

Even had you continued with the *Quarterly Review* on the old footing, we should have been forced to come to this explanation, which I now make in answering your last note. You have always shown that you have at heart the interests of the *Review*, and I sincerely hope that you will concur in thinking that the course which Elwin and I have chosen is the right one under existing circumstances.

Yours faithfully,

JOHN MURRAY.

The Earl of Hardwicke to Mr. Croker.   Extract.

Wimpole, February 26th, 1854.

MY DEAR FRIEND,

What events! I feel confident, indeed I may say I know, that all I previously said and thought, viz., that this war has been brought about by Russian confidence in Aberdeen, and belief (well formed, I think) that the Cabinet hated France and the Frenchman, and would never act in concert and true feeling with him.

The Emperor of Russia dreads the falling to pieces of the Turkish Empire in Europe, for this reason only, that in its stead there would be set up a Christian Empire, Kingdom, or Republic, under the name of Greek. He knows that if that be done, a most formidable barrier would be raised against his steps in that direction, for such a nation would have the religious, as well as the political, sympathy of all Europe; he would therefore rather keep the Sultan in Europe as a more convenient tool for his work.

This was his opinion when he was in England last. He did not scruple to express himself openly on this subject, and he did more at that time that I dare not state, and he felt sure he had settled the question to the exclusion of France.

I think you will perceive in the Blue Book that, in the mind of the Russian a feeling exists that England will play his game; and if he had been left alone with the Turks, this would have followed.

He would in a year have had 150,000 men in the provinces; he would then have raised by secret agency a Greek rebellion, and then marched his troops against the Greek rebels, and have thus become, in the most positive way, the protector of the Sultan in Europe.

This plan is now uprooted, and he is furious. *He has been deceived,* and has a right to complain of Aberdeen and his Cabinet. I think he will now turn his Greek insurrection to his own side and fight it out; that is, up to a certain point. Come what may, I think the Government of the Koran gone in Europe.

Yours most affectionately,

HARDWICKE.

*Mr. Croker to a Correspondent.**

Kensington Palace, October 5th, 1854.

How can you doubt my joy at our successes? I doubted —more than doubted—the policy of the war; I fear, I more than fear, I am alarmed at its consequences; but that does not abate my happiness at the glory of our arms, and at so small an expense of the lives of our countrymen, and, as you add, at the success of our personal friend—"a chip of the old block." My fear and aversion from first to last and *in prospectu* is France. I don't say that Russia is blameless, because the Emperor's own note to Aberdeen and conversation with Seymour prove that he was not sincere in his wish to keep Turkey alive; but that, though it has become a kind of justification of the war, was not at all its immediate cause, which was solely French intrigues, into which our diplomacy was unhappily drawn, and which, I think, might easily have been detected and nullified, and Turkey secured, and Russia checked, by an able minister at Constantinople, or, he failing, by an independent and firm and even high tone at home. I say independent, because our Government has been acting under the undisguised control of the Radical (that is, the whole European) Press, which is leagued against Russia as the *dernière* resource of monarchy. But the die being unfortunately thus cast, no one can deny the activity, energy, and general ability with which the departments of Government have executed their duties.

---

* [There is no superscription on the copy of this letter, and a part of it only exists.]

Mr. J. Winter Jones to Mr. Croker.

British Museum, October 9th, 1854.

MY DEAR SIR,

Mr. Panizzi desires me to present his compliments to you and to ask you if you would have any objection to tell him the name of the person from whom you procured the first collection of pamphlets relating to the French Revolution, which you parted with to the Museum. He understood from you that you purchased them from the bookseller of Marat. Mr. Panizzi thinks it right you should know that it is *Louis Blanc* who desires this information, and that he might wish to make it public, inasmuch as in France they doubt his statement that he has found such a collection in England.

I remain, my dear Sir,

Very truly yours,

J. WINTER JONES.

Mr. Croker to Mr. J. Winter Jones.

Alverbank, Gosport, October 23, 1854.

MY DEAR SIR,

I have delayed for a few days answering yours of the 9th, from my not having been very well.

Be so good as to tell Mr. Panizzi, with my compliments, that my collection of Revolutionary pamphlets consisted of two parts—the first part was formed by myself from various sources of which the most copious was an old bouquiniste of the name of *Colin*, who had been Marat's printer or publisher, and who had in some small dark rooms up two or three flights of stairs, an immense quantity of brochures of the earlier days of the revolution. He had 10, 20, 50, of the same pamphlet, of each of which I would buy but *one*, of course; but I bought, I should think, many thousands of others, of which he had but single copies. What he had least of were the works of Marat—even those which he himself printed—which he accounted for naturally enough—that there were times in which it might be somewhat hazardous to possess them. Though he had been a friend, and I suppose was an admirer of Marat, I found him an honest old creature, intelligent in his little business. It was through him that I found out Marat's sister, as like him, as Colin said, and as from all pictures and busts, I readily believed, as " deux gouttes d'eau." She was very small, very ugly, very sharp, and a great politician. Her ostensible livelihood was making watch springs, but she told me she was pretty easy in her circumstances, and I either gathered from her, or saw cause to suspect, that she had some secret charitable help.

Ever, my dear Sir,

Truly yours,

J. W. CROKER.

Lord Lyndhurst to Mr. Croker.

George Street, October 18th [1854].

MY DEAR CROKER,

The political world is in a most complicated state, and I feel quite at sea.

I am told by an anti-Russian that you are quite Russian, or rather perhaps anti-French. Pray let me know, when you have nothing better to do, what are your views of things in general—a wide range, giving full scope for any amount of political gossip.

While we are trying to pull down the Czar, we are at the same time contributing largely to build up a nearer, and eventually, perhaps, a more formidable power. Still, I wish to drive the Russians out of the Crimea and the Trans-Caucasian provinces, and to compel them to fall back from their excursion to Khiva.

I have a great hankering, too, after the Finland part of the affair.

As you know much about Admiralty affairs, you may tell me whether I am right in thinking that a great mistake has been made in not preparing a powerful squadron of steamers of small draught for the Baltic instead of such enormous vessels. In the last war between the Swedes and the Russians, the contest was carried on principally by fleets of gunboats. In like manner, we might, with a moderate squadron of this description, have been at this moment in possession of the Sea of Azoff, embarrassing the operations and intercepting the Russian communications in that quarter, &c. But this is a small part of the whole, so pray let your pen run glibly over a large expanse of white paper to enlighten and cheer me at this moment, for I am lying with both feet bound up,

teazed by the gout, on a soft bed from which I have no
expectations to escape for several days, and, notwithstanding
the kind attentions of the female part of my family, cannot
boast of being in the highest spirits.

I do not know where you are at present, so I send this to
Moulsey, with directions to forward it; but wherever you
are, I hope sincerely that you are going on comfortably
and well.

Ever most faithfully yours,

LYNDHURST.

Mr. Croker to Lord Lyndhurst.

Alverbank, Gosport, October 20th, 1854.

MY DEAR LYNDHURST,

I take a large sheet of paper, for you have opened a large
field of personal, political, and even prophetical topics.

To what, I suppose, is meant by " my being a Russian "—
that is, disapproving the policy and dreading the consequences
of the Russian war, I must plead guilty. But you have
expressed my feelings more distinctly and truly in saying
that they are against the *French alliance*. I believe, and think
I could prove, that the immediate cause of the misunder-
standing was French ambition and French intrigue. France
had the dexterity to withdraw slily from an aggression so
outrageous that even she could not venture to defend it,
and to drag us as principals into another, and at first altogether different, controversy, in which fortunately—or perhaps
I might rather say unfortunately—the revelation of the
Czar's Memorandum in 1844, and his conversation with
Seymour, came opportunely for the Revolutionary party
throughout Europe, to justify the odium and indignation
which they had already endeavoured to create against Russia,
whom they hated and feared as the chief, if not the only,
power capable of resisting the revolutionary spirit. I never
could understand under what influence it was that the Conservative press—even the most *ultra* of them—joined in the
cry of their old adversaries against their old allies. As long
ago as the scandalous insult to General Haynau at the
brewery in the city,* the most violent of the Conservative
papers took the anti-Austrian and anti-Russian line. Long

* [This occurred on the 4th of August, 1850.]

before Mentzikoff's mission, and while the dissension was still smouldering between France and Russia (England being then quite out of question), all the press became anti-Russian ; and it is a remarkable, and, as far as I have seen, hitherto unnoticed fact, that, *before Mentzikoff had opened his mission,* Col. Ross sent a requisition to Admiral Dundas to move the British fleet into the Bosphorus—an extraordinary proposition at that stage of the debate, for which I have never heard the slightest reason.   My firm conviction (and, as I have said, I think I could prove it) was that the whole affair was produced by the mingled arrogance and dexterity of France, acting on the weakness and bewilderment of Turkey.

I now come to another stage of the affair.   Admitting, for the sake of the argument (which, however, I am far from doing as a matter of fact), that the Czar's Memorandum proves a predisposition on his part for territorial aggrandisement at the expense of Turkey, I think it might rather have been made a guarantee of peace than an excuse for war.   It put (*ex hypothesi*) our Ministers in possession of the *dessous des cartes,* and might have enabled them to restrain and reconcile Russia and Turkey.   On the first movement of the French to inveigle or intimidate Turkey into a violation of her engagements with Russia, England ought, as an *amicus curiæ,* to have advised Turkey of her danger, and told her that, besides the general and well-known aggrandising policy of Russia, *we* had *special* reasons to suspect that the Czar was only looking out for a cause of quarrel, and that the Porte should be therefore doubly cautious not to afford him one, and, above all, not one so unjustifiable on its part as a breach of the most solemn and ancient as well as modern engagements, and as a weak compliance with the new and most unreasonable pretensions of France.   Such a remonstrance, I think, would have steadied Turkey ; while, to the Czar we should have said that, although we admitted that he had been recently ill-treated in the matter of the Holy Places, his memorandum of 1844 showed that he had earlier designs and ulterior projects to which we never could in any way submit, and that, while we should willingly mediate to induce Turkey to do him justice, we would not conceal from him that the principle announced in his memorandum would make us look with suspicion and jealousy at any hostile movement on his part.   This proceeding would either have been successful in moderating both parties, or it would have placed the matter on its *real* grounds—that is, a struggle between France and Russia, in which we should have been spectators, and eventually perhaps mediators, but not parties till some pretensions contrary to the *permanent* balance of power should be advanced by any of the belligerents.

No one can be more a friend than I am to the maintenance of the Turkish Empire, because I cannot imagine what substitute could be found for the Government (even the most imperfect) of the vast and various regions over which it is spread; but I must say that this special chivalry for the integrity of the Turkish Empire, and this zeal for the balance of power, as settled in 1815, come very strangely from France and England, who never before were united in any military or political object, except in the disturbance of that balance of power by the dismemberment of the Netherlands in 1831, and the disruption of Greece from Turkey in 1826; to which let me add the seizure of Algiers by the French, acquiesced in by England, and of the Ionian Islands by England, acquiesced in by France. To be sure it is a proof that nations never blush, to hear those who have robbed Turkey of Greece, and Algiers and the Ionian Islands, and in a great measure of Egypt, complaining that Russia *may* entertain a wish to have a slice on the other side. Nay, we are angrily told that Russia has disturbed the balance of power in the Caucasian regions of Asia—a proceeding that occasions great indignation on our part, who conveniently forget what we ourselves have been doing in the Punjaub on one side, and in Burmah and Pegu on the other side of India; and who have witnessed, without daring to breathe even a sigh of disapprobation, the annexation of Texas, California, and Mexico to the United States. Our newspapers say that no peace shall be made with Russia till we have razed Sebastopol, and taken securities that it never shall be restored. Suppose the *Petersburg Gazette* were to say that peace never should be made with England till she restored Gibraltar to the country of which it is a part, and to which it naturally belongs; that its occupation has not even the excuse of being necessary to England for self-defence, for it is nothing but an insult to and check upon the whole Mediterranean regions? The same may be said of Malta and the seven islands, of Bermuda, and even of the Cape. Where are these doctrines for which we are fighting in the Crimea to end? When we say that we will not suffer the Czar to advance against Constantinople to avenge a series of insults to his religion, how is it that we have no jealousy of the occupation of Rome, and the consequent control over the Roman Church and Papal policy by the French. I have wasted so much paper on the Russian part of the question that I have neither room nor time to enter on the most important and alarming circumstance of our position—the French alliance, which seems to me pregnant with the most awful consequences. Perhaps, by-and-by, I may be able to give you my views on this point. I will now only say that the alliance is and must be "false and hollow," not from the fault or treachery of sovereigns or statesmen, but from the uncontrollable *nature of things*, and that, like the people round Etna, we are planting olives which the next and not distant eruption will destroy.

Ever yours,

J. W. CROKER.

Lord Lonsdale to Mr. Croker.   Extract.

London, November 13th, 1854.

MY DEAR CROKER,

As to Louis Napoleon, I consider him a saviour in putting down the republic; it will be a great blessing if he can be kept where he is. We did not like the Napoleon family, but, taking a selfish way of looking at the state of the world, he is now of use to us. The world has changed its aspect; two great powers have arisen and are increasing in force and strength, Russia and America; and the union of France and England seems necessary to resist them. I do not like the Orleanists, and I think they are the most unpopular of all the different claimants to the throne. I think Louis Napoleon will be well received as a new ally and the extinguisher of a republic. I speak as I feel, thinking that it was the best piece of good luck having such a man turn up. We differ in our old age in politics for once.

We have underrated the power of the Russians; we had not sufficient information to justify the invasion of the Crimea. We are experiencing sad and melancholy losses; as yet the English have had the brunt of the battle, and have suffered accordingly. I am in low spirits as to the result.

I remain, faithfully yours,

LONSDALE.

Mr. Croker to the Earl of Hardwicke.   Extract.

Alverbank, Gosport, November 17th, 1854.

I will not trouble you with a statement of the reasons
which make me think Russia a natural ally, whose power
could do us no direct injury, and could do us a great deal
of good (as it had done in 1812) as a counter-balance to
France, which seems to me to be inevitably and from mere
vicinity, and without regard to the individual character of
sovereigns or ministries, our natural rival and, of course,
natural enemy.   I will not enlarge on that speculative topic ;
but when I came to look at the war *practically*, I could not
help thinking, and I believe saying, that I saw little prospect of advantage in making war on a power whose vitals
were so far out of our reach that the most we could hope to
do was to pare its nails, or at best cut off a finger or wound
a toe ; and that, whatever success we might obtain in the
way of chivalry, there was none to be expected either as to
present profit or ultimate security for the objects we were
contending for.   I therefore approved the reluctance which
the Ministers were accused of feeling to embarking in such
long-handed and remote hostilities, in which, according to
the first laws of physics, the distance increased our difficulties
in almost geometrical progression.

Lord Raglan to Mr. Croker.

Before Sebastopol, Christmas Day, 1854.

My dear Mr. Croker,

I am very much gratified by your cordial congratulations
on the events of the campaign, and the very favourable
opinion you have expressed of my services, with the acquiescence that that opinion is shared by my countrymen generally.
This indeed is highly flattering and encouraging, and, coming
from a friend of your experience, observation, and good feeling, cannot be too highly appreciated.   I am much concerned
to hear that your health is so precarious.   Accept my earnest
hope that your life may, notwithstanding, long be preserved,
and that I may have the happiness of assuring you, *de vive voix*
how grateful I am for all the kindness you have shown me.

The great task, however, confided to the allied armies is
still to be accomplished, and we have to contend against the

difficulties of the season, and many others too numerous to trouble you with.

Believe me, with every good wish,

My dear Croker, very faithfully yours,

RAGLAN.

Lord Lonsdale to Mr. Croker.

London, January 29th, 1855.

MY DEAR CROKER,

I think the present Government ought to be turned out on account of their incapacity and their negligence, which is notorious.

I believe there never was any one more inefficient than the Duke of Newcastle has been.

You think the members engaged in so bad a business that they should be left to the consequences, which must be disastrous. But the public do not understand the thing in this light. The public believe the policy of the war good, but that these men are incapable of carrying it on. If we merely protested, and allowed these incapables to carry it on, the public would regard it as a Ministerial triumph. We can only punish these men in putting them out. The eventual failure of their policy would not punish them, and the policy must be carried out by some one, for we are in the war. Why should we leave so important a matter in hands which are so incapable ? Why should we allow them that which the public would regard as a triumph, though you may regard it as only giving them rope to hang themselves ! There are others that can be Ministers; and do not let it be thought that the only men fit for office are Newcastle and Sidney Herbert.

Truly yours,

LONSDALE.

London, January 31st, 1855.

DEAR CROKER,

There never was a division where the calculators and whips were more out of their reckoning.* Our friends calculated

* [The Aberdeen Ministry were defeated by the totally unexpected majority of 157, on the 29th of January, 1855. The occasion for the division was Mr. Roebuck's motion for an enquiry into the conduct of the

Y 2

upon a majority of sixty. The Government maintained they should have a majority. But everything turned up against the Government in the debate—Bernal Osborne's speech was considered as if the Ministers had determined to resign; Gladstone's attack upon J. Russell ; also a very feeble speech from Palmerston. Altogether, it was looked upon as a break up of the Government, and 107 Whigs and Rads voted against them. Gladstone is in error about 30,000 effective men in the Crimea. There was not half the number a fortnight ago, and I fear by this time not 10,000. Nothing can exceed the misery of the state of our little army, which I almost fear shortly will not exist. I collected some private letters from Colonels, which I have given to Lyndhurst. But whether his motion will come on, I know not. The French Army are as well provided as any troops can be on a campaign, whilst ours are starving. This is to be attributed to the Duke of New-castle. . . . There is no outcry against [Lord Raglan] as yet, as it would partly have taken the responsibility from the Government. But he will be removed upon the change of Government, whoever they are.

Up to this time I know nothing of Lord Aberdeen's conference with the Queen yesterday. I suppose they will try Palmerston. They tell me he is becoming aged fast, that he is deaf and blind, that his hearing and eyesight [are] failing.* I think the Ministry must come to Derby at last.

Truly yours,

LONSDALE.

Monday morning.

My dear Croker,

You are right in your anticipations about Johnny's mission ; his colleagues scouted him, and would have nothing to do with him. Palmerston is busy now, but a Whig tells me he will fail, but they will all rally under Lord Clarendon.

war. Lord Palmerston then formed his first Administration, Lord John Russell and Lord Derby having both failed in their efforts to construct a Ministry. This Government, with many departmental changes, remained in office till February, 1858, upwards of three years, and beyond the term of Mr. Croker's life.]

* [The absurdity of these reports need not now be pointed out. The most striking Parliamentary successes of Lord Palmerston were still before him.]

Johnny is to make an explanation, and give his version of the ousting of the Duke of Newcastle. He will be answered by Gladstone. So war still rages between Whigs and Peelites. Johnny seems to have been willing to dismiss Pam, and again Newcastle, to please the Court.

Some predict Pam will not make a Government. The Peelites are too greedy for places.*

Truly yours,

LONSDALE.

February 2nd, 1855.

MY DEAR CROKER,

Derby has made what the theatrical people call a *fiasco.* He would not make a Ministry from his own friends or his own bat.

Johnny is low at this time, as his move to oust the Duke of Newcastle was ill-managed, and he has a run against him as a shabby intriguer. The offspring of all the old Tory families and merchants have turned Liberals, Whigs, Free Traders—Gladstone, Newcastle, Sidney Herbert, Granville, Porchester. It is the exception to remain a Tory.

There is a principle which is called self-adjustment, and I expect Palmerston will rally the Whigs, with himself at the head; and the formerly excluded Whigs, Lord Grey, Clanricarde, Labouchere, Vernon Smith, and Seymour, will fill up the places vacated by the Peelites. Change of Ministries will be frequent; but a Ministry always will be formed in a week or two.

I am told that the House of Commons is becoming more unmanageable every session, that no division can be calculated upon, that so many of the town members owe no allegiance and vote for popularity. We shall all be beat in a few years if there is not a union of the Tory and Whig aristocracy —and that will only last a few years. Your prediction in the end will be correct as to the [effects of the] Reform Bill, but it has been longer coming about than all of us thought.

Yours truly,

LONSDALE.

* [The Peelites in the Administration, as originally formed, were Mr. Gladstone, Chancellor of the Exchequer; Mr. Sidney Herbert, Colonial Secretary; Sir James Graham, First Lord of the Admiralty. They all resigned on the 22nd of February, 1855.]

Mr. Croker to Lord Hardinge.

West Moulsey, Surrey, February 5th, 1855.

MY DEAR HARDINGE,

I am equally surprised and shocked at the violence and, I am satisfied, unjust outcry which has been raised against the military and naval administrations as to their share in the conduct of the war. Of the *policy* of the war I say nothing; but I feel bound to say, as one who had an official share in the conduct of the last great war, and who has not been an indifferent observer of what has been since done in the two great branches of the service, that I was *astonished* at the celerity, the energy, and the efficiency with which, on so short a notice, so great a force was prepared, collected, and directed to both the Baltic and the East.

The exertion and its results are, I believe, without precedent. They, at least, exceeded what my experience could have led me to anticipate. But it is not to express this general opinion that I write to you, but to notice one particular point on which you and I have had some former communications which you may have forgotten. You are charged, I see, with a special neglect in not having turned your attention to arming the troops with rifles. What you may or may not have done, I know not; but I am sure it was not from inattention to the subject; for when you were at the Ordnance and I at the Admiralty, I happened to hear that the Americans were introducing rifles into their service, and I mentioned to you that I had obtained a pattern of one of their rifles. I remember that you were immediately struck with the fact, and begged me to give you my pattern rifle, promising to give me in return one of our own manufacture. This you did not do; perhaps you were overruled, and did not make any, as we all soon after went out of office; but with the eagerness you then showed to have the rifle copied, I cannot believe that you afterwards grew indifferent and negligent on a subject which struck you so much at first, and of which subsequent experience seemed to have increased the importance. I know not that this reminiscence can be of the least importance, but it has occurred to me that you might not be sorry to have it re-called to your memory.

Believe me to be, my dear Hardinge,

Your friend of lang syne,

J. W. CROKER.

Mr. Croker to Sir James Graham.

West Moulsey, Surrey, February 14th, 1855.

MY DEAR GRAHAM,

Is it possible that *raw coffee-beans* were issued to the troops in the camp ? No doubt it was cheaper and easier, and in every way better, to send the raw coffee-bean to Constantinople, and perhaps even to Balaclava. If it had been sent from England roasted, and still more, if ground, it would have been liable to deteriorate and waste ; but that it should not have been roasted and ground before it was issued to the men in the camp seems utterly incredible. I need not tell you that even if the roasting and grinding could not have been done on shore (where, however, coffee forms an important part of the popular diet), the men-of-war and the great steam fleet in the harbour of Balaclava could have in a week roasted and ground coffee enough to have served the army for a year.

This is so obvious that I totally disbelieve the whole story, but I have seen in the *Times* a statement signed with the name of a person, I think an officer, stating that the fact was true, and that he had seen the coffee-beans strewed about on the snow as, to be sure, they would be if so issued. If this can be contradicted, not a moment should be lost in doing so authoritatively ; if it cannot, if the raw coffee-beans were, even for one day, issued to the troops in camp, I know not what can be said in extenuation of such a blunder, but I know what *will* be said, " *ex uno disce omnes.*" So if the fact can be denied, for God's sake lose no time in denying it.

Yours ever,

J. W. CROKER.

Sir James Graham to Mr. Croker.

Admiralty, February 15th, 1855.

MY DEAR CROKER,

Your Admiralty practice makes you aware that the requisitions from the Commissariat on the Victualling Department are mandatory, and have no discretion in the compliance with them.

I send you the dates and the contents of the varying

requisitions with respect to coffee for the army. The proposal to grind, as well as roast, emanated from this office in an extra official shape, although the duty was not ours. The proposal was adopted. The coffee, ground and roasted, has been packed in air-tight cans; and I believe that the measure has been successful. Coffee is a ration issued for the first time to the British army on foreign service.

Many mistakes, doubtless, have been committed, which experience alone can rectify. It remains to be seen whether Commissioners from Committees of Public Safety will improve the condition of the army, or contribute much to the safe conduct of affairs.

> I am, yours very sincerely,
>
> JAS. GRAHAM.

Mr. Croker to Sir James Graham.

[No date, apparently February 16th, 1855.]

I never for a moment thought that the Admiralty, or any other department at home, had or could have anything to do with the coffee blunder. My enquiry, my wonder, was whether, and if so, by what idiotcy, the raw coffee-bean was issued to the troops in the camp. That is my sole point. From your silence I fear the fact is so,* for which nobody at home can be to blame; but whoever it was at Balaclava or the camp that perpetrated, or permitted such a flagrant absurdity (without sending up a roasting and grinding apparatus with the coffee), ought to be dismissed, or at least censured and recalled for incompetency and want of common sense. It is such things as this—small, as I have said, in themselves but most serious as indications—that drive the House of Commons and the public into these desperate courses of a Committee of Public Safety. If the War Minister cannot deny such a fact, or, admitting it, does not make a flagrant example of the poor idiot who did it, can you wonder, even though you may, as I do, deplore, that the House of Commons should take the matter into its own rough hands?

What I think of these Executive Committees you will judge when I tell you that, in breach of my resolution to

---

* [It is unnecessary to mention now that the fact *was* so.]

have nothing more to do with politics, and, above all, with party politics, I used my best endeavours to induce the two or three friends with whom I thought my opinion might have any weight, to vote against Mr. Roebuck's motion.

One of them answered me with the coffee-beans, and added that he expected to hear next that, instead of flannel drawers, knee-buckles had been issued to the Highland Brigade.

Mr. Croker to Sir George Sinclair.

Bognor, November 25th, 1855.

I have the misfortune, I confess, of differing from you in your estimate of Mr. Urquhart and his case, as I have that also of agreeing with Mr. Bright in his views of the war, though not on his peculiar reasoning. I believe the war was not only unjust in its origin, but utterly wanton on our part.

It has been in its progress extravagant of money and of blood, with no advantage and little glory. Its object seems to be some indefinite *amoindrissement* of Russia, which, whether defeated or attained, seems to me equally certain to revolutionize Europe—probably to set up kingdoms, or, more likely still, republics, of Hungary and Poland—perhaps of Italy, to restore *the France* of Napoleon I., to absorb Belgium and Holland, and finally subdue, and perhaps dismember, our disunited Kingdom. That some such great revolution will be produced by the continuance and extension of the present war I believe, and the only accident that I can imagine to avert it is, what I admit is no improbable catastrophe, a new revolution in France. Of such a revolution I am as certain as I was *all along* of the overthrow of the first Napoleon, but I am far from prophesying, as I did in that case, that *I* should live to see it. Pozzo di Borgo used to say that *he and I* were the only two men in Europe who, in 1810, believed in the future fall of Buonaparte. This was in allusion to a conversation which we had when he came to take leave of me on going to Russia, and when, as he truly related, I told him that, *even then* (before the march on Moscow), Buonaparte was straining a string which would inevitably break, and climbing a pinnacle where both his footing and his head would fail him.

This man's fall is, if possible, more reasonably to be reckoned on than his uncle's.

I am so far from agreeing with Mr. Urquhart's conclusions, that at this moment I should be very sorry of any disturbance of Lord Palmerston. There is nothing that I object to in his Administration that his rivals, nay, his *soi-disant* Conservative rivals, have not countenanced, nay, exceeded, and I am confident that the great *cancer*, Parliamentary Reform, will eat deeper and deeper into our vitals every time it is reopened by a change of Ministry or a dissolution of Parliament.

We now return to the general correspondence of 1854. The first three letters were written in pursuance of a wish which Mr. Croker entertained to vindicate the character of Mr. Pitt from certain charges made by Lord Holland, in his 'Memoirs of the Whig Party.' Mr. Croker's article on this work appeared in the *Quarterly Review* for March, 1854. Among the statements made by Lord Holland was that referred to by Mr. Croker in his letter to the Duke of Rutland, namely, that Pitt was a "partner in the Faro bank at Goostree's." This was a club which succeeded " Almack's," in the same building, and there seems to be no doubt that Pitt frequented it. Mr. Croker proved in his article that there was no foundation for the assertion that he had anything to do with the faro bank.

Mr. Croker to the Duke of Rutland.

MY DEAR DUKE,

West Moulsey, February 17th, 1854.

I have to give you a little trouble, but I hope and believe it will be a labour of love. It has become a fashion with libellers to represent Mr. Pitt as a hard drinker. Now we all know that fifty and sixty years ago, everybody drank at least twice as much as they do now. We know, too, that one night (that of a debate on Lord Howe's promotion as Admiral) he and Dundas came in what was called *tipsy*. But I have heard from several of our common friends that Mr. Pitt was not at all remarkable for habitual excess. Indeed, even on that celebrated night I was told by Sir James Burges, then in the House, that Pitt was not intoxicated at all, and that what gave rise to the idea was that he was actually sick, and went behind the chair to discharge his stomach, which he did, and made as good a speech as ever he did. My own notion is that both the stories were true—that he had had too much wine, and that he got rid of it behind the chair, and was himself again.

I don't like to enquire about individual cases, but I should like to know from your Grace, the only survivor, I believe, of Mr. Pitt's private society, your testimony on this point, that he, like Cato and like others that were not Catoes, may be said "*sæpe caluisse mero.*" I have no doubt, but I do not believe, that it was to any degree *remarkable* or unusual in the society of the day. I am sure that I remember, with wonder, the things of this kind I have seen at a still later day. I see also that Lord Holland, in his insidious way, says that "Mr. Pitt was not guilty of any other vices to excess," as if he was guilty of all to a degree; and he specifies gambling, and that he even kept a faro bank at *Goostree's.* I remember old Lord Carrington told me that they used *to sup* occasionally at Goostree's, but he never said a word about *play,* and the interval in which he ever went to that club was very short—I think he said it was only one year. You were too young to have been at Goostree's, but you may recollect to have heard of Pitt's habits in those early days. Lord Holland also tells a story that George North (afterwards Lord Guilford) met Mr. Pitt at "a country house"—the Duke of Rutland's, I suppose *yours*—and that he came away saying that "he was sorry to find so bad a politician so clever a man." Pitt and George North *may* have met at Belvoir or at Cheveley, and if they did I have no doubt that they found one another very agreeable; but, somehow, I doubt the story altogether, and it is only introduced to disparage Pitt in another point of view. Do you remember anything about it?

Ever, my dear Duke, affectionately yours,

J. W. CROKER.

The Duke of Rutland to Mr. Croker. Extract.

Belvoir Castle, February 24th, 1854.

MY DEAR CROKER,

As to Mr. Pitt's habits of life I can give you no information. I often dined with him when I first began life, for he was my guardian, jointly with the old Duke of Beaufort and my mother, but I have no recollection of having seen any excess in the way of wine on his part. I remember hearing that when he and Harry Dundas got together over a bottle of port wine (or probably two sometimes), the bottle or bottles were always *righted*—an expression in use by an old friend of mine, Chester—but I never heard of any habit beyond that. The same was said of Lord Eldon and Sir W. Scott. Sheridan used to appear now and then in the House of Commons in a state inappropriate for deep debate. But who ever heard that of Mr. Pitt?

Mr. Pitt never was in a country house of mine, unless he was of the party which assembled here on the 4th January, 1799, when I came of age. I know he was invited, but I forget whether his public business allowed him to come. I have no recollection of George North (Lord Guilford).

I yesterday received the correspondence between you and Lord John. There are some stinging expressions *de part et d'autre*, but I certainly think that you have the victory on your side, and that the provocation was all on the other side. The bringing in Moore's poor wife was wholly uncalled for and unnecessary.

Your account of yourself is as favourable as I could desire to receive. "Appetite a little better" denotes improved tone of the internal organs. Then we ought to be getting nearer to a vein of weather more suited to invalids. The winter has been very favourable to me, for I have not had a trace of complaint since November. I am deeply grateful for the mercy.

Ever, my dear Croker,

Your very affectionate friend,

Rutland.

Lord Mahon to Mr. Croker.

Grosvenor Place, February 27th, 1854.

My dear Mr. Croker,

I have no recollection of having heard anything of Mr. Pitt's occasional play in early youth, either from my excellent grandfather, Lord Carrington, or from any other veteran of those times. But I would direct your attention to

the following passage in point from the life of Wilberforce,
by his sons, which you will find in the first volume, p. 18 :—
" We played a good deal at Goostree's ; and I well remember
the intense earnestness which he (Pitt) displayed when
joining in those games of chance. He perceived their increasing fascination, and soon after suddenly abandoned them
for ever."

It is not at all impossible that Mr. Pitt may have kept a
bank at Faro for some one night, since in the passage which
follows the one that I have quoted, Mr. Wilberforce records
that this very thing was done by himself. But remembering
the general tenor of Lord Holland's Reminiscences, I must
say, though with regret, that I cannot consider them adequate
authority for any fact which he does not state from his own
knowledge.

Yours ever,
MAHON.

Lord Lonsdale to Mr. Croker.

March 22nd, 1854.

MY DEAR CROKER,

The Whigs, in their first Reform Bill, had, I conceive, two
objects in view : first, to smash the Tories ; and secondly, by
their new distribution of the elective power, to give increased
influence to the Whigs. Their bill did not prove so effective
as they anticipated, for in the course of time the Tories became
temporarily in the ascendant, and perhaps they might [have
remained there (?)] if we had [had] three or four good men.
The leaders of the Whigs are now attempting another Reform
to effect what the last Bill failed to do.* Their present proposition does not seem to have the same partiality and favour
in it as the last had, as the principal boroughs to be sacrificed
are those of Whig and Peelite interests. As regards the small
agricultural counties, such as Westmoreland, the addition of
the 10*l.* occupation franchise would not have an annihilating
effect, but in the Midland counties, where there are so many
small manufacturing towns and villages, the county representation would be thrown into the hands of the 10*l.* voters. I
believe if this Bill was carried, a large majority of the House

* [Referring to the abortive Reform Bill introduced by Lord John
Russell in February, 1854.]

of Commons under the new Act would be composed of such
men as represent the large towns in Lancashire and the
Metropolitan districts.

I am, truly yours,

Lonsdale.

Mr. S. H. Walpole to Mr. Croker.

House of Commons, March 28th, 1854.

My dear Sir,

Your note having been directed to the Carlton instead of
to 9, Grafton Street, Bond Street, has only just reached me.
You are quite right in your recollections of Midhurst. It
was an old burgess tenure borough, which returned Members
to Parliament without interruption from the beginning of the
fourteenth century; the rights of voting at the time of
the Reform Bill being in the possession of certain old stones,
which were doubtless the remains of ancient burgess
tenements. Whether the burgesses were bought by the late
Lord Carrington, or whether they were compassed within the
space of about 200 acres, I cannot inform you. By the
Reform Act, the right of voting was exclusively vested in
occupiers of the value of 10*l.* and upwards; and the borough
is now, in fact, a district of a county, containing parishes and
parts of parishes, which were so included (as I believe)
simply to favour the Whig interest.*

You are probably aware that Midhurst is the borough
which first returned Mr. Fox to Parliament; but Lord John
has no gratitude on that account, and, with all his devotion to
that old Whig, he is not generous enough to imitate the
example of the great Œnotrian conqueror who "bid spare
the house of Pindarus when temple and tower went to the
ground." Seriously speaking, however, there is a great
anomaly about his bill, which shows how idle it is to draw
any new lines as grounds of disfranchisement. Midhurst has
had sometimes upwards of 300 voters; and it has now less—

* ["There were formerly 120 burgage tenements, which entitled their
respective owners to vote. One of the Lords Montague pulled some of
them down that he might enlarge Cowdray Park, but had stones inscribed
' A Burgage' put into the wall to indicate their sites. Hence it was said
that at Midhurst the very stones voted for Members of Parliament."—
History of Sussex.]

not because there are fewer than 300 10*l*. houses, but because
a great many of them are now occupied by women, and in
several more the occupiers have not cared to claim.   By the
extended franchise which is now proposed, of course it would
have many more than 300, and so the line is partly arbitrary,
and would be in this, as in many other instances, entirely
contradictory to the rule for disfranchisement as now laid
down.

I think you may well look with wonder and alarm at what
is going on abroad and at home.   Very much should I like to
know your views and opinions on the present state of political
affairs.   In some respects we are better than we were ; but
no real good can ever be looked for until two parties are
formed again with distinctive principles.   The Tories joined
with the natural supporters of Sir R. Walpole to turn him
out, and we had no party in the strict sense of the word
for thirty-five years.   The Whigs joined with the natural
supporters of Sir R. Peel to turn him out, and a similar
result seems likely to follow.   It seems to me that the
Conservatives now have only one course which they can take
with honour and safety, viz., to support the Executive
Government, because it is the Executive Government,
wherever they can ; but where they differ from them on
questions of principle, temperately and firmly to maintain
such principles, however unpopular for the time it may make
them.

Believe me, dear Sir,

Yours sincerely,

S. H. WALPOLE.

Lord Brougham to Mr. Croker.

Hotel Frejus, April 19th, 1854.

MY DEAR CROKER,

I have been reading your article—not on Reform, for I had
no time to weigh it well, and therefore deferred reading till
two days hence—but on Holland—and I lose no time in
setting you right about a very important point of history,
namely, the Fitzherbert marriage.   I see you more than half
lean to a belief in it, but you may at once change that into
an entire belief.   I could have proved it in 1820.   I had as
my witness H. Errington, Mrs. F.'s uncle, who no doubt

would have sheltered himself under the privilege of not
committing himself, for he incurred a præmunire by being
present. Mrs. F. herself, in like manner ; and I had a communication from her in great alarm, and I rather think I quieted
her with a promise not to call her ; but of this I am not certain. H. Errington was enough for me, and his refusal would
have been as good as his saying " yes."

It was this, and not at all recrimination, to which I alluded
mysteriously, and in a way that has been much censured,
when I spoke of throwing the country into confusion.
Recrimination of adultery was supposed to be the thing
threatened. Nothing could be more absurd. We had abundant proof of that, but it was of no kind of value ; for who
ever doubted that adultery ? But the other meant a forfeiture of the Crown, or at least a disputed succession, and
I am quite confident, from some things Hutchinson (Lord) told
me, that George IV. was aware of what the real trump was
that I had in my hand.

You know, of course, that the marriage was wholly illegal ;
and Mrs. F. knew it to be so, which explains her say-
ings on the subject. Some too (not lawyers) held that
illegality to make it immaterial. But lawyers well knew
that a perfectly void act every day occasions a forfeiture—as
in all entails, both English and Scotch. T. Moore gives
a discussion between C. Butler and myself at Denman's
table on this point, and his account is correct as to what
Butler and I said. Butler agrees in the law as above stated,
but he adds a thing utterly untrue—that being asked why
we did not bring it forward, we said, " Because we had no
evidence."

We had quite enough to raise the question, which, of
course, was all we could want to do. What was said—at
least, what must have been said—was " That the occasion did
not arise. We were not in danger of being beaten, so as to
play our trump." In fact, we had two escapes—that trump,
and the House of Commons, where I always maintained
I could keep the bill a month in the lobby, or rather as long
as the country were with us, and the bill was persisted in.

I had from Sam Johns the whole history of the F. marriage,
but he would not tell me the parson's name. He said he had
promised never to mention it. He was a man, I think he
said, near Cheltenham. He (Johns) had promised the Prince
to perform the ceremony, and recollected in walking home

a previous promise he had given to Jack Payne (Admiral),
and went back next day to Carlton House and got off his
promise there.

The Prince never forgave him, and never spoke to him
afterwards.

Mrs. F. quarrelled with him for some years, but made it up.
I have other evidence from the Damers, her favourites.

Yours, &c.

B.

Lord Brougham to Mr. Croker.

Thursday, April 27th, 1854.

MY DEAR CROKER,

I grieve to say that before I could even begin the Reform
article, I parted from my copy of the *Quarterly Review* by
lending it to Douro to read to his brother Charles, in his sad
state of eyes (though I rejoice to say the doctor here gives
considerable hopes), and he has taken it away with him.

As to the Fitzherbert marriage, Sam Johns was a person in
whose word and accuracy I could entirely confide. He had
his memory so entire to the last, that when I went over to
see him (he being a good deal above ninety) at Welwyn he
reminded me of dishes at table, and persons present, and
topics of conversation the last time we dined together, and
that so long ago that it was at the St. Albans coffee-house, in
the street near Carlton House, long since pulled down. I was
then (I mean when I went to Welwyn) at Brocket Hall, but
I afterwards saw him repeatedly, both in Hertfordshire and
in town, and came more than once on the subject of the
marriage. He had the particulars from Mrs. F. herself,
who always had the greatest alarm about it, for fear of the
penalties (præmunire, &c.), which she had not been aware of,
any more than of the invalidity, at the time.

She had another reason for being alarmed, namely, the
great favour she was in with the D. of York and others
of the family, who always greatly respected her. I believe
I mentioned her having first quarrelled with Johns, and
afterwards made it up with him, when she happened to pass
him in her carriage in South Audley Street. But the Prince
never forgave him. Mrs. F.'s only fear was of the subject
being publicly broached, and this we know from communications made at the trial in 1820.

In private, at least to her very near connexions, she was very communicative on the subject. Moreover, she never forgave Fox for carrying down the message of denial, and always maintained that he knew the fact. I don't think Fox did forgive the former. I am sure Grey did not. I shall have my memory refreshed on the whole matter as soon as I see G. Damer. With Mrs. D. I have often discussed the subject, especially when my 'Statesmen' was published.

Yours truly,

B.

Mr. Croker to Lord Brougham.   Extracts.

Alverbank, Gosport, July 21st, 1854.

My dear Brougham,

Phrase it as you will—a House of Commons unmanageable, or the country ungovernable—the indisputable fact is that our representative system is not only, as you say, "likely to be brought into disrepute," but is actually so, and will every session become more and more notoriously incompatible with what was called our Constitution.

That result is owing to two causes—first, foremost, and in itself sufficient, was the Reform Bill, which gave the representative element, already even too great (as the passing the bill proved), a power which is swallowing rapidly, not merely all the monarchical authority, but all deliberative functions of a government.

The second cause of the weakness of the Government is the power of the newspapers. This power was always great, but was in general so nearly self-balanced as not seriously to interrupt the functions of a government. Mechanical improvements, extension of education and of business, of literary taste and commercial intercourse, have developed the powers of the press to an enormous influence—an influence the greater because it has become so subtle that we breathe it as we breathe the air, without being conscious of the minuter particles that enter into its composition. But these difficulties of a government from this quarter have been in an incalculable degree increased by the Reform Bill, which has operated in two ways, in many indeed, but in two more prominently; first, its effect on the individual members. The Reform Bill has made seats, and therefore the profession of public life, so precarious that no man can venture to brave the press, and what with the audacity of censure, or the exaggeration of flattery with which it visits individuals, there has grown up, and is still growing, an influence over the conduct of members so imperious that the Speaker, instead of demanding from the Sovereign freedom of speech, had much better ask it from the *Times*.

I dare say you know better than I in my deep retirement can do, how far this goes, but the instances that reach me are at once ridiculous and lamentable. But the second action of the press is still more important. The Reform Bill established the broad principle of governing by representation, and on that basis has been erected into omnipotence what was formerly a valuable subordinate agent, now called public opinion : she was of old the queen of the world ; she has now become its tyrant, and the newspapers her ministers ; that is, they assume that they represent public opinion, and of course the people, in a more direct and authoritative manner, than even the House of Commons. In all the great and in the small questions of the day, from the councils of sovereigns, and the operations of armies and navies, down to the pliability of a soldier's stock, or the early delivery of a middy's letter, the press and its correspondences are now the arbiters. The army is taken out of the hands of the sovereign, virtually, for a long time past ; now avowedly. I don't otherwise complain of that, but as another innovation on our old constitution. I admit the necessity of a responsible minister in the army or in the navy. My regret and alarm is that I see all ministerial functions either yielded to or usurped by Committees of the House of Commons, and even more undisguisedly by editors of newspapers.

Ever yours sincerely,

J. W. CROKER.

Mr. Croker to Lord Monteagle.

Alverbank, Gosport, September 21st, 1854.

MY DEAR MONTEAGLE,

I never suspected your memory or your wish to forward my search, but I did apprehend what I think will turn out to be true, that all the boastings we have heard about the new system of keeping our national records are palaver and hum-

bug. Mr. Secretary Johnston * is a remarkable character in
our political, literary, and anecdotical history ; his name is in
our best histories, our best poetry, and the vicissitudes of his
life ended in a persecution under Queen Anne, and a pension
under George I., and a kind of Court favour, *otium cum dignitate,* under George II. ; and yet I dare say our well-arranged
public records will not afford you, an official and authorized
enquirer, any particulars of that pension, which was the final
remuneration, and I believe only means of existence, of this
once influential and remarkable man.   These are the kind of
details that carry us back into the private life and individual
character of historical personages, and excite in my mind,
pro re natâ, a (perhaps you will think it) morbid curiosity.   I
shall therefore be glad if your enquiries shall enable me to
complete the history of James Johnston, and to explain two
or three at once obscure and striking passages of Pope—obscure
as to their substance, but striking in expression.   It may
facilitate enquiry to state that Johnston died in 1737, ætat.
93.   And the short line in the 'Gentleman's Magazine' that
announces his death, is nearly all that we know of him from·
the death of William III.

Talking of pensions, I wonder whether at my death (almost
miraculously adjourned for now three years) my poor wife
will recover the pension of which she was—an unprecedented
and I believe solitary exception—deprived during your
administration.†

I quite agree in what you say of the potato crop.   Virgil
indicated the governing principle fifteen hundred years before
potatoes were discovered.

" Pater ipse colendi
Haud facilem esse viam voluit, primusque per artem
Movit agros, curis acuens mortalia corda."

---

* [The first edition of Pope's Works has J——n, meaning no doubt
old Mr. Johnston, who had been King William's Secretary for Scotland.
He retired from public life on a pension, and fixed himself in an elegant
villa at Twickenham (since known as Orleans House), where he amused
himself with horticulture, but neither neighbourhood nor similarity of
taste could reconcile Pope to the old Whig.   He was a cousin of Bishop
Burnet, and was recommended by him to King William.—*Note by Mr.
Croker for his edition of Pope's Works,* vol. iii. pp. 64, 65.]

† [This pension was recovered for Mrs. Croker after her husband's
death.]

A livelihood that can be obtained by what is called a labourer, clad in the rags of a long great coat, working with one hand while the other is in the pocket of what once were somebody else's breeches; such a livelihood, if it even keeps the body alive, must kill all energy and intellect, and reduce the man to the condition of the brute, living and contented to live on the spontaneous produce of mother earth— "that man is of the earth, earthy;" and the nearer that his aliment approaches to spontaneity, the nearer he approaches to the beasts of the field. Think of the various processes that improve and transform the grain of wheat into bread—the plough, the harrow, the reaper, the carter, the bailiff, the salesman, the miller, the baker—and compare it with the single-handed Paddy, who makes a hole in the ground to receive half a potato, and at the end of six idle, do-nothing months expects to dig up ten, which are to be his sole maintenance for a whole year.

Ever yours,
J. W. CROKER.

Lord Strangford to Mr. Croker.

London, October 21st, 1854.

MY DEAR OLD FRIEND,

I am sick of all I see and hear! All the ancient historical notions under the shade of which you and I have grown old and respectable, are being rapidly swept away. Chateaubriand—sometimes speaks truth, and never more so than where he says, " Nous sommes sur les bords d'un monde qui finit, et d'un autre monde qui commence." What a frightful thing this " commencement " will be!

This is Trafalgar-day! You and I are old enough to remember it. Does anybody else, in these days of philanthropy and amalgamation, venture to do so? This story of the 'Hougomont' transport being re-baptized into the Marshal St. Arnaud is quite delightful. A lord of the Admiralty, whom I met at dinner last week, told me that there had been some difficulty made about this change of name by the owner of the 'Hougomont,' as the vessel had, under its original name, been a part of some property settled on his daughter at her marriage; but that they had got over it by engaging at the Admiralty or Transport Office that the new name was only to last for six months, by which time it was supposed that the war would be over.

What do you think of Dizzy as the leader of the Protestant party? Lord Derby disapproves of the thing altogether. God bless you.

Ever yours affectionately,
Sp.

Mr. Lockhart to Mr. Croker.*

Abbotsford, November 19th, 1854.

My dear Croker,

If there had been anything comfortable in my own condition, or, as far as I understood it, anything in yours, I should not have been at all likely to drop the correspondence that had been for so many years one of the chief and most regular amusements of my life.

My health and spirits both gave way about two years ago. My immediate relations and friends thought something of Robert† Hay's Roman proposal, and although abhorring travels, I submitted to the experiment; but the appearance of benefit was slight and fleeting, and before the usual period for English tourists to return home, I found various warnings that it would be prudent for me to do so. Since then I have continued to lose strength almost without interruption, and my usual state is that of the most complete childish helplessness in body, and almost equally so in mind. I am not, however, aware that my reasoning soundness is disturbed, unless by occasional medicine which often confuses my memory.

I spent the latter part of the autumn at my brother's in Lanarkshire, at which time I was by no means so very low as I am now; but between the decay in my own physical powers and the temptations of the Hope Scotts being established in Scotland, I saw no reason for refusing myself the pleasure of being under the same roof with my nearest

---

* [This letter is signed, in a feeble hand, by Mr. Lockhart, and was certainly one of the last letters signed or dictated by him. He died on the 25th of November, six days after it was written. An interesting account of his last days will be found in the *Memoirs of James R. Hope-Scott*, 1884.]

† [Robert Hay, for a long time Under-Secretary to the Colonies. He was an old friend of Mr. Lockhart's, had long been in the habit of passing the winter in Rome, and had invited Mr. Lockhart to join him there.]

and dearest relations, not excluding Charlotte's baby, who is a particular delight to me.

Even a short letter is a considerable exertion. My daughter will let me summon her assistance as my amanuensis some day soon again. Meantime I suppose enough has been said to leave you with the clear impression that it is not possible for any of my inspectors to have reached a humbler notion of my prospects than I have long myself been content with. Charlotte joins me in kindest regards to Mrs. Croker, and I hope when our hands fail altogether, that theirs may still continue to maintain the usual offices between our families.

Meantime, believe me,

Ever yours truly,

J. G. LOCKHART.

Mr. Croker to Lord Brougham.

Alverbank, Gosport, December 3rd, 1854.

MY DEAR B.,

Poor Lockhart departed as quietly and happily (since we were to lose him) as could be wished, and in the circumstances he and his friends would have chosen for him—in the arms of his daughter and at Abbotsford ; and his last hours were cheered in fondling his grandchild, the only relic of his blood and of Sir Walter's. He was buried on the 1st of December in Dryburgh Abbey, by the side of Sir Walter. It seems strange that six friends, who, all in good health, and all having every prospect of surviving me, took the trouble of paying me visits when they thought I was near my departure, should have all gone before me—the Duke, Londonderry, Sir Byam Martin, Lockhart and two others whom you did not know.

I am like you, and I believe even more than you, alarmed about this terrible war—grieved for what we have lost—little consoled by ruinous victories, and trembling to think how near we may be to a more awful and decisive catastrophe. God avert it ; in fact, the fate of our army is in the hands of God, not of man. On His providence, vulgarly called accident, it now depends whether a man may be saved.

Ever yours,

J. W C.

CHAPTER XXX.

1855–1857.

MR. CROKER'S old friends were now rapidly passing away, but most of them continued on affectionate terms with him to the last. The Duke of Rutland corresponded with him while he was able to hold a pen in his hand; and the chief companion of Mr. Disraeli in his early scheme for the Re-generation of England, felt it a matter of duty to write to Mr. Croker to tell him how greatly his father had loved him, and how sincere was his own " admiration and respect." Such was the feeling with which Mr. Croker was regarded by those who had been closely associated with him for nearly

half a century, and who were best able to form a right
judgment of his character.   They never wavered in their
attachment to him.   There are men and women still living
who were his intimate friends and associates, and they continue to regard him as one of the best and truest friends they
ever had.   No doubt, he was not the same to all men.   To
strangers, or towards persons whom he disliked, his manner was
sometimes overbearing and harsh.   The deference with which
his opinions were usually received rendered him impatient of
contradiction, and age and infirmities doubtless aggravated
the natural sensitiveness of a nervous temperament.   But
every one who had more than a superficial acquaintance with
him was well aware that he had done a thousand kindly acts,
some of them to persons who little deserved them at his
hands, and his private accounts show how generous he was
to all who came to him in necessity or distress.

In spite of the sufferings which he was called upon to
undergo in these later years, his spirit never flagged.   He
kept to his work, and although death was constantly within
sight, he did not fear it, or allow it in any way to interfere
with the performance of the daily duties which he prescribed
for himself.   To give up work, and to acknowledge in one's
own heart that all is over, and that nothing more can be done
on this side the grave, is a miserable way to precipitate the
end.   Mr. Croker was prepared for the end, but he was disposed
to wait patiently for it, and meanwhile to do what was to be
done with all zeal and earnestness.   His literary work never
failed to be a source of solace, and his interest in public
affairs never abated.   He did not write so much as of old,
but few questions of importance passed by him unnoticed.
Seldom did he allow any statement reflecting on the reputation of his old friends—especially the Duke of Wellington—
to pass unchallenged.   One of the last letters he wrote was

prompted by the desire to prevent a misrepresentation of the Duke's political character from passing into history.

Two of the letters which immediately follow recall familiar names in this correspondence. They were, of course, written by the sons of the distinguished men who had been among the early friends of Mr. Croker.

The Duke of Wellington to Mr. Croker.

3, Upper Belgrave Street, February 25th, 1855.

My dear Mr. Croker,

It is not so easy to say who is to blame for the misfortunes in the Crimea, and all suspect according to their antipathies.

Routh, my father's friend, tells me that it is *not* the system, but the non-instruction of the men employed. Virtuous creature!

For my part I suspect that there has been no loss or non-arrival without proportionate gain to some rascal contractor or carrier; and yesterday I heard a curious confirmation of my fancy. In my defective way, I overheard Clarendon accounting "for the medicines being under the shot." They were *not* under the shot, but under 130 tons of cargo smuggled into the ship by the captain, which naturally he wished to keep quiet until he sold it, and therefore would not disembark the medicines.

This accounts for the Duke of Newcastle's firmness in asserting that the medicines were not under the shot. Remedy: send a supercargo, and never spare an evil-doer *when he can gain by it.* I would take his gaining by it a proof of intention.

I think you are rather a funker about newspapers. There are two things in our favour against them.

They cannot come to agreement till their customers agree; and in England they depend on a daily sale; an *abonnement*, as in France, would make them more formidable, for it would give their malice independence as long as the *abonnement* lasts.

The system of sending correspondents is fatal to any military operation on land, and a reason for confining ourselves to ships. The minister might say, "that as the people of England countenance such a system, he declines the responsibility of sending an army."

Going to the Crimea at all with such a force, and during the short interregnum between autumnal fever and winter, was the front of the offending.

Napoleon must be forgiven; his position required a *coup*; but there can be no reason but personal ambition which could induce Newcastle and the Government to obey the *Times*. The *Times*, like Napoleon, depended on a *coup*, and it might have succeeded in upsetting a minister, but it could not have forced an unwise expedition. Surely the consideration of such an expedition must be on cool contemplation of chances; and when a man is convinced that they are against the enterprize, he ought to say so.

It seems that, although Napoleon was so much in favour of it, his generals were against it, and the English carried it.

Now, however successful the allies, the French must have all the honour, as our numbers and physique are so low.

Not a word can be said against our fighting, however, which may be wholesome some day against our allies.

Yours sincerely,

DOURO.*

Lord Aberdeen to Mr. Croker.

Downing Street, January 6, 1855.

MY DEAR CROKER,

Your letter contains a melancholy picture of the truth. I never recollect anything like the present state of the daily press; and I know not what may ultimately be the consequences. I fear, however, we must admit that all hope of a remedy is vain, at least it entirely passes my power to provide one. I well recollect the days of the *Courier* to which you refer, and am fully aware of its prompt and successful efforts in the cause of truth. But you were young, active, and able, and you had useful fellow-labourers. I should not now have the least notion how to organise a system of counteraction of this kind. I can easily understand why I

---

* [The second Duke of Wellington, who died suddenly at Brighton, on the 13th August, 1884, continued to use the signature " Douro " for some little time after his father's death.]

should be, almost exclusively, the object of these attacks. Whatever may be the qualities of different ministers, I am the bond by which they are united together. That once destroyed, the whole fabric falls to pieces. This is not, however, a Ministerial question. Ministers must always expect to be treated with injustice, but it is new to see our naval and military commanders held up to public scorn in this fashion.

The power of the press for good and for ill has been steadily progressive, and will probably continue. My great hope is in the good sense of the people of this country, who are also becoming more enlightened every day, and better able to distinguish the good from the bad. We must educate by all the means in our power; and we shall be able to trust the people more safely with their own concerns. Many changes of popular opinion have taken place in our day, and we need not altogether despair of seeing a salutary impulse given by apparently inadequate causes.

Ever, my dear Croker,

Truly yours,

ABERDEEN.

Sir Robert Peel to Mr. Croker.

Drayton Manor, Tamworth, February 2nd, 1856.

MY DEAR MR. CROKER,

It is indeed years since last we met, and although circumstances unfortunately led to an interruption in the relations of a once most intimate acquaintance, I cannot but look back with pleasure to the time when you were a familiar friend beneath this roof; it is therefore a source of much gratification to me to acknowledge the receipt of your letter of congratulations on the occasion of my recent marriage, and whilst appreciating your expressions of the present with the happiest recollections of my earlier years, I thank you warmly and heartily for your good wishes for the future honour and welfare of my family.

I remain, my dear Mr. Croker,

Yours very faithfully and truly,

ROBERT PEEL.

Mr. Croker to the Duc d'Aumale.

West Moulsey, April 5th, 1855.

SIR,

Your Royal Highness is, I believe, aware that in my
enquiries after our great poet Pope, I have found one line,
which has perplexed all his critics, in which he describes a
view of your Royal Highness's present residence as ex-
hibiting, when seen from the river, two statues of a *dog* and
a *bitch.* No such statues have been visible for an hundred
years, and people have been puzzled to make out what they
were, and where they could have been. They have been
looked for and enquired after in vain. At last I have
ascertained that they stood, and actually do stand, on a wall
of your Royal Highness's garden towards the Thames, but
so overgrown with ivy as to be totally hid, and offering
only the appearance of two ivy bushes which give no idea
what they originally were. Your Royal Highness's personal
goodness to me and your known love of literature induces
me to hope that you will permit this curious point to be
elucidated. If my health, which is still very precarious,
allows me, I would do myself the honour of paying my
respects at Orleans House any day next week that you would
allow; or if I should not be able to accomplish that object,
I should hope that your Royal Highness would consent to
allow me to have a drawing made of the statues.

J. W. CROKER.

The Duc d'Aumale to Mr. Croker.

7 avril 1855.

Le chien et *la chienne* existent en effet dans mon jardin,
mon cher Monsieur. Ils ornent les murs de mon potager, et
je les ai fait récemment dégager de la masse de lierre qui les
cachait. Leur existence m'a été révélée par un clergyman qui
m'a fait demander, il y a quelques mois, la permission de les
dessiner. Malheureusement, je n'étais pas chez moi, en sorte
que je n'ai pas pu savoir de lui quel genre d'intérêt s'attachait
à ces deux petites statues, et Pope ne m'est malheureusement
pas assez familier pour que je puisse faire la découverte à
moi tout seul. Vous serez donc doublement aimable en

venant nous expliquer cela vous-même, et en nous pro-
curant le plaisir de causer quelque temps avec vous. Nous
déjeunons à midi. Samedi prochain 14, vous conviendrait-il?
ou bien quelque autre jour, à votre choix, de la semaine qui
commence le lundi 16 ?

Toujours heureux de me retrouver en rapport avec vous,
et de vous assurer que je suis, bien sincèrement,

Votre affectionné,

H. D'ORLÉANS.

Dean Trench to Mr. Croker.   Extract.

Itchenstoke, Alresford, September 24th, 1855.

MY DEAR SIR,

Certainly the answers of the candidates generally revealed
to me a depth of ignorance, in respect of English literature
among our young men, of which I had no conception. In
one of my questions I ask who were the authors of a few
of the best known poems in the language. I received the
following answers, which I gathered out of the papers as I
read them. I was assured that 'The Fairy Queen' was
written by Chaucer, by Thomson; 'Canterbury Tales,' by
Goldsmith, Gray, Dryden; 'Comus,' by Pope, Dryden,
Beaumont and Fletcher; 'Absalom and Achitophel,' by
Milton, Hannah More, Shakespeare, Byron; 'Essay on Man,'
by Newton, Dryden, Burke, Milton, Locke, Swift, Prior;
'Dunciad,' by Sterne, Akenside, Beaumont and Fletcher,
Dryden; 'Hudibras,' by Gower, Pope, Fielding, Ben Jonson,
Shakespeare, Samuel Johnson; 'Task,' by Coleridge, Gold-
smith; 'Excursion,' by Crabbe, Thomson, Tennyson, Swift,
Gower, Goldsmith; 'Thalaba,' by Swift, Pope, Shenstone,
Cowper, Byron, Coleridge.

I would not have troubled you with these particulars but
that your letter indicates an interest in the subject, and
the document is, I think, a curious one in its way.

Ever very faithfully yours,

RICHARD C. TRENCH.

Memorandum by Mr. Croker.

As I can speak decisively on the question lately raised as to Mr. Thomas Scott's share in the 'Waverley Novels,' I think it my duty to do so.

Early in my acquaintance with Walter Scott, and soon after I had become Secretary of the Admiralty, he asked me to obtain some Colonial office for his brother Thomas; in addition to a statement of his position and circumstances, not necessary to be repeated, he said that, besides being a very good fellow, he had a great fund of local Scotch anecdotes and stories, which perhaps might be turned to account in the *Quarterly Review*, which had been recently established, and in which he and I took a common interest. Without reckoning, I confess, much, or indeed at all, on Tom's literary value, I was anxious to gratify his brother, for whom (as I believe every one did) I had felt a peculiar regard from the moment that I made his acquaintance. I accordingly applied to the late Lord Bathurst, then Secretary of State, for some situation in the Colonies, which his Lordship had very soon an opportunity of giving in Canada. Tom on this came to London to receive his appointment and prepare for his emigration. I, of course, saw him, and must again confess that I discovered no indications of the latent spirit that was soon after manifested in "Waverley." I never thought again of Tom Scott's story-telling till after I had myself heard with great wonder Sir Walter's almost spontaneous and quite unequivocal denial of the authorship at the Prince Regent's table. This declaration so staggered my former belief, I might say certainty, that Walter was the sole author, that I set about conjecturing how it could be reconciled with what I still had little doubt was the substantial fact, and then I recollected what he had told me of Tom's store of Scottish stories, and I was inclined to suppose that Tom might have furnished the original matter in such a degree as to warrant Walter in attributing the authorship to him. I believe this solution occurred to others as well as to me, but it soon vanished before successive evidence, and at last the public avowal; after which I reminded Walter that such an impression as to Tom had naturally received some countenance, as his communication had been made to me long before the "Waverley" mystery, and could not have been designed to mislead.

Sir George Sinclair to Mr. Croker.   Extract.

Thurso Castle, November 20th, 1855.

My dear Croker,

Our weather has been, in general, calm and moderate. My beloved daughter is one of the kindest, most affectionate, and most devoted, as well as intelligent, of human beings; and I may with truth say, that

> " The busy day, the peaceful night,
> Unfelt, uncounted, glided by;"

and I often regret the years misspent in faithless courts and fawning senates—neither doing nor deriving any good.

I would much rather learn from you what you think of the present state of public affairs, than trouble you with any lucubrations of my own.   There seems to prevail a fatal mediocrity in every department—in the Cabinet, no Chatham; in the navy, no Nelson; in the army, no Wellington; in the church, no Luther.   " I am only a lodger," as the Hibernian said when the house was on fire.   But I must say that I think we are in great jeopardy both at home and abroad, and I have little doubt that both here and in France an awful financial crisis is near at hand, which our shallow and self-conceited ministers are quite incapable to parry, or even to palliate; and no other party possesses, or I fear merits, national reliance and respect.

My dear Croker,

Your very sincere friend and well-wisher,

George Sinclair.

Mr. Drummond to Mr. Croker.

St. James's Place, February 14th, 1856.

My dear Croker,

I have had great pleasure in presenting your address,* and it was an additional gratification to see your handwriting as good as ever, whereby I hope you are stronger than when you last wrote to me.   It seems to me that the refusal to keep the churches in repair is as infidel an act as the nation can commit, and far worse than refusing to pay tithes.

* [Probably a petition to the House of Commons on the church-rate question, drawn up by Mr. Croker.]

As to the war, its popularity arose from the strong instinct amongst the revolutionists that Russia is the great representative of the Conservative principles; hence their hatred of the Empire; and they expected that it would not cease until it had blown up into a flame all the dominant nationalities. I think still that when we come to the last sealing of the treaty something will occur to unsettle it. The Emperor of the French is determined to have it: Palmerston is as determined for war.

Our Conservative (!) lords seem blowing up their house about their own ears. Voting by proxy in criminal cases, appellate jurisdictions, &c., &c., will all now be discussed, questioned, and altered.

Always yours faithfully,

HENRY DRUMMOND.

Lord St. Leonards to Mr. Croker.

[No date.]

MY DEAR CROKER,

If I were you, or rather if I had your task * before me, I would not refer to the ancient law, which would require explanation. Strictly speaking, the power of entailing is not confined to one or two generations.

What you wish to explain may be put thus, although you will explain it much better.

The author is incorrect in stating that the right of primogeniture is derived from the liberty of bequeathing. The law, in the absence of any disposition by act *inter vivos* or testamentary disposition, gives real property to the eldest born. But an entail may be created by deed or will, and if left undisturbed by the successive owners under the entail, may continue by law until the whole line provided for is exhausted. The inconvenience resulting from too much land being placed *extra commercium* by entails is avoided by enabling tenants in tail, who were unborn when the entail was created, upon attaining twenty-one, with the concurrence

---

* [An article appeared in the *Quarterly Review*, No. 165, on Entails of Land (June, 1848). It was not written by Mr. Croker, but he may have had some hand in it, and this letter was perhaps designed to help him.]

of the previous tenant for life if there be one, to bar the estate tail and all remainders over, and to acquire the fee-simple or entire ownership over the property. Other modes of settlement by the English law are subject to rules which, in order to guard against perpetuities, require the estates created to be capable of vesting within a fixed and limited period. These powers, whilst they tend to keep large properties in the heads of families, lead to no serious mischief, for the power of releasing the estate from its fetters soon arrives, and the habits of the people lead to resettlements of the property upon the like footing.

I hope this sketch will assist you in your note.

Ever very truly yours,

ST. LEONARDS.

Mr. Croker to Lord Lyndhurst.

West Moulsey, Surrey, February 21st, 1856.

DEAR LYNDHURST,

Occupied as your mind must be, I think it worth while to intrude on you for two minutes at most.

I very much doubt either the constitutionality or the rationality of the new doctrine that the High Court of the House of Peers should be exclusively, or even over-proportionably, a Court of Lawyers. Cases come there only after all the lawyers in the land have debated and differed, and it seems to me most wholesome that the question should be brought before a tribunal not destitute of the highest legal authorities, but comprising also the natural good sense of the best educated body of men in the kingdom, the most interested in the due execution of justice, and the highest and farthest above any private feelings that might warp it : it seems to me like a final trial by the most special and respectable jury that the country affords ; and if they think that on any point they have not legal authorities within their own circle, the Constitution provides for them the assistance of the judges to advise, though not to vote.

In short, I believe this life peerage to be as irrational and unconstitutional as it is illegal, and I persuade myself that Lord Coke's dictum about it is not a dictum, but a deduction from premises which he lays before us, and of which the major, the minor, and the middle term, are all notoriously false, and therefore so is—*pace tanti viri*—the conclusion.

I heard with great delight that you were in the former debate as brilliant and vigorous as you were at forty-four.

With kindest regards to my lady, I remain, as I have been for thirty years,

Your affectionate and admiring friend,

J. W. CROKER.

*Lord Strangford to Mr. Croker.**

Monday.

MY DEAR CROKER,

I have been very ill since I wrote to you last week. My *Nemesis* still pursues me. On Thursday I had the misfortune of losing the last legacy of my poor dear daughter Sligo, at Westport, the most gifted little being I ever beheld; so preternaturally gifted in truth, that one might have safely predicted that she would not be long for this world of sin and sorrow. On the same day I lost my dearest and oldest friend (except yourself), Lord Stanhope, after an uninterrupted intimacy of forty-seven years. My darling little grand-daughter had just completed her sixth year.

Ever yours affectionately,

S.

Mr. Croker to Lord Campbell.

West Moulsey, Surrey, 20th February, 1856.

MY DEAR LORD,

I have just received your speech on the life peerage,† and hasten to thank you for this mark of your remembrance of

* [This appears to be the last letter which Mr. Croker received from his old friend. Lord Strangford died on the 29th of May, 1855. The letter on p. 358 is from his son, the well-known George Smythe, of the "Young England" party, who survived Mr. Croker only a few months. The Strangford peerage became extinct in 1869.]

† [This discussion arose in consequence of a life peerage having been granted to Baron Parke, under the title of Lord Wensleydale. The House of Lords, upon a division, decided that the letters patent could not enable "the grantee to sit and vote in Parliament," and finally the Government created Baron Parke a peer in the usual way, and the Lords gained their point.]

2 A 2

an old acquaintance whom you might have been well excused for thinking out of the world. I am, however, still alive, and as susceptible of a life peerage as Mr. Baron Parke, and as likely I hope to enjoy one. This affair has its grave and its ludicrous face, but one aspect that I have not yet seen noticed combines both.

The pretence of the measure is to introduce an accession of sound law (much needed it is alleged) into the House of Lords, and the "learned pundit" selected for this great purpose, and whose presence is to give learning to the House and confidence to the public, exhibits his competence by advising and accepting what every lawyer in England, except the two parties who have concocted the patent, pronounce a gross illegality. This is stumbling at the threshold with a vengeance, as Sir Thomas More said when he was about to lose his head; and the same may be said of Sir James Parke, who has very evidently lost his in his eagerness to get a coronet to put on it.

But on looking closer into Coke's dictum, I think I see that it is not so much a *dictum* as a *deduction*—a very different thing; for little weight as I think even his *dictum* would have in the present state of our Constitution, and after two centuries of practical dissent from it, still that *dictum* of such a man would carry, as it has hitherto done, considerable authority; but if it be only as I think, a deduction from premises, it is of no more value than the premises may warrant. Now, on reading all the paragraphs attentively and in connexion, it seems to me that Coke states the argument thus: a woman may obtain a life peerage by marriage (which I deny in any other sense than that all peerages are peerages for life); but having made this conundrum, for it really is no better, he proceeds to complete his syllogism thus—I quote his *ipsissima verba* :—

"And as an estate for life may be gained by marriage, so may the king create either man or woman noble for life."

The argument, you see, is a gross *non sequitur ;* for even if the premises were true, the conclusion is much wider than they. But that is not all, for the premises are notoriously false : a woman does not obtain a life peerage, for Coke immediately after states that she forfeits it by a second marriage with a commoner, and so it is not for *life.* But again, the original peerage which she shares with her husband is no more a life peerage than his—it is an hereditary peerage, which both enjoy physically for their *natural lives*, but which descends to their joint heir, and not two peerages, one on the man and one on the woman.   I do not know whether I make myself understood, but it seems to me that Lord Coke's *dictum* is merely a deduction from premises, of which the major, the minor, and the middle terms are all false—it is but little better than, as I have said, a conundrum on the word *life*.   The peerages to unmarried women for life is quite another matter, for in the first place it does not affect the real point at issue—sitting and voting in Parliament; but in the next the legality of such creations might, in spite of the harlotry precedents, be reasonably doubted, and they might be rather assimilated to that exercise of royal favour that bestows rank by a notice in the 'Gazette.' But it is observable how cautiously this prerogative has been used of meddling with the *peerage!*

Take the instance that Lord Clarendon's mourning the other day suggests.   He succeeded his uncle; his mother was Mrs., and his brothers and sisters Misters and Mistresses Villiers.   Well, a notice in the Gazette gave the brothers and sisters the rank of Earl's children, and we had My Lady Theresa and the Honourable Charles and the Honourable Henry, and a very proper exercise of a decent and reasonable prerogative—but was it decent or reasonable, if it could have been helped, that the mother of these lords, ladies, and honourable gentlemen should have lived and died plain Mrs. George Villiers?   I myself do not see why she should not have had the Gazette courtesy rank of an Earl's widow, but I suppose they have been afraid of meddling with titles really belonging to the peerage; for what was conferred on the sons and daughters was only *rank* at court, which might be given, and was given, in the Fitz-Clarence cases, where there was no question of peerage at all.   But why, then, if life peerages to women were legal, was not a life peerage of Countess of Clarendon conferred on Mrs. Villiers, which would have placed her and her sons and daughters all in their natural positions?   I really believe that if it had been thought possible, so simple and reasonable a solution of the difficulty would have been adopted.

You see my pen has run away with me, and I have returned you an essay, almost as long, longer indeed than the portion of your speech to which it refers, but I have ventured to do so, not only in the hope that my hints from my hermitage may be not altogether useless, but also to shew your lordship that I am not ungrateful for your kind recollection of me.

Believe me, my dear lord, very sincerely yours,

J. W. CROKER.

The Hon. G. S. Smythe (Seventh Viscount Strangford) to Mr. Croker.

May 30th, 1855.

MY DEAR MR. CROKER,

It is my painful office to inform you of the death of your old college-friend, and world-friend, and Tory-friend, Lord Strangford, my father.

During the last few days of his life he was perfectly calm, still, unconscious and lethargic. From this night sennight, up to Friday night last he suffered in great agony from indigence (*sic*) and default of respiration. But for ten days preceding the end he was utterly incompetent to write, or indeed shape his thoughts into form, or I am sure, sir, that he would have, in farewell, written to you.

Since the death of Mr. Canning you have ever been his intellectual chief; and from boyhood I remember that every solecism of my puerile English, or sciolism in more ambitious nonage, were met by the correction, "What would Croker say?"

Two or three years ago, I believe that the reminiscences of long-past years and Trinity days were revived and re-riveted in the bonds of a retrospective sympathy and warm agreement as to the causes and results of modern politics.

At any rate I am sure that my father greatly loved you; much looked up to you as a king in letters; was always seriously and gravely concerned when you were ill (as you were, sir, a few years ago); and these reflections must stand my excuse for intruding upon your retirement, to give you news so painful.

I am, Sir, with great admiration and respect,

Your obedient servant,

G. SYDNEY SMYTHE.

Mr. Croker to Lord Strangford.

Alverbank, Gosport, June 2nd, 1855.

MY DEAR LORD,

I have only this morning received your, I may almost venture to call it, welcome letter, which, by a post-office mistake, had been, it seems, sent to Faversham. I venture to say *welcome*, because, as I already knew the worst, I was anxious to hear some of the details, and am thankful to have heard that the last days and hours were without suffering. It was also some consolation to find that our old and mutual friendship and affection is duly appreciated by the person most sure to know, and best entitled to express, his feelings. Of that friendship and affection, which had lasted fifty-seven years, I had had abundant proof that his share was as cordial as mine towards him; but I could hardly have expected that his partiality for me was in other respects so much greater than I could deserve.

I had heard about the middle of April that he was not well, and I took an early opportunity, the first and the last I had, of calling on him, and was glad to find him better, both in health and spirits, than I had been led to expect, and he even arranged to spend a few days here about this time. We talked of old times and recent times, of his domestic afflictions and hopes; of the children he had lately lost, and of those that remained—all with his usual good sense and good feeling. You are aware that during my illness, when he had a prospect of more years of life than I had of weeks, his good-nature often brought him to see me.

I conclude by thanking you very sincerely for your own feelings towards me, and wish I could hope for an opportunity of cultivating, for the short space that is probably left to me, the friendship of your father's son.

I am, my dear Lord, most gratefully and faithfully,

J. W. CROKER.

Lord Lyndhurst to Mr. Croker.

George Street.

[No date. Probably February, 1856.]

MY DEAR CROKER,

I was charmed at receiving a letter from you, and the more so as it appeared from the contents that you are as alive to what is going on among us talkers as ever. Brougham assumed his old tone in the debate—active and energetic. Campbell and St. Leonards were piano in voice, but they have published their speeches, and they tell well. I think we have saved the Peerage, but we must endeavour to construct a golden bridge for the retreat of our opponents. This affair, and the subsequent proceedings in the House of Commons have tended to damage the Palmerston Ministry, and if the peace should turn out not to be quite satisfactory, they will hardly be able to stand their ground. Peace, I presume, there will be at all events. The Emperor, I hear from Paris, is determined to bring back his army from the Crimea. I passed four months in the Champs Elysées, not disagreeably, though the want of my walking powers interfered with the usual enjoyments. Pray, when you come to town, look in upon Lady L. and myself; we should both like to have a little chat with you, which always leaves an agreeable impression.

Ever yours faithfully,

LYNDHURST.

Lord Palmerston to Mr. Croker.

Piccadilly, February 6th, 1856.

MY DEAR CROKER.

I have not read Montalembert, and have no clue but your letter to guide me in guessing which "few words" of mine he honours with his approbation ; but as people generally think a speech good in proportion to their agreement with its arguments and object, I conclude that he alludes to a speech of mine in 1829 on the Catholic question and in support of Peel's Bill.

You were a better prophet than I am, for I certainly did not contemplate the possibility of my having to form a Government till a very short time before I was called upon to do so. As to the two things you want us to do, I think on the whole the chances are that we shall accomplish the first, and I should be very glad to be able to do the second. I am inclined to believe that the Russians mean peace ; and I have always thought the Succession Tax, though imposed by a great name, a financial error, and at variance with the plainest principles of political economy. But if the tax was to be

maintained, there was a great difficulty in resisting its application to landed property.

I hope I may look upon your letter as a proof that you
continue well.

Yours sincerely,

PALMERSTON.

Mr. Croker to Lord Palmerston.

Kensington Palace, April 25th, 1856.

MY DEAR PALMERSTON,

I have been ill ever since I saw you, but am better, and
expect to return to my rural exile next Monday; and as I
can't *prophetize* when I may ever have another opportunity, I
should like to see you again before I go, if you could give me
another twenty minutes next Sunday. I have not been well
enough to see any one from whom I could hear what the
world is saying; but what I read of the debates and newspaper criticisms only increases my despair of the possibility
of governing this country, and my sincere sympathy for
those who have to deal with that captious, jealous, inconsistent
and ungrateful tyrant that calls itself the "public." I do not
say, "God send you a good deliverance," because I believe that ᵥ
what might seem *your* deliverance would inevitably and
most seriously increase the general danger. The last words
the Duke of Wellington said to me in contemplation of my
probably going before him (who, however, went the following
week), were :—" But at least, my dear Croker, it is some,
consolation to us who are so near the end of our career
that we shall be spared seeing the consummation of the ruin
that is gathering about us."

Yours sincerely,

J. W. CROKER.

Mr. Croker to Lord Palmerston.

Alverbank, Gosport, July 8th, 1856.

MY DEAR PALMERSTON,

I see by the papers that Prince Jerome has some law-suit
concerning the legitimacy of his children by his first marriage.
I don't suppose that *we*, English, can have any concern with

the affair, but *if* we have, you may like to know that you
have, I believe, in the Foreign Office some information on
the subject, for happening last week to be looking over some
old papers, I found a copy of a letter from Serrurier, then
French Minister in America, to the Duke of Bassano dated
14 Janvier, 1813, giving an account of " the Act of the State
of Maryland," dissolving the marriage between " Jérome and
Elizabeth Bonaparte," but preserving the legitimacy of the
issue of the marriage.   Serrurier enters into some details as
to Miss Paterson's views, who throws herself on the goodness
of the Emperor.

I forget how or why I came to have a copy of this letter,
but suspect that it was intercepted by the allies in the Saxon
Campaign of 1813 (as several other despatches were), and
that it having somehow reached me, I preserved it as a *pièce
historique.*   But I can have no doubt that either the original
or a copy must have reached the Foreign Office ; and, if the
matter is worth enquiring after, will no doubt be found there
under the date of March or April, 1813.

There has been an old tracasserie between Jerome and Louis
Napoleon about the position of Jerome and his son in relation
to the *Empire,* and this law-suit is probably a branch of it.

Ever sincerely yours,

J. W. CROKER.

Lord Palmerston to Mr. Croker.

Broadlands, October 16th, 1856.

MY DEAR CROKER,

I have received yours of the 12th.   I was very sorry that
your young friend * was not one of the three at the top of
the list.   He may, nevertheless, have been in fact as good as
the more successful competitors, for these examinations
cannot from the nature of things and the constitution of man
be as accurate measures of relative ability and attainments
as a foot rule would be of relative height, but at least they
so far secure the interests of the public service as to make it

* [This refers to a competitive examination for a clerkship in the
Treasury, for which Lord Palmerston had given a nomination to Mr.
Croker Barrow, the present Sir John Barrow.   He took the sixth place
among nine competitors for three appointments.]

certain that those who succeed are young men of capacity and attainment, while by the method of appointment formerly adopted no such certainty could be had.

Yours sincerely,

PALMERSTON.

Lord Lyndhurst to Mr. Croker.

[No date.]

MY DEAR CROKER,

I have just seen Charles Greville *—lately from Paris. The French seem to have taken part with the Russians against the Austrians. We, however, stuck to these, our ancient allies, particularly upon the question of the New Boundary, which, I am sorry to say, comprehends less than was originally intended. The Austrians, therefore, and we are upon the best possible terms. I hope it may continue. The balance of our warlike account is not very agreeable. We have spent a hundred millions, and have increased the influence and consolidated the power of a nation which has, and always will, hate us. We shall wilfully harm ourselves if we omit to take every precaution to guard against what sooner or later will happen—a dispute with this very formidable Power. France is evidently courting Russia, and will probably beat us as usual in that game. We must look to ourselves alone for security.

Yours ever faithfully,

LYNDHURST.

The Duke of Rutland to Mr. Croker.†

Belvoir Castle, September 14th, 1856.

MY DEAR CROKER,

You will readily understand my long silence, and especially my having let several days elapse without answering your

---

* [Author of the ‘Journals’ published in 1874. Mr. Greville died in January, 1865.]

† [These letters are given as the last memorials of another of Mr. Croker's very old friendships. The Duke died on the 20th of January, 1857, a few months only before Mr. Croker. They had been staunch friends for upwards of fifty years.]

letter of the 24th August, so kindly enquiring after me. The fact is, 1 do not like that a friend such as you have ever been in sincere attachment to me, should be addressed by any amanuensis in lieu of myself, and yet I have had so much pain and suffering since that date, that I have failed on several occasions when I have been going to write to you.

I have been confined to bed seventeen weeks, getting up for three hours in the evening lately. My own opinion is, that I shall never get rid of this illness. Every organ in the system has been attacked in its turn, and how I have survived so long I know not. Yet my doctor and those who have seen me seem to have no apprehensions of immediate danger, though some weeks since my doctor told me I was very seriously ill.

Well, as to yourself! I was made most happy by the tone of your letter written in August. Think of your talking of walking the stubbles! How your energy would have been thrown away, for scarcely a partridge is to be found, and my doctor, who is the only *tirailleur* here (and, indeed, except dear John, my only guest), can find very little to shoot at. Yet he is wild after the diversion, all gouty as he is. At Longshawe the game is boundless.

Ever believe me, my dear Croker,

Your most affectionate friend,

Rutland.

The Duke of Rutland to Mr. Croker. Extract.

Belvoir Castle, September 17th, 1856.

My dear Croker,

·My sickness is such that I can never depend upon myself for one hour as to capability of application to any subject. My conviction is that I can never again have health that will give a charm to life, and yet I am most desirous of some slight prolongation of life, with a decent share of health and strength, for the purpose of showing how zealous I am to evince deep contrition and remorse for the poor amount of good which I have done during a long life, compared with the means, capabilities, and capacities so mercifully and graciously bestowed upon me. Your letters are ever interesting to me, and are always welcomed heartily, especially when they give such an account of yourself as you did three weeks since, and which tone I hope you are again enabled to entertain.

The Duke of Bedford writes me word that he saw great improvement in Ireland during his late visit there, and my relation Carlisle is very popular. He is sure to be popular wherever he goes, but with some he is said to be thought too volatile, and to aim too much at youth gone by. He danced down a long set one night last week at a ball, and appealing to the host of the Court (Mr. Connellan) for applause, he asked if he (Mr. C.) had left off dancing, when the reply came back, " Yes, my lord, and marbles too."

How long do you mean to remain at Alverbank? Have you made an arrangement comfortable to yourself on giving up Moulsey? I remember being struck with the perfection of its arrangements, and especially of your library.

Ever believe me, my dear Croker,

Your most affectionate friend,

RUTLAND.

The Duke of Rutland to Mr. Croker.

Belvoir Castle, November 17th, 1856.

MY DEAR CROKER,

I go downwards each day. My legs, feet, and thighs are swollen beyond measure. I have had to send to many places (Nottingham at last) for stockings that will draw on. There is much pain over the whole body, and I dread the arrival and passage of each night. The fits of coughing issue a sound such as I never before heard. I think another two days will be as many as I can endure, unless a favourable change takes place. If I was better prepared for the awful change, I should be far more comfortable and easy.

We are in a curious position abroad. I hear that the French Emperor is as strong as ever in his friendly feeling towards England, and that he is very angry with those of his Ministers who have been playing a false game, and have endeavoured to curry favour with him for Russia, viz., Morny and two or three others. The affair of Fontainebleau is entirely attributable to his English disposition. The Duke and Duchess of Beaufort, and some others of our noblesse, were to have been of the party, and are sorely mortified by the disappointment. We have very few pheasants, to the disgrace of the keepers, for the expense at which the game will have been preserved amounted to 2000*l.* last year, and there is very little to show for it.

Ever, my dear Croker,
Your truly affectionate friend,
Rutland.

My hand has become so unsteady that I can scarcely guide my pen, and shaving is becoming a most dangerous employment, but still I have always performed it as yet. Make my best remembrances to your fireside circle.

The Duke of Rutland to Mr. Croker.

Belvoir Castle, December 28th, 1856.

My dear Croker,

I had been wondering what had made you silent—you knowing how much gratification I derive from your letters—when I received the unpleasant solution of your silence in the account of your not having been so well. I must therefore entreat that I may have very shortly a further, and I hope a better report of your health. You have recovered so completely from a worse state than you describe that I will even hope you may be able to shake it off. I can give you no good news of myself, for each night before going to bed I have asked Dr. Parsons whether I shall live till the morning. My cough continues most distressing, and the action on the chest is so embarrassing as to breath that I have not gone to bed the three last nights.

I shall leave a curious state of Europe behind me; and what is to happen who can say? If the King of Prussia moves as he says he will, all the European nations must, ere long, be again at war. I hear that M. de Morny is dissatisfied with his position at Petersburg, compared with that in which we have placed our Minister at Paris. We (the Lord Lieuts. of Counties) have received the fill-up to complete the regiments of the several counties as soon as may be practicable, and I have drawn the money for the accomplishment of the object. There seems to be a hankering for fighting among the nations of Europe. Even Prussia, that held off so long, has at last indulged the fancy, when the great folk had finished their fancy in that direction. If Prussia perseveres I hope she will have a good drubbing; she deserves it.

Ever, my dear Croker,

Most affectionately yours,

RUTLAND.

Mr. Croker to Lord Lyndhurst.

Alverbank, Gosport, November 27th, 1856.

MY DEAR LYNDHURST,

Do you *still* remember what you once reminded me of, the dinner that Canning gave you and me when he was settling his Administration ? After you and he had discussed several persons and allotted several offices, in which I perhaps *too saucily* gave my poor opinion, you said to me in a tone of pleasantry, " And now, Croker, that you have settled almost all the offices of the State, what do you mean to *take for yourself ?* " Though this was a mere pleasantry, I answered, if not seriously at least sincerely, that circumstanced as I was, I could not change my position ; and Canning (I think), reluctantly, and you also, acquiesced in my motives.

If you remember this, I should like much to possess your testimony to that effect, and my kind lady would, I think, not regret the trouble of writing it for you.

I often hear of you and her, and lately from Paris, and glad to hear all that is agreeable as to your spirits, and nothing disagreeable of your health. In plain truth, people look on you as a miracle.

I am glad to say that I have some hopes of being more a witness of your juvenility than I have lately been, as we mean to take our *permanent* abode at Kensington Palace ; and though my state is precarious, it is not seriously uneasy for the moment, and promises me, please God, the power of seeing you more frequently.

What a week of excitement that was when you and I saw so much of each other, while Canning was making his arrangements. Kindest regards to the lady so deservedly dear to you, and to me so undeservedly kind.

Ever, my dear Lyndhurst,

Affectionately yours,

J. W. CROKER.

Lord Lyndhurst to Mr. Croker.

George Street, December 2nd, 1856.

MY DEAR CROKER,

Those were joyous days—days of hope and expectation. I well remember the conversation to which you refer, and Lady Lyndhurst reminds me that I have more than once mentioned it in her presence. We are charmed with the account of your intention to fix your residence so near us; you know how much we relish your conversation and society. We find London suits us extremely well at this season; we left Paris at the beginning of November in hopes that this would be the case, and we have not been disappointed. At this moment of all others I should delight in an hour's conversation with you—there are so many matters to discuss and consider. If you have no better employment, and are not likely to come to town soon, perhaps you will favour me with a sketch, however slight, of your view of our actual situation and future prospects. Everything appears to me, if I may so say, *loosened ;* the attraction of cohesion gone, the parts of the system floating here and there, and I am asking myself and others in what will all this end; to what are we, in the language of our Foreign Minister, drifting at home and abroad ? Rise, my Apollo, and throw a little prophetic light upon these matters which you from your observatory are so capable of doing.

Yours faithfully,

LYNDHURST.

*Lord Hatherton * to Mr. Croker.*

Capesthorne, December 26th, 1856.

MY DEAR CROKER,

I am sorry not to have answered your letter dated the 1st (but which did not reach me till several days after that date, if I remember rightly) as soon as I expected I should have done. But I have not yet had a day at home to search for that memorandum, which I am anxious to copy for you.

I am now in old Davenport's house—you remember him in

---

* [Lord Hatherton sat in the House of Commons for Staffordshire many years. His first wife was a daughter of another of Mr. Croker's old friends, the Marquis Wellesley.]

the House of Commons. Don't you now see him *up*, stroking his hat, and stammering out a sessional speech about the ruin of the silk trade, with old Egerton on one side, and the excellent Gaffer Gooch on the other?

Alas! I can think of nobody of that date who is not gone. Even the young men of those days are no more—Peel, Goulburn, Fitzgerald. I ought to look much older than I feel. There is not now one peer owning property in the county of Stafford, except Lord St. Vincent, nor one squire of 1000*l.* a year, living, who was in possession of his property when I entered on mine in 1812 ; nor one trading firm that has not changed its name! And here I still am, well; once the county's member, now its Lord Lieutenant, and its father with a vengeance. I dare say this is singular in my case ; but the singularity goes farther. I am only the fifth proprietor of my property since the time of James I. I believe I am the only peer of whom that can be said. My immediate predecessor (old Sir Ed. Littleton) commanded a company of the Line, in garrison at Chester, at the time of the Rebellion, 1746.

Yours ever sincerely,

HATHERTON.

It will have been gathered from various allusions in the foregoing letters that Mr. Croker's health had gradually been declining, and that there were circumstances connected with his condition which occasionally gave his friends great anxiety and alarm. He was a sufferer from a disease of the heart, which manifested itself in fainting fits, sometimes very severe, and so long protracted that recovery seemed almost impossible. It was in the year 1850 that this malady first appeared, and the physician who was consulted thought it wise to reveal to Mr. Croker the true nature of the warning which had come to him. In a letter written to Lord Londonderry, he remarked: "I have had ever since my youth a disposition to faint on very slight provocation, and I have actually fainted four or five times in the last eight or nine months without any cause, and as yet without any consequence. But my doctors, though they seem not to know what the matter is, advise me to be more sparing than I used to be of mental exertions."

Undeterred by the gravity of these symptoms, Mr. Croker continued to work with his usual energy at every enterprise which he took in hand. His annotations of Pope always afforded him congenial occupation. A year after the first attack, the fainting fits returned with increased violence, and from the middle of November, 1851, till March, 1852, he never knew what it was to pass a single day without two or three of these fits, and he sometimes had twelve or fourteen. He also suffered from agonising pains, which were supposed to have their origin in neuralgia. But "neither of these most trying complaints drew from him one murmuring word." * He was aware that in this sleep which so nearly resembled death, he might at any moment pass into another state of being, but he was accustomed to say, "I have no fear of death. It is but like going out of one room into another." His pulse was seldom above 30, and often fell to 23. As soon as the attacks passed away, he went to his desk again and resumed those pursuits which were dearer to him than life—an article for the *Quarterly*, or some notes for the edition of Pope, which he worked at almost every day, although he had no hope of living to complete it. "The result," he wrote to Sir George Sinclair in 1852—when he was unusually weak and low— "is in the hands of God, and is probably not distant. I await His pleasure, not merely with resignation, but with gratitude that in my seventy-second year I have neither bodily suffering nor mental decay, and that I am fondly and care-

---

* From a letter by Lady Barrow to the Editor. For the particulars concerning Mr. Croker's illness and last days, the Editor is indebted to this lady, and to Miss Boislesve, who acted for some years as Mr. Croker's amanuensis, and attended him with great fidelity and affection until his death.

fully watched over and supported by a circle of wife and
children* as anxious and affectionate as ever man was blest
with.   Adieu ! Receive my best wishes, and if we are not to
meet again, continue your kindness to my memory."

But the end was not so near at hand as he thought. After
a time, indeed, he became in some measure accustomed to
the mysterious visitations which so suddenly transported
him to the border-land "between two worlds." His general
health was good; his intellectual faculties were as acute as
ever; "but," says Miss Boislesve, "at any moment, without
any warning whatever, he felt faint, and sometimes completely lost consciousness for a few seconds, sometimes merely
felt the passing feeling; but even when he lost consciousness,
he woke up perfectly well aware that he had fainted, but
able to go on with what he was dictating as if nothing had
happened.   He could even finish the sentence he had begun
not having lost the thread of his ideas in the least degree.
All this time his patience never failed. His love for his
family and friends was something wonderful. He was always
thinking of what could please and amuse the young people,
entering into all the pleasures he had planned for them with
as much zest as any."   In like manner, Lady Barrow speaks
of his "wonderful patience, and his gratitude for any little
attention to his comfort." "My constitution," he wrote to
Lord Palmerston, "has learned to accommodate itself to
circumstances, and I seem to live as comfortably on a pulse
of 30 as I used to do on one of 70. I am thankful for the
mercy I experience, but not blind to the peril, and to the
inevitable termination. Though I walk and drive out, and
receive and even pay visits, my tether is very short." And
to Lord Londonderry he wrote (in September, 1853), " I
thank God for the absence of all suffering, and the enjoy-

---

* The children of Lady Barrow.

ment of much domestic happiness. I have a good many young people about me, and I sit up sometimes thrice a week to see them dancing polkas and playing charades."

Although during the last two or three years of his life he had ceased to contribute to the *Quarterly*, he watched every number with undiminished interest, and kept up a friendly communication with his old friends. The following letters are among the last which he wrote :—

Mr. Croker to Mr. Murray.

Kensington Palace, February 14th, 1857.

DEAR MURRAY,

I have been so very ill as to have been unable till yesterday to look at the Raglan article in the last *Quarterly*, of which I heard a good deal, and which was sure to interest me. In reading it, however, I find a statement that the Duke of Wellington " had been often heard to say in after years that there were two or three periods of the battle of Waterloo when he thought it all over with us." I am very curious to know the reviewer's authority for this statement. There were few persons to whom the Duke talked so often and so fully of Waterloo as to me, and I can assert that not only did he never say anything of the kind to me, but when he has been asked, as he was *directly by me*, and often by others in my presence, whether he was at any period seriously alarmed for the result, would always answer, " *Never.*"

In Lord Ellesmere's little sketch of his life, p. 39, you will find his evidence to the same effect, and I think I also may appeal to any other person who has conversed with the Duke on the subject, whether he ever gave any colour to such an inference. I can positively assert that Alava, Lords Hill, Anglesey and Raglan, and all that I have ever talked with on the subject, united in stating that neither the Duke's confidence in the result nor their own ever for a moment varied.

It would have been no wonder, and still less disparagement, if during so long and complicated and diversified a struggle there had been fluctuations of hope, moments of doubt; but it was one of the greatest marvels of that day that

in point of fact there was not, neither in his own calm judgment, nor in the congenial and confiding feelings of all those
who were around him.

I write with difficulty and in great pain, but I am anxious
to record my evidence on this particular point which had
from the first excited my surprise and curiosity, and which
turned out to be, as I thought and think, peculiarly characteristic of the steady lucidity of a mind that rose clear above
the clouds of the battle accumulated below.

Ever yours,

J. W. CROKER.

Mr. Croker to —— (probably Lord Brougham).

June 13th, 1857.

I am by no means surprised at the quiet and even gay
aspect of Paris. Despotism is the paradise of the infinite
majority of the people. It has no drawback but taxation ;
but if (as it certainly does occasionally happen) the taxation
should repay itself or help to reproduce the elements of taxation in pleasurable or plausible forms, as in Paris for the
last few years ; if, I say, taxation can be so *sugar-plummed*
nothing can be for the moment more agreeable to the feeling
and taste of the nation, or more conducive to a temporary
prosperity. The brilliant bubble will burst, but meanwhile
"*Vive l'Empereur ;*" and this is a kind of prosperity that
nothing but a despotism can bestow. Any form of legitimacy,
or even legality, would be forced to surround itself with
something of independent co-operation, and the minutest
grain of independence in the lowest tribunal, or most humble
rouage in the whole system, would be the germ of a general
break up. Louis Napoleon is, as his uncle was, dancing the
tight-rope. So I said, so I wrote, of the uncle in 1809, and
1814 fulfilled my prophecy. What the anno domini of the
nephew's tumble is to be, some, perhaps very small, events
will decide ; I am sure it is not distant, and I am sorry for it,
for with all my old prejudices in favour of constitutional
Government, I shall think it a great pity if a few dozen
literary adventurers and *émeutiers* should again get the upper-
hand, and prevent the vast majority of the French people
from enjoying that species of government which, after all, I

believe to be the most conducive to their general happiness.
Freedom of speech, liberty of the press, *habeas corpus*, trial
by jury, are as essential to government in England as, I
believe in my conscience, they are incompatible with any
government in France ; therefore I repeat *"Vive l'Empereur."*
You Whigs are like quack doctors who have but one specific
for all constitutions, and you have been endeavouring to
revolutionise "mankind from Indus to the Pole" only because
it suited our traditions, our tempers, and our wants to have a
Revolution in 1688.

Mr. Croker to M. Guizot. Extract.

Kensington Palace, July 14th, 1857.

In the letter to which I was replying, you blamed the
Duke of Wellington for his indiscreet declaration against all
reform, and attributed to it the mischief that followed. I was
a witness of the whole game—the *dessous des cartes*, as well as
what was public, and I do assure you that that declaration had
nothing whatsoever to do with the events that followed. The
reform clamour had not been for many years so low as it
then was, and the defeat of the Duke's Government arose
entirely from his and Peel's unhappy defection from their
principles and their party by the concession of Catholic
emancipation.

I am an impartial judge on that point, for I had been all
my life a steady supporter, both in the press and in Parliament, of Catholic emancipation. It was the only point on
which I differed from Peel and the Duke, and that was the
reason why, when they resigned in 1827, I found it impossible
to go with them, as Mr. Canning and I had always agreed on
that point. In the natural course of politics, when that question grew too strong to be resisted, the anti-catholic ministers
should have retired, and the Whigs should have been allowed
to come into office and to carry their own great measure ; but
when Peel and the Duke unhappily and unfairly cut that
ground from under them, they were forced to lay hold of the
next great question on which something was left for them to
do ; and they were driven back upon Reform, which was in a
very slumbering state, but of so combustible a nature that
when the match was once applied it blazed up and exploded
with a fury that surprised, and astonished, and alarmed those

who had introduced it, as some leading men of that Cabinet have honestly confessed to me.

But though the Duke of Wellington had made the original mistake of doing what was right to be done, and perhaps inevitable, and what I individually approved, but which ought to have been done by the Whigs, the Duke, I say, saw that one false step should not be followed by another, and that another concession would have been only followed by other demands, each growing more irresistible by every success that was obtained.   He was therefore in as nearly as possible the same situation that Louis Philippe and you were upon your own subject of reform ; some portions of the demands of your opposition were plausible enough, and you would, as abstract propositions, have seen no great harm in conceding them ; but if you had once begun to make such concessions, all the rest would have followed, with the additional mischief of discrediting the King and his ministry.   You would not have much cared as to what rate the electoral franchise should have been fixed, but you knew that even the most moderate concession would, in the then temper of men's minds, involve virtually the abandonment of your position.   What great harm was there in the proposed banquet ?   None at all, as a single fact, but it was a defiance of the Government which it was absolutely necessary to resist ; and this was so true, that we now know that the leaders of that movement (who only wanted your places, and not a revolution) were in their own minds as much alarmed as you were, and found themselves most reluctantly dragged into the vortex.   I told all this to Louis Philippe himself, as, I believe, I also did to you, and I consoled the King in some of our long conversations at Claremont by showing him that his and your resistance to the banquets had only accelerated a catastrophe which (accompanied by a loss of your characters) would have equally occurred if you had been so pusillanimous as to yield, and the wise old man actually embraced me, *avec effusion,* as you say, at the view I had thus opened to him : and it was on those principles that I, at the time, defended you in the *Quarterly Review,* when there was an outcry made against you for having precipitated things by your indiscreet resistance, and it is on this principle that I now defend the Duke of Wellington against the very same reproach which you have directed against him, and if I had room, or time, or strength to pursue the subject, I am convinced that I could prove that nothing could be more

analogous, I might almost say identical, than the conduct
of the Duke of Wellington and Monsieur Guizot on those
respective occasions.

This was what I was anxious to say to you, and I shall
conclude with assuring you that I am deeply sensible of the
affectionate sympathy which your letter shows for my present
condition. I can hardly hope that I shall ever see you again,
but while I live, I shall never cease to pride myself in the
title of being your friend, and by thinking that to the best of
my abilities I did justice to both your personal and political
character.

Believe me to be, mon cher ami,

Most affectionately yours,

J. W. CROKER.

On the 1st of August, 1857, Mr. Croker dictated a letter
to the Home Secretary * concerning the final disposition of a
collection of papers which Horace Walpole found at Lord
Hertford's seat at Ragley, in August, 1758. These papers
related to the lords Conway, who were Secretaries of State to
James I. and to Charles I. and II. Walpole had once
intended to make a selection from the documents for the
purpose of publication, but he abandoned the idea, and the
third Marquis of Hertford handed a great part of the papers
over to Mr. Croker, reserving for himself a number of
autographs. Mr. Croker came to the conclusion that the
State Paper Office and the British Museum were the proper
homes for the collection, and he offered to present them to
those departments.

Sir George Grey to Mr. Croker.

Whitehall, August 7th, 1857.

SIR,

I beg to acknowledge the receipt of your letter of 1st
instant, and of the two volumes which accompanied it, con-

---

* Sir George Grey.

taining an index of the curious and valuable papers described in your letter.

I have much pleasure in conveying to you the best thanks of Her Majesty's Government for the interesting information which you have given me with regard to these papers, and for the proposal you have made as to the disposal of them. Her Majesty's Government will gratefully accept your offer of placing that portion of them which may be considered as valuable State Papers in the State Paper Office, and I have no doubt that the trustees of the British Museum will gladly receive such of them as are merely private, though relating to subjects of interest, with a view to their being deposited among the manuscripts in the Museum. In accordance with what I understand to be your wish, I will either direct that some competent person from the State Paper Office shall wait upon you to receive these papers, and examine them, with a view to the distribution of them between the two depositories, or, if you should prefer to transmit the entire collection to this office, I will take charge of them, in order that they may be examined and disposed of in the manner which you have suggested.

I have the honour to be, Sir,

Your obedient servant,

G. GREY.

Mr. Croker to Sir George Grey.

St. Alban's Bank, Hampton, August 9th, 1857.

SIR,

I am very much gratified by the approbation which Her Majesty's Government have been pleased to signify to me of my proposal concerning the Conway papers.

I have been experimentally removed hither by the advice of my physicians, and I have not any clear recollection of what the bulk of the papers may be; I shall, however, have them looked at to-morrow or next day and shall acquaint you, perhaps in a postscript to this letter, with the size of the box or case which may be necessary for their removal; and when it is provided it may be sent to Kensington Palace, where Mrs. Croker's servant will have directions to deliver the papers to the person who may be sent to receive them.

There is a further observation which I think it right to

make for the use of those who may have to arrange the papers. I have mentioned in my former letter that several of probably the most curious of the papers have been formerly disposed of as curiosities. But of any that have been so moved since I have known them, I hope, and indeed am pretty certain, that I had copies made to replace them, so that for literary or historical purposes nothing is lost.

I have the honour to be, &c.,

J. W. C.

St. Alban's Bank, Hampton, August 9th, 1857.

Sir,

With reference to my other letter of this date, I beg leave to add a further stipulation, of which you will no doubt see the propriety, which is, that if on examination of the Conway papers anything like title deeds or other documents connected with the property should have found their way into the collection, they should be carefully put aside and returned to Lord Hertford, whom I have apprised of this stipulation.

I have the honour, &c.,

J. W. Croker.

It will be observed that the last two letters are dated from St. Alban's Bank, Hampton. This was the house of his old friend, Mr. Justice Wightman, where Mr. Croker had come to spend a few weeks, both his own houses having been let. He went there on the 5th of August. "We drove down," writes Miss Boislesve, "from Kensington Palace.* On arriving, he went straight to the library, as he always did on first arriving anywhere. The next day the Barrows arrived, and he was quite pleased to find himself surrounded by his family. He was very fond of all those children."

On Monday, the 10th of August, he worked all day at his notes on Pope, and was perfectly happy among his books and papers. "His old friend, Mr. Beresford," says Miss Boislesve,

---

* Where, as it has been stated in previous chapters, Mrs. Croker had apartments for many years, and where she died on November 7, 1880.

" spent an hour or so with him, talking of old times. I had gone to Kensington. On my return, he greeted me, as usual, with pleasant words of welcome, and told me he had had a very good day, and his voice was as cheerful as his looks. After dinner he asked me to write two letters under his dictation, one to the late Lord Hertford,* about the Conway papers ; the other to Sir George Grey, about the same papers being sent to the British Museum.

" We (Mrs. Croker, Lady Barrow, and I) then took leave of him, while he was being put to bed by his servant, intending to come back to him in a few minutes. Hardly had we time to get down-stairs when the handbell rang violently. We ran up—I entered the room—saw he was fainting, jumped on his bed, and held his head—but it was all over. In an instant he had gone to his rest. His servant said that he merely exclaimed, ' Oh, Wade ! ' just as he was putting him into bed."

Thus, then, he passed away, in the manner which he had always desired—surrounded by those whom he loved the best, and yet spared the pain of protracted parting and farewells. A little while before, some one had remarked in his presence that " death was an awful thing." " I do not feel it so," he said ; " the same Hand which took care of me when I came into this world will take care of me when I go out of it." In this hope he died, as he had lived. The record here presented would be sadly incomplete—would, indeed, be wholly misleading as to Mr. Croker's true character—if great stress were not laid upon the incalculable value and importance which he attached to a firm and unfaltering belief in the revealed truths of the Christian religion. It was in that faith that he sought and found consolation and hope under the great sorrow which had befallen him in the

* The fourth Marquis, who died in August, 1870.

loss of his only son. " It is one of our greatest comforts,"
wrote Lady Barrow to Sir George Sinclair, " to know that his
faith and hopes were entirely fixed on the true foundation of
our blessed Christian faith, and the fruits were indeed apparent—the submission to God's will with which he bore acute
and lengthened sufferings." Among his papers there is a
prayer which he was accustomed to use, and which he had
composed two days after death had bereaved him of his son,
and cut off " the desire of his eyes at a stroke." The same
feeling which is breathed in this prayer animated him to the
end of his days, and enabled him to look forward to the short
passage which, for him, lay " between one room and another,"
with a tranquil mind :—

" Grant, we beseech Thee, that the death of our dear, dear
child may awaken us, his unhappy parents, to the prospect of
eternal life; and that this our temporary affliction may so
chasten and correct our hearts, as to make us, when our trial
shall come, less unworthy of that eternal mercy into which
we humbly trust that our little innocent is received; and
we, with all our souls, beseech Thee, O merciful GOD! to
strengthen our good intentions, to control our worldly pro-
pensities, to forgive us our past offences, and by Thy grace so
to regulate our lives in this perishable world, that we may
indulge the blessed hope of meeting our beloved child where
pain and death cannot come, and where love endureth for
ever! For which we hope and pray through the mediation
of our Saviour Jesus Christ. Amen."

The Bishop of Exeter to Mrs. Croker.

Durham, September 7th, 1857.

MY DEAR MRS. CROKER,

If I have forborne hitherto to write to you, you will, I am
sure, attribute my silence to its true cause : unwillingness to
intrude upon you in the early days of your bereavement.
Accept now my very sincere condolence on an event which
has fallen in all its heaviness upon you, but which has also

been felt as no light sorrow by the wide circle of friends who knew and loved him for whom you mourn. The greatest and surest consolation even to yourself must be the remembrance of that unswerving faith in which he lived and died. But you have the further comfort of knowing that all that untiring love and watchfulness could do in lightening the sufferings of his long protracted illness, and contributing to his comforts, was most affectionately performed by you. May it be long before you need similar attentions. This consideration is more strongly impressed upon myself by my daily experience of the same love, evincing itself in the same way, and forming my chief worldly happiness now that I am in my eightieth year. Let me hope, if it please God still to prolong my life and strength to another spring, that I may have the gratification of assuring you in person of my deep sympathy and warm regard.

Mrs. Phillpotts and my daughter unite with me in every kind wish.

> Believe me, my dear Madam,
> Your very faithful and attached friend,
> H. EXETER.

INDEX.

SINGLETON.

Singleton, Archdeacon, ii. 9.
Slane Castle, George IV.'s visit to, i. 206.
Slavery, abolition of. Peel's opinion, i. 116, 294.
Smith, Sir Sidney, his character criticised by the Duke of Wellington, i. 348.
——, Adam, anecdote of, ii. 31.
——, James, letter to Croker, i. 18.
Smith-O'Brien, Mr., iii. 7.
Smythe, Hon. G. S., announces the death of his father to Croker, iii. 360.
Soldiers, English, Scotch and Irish, different characteristics of, i. 353.
Somerville, Mrs., recommended for a pension, ii. 257, 273.
Sontag, Mdlle., described, i. 417
Sophia, Princess, i. 360.
Soult, Buonaparte's opinion of, ii. 307, 370—Wellington's opinion, ii. 277.
Southey, Robert, accepts the Laureateship, i. 49—his 'Life of Nelson,' 50—proposed 'Book of the State,' 276—as a political writer, ii. 410—letter to Brougham, 259—pension, 275.
——, Croker to, i. 50, 276.
Spa Fields riots, i. 99.
Spain, British force sent to, in 1826, i. 321.
Spanish aggressions, i. 321.
Sparks, Jared, and the map of the boundaries of the United States, ii. 398.
Spearman, Sir A., i. 405.
Spencer, Lord, ii. 242, 246—and the Cabinet, 347 (see Althorp).
Spencer, Sir B., anecdote of, ii. 123.
Spring Rice, Mr., describes Croker's speech on the Catholic question, i. 131—ii. 77—proposed as Speaker, 263.
Stael, Mme. de, described by Croker, i. 326.
Stamp Act, ii. 305.
Standard, the, paragraph in, i. 397, 399—ii. 116—on the Corn Laws, iii. 39—as organ of Tory party, iii. 83.
Stanley, Lord, i. 420—refuses to join the Ministry in 1835, ii. 248, 250, 256—his position with Sir Robert Peel, 257, 269, 282, 300, 302—speech on Corn Bill, iii. 69—looked to as leader, 70, 74, 76, 90, 305—on the rate of navvies' wages, 88—payment of Irish priests, 106—

SUTTON.

object of the 'Peel' pamphlet, 114-117—on the Corn Laws, 133—political prospects in 1850, 219—difficulty of forming a Government, 231—on 'Protestantism, Protection, and down with the Income Tax.' 237.
Stanley, Lord, Croker to, iii. 80, 105, 111.
Stapleton, Mr., Canning's private secretary, i. 381.
Staremberg, Count, anecdote of, i. 331.
Statue of the Duke of Wellington, ii. 326—disputes about its site, 327.
Stewart, Charles (afterwards Marquis of Londonderry, q : v), intrigues against the Duke of Wellington, i. 346.
Stopford, Dr. (Bishop of Cloyne), and Mr. Phillips, i. 8.
Stormont, Lord, i. 290—ii. 151, 154, 166.
Stowell, Lord, notes on Johnson, ii. 27, 35.
Strachan, Sir R., and Lord Hertford, ii. 415.
Strangford, Lord, "Young England," 7—on the Duke of Wellington's statue, iii. 128—on Croker's article on the 'Memoirs of Moore,' 297—George IV.'s generosity to Sheridan, 299—the *Hougomont* transport re-named, 343.
Strangford (7th Lord) announcing his father's death, iii. 360—Croker to, 361.
Strathfieldsaye, ii. 150, 207, 231, 306.
Stuart, Villiers, on the Catholic question, i. 418.
Stuart, Sir W., ii. 308.
Studios, the, in 1828, i. 411.
Sugar duties, ii. 68—iii. 137.
Suisse, Nicholas, valet to Lord Hertford, ii. 415—suspected of dishonesty, 417.
Sumner, Mr., i. 210, 357.
Sussex, Duke of, ii. 249.
Sutherland, Duke of, ii. 199.
——, Duchess of, ii. 293.
Sutton, Charles Manners, i. 121-160—letter to Croker on the illness of his son, 122—Prime Minister, ii. 147, 161, 164, 167—refused a peerage, 186—elected Speaker, 200—Baronet, 213—proposed as Speaker, 262—defeated, 266—made a peer, 266—raised to the peerage, 266.

www.ingramcontent.com/pod-product-compliance
Lightning Source LLC
Chambersburg PA
CBHW030820110726
47900CB00006B/1683